The Blacknock Woman

By the same author:

Where the Fresh Grass Grows (1955)
A Path to the Bridge (1958)
The Van Langeren Girl (1960)
A Touch of Thunder (1961)
A Time to Retreat (1963)
Genesis 38 (1965)
A Mission for Betty Smith (1967)
Messiter's Dream (1990)
The Cross of San Vincente (1991)
The Singing Stones (1993)
Covenant with Death (1994)
Shadows on the Sand (1995)
The Travelling Dead (1997)

Non-fiction

Transformation of a Valley (1983)

THE BLACKNOCK WOMAN

Brian Cooper

Constable · London

First published in Great Britain 1999
by Constable & Company Ltd
3 The Lanchesters, 162 Fulham Palace Road
London W6 9ER
Copyright © Brian Cooper 1999
The right of Brian Cooper to be
identified as the author of this work
has been asserted by him in accordance
with the Copyright, Designs and Patents Act 1988
ISBN 0 094 79460 X
Set in Palatino 9 pt by
SetSystems Ltd, Saffron Walden, Essex
Printed and bound in Great Britain
by MPG Books Ltd, Bodmin, Cornwall

A CIP catalogue record for this book
is available from the British Library

FOR WINIFRED

There is a tide in the affairs of women
Which, taken at the flood, leads – God knows where

Lord Byron: *Don Juan*

CONTENTS

AUTHOR'S NOTE

Blacknock exists. So do Blakeney and Morston, Stiffkey and Wells, but those readers who search for Medford on their maps will be unsuccessful. It is a mixture of many villages on the north coast of Norfolk, a place conjured out of imagination, and the folk who live between Greystoke Farm and Three Farthing Hill are mere creations of the mind.

Those familiar with the coast will no doubt have heard of the Blacknock legend, but those who are still unaware of its magnetism and wish to know more about its desolate beauty and the ever-present threat of its swift-running tides should turn to Alan Savory's book, *Norfolk Fowler*, where I first read the tale of the woman whom I blessed with the name of Mary Bunn.

PROLOGUE
THE MIST

And the sea gave up the dead which were in it

The Revelation of St John the Divine: 20.13

There are nights in early summer on the north coast of Norfolk when the mist from the marshes drifts in to lie at first light like a silver sea across the surface of the fields. It wraps itself around the old brick-and-flint barns and cowsheds and, invading the villages inch by inch, cloaks the small gardens, hides the cottage walls, envelops the windows, and curls like smoke around the roof-tiles and chimneys.

On such a May morning in 1951 it lay low and dense across the village of Medford. It all but hid the church of St Mary the Virgin in its hollow beside the Dutch-gabled rectory, wreathed the twists and turns of the narrow coastal road, and completely obscured the river, flowing sluggishly to the sea beneath the flint-walled bridge.

It lay so thick on Liggerbeck Hill that the end of Deep Lane – one of the tracks that probed out like fingers to the marsh – was almost lost to sight, and if anyone had ventured down it to the edge of the saltings, he (or, at that hour in Medford, more likely she) would have seen nothing but a few yards of tangled brown marsh plants, and rivulets oozing water beneath the flood tide.

Then, as the sea began to ebb and the sun rose above Blakeney to penetrate the mist, the dull grey shroud that had lain across the coast slowly dissolved. It lifted from the river, from the bridge and the church and the flint-pebble cottages. It lifted from the long, straight stretch of Deep Lane and from all that lay beyond.

As the waters drew back and the sun climbed towards its zenith, they laid bare the marsh: three-quarters of a mile of desolate beauty – sea lavender and sea aster, scurvy grass and purslane, pools and winding creeks – extending as far as the eye could see to the edge of the sand.

The sand itself was lost in the distance, but it spread a further mile to the low-water mark, seamed by the channels of Broad Sand, Sickle and Flat Bed Creeks, and lying between them a dull patch of mud that was known as Blacknock.

The receding sea exposed it, covered in eel-grass and rich in the cockles for which Medford was famous. But it exposed something more.

There, amid the long, green pennants of eel-grass, lay the body of a woman, naked, half-curled, with one arm stretched out and the fingers extended, as if in a last convulsive attempt to cling on to life.

But all to no avail.

The sea rushes in across the sands at Medford, deepening the creeks and filling the channels that meander through the marsh; and out on Blacknock, even in the sun, the end of Deep Lane is nothing but a barely visible line that lies between the shore and the wide Norfolk sky.

And there are nights in early summer when the mist comes down, the line disappears, and such life as remains buries itself, like the cockles, in the mud.

I
THE MYSTERY

Call me what instrument you will, though you can
fret me, you cannot play upon me

William Shakespeare: *Hamlet*

1

The phone on the desk in front of Mike Tench rang at half-past ten the following morning. Lifting the receiver, he heard Ledward's voice.

'Good morning, Chief Inspector.'

He was mildly surprised. The pathologist was a taciturn man who suffered from insomnia, and normally failed to surface at such an early hour. On the rare occasions when he did, he was fretful, irascible and addicted to nothing more extravagant than grunts of denial. In contrast, he now seemed almost expansive.

'I trust you slept well, Chief Inspector,' he said.

'I did.' Tench was wary.

'I'm glad to hear it,' Ledward said.

'And you, Doctor?'

'Yes. For once, Chief Inspector, I can say that I did. Such a happening is in my case regrettably rare, but I woke this morning feeling suitably refreshed and ready to face the problems that plagued me last evening . . . They prompted me to ring you.'

Tench stifled a groan.

'I think, Chief Inspector' – Ledward was quite immoderately cheerful – 'you should come and take a look at one of my lodgers.'

'Male or female?'

'Female. No identity. Allegedly drowned.'

'Allegedly?'

'So I was led to believe.'

'But she wasn't?'

'In my considered opinion, no, she wasn't, Chief Inspector. Drowning is one of the most difficult diagnoses to make when performing an autopsy, but in this case the positive signs are all absent. I've had to look elsewhere for the cause of death.'

'And . . .?' said Tench.

'My conclusions can only be tentative, Chief Inspector, but she was certainly dead prior to immersion.'

'You mean . . . it could be murder?'

'Who knows?' Ledward's answer was entirely predictable. 'But I think you should bear the possibility in mind.'

Tench pushed aside his files.

'I'll be with you in a quarter of an hour,' he said.

*

He stared down at the woman on the slab.

'Early thirties.' Ledward was terse. 'Five feet two, green eyes, auburn hair, roughly eight stone. Washed up on the beach at Medford. She was dead on arrival at Holt Cottage Hospital, but the medical staff failed to diagnose cause. They passed her to me for further examination.'

'And you say she didn't drown.'

'The signs are all negative. No frothing at the mouth, no distention of the lungs by water and, most important, no diatoms.'

'Diatoms?'

'That's right. Microscopic algae. Common in both fresh and salt water. If she'd drowned, they'd have penetrated the membranes of the lungs, and the circulation system would have carried them round her body. I'd have found them in distant tissues: in the kidneys, the liver and bone-marrow, and possibly also inside the brain. If her heart had still been beating when she was submerged, the diatoms would have been there. They weren't, so she must have already been dead.'

'Then how did she die?'

'Ah, well' – Ledward stroked his chin – 'there we enter the world of imponderables, Chief Inspector. Let me say first of all that people can die from immersion in water without actually drowning. They can die from shock or vagal inhibition, but if that were the case I'd expect to find some corroborative signs.'

'But you didn't.'

'No, I didn't.'

'And so?'

'As I said, I looked elsewhere.'

'And you came to some conclusion?'

'A tentative one.' The doctor looked down his nose. 'You know me, Chief Inspector. I'm always very careful not to speculate on matters as vital as this. I wouldn't like what I say to be taken as gospel.'

Tench nodded. 'Of course not.'

'You won't find it in my autopsy report, and it's not for press consumption.'

'That's understood, Doctor . . . What did you conclude?'

'Take a look at this.' Ledward leant over the body and peeled back the lips. 'Bruising,' he said. 'Must have been caused by contact between the lips and the teeth. While she was alive . . . And these faint contusions. You see them? Here, on the cheek. They're all tell-tale signs, and they corroborate other findings. I think this woman died from anoxia, Chief Inspector: deficiency of oxygen. Someone suffocated her. Someone of considerable strength. There are no marks elsewhere on the body to indicate a struggle, so the person who killed her must have been strong enough to hold her motionless, place a hand over her nose and mouth and keep it there. If the pressure were sustained, that would be enough. She would die from a lack of oxygen to the lungs.'

Tench bent down and peered at the marks.

'You said it could be murder and you've made that clear enough, but could it have been an accident?'

'You mean could she have been killed by someone who was merely trying to stop her from making a scene? Yes, it's possible.'

'But not likely.'

'I didn't say that.' Ledward was back to his old cautious self. 'It would depend on the relative strengths of the participants. The pressure, as I said, would have to be sustained.'

'For roughly how long?'

'For as long as it took her to die, Chief Inspector. Not knowing what happened, I'm not prepared to go any further than that. But I will say this. To deprive people of oxygen kills them quickly. They lapse into unconsciousness in less than two minutes, and after that death can supervene at any time.'

'Are there any signs of a sexual assault?'

'As far as I can tell, none whatsoever.'

Tench was thoughtful.

'I suppose,' he said, 'it's impossible to tell precisely when she died.'

'Quite impossible, Chief Inspector. You know that all too well. I can suggest a range of times, but that's as much as I can do. Death was certified at Holt at 11.58 yesterday morning, but she died, according to my estimation, between twenty-four and forty-eight hours before that and from the evidence of maceration, I'd say that she hadn't been long in the water. Perhaps eight to twelve hours. No more than that.'

2

His old Chief, John Lubbock, now retired to a coastal cottage at Cley, had once told Mike Tench that if he wanted to know anything about anyone who lived in a Norfolk village there was only one man to ask.

'Get on to the local flatfoot,' he'd said. 'You'll find that he's always a mine of information. Long-standing coppers like Ezra Dodds at Stiffkey and Jack Bates at Medford have lived in the place for years. There isn't much they don't know about what goes on.'

So when, an hour after parting company from Ledward, Tench and Sergeant McKenzie drew up in front of the police house at Medford, the Detective Chief Inspector was prepared to approach Constable Bates with all the deference, not to say reverence, due to a man whose local knowledge, according to Lubbock, was encyclopedic.

And not only that. Though he'd never met Bates, he'd heard a good deal about him. A legend on the coast, he reputedly stood a good six feet five in his regulation socks, was broad as a barn door and strong as an ox, took size eleven boots and ruled Medford all the way from the weir at Greystoke Farm to Three Farthing Hill and, so it was said, ruled it simply by his presence.

Not that he had much in the way of crime to contend with. The village was normally a peaceful place. There'd been little excitement since a day in September fifteen years before when young Charlie Washbrook had had to be forcibly detained after setting Joe Muskham's hayloft ablaze.

Since then Medford had drowsed in the sun, and for most of the time Bates had been content to drowse along with it, save on those evenings when old Eli Craske, drunk in his cups, had threatened to break up the local alehouse. On such occasions the constable, tempering his undoubted authority with compassion, had firmly steered him home and put him to bed.

The police house was the usual brick-and-flint cottage with a white wooden porch, and the garden, like that at Stiffkey, was immaculately tended. The lawn was trimmed, the gravel paths were aligned with a military precision, the flower beds were neatly hoed, and there wasn't an errant plant to be seen.

Constable Bates, however, was less than immaculate. Dressed in an old shirt with the sleeves rolled up, a mudstained pair of trousers, and boots which could well have been discarded at the time of Charlie Washbrook's arrest, he was on his hands and knees by one of the flower beds, grubbing with his fingers for what appeared to be a non-existent weed.

Unperturbed at the sight of the Chief Inspector, he rose to full height and extended a much-contaminated hand.

'Good to meet ye, sir,' he said. 'Reckoned as there'd be someone from Norwich around at some time today.'

Tench took the hand, steeling himself to show no reluctance. Bates shook it firmly.

'Like as not ye'll be wanting to see Surly Sarah.'

'If you say so, Constable.' Tench hadn't the faintest idea who she was, but he was willing to accept that this village mandarin had a cogent reason for introducing her at this point. 'Did you say Surly Sarah?'

'Aye, sir, that's right. Old Sarah Clogston. It were she as found the body.'

'You mean down on the shore?'

'Aye, sir. Out at Blacknock. Brought her all the way back to the end o' Deep Lane, and that's a good mile. Nay, it's mebbe nearer a mile and a half.'

'She carried the body a mile and a half?'

'She did indeed, sir, and that's all of a fact. Slung the poor creature up on her shoulder and tramped all the way across the sands and the marsh.'

'On her own?'

'It's the truth, sir. Sarah's not one to be asking for help.'

'She must be remarkably strong for a woman.'

'Must be a bloody Amazon,' McKenzie remarked.

Bates gave a shrug.

'Aye, she's big and brawny, but there's others as big. It's just as she's used to be toting heavy sacks. They all of 'em are. There's a knack to it, Sergeant.'

'All of them?' said Tench.

'The cockle women, sir. They go out at low tide and bring back the cockles in sacks across the marsh. Blacknock's a rare place for cockles.'

'I'd have said that was man's work.'

The constable nodded.

'Mebbe you would, sir. Mebbe you would, but not here in Medford. Men are out on the land. It's women's work, cockling.'

Tench scratched his head.

'So this Surly Sarah was gathering cockles out at Blacknock, came across the body, and carried it a mile and a half to the village?'

'To the end o' Deep Lane, sir.'

'And what did she do then?'

'Set it down on the very edge o' the marsh, sir, and came to fetch me.'

'What time was that?'

'Just afore eleven, sir, yesterday morning. Low water were due at 10.18.'

'So you rang for an ambulance?'

'Right away, sir. It's normal procedure. We get bodies washed up reglar like all along the coast, and there's naught we can do. I got out the bike and cycled straight down, but the woman were clearly dead.'

'And what about Sarah – what's her name – Clogston?'

'Asked her what she knew and then packed her off home, sir. But reckon you'll be needing to get her own tale.'

'Yes, you're right.' Tench glanced at McKenzie. 'Reckon we will, Constable. Where does she live?'

'Drove Street, sir. Down by the river. But I'd best be going with you. She don't talk to furriners.'

'Surly, is she?'

'Aye, sir. Surly's the word. Ye'll not be getting much out o' Sarah 'fore Christmas, save she sees me.'

21

3

A quarter of an hour later, with Bates in the lead – by that time immaculately uniformed and helmeted – they crossed the river bridge and advanced on another brick-and-flint cottage.

'This Clogston woman,' said Tench. 'Is she married?'

The constable stopped.

'Was, sir, once. Wed to Sam Clogston. He were a whelker. Drowned twenty year ago now, crossing the bar at Wells in an autumn squall. She's not spoke much since.'

He took three measured steps forward and knocked on the cottage door.

'Best let me do the talking, sir, afore ye get round to asking any questions. She knows me from nigh on thirty year back, and I know her. Had to deal with her a time or two. Might be a help.'

Tench retreated a pace.

'Right. Carry on, Constable. You smooth the way.'

'Won't be easy, sir,' said Bates. He peered through the window and rapped on the pane. 'Sarah!' he shouted. 'It's me, Jack Bates. Open the door.'

There was a sound of shuffling footsteps inside and the door opened six inches to reveal a toothless mouth, a face etched with creases and roughened by exposure to Norfolk winds, a thatch of grey hair drawn back across the temples, and two eyes as piercing as a couple of gimlets. They bored into Bates.

'What yew want?' The voice was harsh and the tone uncompromising. 'Ent no time ter be mardlin'. Yew know tha'.'

Bates stepped to one side.

'This is Mr Tench,' he said. 'He's come all the way from Norwich just to have a few words.'

The eyes swivelled towards the Chief Inspector and stayed there.

'He's a furriner. Don' talk to no furriners.'

'Mr Tench is a gentleman.'

'Mebbe.' Sarah Clogston wasn't given to swift surrender.

'He've a mind to hear what happened out at Blacknock yesterday.'

'Do he now?'

'He does, and he'd like you to tell him.'

'He's a furriner. Ent his business.'

'I'd very much like to hear, Mrs Clogston,' said Tench.

The grizzled head nodded towards Constable Bates.

'Then reckon tha'd best be larnin' from Jack. He know. Writ it all down, he did, word arter word.'

'You'd be doing me a favour, Mrs Clogston, you really would.'

'Don' talk to no furriners.'

'Then talk to Jack, not to me. I'll just listen.'

The eyes flickered doubtfully. Bates seized his chance.

'Come on, Sarah,' he said. 'Ye can tell me agen. Reckon tha's like to be simple enough.'

The door creaked open another six inches.

'Ent a-gorn ter tell furriners all o' my know.'

'How about a cup o' tea? We're all a mite thirsty. An' a clutch o' they currant buns that's a-bakin'.' Bates sniffed the air. 'Masterpieces they are.'

The door opened still further. It revealed the full Sarah Clogston, resplendent in a heavy black skirt, thick worsted stockings and a black woollen shawl thrown across her shoulders.

'Tha's a rare botty bugger, Jack Bates,' she said, 'an' tha talks a load o' squit, but tha's mebbe right.' She looked Tench up and down. 'He do look a mite squinny. Ent a deal thicker'n two boards clapped togither. Reckon he could do wi' some wittles inside'n. Ye'd best step across, but I ent a-gorn ter talk, not yit I ent. An' tha' gret lummox' – she nodded at McKenzie – 'he ent comin' in. He look sour as a wedge. Reckon as he'd gi' ye a ding roun' th'lug-hole soon as say arternoon.'

Tench turned to the sergeant.

'Go and take a look at the river, Mac,' he said 'And get on to Gregg. I want him down here, and Sue Gradwell. Tell them to make it sharp.'

4

There's a long-running tale that, if you happen to be lost in the Norfolk lanes and ask a countryman the way, he'll look at you with an air of mistrust and reply with another question: 'What d'ye want ter know fer?'; as if, tramping the wilds, you might well be secreting a bomb in your rucksack and nursing some plot to blow up the village.

It's a tale designed to encapsulate, with a touch of wry humour, the Norfolk villagers' suspicion of what they term 'furriners': folk who were born and bred in the 'Sheers': outside East Anglia, perhaps outside Norfolk, or even in extreme cases outside the bounds of their immediate locality.

Mike Tench had heard it repeated all too often and, since arriving in Fakenham five years before, he'd been more than once reminded that he was very much of a 'furriner'. Born and raised in one of the dingier districts of Manchester, where his father was still a Church of England canon, and with little experience save two years at Cambridge and a further five in the army, he'd been transferred to Norwich to train for the CID under Detective Chief Inspector John Spencer Lubbock; and the Chief's opening question had informed him, in no uncertain terms, precisely where he stood. 'How long have you lived in Norfolk, laddie?' he'd asked; and when Tench had told him a matter of months, he'd said, 'Right. You'd better start taking notes. You've a hell of a lot to learn.'

He'd learnt, but learnt the hard way; Lubbock's methods of training were far from gentle; but he'd soon come to realize the desperate truth of the older man's assertion. It had taken no more than his first crass mistake for Lubbock, who'd lived in the county for all but sixty years, to make clear to him just how much he was lacking in local knowledge.

'You're in Norfolk now, laddie,' he'd said, 'and it's a very different place from that sprawling mass of houses and factories and junk where you were born and brought up. You know what Norfolk is? It's a million plus acres of medieval England, flat, exposed and yet curiously secluded. It has marshes and fens, wild heaths and woodlands, and long, sweeping roads that run for miles between bare, deserted fields. The population's sparse and most Norfolk folk live out their lives in rural communities: villages, laddie, and villages that are isolated, small and reclusive. There are seven hundred of them, scattered far and wide across the million acres; and you'd best be prepared, because in every single one of them you'll be viewed with suspicion. One glance from behind the curtains and they'll know you're a furriner, and you'll be lucky if you get them to open their doors an inch, let alone their mouths.'

Because of that, Constable Bates's assessment of Surly Sarah had come as no surprise, and the sight of a pair of suspicious eyes peering at him round the jamb of a door had done nothing to disconcert him. He'd seen eyes like that many times before, in numerous villages on the north Norfolk coast.

But Lubbock had gifted him with more than a mere smattering of local knowledge. He'd also taught him the virtue of patience. 'Unravelling a murder can be a long-drawn-out business, laddie,' he'd say. 'You've got to have patience. Let people talk. Listen to what they say and don't interrupt. Listen and keep on listening. Somewhere among the many thousands of words, there's bound to be an idle snippet of information that'll prove in the end to be worth its weight in gold.'

So, in Sarah Clogston's claustrophobic parlour, sitting in her old wooden rocking-chair, sipping her tea and munching a currant bun, he was quite content to let Bates do the talking as the constable, with commendable patience, coaxed her into telling them once again what had happened the day before at Blacknock.

5

It took a long time. Not that Mrs Clogston was inclined to modesty, but she was, like many of her kind, instinctively tight-lipped, and she couldn't see why Bates and this furriner from Norwich were making such a fuss over what was a far from unusual occurrence. They'd had drownded bodies washed up afore, an' she were carryin' sacks o' cockles every blessed day, weren' she, up fra' Blacknock? They was allus weighin' a duzzy sight more ner a slip of a girl. An' tide were by tha' time nigh on th'turn. Wouldna bin right ter leave th'poor mite ter be swished out ter sea anorl, would it? There were on'y one thing as she could be a-doin', weren' there? Tek up th'poor soul an' bring her ashore.

To such ethical questions Bates made no response. He clung to his own predetermined line, and with true Norfolk doggedness refused to be deflected.

What time had she set out for Blacknock yesterday?

Sarah was vague.

What kind of a question were tha' ter be askin'? How i' th'name of ol' Nick could she tell wha' th'time were? Didn' go by no clocks. Allus went by th'tide, aye an' th'weather. It were late, that it were. She'd had ter bide on till th'fog were a-liftin'. Nay, more ner tha'. She'd had ter bide on till she were sure as it weren' a-droppin' agen. Once as sun were strong enough to burn un away, she'd set out fer th'marsh.

On her own?

No, she weren' on her own. Fanny Bredcocke were with her.

They'd gone straight to Blacknock?

Now that were another rare question to be askin'. Had he gone shanny? Course they'm not goin' straight. Tha'd have ter be dawzled ter go straight on th'marsh. If tha went straight, tha sank. No, tha went on th'sosh, twistin' this way an' tha' like any ol' tosspot out o' th'pub. On'y way ter kep livin'. He should know tha'.

Bates took the rebuke with a stolid composure.

But they were aiming to get to Blacknock?

Had ter be, aye. Bes' cockles there.

So they'd picked their way across the marsh and the sand. Then what had happened?

Contempt had made Mrs Clogston for once almost voluble. Now, without any warning, she reverted to Surly Sarah.

Wha' fer did he want ter know all o' this squit?

Mr Tench had to know.

An' what were it all ter do wi' a furriner fra' th'Sheers?

Bates was inflexible.

It were rules. So what had happened?

Poor little mawther were layin' there, drownded. Weren' that enough?

Were there any clothes about? Had she seen any?

That she hadn't, no. Not so much as a stitch.

Just the body? Nothing else?

An' wha' more were there like ter be?

Footprints? In the mud?

Mrs Clogston dismissed him with a glance of disdain.

'Jack Bates,' she said, 'tha gits worse an' worserer. Tha's no more sense ner a May bloody gosling. Does tha think there'd be footprints wi' tide a-swishin' an' swoshin' all night? Tha mus' be right dawzled.'

It took Bates what seemed an interminable age to prise out the facts.

No, Fanny Bredcocke hadn' bin there when she'd lit on th'body. She were closer inshore. Passed her on th'way back, cocklin', she did. An' th'other women, too.

Who were they like ter be? Well . . . there were ol' Molly Middleton. Her fer a start. An' Alice Burgeys. She were along. Aye, an' Rose Starlin', an' Yelda Thober, an' tha' slummockin' gret mawther, Betsy Girdlestone . . .

Nay, she weren' axin' they fer no hand. Not they lot o' knap-kneed mawkins. Ent a-gorn ter do tha'. All she do were ter hoick up th'poor dead critter an' then drop her down sharp at th'end o' Deep Lane. An' weren' it time they buggered off an' left her ter do th'fettlin'? She weren' partial ter mardlin' wi' furriners all day.

Bates was unmoved. He drained his cup and took another currant bun.

'Reckon there's a mite more tea in that pot,' he said. 'Pour me another cup. It be thirsty work, mardlin'.'

6

Detective Sergeant Bill McKenzie leaned on the bridge parapet and looked at the river. It provided him with nothing in the way of inspiration.

Knocking on fifty years old, broad, overweight and heavily moustached, McKenzie was one who preferred the city lights to those less well illuminated parts of Norfolk that he dismissed as 'the sticks'; and he had, in particular, a strong aversion to those parts of 'the sticks' that he contemptuously called 'the swamps'. Medford was in the sticks, way out in the sticks, and it was also in the swamps.

He eyed the trickling stream with a growing sense of boredom that did nothing to whet his appetite for Medford. How anyone with even a spark of life could choose to live in such a morgue was beyond his comprehension. Another ten minutes and he'd begin to feel rigor mortis setting in.

He shifted his position, turned his back on the river and lolled against the bridge. Medford slumbered in the sun. The only things that moved were a mangy brown mongrel sniffing at a milestone and the wisps of smoke that rose from the cottage chimneys. There was no indication from Sarah Clogston's door that it was likely to open; no sign indeed that Drove Street was about to reveal anything that might stir his listless eyeballs into activity. The mongrel had apparently come to the same conclusion. It wandered round a corner and vanished from sight. There was nothing, it seemed, that was worth a second sniff, let alone a second glance, in the whole of Medford.

It was thus in perverse disregard of their presumptions that, at that very moment, something should occur which merited a good deal more than a glance.

It was the sound of her high heels tapping on the road that first alerted McKenzie to the fact that Medford embraced more than mange-ridden dogs of patently doubtful extraction and Surly Sarahs who slammed their doors against furriners.

Dressed in a close-fitting, cream linen bodice and skirt that emphasized the swell of her breasts and the slimness of her waist, she turned down to the bridge from the coastal road and came tapping towards him. She wore a small pill-box hat with a diminutive feather, and the modest slit in her calf-length skirt revealed the promise of shapely legs above a pair of irreproachable ankles. Clutching a strapless handbag, she walked past him without a glance. She gave him no greeting, flashed him no smile. She ignored him completely.

Which, to McKenzie's way of thinking, was strange to say the least. The sight of this apparition sprung from the swamps had affected him much as a sight of Aphrodite rising naked from the waves. It had left him bemused. He'd stared at her as she approached, and he'd continued to stare as she crossed the bridge and passed him; and his long and varied experience of women had led him to expect some kind of reaction. Women were normally conscious of such a stare. They either smiled, or caught his eye and glanced hurriedly away. But she had done neither. She'd seemed utterly oblivious to the fact that he was there, lounging against the parapet and stripping her as naked as Aphrodite might have been. As far as she'd been concerned, he could well have been no more than a stain on the wall where the mongrel dog had lifted its leg.

He was predictably intrigued. With little else to do but look at Medford's less than captivating river, he watched her receding figure with a lazy fascination till a bend in the road detached her from sight.

He was still gazing at the point where he'd seen the last erotic sway of her hips when the door of the Clogston cottage opened with the creak of an ancient weatherboard to reveal the full glory of Constable Bates and, behind it, the shadowy outline of Tench.

They walked across the road and joined him on the bridge.

'Any sign of Gregg and Sue Gradwell?' said Tench.

'Haven't seen them yet.' McKenzie waved a hand. 'Told them to wait at Bates's place until we got back.'

Tench leaned on the parapet and looked at the river.

'Peaceful, isn't it?'

'Idyllic,' McKenzie said. 'I've always thought of retiring to a village like this. Nothing ever seems to happen. You can stand here and dream.'

7

At that very moment, five miles along the coast, ex-Detective Chief Inspector John Spencer Lubbock knocked out his pipe in a battered tin ashtray, hauled himself out of his only armchair, armed himself with his cherrywood stick and locked the door of his cottage below the church at Cley. Then, backing his old Morgan three-wheeler out of the brick store-shed he used as a garage, he drove down to the village and turned left on the coastal road that led to Blakeney.

He crossed the river, climbed the hill and, in less than a mile, reached the twin-towered church of St Nicholas, once equipped with a lantern to guide mariners into what, centuries before, had been a thriving harbour. But his business that afternoon was not in the church. He drove past it, past the road leading down to the quay, past the brick-and-flint houses and pebble-walled gardens till, on the long, straight stretch that reached out to Morston, he drew to a halt by a five-barred gate at the foot of Kettle Hill.

There he wound himself out of the cramped driving seat, leaned on the gate and, with slow, methodical finger movements, began to fill his pipe, gazing up all the time at the black-towered windmill with its white cap and sails on the crest of the hill.

He surveyed it with a measure of self-satisfaction, not to say pride. When he'd inherited it four years before, along with the cottage, the granary, stables and cart-lodge, it had been nothing more than a smoking ruin, the cap and sails burnt away, the cast-iron windshaft, the brake wheel and the gearing to the burnt-out fantail exposed, the window apertures blackened above and around where flames had pierced the tower and licked along its wall. Inside there'd been nothing but the metal machinery warped by the heat, and a maze of charred timber choking what had once been the basement store.

Now it presented a very different aspect. He'd spent the remainder of his legacy on restoring the mill. It had taken three years, but right at the end of the previous summer the last of the sails had been hoisted into place and he'd ordered the first consignment of grain. Now, every weekend, the sails turned in the breeze that blew from the sea, the newly-fitted burr stones ground the grain into flour, and the cottage, refurbished, had been let to the first of his summer visitors: holidaymakers who came to tramp the coastal paths, sail their dinghies down the creeks to the sea, or simply to watch the birds that nested on the shingle or frequented the marsh.

Striking a match and cupping his hands, he lighted his pipe, drew on it several times and expelled a cloud of smoke that drifted towards the mill. Then he pushed himself up, opened the gate and drove up the slope.

The cottage door was ajar, so he tapped on it gently. There was no response from inside, so he knocked a second time, louder than before. There was still no reply.

He stood back and looked around. As far as he could see, there was no one about.

He walked across to the stables and peered inside. The place was empty, and so were the granary and cart-lodge.

He trudged back to the cottage and looked through the windows. There was no sign of life.

With some hesitation, he pushed open the door and stepped inside. There was no one in the parlour, in the kitchen, the bedroom, or the washhouse at the back. He examined the drawers and cupboards, lifted the coverlet and looked under the bed.

For a moment he stood outside, undecided what to do. Then he locked the cottage door, drove back down the hill, closed the gate behind him, and with one last searching glance at the mill pulled on to the road and turned towards Blakeney.

The ex-Detective Chief Inspector had, it seemed, like McKenzie, encountered the unexpected.

McKenzie, expecting to see nothing, had been blessed with a vision that had left him entranced, whereas Lubbock, expecting much, had found nothing at all.

And it had left him bewildered. So much so that he stopped at a phone box in Blakeney, where he dialled the operator and asked for a number.

Not that that did anything to lessen his perplexity. He emerged tight-lipped and, starting up the car, missed a gear and stalled the engine.

29

He swore at himself – something he rarely did – and then, muttering into his long-expired pipe, set off again for Cley.

8

'We've got two immediate problems,' Tench said, as they made their way back towards the police house. 'We don't know who the woman is, and we don't know where she went into the sea.'

'Reckon as it's most times the same, sir,' said Bates. 'Body's washed up, an' we're asking the same two identical questions. Find the answer to one an' it's like as not the second'll be solving itself.'

Tench stopped in his tracks. 'Then we'd better start looking for answers, Constable. You've had no reports of anyone missing?'

'No, sir. Can't say as I have, and I'd be knowing for certain if anyone were. Word's getting around sharpish here in Medford. Travels like the speed o' light ye might say. No, sir, she won't be from Medford an' that's a fact. I took a good look, an' her face weren't familiar.'

'Then it's likely she was dumped in the water somewhere else. The point is, where? According to what the pathologist says, she'd been in the sea between eight and twelve hours. Now you know the coast well and the way the currents run, so where would you say she went in? Make a guess.'

Bates stroked his chin. 'Currents run to the east, so it'd like to be somewhere to the west, sir, for sure; but where, well, that's a different kettle o' fish. Ten hours is no time at all, an' water were passably still Monday night. Could be Wells or Holkham, even Brancaster mebbe. On the other hand . . .'

'What?'

Bates gave a shrug. 'There's a tale as goes around these parts,' he said, 'about ol' Mary Bunn.'

'And who's Mary Bunn?'

'She were one o' the cockle women, years ago, sir. They say she were cockling out on Blacknock when all in a trice the mist come down an' she were lost wi' nary a speck o' light to be guiding her back. The whelk boats from Wells, they were lost in it too, an' come crawling in, all of 'em, feeling their way through the fog along the coast. The men aboard said they heard a woman sobbing out on Blacknock, but they daren't get too close. They reckoned it were Mary trapped on the mud wi' the tide coming in, an' her knowing it were rising so fast she'd no chance. Nor had she, sir. They found her next day, a-drowned on Blacknock.'

'She was still there?'

'Aye, sir, so the tale tells.'

'The tide hadn't shifted her?'

'No, sir, that it hadn't. And the weather that night were the same as 'twere Monday. Still an' misty. So I'd not be ruling out that she were left on Blacknock.'

McKenzie frowned.

'You mean someone could have carried her out across the marshes and dumped her there?'

Bates nodded. 'Aye, they could. I'm not saying as they did, but I reckon ye'd both of ye be well advised to keep the notion in mind.'

'She was carried back,' said Tench, 'so she could have been carried out.' He turned towards Bates. 'Are we looking for someone with local knowledge? Someone who knew the tracks across the marsh?'

The constable removed his helmet and scratched his head.

'Let's put it like this, sir. There be few sane bodies apart from the women who go out there reglar as'd think o' toting such a weight across the marsh, an' it'd like to be mighty dangerous even to try it. Ye'd need it to be light an' ye'd need to know the way. There's rotting timbers thrown across the creeks. One step left or right an' ye'd be sinking in the mud.' He paused. 'But that's not to say as it couldn't be done if ye were desperate enough to be rid of a woman ye'd like as not murdered. Monday night were bright moonlight afore the mist come down. Set off atween the tides, watch every step, an' ye might well make it out there an' back agen alive. But ye'd have to be driven by a fear that were greater than any fear ye might have o' the marsh. If ye want my thinking, sir, then it's this. It's not a trip I'd be caring to make any time, not without a guide. Blacknock's no place to get on to an' off unless instinct's telling ye which route to take. An' ye never know wi' the mist. It comes down sudden like, an' if ye're out there ye lose all sense of what's around. Ye could be walking to the sea, not making for the land.'

He donned his helmet again.

'No, sir,' he said, 'if ye're out on Blacknock in a blanket o' fog, then, like ol' Mary Bunn, ye may as well sit down an' sob till ye die There's not much else ye can do.'

9

Jack Bates was a bachelor, and it had long been noised around Medford that he'd chosen to embrace a celibate life because, way back in time, he'd suffered a bitter disappointment in love and still carried a torch for the woman who'd thoughtlessly spurned his attentions.

Whether this was true remained a matter for speculation, but it was undeniable that, since arriving in the village, he'd maintained a rigidly neutral stance in the face of much attention from a long line of eligible Medford spinsters.

Such love as he'd displayed had been concentrated, not on the fairer sex, but on his job, which he performed with a meticulous efficiency; his garden, where the plants were regularly cleansed of weeds and planted with a regimental precision; and his parlour, which was filled with highly polished brassware and dusted with a frequency that left no occasion for the merest speck of grime to soil its unremittingly impeccable aspect.

To McKenzie, whose bachelor flat on the outskirts of Norwich was a chaos of empty beer bottles, unwashed crockery and long-discarded copies of the *Eastern Daily Press*, it appeared to be a room designed, above all, to engender discomfort. It needed a few things flung about at random to make a man feel at home. As it was, he felt like a very large bull sniffing the air of a small china shop.

What made him feel even more out of place was that none of the others seemed aware of their untouchably immaculate surroundings. Tench had pulled out a spindle-legged chair from a corner and stretched out his legs, while Gregg and Sue Gradwell, summoned from Norwich, had already commandeered the two deep armchairs, and relaxed in them with every appearance of comfort. Since Bates was rooted firmly behind his desk, the only seat that remained was a small wooden stool. He squatted down on it, his knees distressingly close to the level of his chin, and felt more than ever like a displaced person picked up and dropped in an alien land.

'Cosy little den you've got, Constable,' said Tench.

'Serves its purpose, sir,' said Bates.

Tench pulled out his notebook. 'These women that Mrs Clogston mentioned. If we question them, which of them's likely to talk?'

Bates looked down his nose. 'Not many, an' that's a fact. They don't take kindly to folk interfering. Reckon as Yelda Thober's got a mite more gab than the rest o' the bunch. Gather cockles they may, but they're tight as clams when it comes to the talk. Ye'd best be leaving 'em to me, sir. I've known 'em for years.'

Tench nodded. 'Right. Now supposing the body was dumped here in Medford. You said it was possible, but whoever chose to do it must have set off between the tides. What time was low water on Monday night?'

Bates opened a drawer in the desk and took out his tide tables. 'Eight minutes to ten, sir,' he said. 'High water were ten past four Tuesday morning.'

'And sunset?

The constable reached for another book, and ran his finger down a column of figures. 'Near enough half-past eight, sir. 8.28.'

'And it was moonlight on the marsh?'

'Clear and bright, sir, aye, till the mist come down. That'd likely be three in the morning, thereabouts.'

'So any of your cockle women could have made it out to Blacknock and got back again safely if they'd set off from Deep Lane just after sunset.'

'They could, sir, aye. But . . .'

'You wouldn't like to think that any of them did?'

'Not in character, sir.'

'You're sure of that, Constable?'

'As sure as a man can be. I've known all of 'em nigh on thirty year, sir. Seen 'em grow up.'

Tench nodded again.

'Right. That means we're left with your other possibility. A desperate man, strong enough to carry a body that far, knowing the tides, using the moonlight and watching his step.'

Bates gave a shrug. 'Could be done, sir.'

'And if it was, would anyone have been likely to see him?'

'Doubtful, sir, doubtful. There's not many houses look out on the marsh, an' village folk hereabouts pulls their curtains at sunset an' shuts it away. It can look mighty lonely like once the light goes.'

'But he could have been seen.'

'He could, sir, aye, but only by chance.'

'Then we'd better make sure, one way or the other.' Tench turned to McKenzie. 'Mac,' he said. 'You and Gregg and Sue Gradwell. House-to-house here in Medford. Split the village between you but concentrate first on the houses near the marsh and those close to Deep Lane. We need to know if anyone saw anything unusual on Monday night; maybe heard a car or happened to see one parked; caught sight of folk wandering about in the dark when they should have been at home. You know the form . . . I'm off back to Norwich to report to the Chief Super.' He pushed himself up. 'Keep in touch with Bates and let me know how things go. And as soon as I've gone, give Lock a ring. He's manning the phone. Tell him I'm on my way.'

10

Prior to Lubbock's retirement, Detective Chief Superintendent Hastings had worked closely with him for more than ten years, and their relationship had proved to be not merely productive, but also congenial.

An odd kind of intimacy had grown up between them. If there was one thing that Lubbock detested, it was deviousness. He warmed to fair dealing, and he'd soon decided there was nothing that was even remotely devious about James Francis Hastings. He was a man you could turn your back on with unfailing trust, a man who never pulled rank, who argued his case gently, succinctly, but always with an ultimately disarming logic; a man who could be worked under, a dispassionate colleague and often a friend.

For his part, Hastings had immediately taken to this solid, slow-moving, unemotional figure. He knew how much his monthly crime statistics owed to his Chief Inspector's uncanny success in solving the most intractable of crimes, and he respected him for it. How he did it Hastings could never quite fathom. Even without a wealth of evidence to support him, Lubbock always seemed to have a built-in compass which turned him in the right direction: towards the killer and the motive that had led him to kill. Because of that, he'd valued his opinions, forthright as they'd been, and irrational as, on more than one occasion, they'd seemed.

Most of all he'd valued his character assessments. When it came to appraising his junior officers, Lubbock had almost always proved to be right, and never more so than in the case of Mike Tench.

He remembered the day, some four years before, when Lubbock had suggested that Tench, then merely a fledgeling sergeant, should be packed off to Italy to deal with a particularly difficult case.

He'd demurred.

'Surely, John,' he'd said, 'he's far too inexperienced.'

But Lubbock had had his own very different views.

'He's bright, he's conscientious and he won't let us down. He knows that part of Italy. He was stationed there at the end of the war. And he speaks a certain amount of Italian. He's equipped to do the job and if, as you say, he lacks the experience, then what better way of giving him what he needs?'

He'd still had his doubts.

'You think he's up to it?'

'Oh, yes' – Lubbock had been firm – 'he's up to it all right. Believe me, sir, Tench is going to climb fast. In another six months you'll be ready to put him up for DI. In another twenty years he'll be sitting in that chair that you're sitting in now; if not here, then somewhere else. And, at this early stage, it might be worth gambling on a future Detective Chief Superintendent.'

Well, he'd gambled. Tench had gone, and he'd wrapped up the case; and six months later, almost to the day, he'd put him up for promotion. He'd been a Chief Inspector now for all of twelve months, and in that time he'd matured out of all recognition.

As he looked at him now, face to face across the table, he admitted to himself that Lubbock had been right. Tench had risen fast, and he was going to rise further.

'So, Mike,' he said, 'what's the problem with this woman who was washed up at Medford?'

Tench took a deep breath.

'The problem's Dr Ledward's diagnosis, sir. He's sure she didn't drown.'

'He's positive?'

'Seems to be.'

Hastings laid down his pen.

'Well, Reg Ledward isn't one to jump to conclusions. We both know that. How does he say she died?'

'Anoxia, sir. He thinks she was suffocated, then she was dumped.'

'You'd better give me a run-down.'

'Right, sir.' Tench summarized the little he knew.

Hastings frowned. 'This Clogston woman. Are you telling me she carried the body back across the sands and then across the marsh? A mile and a half?'

'Roughly that. Yes, sir.'

'Seems hardly believable.'

'She's used to carrying sacks of cockles, sir. They all are, the women who gather them.'

'Yes, I've heard they're a breed on their own,' Hastings said, 'but even so . . . You've questioned her?'

'Yes, sir.'

'And what did she say?'

'Not a lot.'

'Reluctant to talk?'

'Mouth like a mantrap, but I wouldn't think there's anything dodgy about her.'

The Chief Super laced his fingers underneath his chin.

'So we're looking at a possible murder.'

'A suspicious death, sir, at least.'

'And we don't know who the woman is.'

'Not yet, sir, no, but it doesn't seem likely she came from Medford, though she could have been dumped there. No one's been reported missing in the village, and Constable Bates didn't recognize her.'

Hastings pondered.

'Well, we're not likely to make much headway till we know who she is. That's the first priority. So what are you going to do? Use Ransome?'

Dave Ransome reported crime for the *Eastern Daily Press*.

'Seems the best bet, sir. We'll let him have an artist's impression of the woman. He's got enough clout to give us a front-page spread. Apart from that, all we can do is circulate local forces, trawl through the missing persons files and wait for someone to get worried enough to ring us. McKenzie, Gregg and Sue Gradwell are doing a house-to-house in Medford, and Bates is interviewing the rest of the cockle women there.'

35

'Incident room?'

'For the moment, sir, I think the police house in Medford. It's right on the spot. Once we know who she is, we may have to change it, but till then . . .'

'Medford . . . That's close to John Lubbock's place, isn't it?'

'Yes, sir.'

'How close?'

'Five miles at a guess.'

'And what about that mill of his? Kettle Hill?'

'Even closer, sir.'

Hastings narrowed his eyes. 'Are you thinking what I am?'

'Trying not to, sir.'

'He hasn't made contact?'

'Not yet, sir, no.'

'But it's likely?'

Tench gave a shrug. 'You know Mr Lubbock. Once he scents a murder and knows I'm involved, he'll make it his business to offer me the wisdom of his long experience. He's never been known to fail.'

'Still can't bring himself to believe you can solve it on your own?'

'He's never retired, sir. We both of us know that. You always said that he'd a nose for a murder. Well, he has. It's still sniffing.'

'Not yet, though.'

'No, sir, not yet. For the moment this is just another body washed up on the shore. But when he opens his paper tomorrow morning . . .'

'That'll be D-Day.'

'Who knows?' said Tench. 'Perhaps he'll have a sudden transmogrification. Decide he's too old to be mixing it with killers.'

The Chief Super smiled and then shook his head.

'If I know John Lubbock, nothing short of a miracle's going to keep him off the scent when he shakes out his *Eastern Daily Press* tomorrow morning.'

'And the age of miracles is past?'

'Long ago, Mike. Long ago. So keep me up to date and keep your fingers crossed.'

Tench didn't cross his fingers, for the simple reason that he had no time.

Detective Constable Lock was waiting to see him outside his office. He opened the door.

'Yes, Desmond?' he said. 'Something to report?'

'This Blacknock woman, sir. She's been identified.'

Tench stared at him. 'She has?'

'Yes, sir. Half an hour ago.'

'Who is she?'

Lock was a conscientious young man. He pulled out his notebook. 'Name of Mallalieu, sir.'

'Local?'

'No, sir. From somewhere down south.'

'Then who identified her?'

Lock seemed to hesitate. 'Well, actually, sir . . .' he said.

Tench waited. 'Go on.'

'It was Mr Lubbock, sir. Rang from the mortuary. Told me to say he was on his way to see you.'

11

As a matter of fact, Lubbock had already arrived. Even as Lock spoke, he was manoeuvring his car into a vacant corner of the station compound, and five minutes later he was seated in Tench's office, stoking up his pipe.

'So she didn't drown,' he said. 'I thought not, when I saw her. What killed her then, laddie?'

'Ledward says anoxia. She was suffocated. That's his diagnosis.'

'Well, Reg Ledward never says anything till he's sure, and even then he makes it sound as if he might be mistaken. If he says she was suffocated, you can take it as gospel . . . Accident or intent?'

'Could be either,' said Tench, 'but someone certainly dumped her in the sea. So tell me about her.'

Lubbock drew on his pipe and expelled a rolling thunderhead of smoke.

'Looking back on it, laddie, there's not much to tell . . . You know I intended to let the mill cottage to holidaymakers?'

'You said so, yes.'

'Well, a fortnight ago I put an ad in the *EDP* and in a couple of the nationals. Then last week – it was Wednesday – this woman came knocking on my door at Cley. Wanted to take the cottage for a fortnight. There seemed no reason not to trust her; she offered to pay two weeks' rent in advance; so I drove her across to Kettle Hill in the Morgan, showed her around, fixed up for bread and milk to be delivered, and gave her the key.'

'And she settled in all right?'

'Appeared to do, yes. I went round to see her the following day, and she seemed happy enough, so I left her to it. Then today I thought I'd better pop in again just to see how things were going.'

'And?'

'She'd disappeared. The cottage door was standing open, but the place was empty. Not a trace that she'd ever been there at all. I went through all the drawers and cupboards. Cleaned out. She'd brought a suitcase with her. That was missing too. Looked as if she'd simply packed up and walked away. No word to me. I couldn't understand it. Then I remembered that report in the *EDP* about the woman washed up on the beach at Medford, and began to wonder. She was a stranger to the area. Could easily have gone walking out on the marsh and got caught by the tide, so I thought I'd better take a look at the body. It was her, no mistake. Then I heard that you and the lads were out at Medford. That made me put two and two together.' Lubbock laid down his pipe. 'Looks as if we might have a murder on our hands, doesn't it, laddie?'

'You're sure it was her?'

'Positive. No doubt about it.'

Tench reached for a sheet of paper and took out his pen.

'Then who was she?'

'Gave her name as Veronica Mallalieu.'

'Where from?'

'Southampton.'

'Did she give you an address?'

'45 West Hammerton Way. Gave me a phone number, too. Southampton 9599.'

'Well, at least that gives us a start. We know who she is.'

Lubbock retrieved his pipe.

'Don't jump to conclusions, laddie. I wish to hell we did.'

Tench gave a groan. 'Go on,' he said. 'Tell me.'

'On the way back home, I stopped off at a phone box in Blakeney. Asked the operator for Southampton 9599.'

'And?'

'No such number. So when I got back to Cley, I rang up Joe Feltham, an old colleague of mine in Southampton CID.'

'No West Hammerton Way?'

'Non-existent,' said Lubbock, 'and there's no Veronica Mallalieu on the electoral register, so it looks very much as if our suffocated friend didn't want herself traced. The question is why, and what was she doing here that made it so imperative that no one should know she was up here at all?'

II
DEEP WATER

Under every deep a lower deep opens
Ralph Waldo Emerson: *Circles*

1

At 2.35 that same afternoon, as Tench was nearing the outskirts of Norwich, PC Harris, the resident constable at Blakeney, received a call from a Mr Geoffrey Wellbridge of Sparrow Hill House at Sibthorpe. It reported a break-in.

Steve Harris was young, athletic and, unlike McKenzie, still enthusiastic. Throwing a leg over his motorbike – a recent acquisition – he pull-started it into life, crackled his way along the straight stretch to Morston, turned left beyond the church, and in a matter of minutes was approaching Sibthorpe.

Sparrow Hill House was a somewhat grim Elizabethan mansion with two projecting wings, a pair of stepped gables and mullioned and transomed windows. Empty and neglected during the war years, it had been rented by Wellbridge some six months before, but little had been done since then to cut the rank grass that had overgrown the garden or to trim the branches of trees that all but obscured the drive and hid the house from the road.

Harris knew little about Wellbridge himself, apart from what village rumour had from time to time told him. He'd apparently been working abroad, had married there, brought his wife home with him and settled down at Sibthorpe because, so it was said, he'd grown tired of the hills and Norfolk was just about as flat as anywhere in England.

Harris wound along the drive beneath an archway of leaves, parked his bike by the weatherbeaten door and pulled on the bell. It rang somewhere deep in a cavernous interior; then the door was wrenched back, and he found himself facing a wiry, dark-haired, middle-aged man with a face burnt brown by exposure to the sun: long exposure at a guess, for six months of Norfolk winter had done little to fade the tan.

'Ah, Constable,' he said. 'Please step inside.'

'Mr Wellbridge?'

'That's right.'

'You reported a break-in, sir.'

'Yes. That's correct. Would you like to come this way?'

He led Harris down a long, vaulted hallway and threw open a door. 'See for yourself,' he said.

The room was extensive. Oak-panelled with a large recessed fireplace, it was clearly used as a sitting-room and study. There was a deep three-piece suite, a weighty oak table, and in one corner a knee-hole desk. French windows, wide and high, revealed an unkempt lawn hemmed in by conifers.

But, apart from the heavy furniture, the place was in chaos. Paintings, photographs and ornaments lay smashed about the floor; books had been ripped from their covers; cushions disembowelled; drawers emptied and tossed aside.

'And there's a window broken in the kitchen,' Wellbridge said. Harris examined it. It was clear the break had been done from outside.

'Have you any idea, sir,' he asked, 'who might have been responsible?'

Wellbridge shook his head. 'Not the remotest.'

'No one who might have had a grudge to work off?'

'I don't see how there possibly could have been Constable. We've only been living here for six months, and we've kept ourselves very much to ourselves. We don't know many of the people around.'

'No disagreements with any of the locals?'

'Not that I know of. Why should there be?'

Harris led the way back. 'You found the room like this, sir?'

'I didn't. My wife did. She's been away since Saturday. She has a friend in King's Lynn, and she's been staying over there. She came back this afternoon, and this was what she found. She rang me in Holt. I run a timber business there.'

'What time did she get back, sir?'

'She rang me at round about two o'clock, so it must have been five or ten minutes before that.'

'And you came straight home?'

'Of course I did. Right away.'

'You travel into Holt every day?'

'Yes. I leave about eight. It takes roughly twenty minutes.'

'And you left at eight this morning?'

'Promptly at eight.'

'And everything was normal?'

'If you mean was the place wrecked, no, Constable, it wasn't.'

Harris looked round the room. 'Is there any damage anywhere else?'

'No. Just here.'

'And is there anything missing?'

Wellbridge nodded. 'Yes, there is.'

Harris took out his notebook. 'Can you give me a list?'

'I don't need to, Constable. There's only one thing been taken. A prayer-wheel.'

'A prayer-wheel?'

'That's right. A Buddhist prayer-wheel. The kind that's carried by the faithful in Tibet. I brought it back with me from India.'

Harris had never heard of such a thing. 'Can you describe it, sir?'

'Well, it's not really a wheel. It's a revolving copper drum on the end of a stick. The drum's hollow. It holds a roll of paper printed with mantras –

Buddhist incantations. People carry them about and turn them as they pray. Each revolution of the drum represents a mantra. It's an aid to concentration.'

'Valuable, sir?'

'Intrinsically, no. It's just wood and copper, embossed with designs and decorated with coloured beads.'

Harris was puzzled. 'Then why, sir, would anyone want to steal it?'

Wellbridge gave a shrug and threw out his hands. 'I haven't the foggiest notion,' he said. 'Your guess is as good as mine.'

2

If Steve Harris was puzzled, Tench felt he was lost in the middle of a maze. He frowned across the desk at his old Chief Inspector.

'She didn't tell you why she wanted to rent the cottage?'

'No, and I didn't ask her.' Lubbock dragged on his pipe. 'In any case, it wouldn't have done much good if I had. If she was so keen to keep her name a secret, she wouldn't have told me why she was there.'

'And you've no idea what she'd been doing all week?'

'Not a clue. Hadn't seen her since Thursday.'

'You said you fixed up for bread and milk to be delivered. Who by?'

'Milk from the farm down at Morston Bottom . . .'

'Walter Bolding?'

'That's right.'

'And the bread?'

'Leo Wickstead.'

'Wickstead in Stiffkey?'

'Used to be there. Still owns the shop, but he moved across to Medford a couple of years back. Wanted to expand.'

'I'd have thought he'd have wanted to slim, not expand. Is he still as fat as ever?'

'Much the same,' said Lubbock.

'Then he needed a bigger shop. He and his wife could hardly move around in that little place at Stiffkey.'

'Well, as far as the shop's concerned he's no better off at Medford. If anything it's smaller, but he's got a bigger bakehouse and doubled his trade . . . Anyway, I made arrangements with both of them – him and Walter Bolding – early this year. You know them. They're reliable. You met them at the time when the mill was burnt down.'

Tench remembered. He remembered the smell of Mrs Bolding's roast

43

beef, sizzling in the stifling heat of her kitchen, and the taste of Emmy Wickstead's butterfly cakes. He hadn't expected them to come back to mind in connection with a body washed up on the shore.

'Then we'll have to speak to Walter,' he said, 'and to Wickstead. They may have seen something. Any other likely callers?'

'Can't think of any, laddie.' Lubbock bit hard on the stem of his pipe. 'She wouldn't have been getting any letters, I'd imagine, but it's worth checking up with the postman at Blakeney.'

'He's a regular?'

'Yes. Elderly chap. Been delivering there since well before the fire. Fred something or other. Don't know his surname. The Boldings may know. He delivers there too.'

Tench thought for a moment.

'You said you drove her to Kettle Hill in the Morgan. How did she get to you?'

'Took a taxi from Holt. Paid it off at the door.'

'Then she had no transport of her own?'

'Not that I could see.'

'Kettle Hill's pretty isolated, isn't it?'

'Nearest place is the Boldings' farm, and that's a mile away.'

'And you think she came here with some purpose in mind?'

'Must have done, laddie. She was secretive enough.'

'Searching for something?'

'Or someone. Who knows?'

'Then how did she intend to get about while she was here? It's quite a distance to walk, even into Blakeney.'

'Perhaps she did walk. She seemed fit enough ... And there's a bus service runs along the coastal road.'

'I suppose so,' said Tench.

'She could have hired a bike.'

'If she did, where from?'

'Closest place is Bretland's cycle shop in Blakeney.'

'Then we'd better check it out. A stranger to the area riding a bike could well have been noticed.'

Lubbock pulled out a waste bin from under the desk, and knocked out his pipe.

'They all need to be checked: the Boldings, Wickstead, Bretland's, the postman; but there's another thing, laddie. If she was murdered as Reg seems to think, then someone, God knows who, cleaned out the cottage. We've no proof at the moment that that was where she was killed, but wherever it happened the killer must have paid a visit to Kettle Hill afterwards and taken away her belongings. He must have opened all the drawers and the cupboards and fingered every doorknob. That's not to say that he wasn't wearing gloves, but he could have left a trace. So the first thing to do is . . .'

'Get Lester down there.'

Sergeant Lester was in charge of the scene-of-crime squad.

'Right away, I'd say. He's still got five hours of daylight left. Four by the time he gets there. Let him loose on the place, see what he can find. The rest can wait till tomorrow.'

Tench reached for the phone.

'We need to know who she was.'

Lubbock pocketed his pipe.

'Well, we don't know,' he said. 'But we will. Give it time.'

3

At that moment, in Medford, Detective Sergeant Andrew Gregg was standing in front of a small corner shop, looking up at the sign that stretched across the window.

'Leo Wickstead,' it read, 'High-Class Baker and Confectioner.'

Gregg was young, tall and discreetly ambitious. He was also an optimist. He rose each day, whatever the weather, with the firm conviction that things would go well, and since the sun was shining brightly on Medford that afternoon he'd seen no reason to feel other than cheerful when he'd begun the house-to-house by rapping on the door of the first brick-and-flint cottage at the end of Main Street.

Since then, however, his expectations had progressively declined. It was not that, like McKenzie, he took a jaundiced view of Medford. It was simply that on Monday night no one in Medford had noticed anything unusual. The village, it seemed, once the light began to fade, drew the curtains across its windows and retired into deep hibernation till the dawn. Huddled in its parlours, life passed it by, and passed unrecorded.

He hadn't a great deal of hope that Wickstead would prove to have been more perceptive, but he wasn't inclined to waste any more time. Placing the flat of his hand against the shop door, he pushed it open and stepped inside.

There was very little space: too little, in fact, to contain Wickstead, his wife, three gossiping customers, the shelves of crusty loaves and the range of glass-topped cases that seemed to hold more varieties of cake, bun and doughnut than Gregg had ever seen in such reckless compaction.

This was, first of all, because Wickstead was not merely high-class but globular; and second, because his wife was of similar girth. Standing as he

45

did in his square-fronted apron with his back against the shelves, his paunch brushed the counter, threatening, as he swivelled and clutched at a loaf, to sweep into nether darkness a plate piled high with butterfly cakes; while she, red-faced, cheerful and bulging in all the most appropriate places, continually strove, though clearly short of breath, to twist and turn and operate the till in what little space was left.

It was, thought Gregg, like watching the movement of two balloons perilously close to spontaneous detonation; and, as Tench had once done, he found himself following each of their ponderously balanced revolutions, beguiled by the fancy that both of them might at any moment explode, wrecking the shop and depositing everything, loaves, cakes and customers on to Liggerbeck Hill.

It was a crotchet that proved to have no foundation. The Wicksteads survived, the customers dribbled away one by one, and he was left face to face with Wickstead himself, who, in the aftermath of service, rocked from side to side like a tumbling-toy and placed two hands on the counter for support. 'Right then,' he said. 'What you arter, boy?'

Gregg produced his card.

'Detective Sergeant Gregg, sir. Norwich.'

Wickstead took the card, adjusted the rimless pince-nez that dangled from his neck on a loop of black ribbon, and studied it closely. 'Tha' don' answer the question,' he said. 'What you arter?'

'A little assistance, Mr Wickstead. Nothing more.'

The baker eyed him suspiciously. ''Bout what?' he asked.

'We're making inquiries about the body washed up on the shore yesterday . . .'

'Don' know nothin' about tha'.'

'And about Monday night.'

'What about Monday night?'

An elderly woman armed with a basket shuffled into the shop. Gregg glanced at her and then turned back to the counter. 'Is there somewhere we could have a little talk on our own?'

Wickstead looked him up and down. 'Aye,' he said. 'Mebbe. Worth movin', is it?'

'Better, sir, yes.'

The baker gave a deep sigh. 'Sure about tha'?'

'Better with just the two of us, sir, don't you think?'

'Mebbe. Mebbe not.' Wickstead still seemed reluctant to move, but after much thought he fetched another deep sigh, and with one hand on the counter and the other on the shelves he eased himself round till he was facing his wife. 'Best go back o' th'shop then,' he said. 'Come you wi' me, boy . . . Emmy, back up!'

It was only then that Gregg understood his reluctance. Movement within the shop could, so it seemed, only be achieved by pre-calculation. The

Wicksteads, to pass one another in the narrow space between the counter and the shelves, had to execute a kind of physical self-compression, inhaling deeply at the very moment when they squeezed past each other. This proved to be a major operation and was only achieved at last with considerable effort, much puffing and blowing and a sound like a cork coming out of a bottle.

Mrs Wickstead in particular, wedged against the counter, turned red in the face and appeared to be on the point of imminent combustion. Gregg watched her with fascination, Wickstead with more than a little concern. As she staggered free he put out a hand to steady her. Then he smoothed down his apron and waved Gregg through. 'Ent worth it,' he said, 'all this arslin' around. Emmy an' me, we ent like you young uns, straight up an' down as a yard o' pump water. So ye'd best not be axin' a load o' squit, boy, or I'll be chargin' ye fer time.'

4

If the front of the shop was small, the back was even smaller, and such space as there was appeared to be consumed by a multitude of white-dusted sacks of flour and a heavy deal table stacked with baker's trays. Wickstead swept them aside, lowered himself at some peril on to a stool, wiped his pince-nez on a large scarlet handkerchief, clipped them back on his nose and looked at Gregg with some impatience. 'Right then,' he said. 'What be all this spufflin' about Monday night?'

The auguries, Gregg admitted, weren't exactly hopeful. Nonetheless he persisted. 'We're making some inquiries in the village, Mr Wickstead.'

'Waste o' time, tha'.'

'Then you didn't see anything unusual on Monday night, Mr Wickstead?'

'What like, boy?'

'Someone wandering around, a car parked where a car wouldn't normally be. A stranger perhaps . . .'

Wickstead shook his head. 'Emmy an' me, we'm in bed at nine sharp. There ent a deal ter be sittin' aroun' fer i' Medford, an' we ent ones fer mardlin', her an' me. Bakers is early risers, boy, has ter be. Same every mornin'. Four o'clock on th'dot. An' we sleeps like a couple of ol' dead logs.'

'But you do run a shop, Mr Wickstead.'

'Aye.'

'And trade's good?'

'Fairish. An' that ent far wrong.'

'Regular customers?'

'Aye. Village folk.'

'What about strangers?'

Wickstead was seized by a sudden fit of sneezing. He quivered like a jelly on a cardboard plate, and the pince-nez dropped from his nose with a clatter. He picked them up, blew his nose thunderously into the scarlet handkerchief, wiped his eyes and wheezed like a faltering donkey-engine. 'Flour dust,' he said breathlessly. 'Gets in the toobs. Wicious stuff, flour dust. Worse'n pneumonics. Buggers things up good an' proper, it do.' He thrust the handkerchief back in his pocket and adjusted his bulk to a safer position. 'Trade was it, boy?' he said.

'Customers, Mr Wickstead. Strangers in the shop.'

'Oh, aye. Furriners. Not a deal o' they, no. Comes a-garpin' odd times, but they ent much fer spendin'. Don' see a lot of 'em 'cept passin' by.'

'You haven't seen any in the last few days that made you at all suspicious?'

Wickstead sniffed. 'Ent got th'time ter be axin' why folk do this an' not tha'. Them as do's like ter find 'emselves all of a muckwash, an' tha's a bloody fact.' He straightened his pince-nez and stared at Gregg. 'Reckon ye never baked a loaf, boy. Right?'

'Can't say that I have, sir.'

'An' when it come to bakin' ye don' know a bee from a bull's arse. Right?'

All Gregg could do was confess with a shrug that his knowledge of loaves was hardly exhaustive.

'Ye're all up at Harwich, boy, ent ye? Tha's truth on it.' Wickstead braced himself with both hands on the table. 'Then reckon a'd best be puttin' ye ter rights. Bakin' loaves be an art like. It ent ter be rushed. Nor be mekkin' they botty little buns an' they butterfly cakes as ye'll need ter be tekkin' a bag when ye go. Then there be sellin'. Ten hours a day. An' eatin' an' sleepin'. Necessitous, they be. An' all muxed up tergither ye know wha' they mean, boy?' He heaved himself up off the stool with a groan. 'They mean as a'd be shanny ter let ye go slarverin' on about furriners an' Emmy an' me wi' not a second ter spare . . . Ye can tek it as gospel. There ent no furriners prowlin' roun' Medford a-doin' dark deeds. There be more on 'em, true, now as summer's a-comin', but all they be doin' is garpin' aroun'. Naught else, boy, naught else. Not buyin' fer sure, an' tha's a bloody fact . . . Ye're jus' wastin' yer own time an' Emmy's an' mine. So reckon as ye'd best be away back ter Norwich, an' let them as has work ter do git on an' do it.'

Gregg gave up the struggle. He took a deep breath. 'If you say so, Mr Wickstead.'

'Sure on it, boy, an' tha's God's hones' truth.' Wickstead swayed on his feet and turned towards the shop. 'An' don' you be fergettin' they butterfly cakes. They be Emmy's best bakin'. Couple o' bags ye'll be tekkin', a reckon. Tha' be fair charge.'

They watched him go, armed with two paper bags.

Emmy looked at her husband. 'What he be wantin'?'

'Axin' 'bout furriners.'

'Yew tell him then?'

'Wha's ter tell?'

'Yew know. They sacks.'

Wickstead wheezed heavily.

'Sacks?' he said. 'Sacks? An' why should a be romentin' on about sacks? Wha' do he want ter be knowin' about they fer? Hones' ter God, gal, reckon there be times when yew ent got more sense'n a May bloody gosling. Tha gits shannier an' shannier, bugger me if tha' don'.'

5

'This prayer-wheel, sir,' said Harris. 'Where was it kept?'

Wellbridge gestured towards the corner of the room. 'It was lying over there. On top of the desk.'

'Not in a drawer?'

'No. It was a bit of a curio, but there wasn't any reason to hide it away. I suppose you could call prayer-wheels collectable items, but they're not exactly in short supply. You can pick them up for next to nothing in Indian bazaars.'

'And you're absolutely sure it's the only thing missing?'

'As far as I can tell. It's difficult to say for certain because the place is in such a mess, but I didn't keep anything of value in here. Apart from our passports.'

'And those weren't taken?'

'No, they're underneath here.' Wellbridge bent down and raised the edge of an upturned drawer.

Harris saw them and gave a nod. He looked around at the carnage. 'It seems to me, sir,' he said, 'that there can only be two possible reasons for this. Either someone set out to do wilful damage . . .'

'And that's most unlikely.'

'Or else they were searching for something they thought was here: something they couldn't find . . .'

'And wrecked the place out of sheer frustration?'

'It's possible, sir, yes ... You say you can't think of anyone who might have had a grudge.'

'No, I can't.' Wellbridge shook his head firmly.

'Then can you think of anything an intruder might have possibly hoped to find? What about money?'

'We don't leave much around. There was ten pounds in notes in one of the kitchen drawers. It's still there, Constable. Hasn't been touched.'

'Anything else? Cheque books? Valuables of any kind?'

'We both had our cheque books with us, and the only thing of any real value in the house is my wife's jewellery: a string of pearls, a diamond pendant and an amethyst bracelet.'

'And they weren't touched either?'

'No. They're still upstairs in her bedroom drawer.'

'And there's nothing out of place anywhere else except here?'

'Not that I can see.'

Harris scratched his head. 'Then it looks as though this person, whoever he was, smashed the window in the kitchen and made straight for this room. The question is, why? Can you think of a reason?'

Wellbridge threw out his hands. 'I only wish I could, but I just can't believe there was anything here that anyone would want to steal. Let alone break in for the purpose of searching.'

Harris slipped his notebook back in his pocket. 'You say it was your wife who was first on the scene?'

'That's right.'

'Is she here?'

'Yes, she's having a bath. I think the sight of this room made her feel that she needed one. You'd like to have a word with her?'

'If possible, sir, yes.'

Wellbridge moved towards the door. 'I'll ask her to come down.'

She came swathed in a pink bathrobe, towelling her hair: a slim, shapely woman, very much younger than Wellbridge himself.

'Deirdre,' he said, 'this is Constable Harris. He'd like to ask a few questions.'

'Why should he want to do that?' Her voice was soft and low, almost a whisper. 'You've told him what happened, haven't you?'

Harris gave her what he hoped was an apologetic smile. 'It's routine, Mrs Wellbridge. Nothing more than that. You were the one who discovered the damage. I have to speak to you.'

She drew the robe more tightly around her, swept a broken picture frame off the settee, and perched on the edge.

'OK,' she said. 'Speak.'

'I gather you've been away since Saturday, ma'am.'

'Yes, I have.'

'What time did you get back here?'

She gave a little shrug. 'I suppose it was just before two o'clock.'

'What did you do?'

'Unlocked the door and came in, Constable. What else would I do?'

Harris restricted himself to a nod.

'Once you were in, where did you go?'

'Straight to the kitchen.'

'Did you notice the broken window right away?'

'I could hardly miss it. I was treading on glass.'

'So what after that?'

'I pulled open the drawer in the kitchen table. I keep small amounts of money in there.'

'Ten pounds?'

'Yes, ten. It was all in pound notes.'

'I'd hardly say that was a small amount, Mrs Wellbridge.'

'You wouldn't?'

'No, it doesn't seem so to me.'

She gave another shrug.

'Does it matter?' she said. 'It hadn't been touched. That's the important thing.'

'Then what did you do?'

'Started to look around. This was the nearest room so I came in here.'

'And found it like this?'

'Exactly like this.'

'You telephoned your husband. When did you do that?'

'As soon as I'd looked in the other downstairs rooms and checked in the bedroom . . . Maybe five minutes later . . . What's the point of all this?'

'I'm just trying to get a picture of what happened, Mrs Wellbridge.'

She sighed. 'You'd be better advised to find the little sod that did it.'

There was something in her voice and the words she used that stopped Harris in his tracks. He frowned. 'Have you someone in mind, ma'am? Someone in particular?'

'Well, of course I have,' she said. 'Hasn't my husband told you? There's only one person who could possibly have smashed the place up like this. It's that half-witted boy from the farm up the road.'

'You mean Danny Sprot?'

She looked straight at him.

'If he's the one they call Daft Danny,' she said, 'yes, I certainly do. So I suggest you arrest him . . .'

6

A mile away, in Medford, WDC Susan Gradwell raised the brass knocker on a large detached house of Georgian aspect, rapped sharply twice, took a step backwards and waited for some response.

Sue Gradwell was young, intelligent and self-possessed. Her fair hair was swept back and pinned in a pleat; her eyebrows were delicately pencilled; and her lips, the upper one very much the Cupid's bow, needed little to enhance them. She was healthy, lissom, and possessed of a figure sufficiently curvaceous, as she very well knew, to act as a lodestone for the eyes of male colleagues whose lusts were unfulfilled.

As far as she was concerned, they were likely to remain so. There wasn't one of them she'd ever, in her wildest fancies, felt tempted to spend an evening with, let alone a night. She'd resigned herself, long before, to the growing conviction that none of them had the slightest idea what it was like to be the solitary woman in an outfit that was trimmed to serve the whimsies of men. Their genes, she'd concluded, were programmed in some peculiar way that made appreciation of a woman's viewpoint utterly impossible.

When she'd joined the CID she'd imagined herself as a kind of pioneer, bringing something to a totally masculine squad that had thitherto been lacking; solving the odd intractable case by a typical flash of woman's intuition; appraised as an asset in the fight against crime, and possessing a talent unique in itself that no one would possibly dare to misappropriate.

But it hadn't turned out to be quite like that. It was true she'd been regarded as something unique, but her singularity had been that of the only sex object within easy vision: a slip of a girl, first to be ogled and then dismissed as a mere scrap of frippery to be tacked on the fringe of a squad of complacently self-sufficient men.

She'd spent most of her time proving her male associates' all too plausible thesis that the most mundane, petty and boring tasks were purposely designed to be done by women. She'd held the hands of bereaved wives and mothers, tended weeping sisters and calmed bewildered children. She'd returned victims' clothes to grieving relations, answered the phone in the CID room, typed out innumerable statements from suspects, and done little else but run errands for those who refused to bother themselves with the routine chores; and when, six months before, more out of boredom than anything else, she'd decided it was time for once to use her own initiative, she'd been left battered and bound on an airfield runway, lucky to escape death at the hands of a man who'd revealed himself as a multiple killer.

For a few days, lying in a hospital bed, she'd been a heroine, if a misguided one; but, once back with the squad, nothing seemed to have changed. All the men she worked with, McKenzie, Gregg and Lock, Ellison, Rayner and Spurgeon, even the Chief himself, if not misogynistic, still clung to the belief that God had designed women to do this and men to do that, and this was always the more tedious, uninspiring and unproductive. It hardly mirrored the kind of work she'd joined the CID to do.

The afternoon she'd spent in Medford had proved to be no exception. Constable Bates, she could only deduce, had drawn up a list of all the people in the village who closed their curtains, switched on their lights and shut themselves off from the world every day of the year once the light began to fade. She'd trailed from cottage to cottage and met with the same negative response at each door. No one had stepped outside after half-past eight, no one had even peered through the slits in their blinds. They'd retreated behind their brick-and-flint walls, eaten their suppers, gone to their beds, slept the sleep of the just, and never given a thought to the rest of Medford till the following morning. Jack the Ripper, it seemed, could have prowled the village for hours, and left in the dawn without a single speck of blood on the blade of his knife.

She looked down at the list. She'd done twenty-two houses, and this was the last. The Meals. Its owner a Hilary Burcham. No Mrs or Miss. Probably some old biddy who never stirred out. Slept all the night and half of the day. Even if Mrs (or possibly Miss) Burcham was alive and awake, which didn't seem likely, the chance of retrieving a vital clue was no better than it had been at any of the other twenty-two places where she'd wasted a whole afternoon of her life.

She took a step forward and rapped a second time. Half a minute ebbed away, and she was just about to leave The Meals to its silent slumbers, when a window in the attic was suddenly wrenched up, a man's head appeared, and a resonant voice called down to her, 'Wait!'

She waited, the head was withdrawn, only to reappear after what seemed to her an excessively long interval, and the voice, deep and vibrant, rolled down to her again. 'Abject apologies, dear lady,' it said. 'Urgent business. Had to be dealt with. Now tell me. What can I do to assist?'

She looked up, shading her eyes against the sun. What she saw was a head of flowing white hair, and underneath it a wrinkled, weatherbeaten face, and a pair of nut-brown arms resting on the sill.

'I'm looking for a Hilary Burcham,' she said.

Whoever the man was, he seemed vastly amused. 'Then look no further, dear lady,' he said.

'You're Hilary Burcham?'

'The very same, madam. Hilary James Marmaduke Burcham. Baptized, I

53

might add, by the Bishop of Norwich, seventy-five glorious summers ago. And that being so, what can I do to help?'

She held up her card. 'Police, Mr Burcham. CID. I'd like to ask a few questions.'

'You would?'

She nodded. 'If it's convenient.'

Burcham produced a watch and studied it intently. 'Difficult, dear lady. Held up at Peterborough. Ten minutes late. Due at Ely in less than a quarter of an hour. Still, nil desperandum. Might just be done. Courtesy to the travelling public, that's always the watchword. Can only offer my deepest regrets. Impossible to leave here before we reach Ely. Safety regulations. Movement restricted at times such as this. Afraid you'll have to find your own way by the road. Should be no problem. Directions clearly posted. Easy to read. Straight up Carrow Hill, under the Wensum Bridge and then follow the signs to Norwich. Entrance below. Just open the door.'

The window slammed down, then it jerked up again. He leaned out and waved.

'More apologies,' he said. 'You'll need a penny for the turnstile. There's a label on the tin.'

7

It was curiosity more than anything that made her persist. That and a desperate determination to salvage something from what had been, until then, a wasted afternoon.

The man was clearly eccentric, if not plainly mad, but long hours of fruitless questioning all over Norfolk had taught her that it wasn't always the sane, responsible people who vouchsafed the most significant scraps of information. It was often the unconventional: those who lived in their own little offbeat worlds, kept unusual hours and were wide awake when other folk slept. There was no indication that Mr Hilary James Marmaduke Burcham made a habit of wandering the side lanes of Medford when the full moon happened to be shining on the marsh, but on the other hand there was no solid evidence to show that he didn't. Whatever the urgent business was that claimed his valuable time, it was, she decided worth a further few minutes' investigation.

She turned the knob on the door and stepped warily inside. Ahead of her was a hallway that led to a flight of stairs, and at the bottom a turnstile that looked to have been imported from a decaying seaside pier. The paint was green and chipped, and resting on top was an old cocoa tin with a cardboard sign that read 'PLEASE PLACE A PENNY IN THE SLOT AND WALK THROUGH.' She peered into the tin. It held a single copper coin.

The hallway was wide, and it was possible to walk round the turnstile at either side, but she followed instructions, dropped the penny in the slot and pushed through the barrier. On the wall of the stairs were two further signs printed clearly in black. The first said 'CARROW HILL'. The second bore the word 'NORWICH' with an arrow pointing upwards.

She set foot on the bottom stair and then stopped. From way up above came a deep continuous rumble. It seemed to travel round the house, growing louder, then fading away into distance; repeating itself, time after time. It sounded as if some juggernaut were pounding through the attics.

She leant on the banister rail and listened. Then she gave a little smile, half in amusement and half in relief. She knew what she was hearing. She'd heard it too often before to be mistaken.

Born and raised in Nairobi where her parents had occupied a flat in the embassy, she'd been sent back home to a boarding school in Sussex and had had to spend most of the summer vacations with an uncle and aunt who lived with their two young sons in an echoing Norfolk rectory. The boys had claimed an empty upper room for themselves, and that same continuous rumbling sound had become a familiar accompaniment to the long, hot days she'd spent with the family.

Mr Burcham, like her cousins, was merely indulging his own fascination with mechanical toys. As was the case with others who shared his addiction, he just hadn't grown up.

She took a firm grip on the banister rail and began to climb the stairs.

The first-floor landing carried another sign: 'NORWICH STRAIGHT AHEAD', and at the foot of the second flight were two more printed in glaring red: 'TAKE CARE WHEN PASSING UNDERNEATH THE BRIDGE' and 'THE COMPANY ACCEPTS NO RESPONSIBILITY FOR INJURY'; while the exit from the stairs to the second landing was blocked by a sheet of boarding supported on trestles and bearing the legend 'WENSUM BRIDGE'.

She ducked underneath it and straightened up in time to see a locomotive and tender, four carriages and a brake-van emerge from a tunnel entrance in the wall, clatter past her at speed and disappear through a similar hole by a door that carried yet another sign, this time in blue: 'ALL PLATFORMS THIS WAY'.

By the time she'd negotiated three trestle-lined rooms and the train had sped past her twice, she was beginning to wonder whereabouts in the house Mr Burcham had chosen to locate Norwich station.

She found them both at last in a room at the back overlooking the marsh. He was standing behind a table that held a switchboard and a battery of finger-length levers, while in front of him spread a dizzying complex of rails with station buildings, sidings and enough rolling-stock to compound another two dozen trains. On the wall at his back was a notice that read:

'DO NOT CROSS THE LINE EXCEPT BY THE FOOTBRIDGE'; the one that faced him was plastered with railway timetables, in the middle of which like an island set in a paper sea, was a large, clear-faced clock; and directly above him hung a microphone, suspended on a pulley from the whitewashed ceiling.

At that moment the train burst into the room from yet another tunnel, slowed as it approached the station and drew to a halt at one of the platforms. Burcham reached up, pulled the microphone down, and announced in his normal booming voice, magnified to almost unbearable volume by means of some cunningly hidden loudspeaker, that this was Ely and the train now standing at platform two was the 4.25 to London, stopping – and here he took a deep breath – at Cambridge, Shelford, Whittlesford, Chesterford, Newport, Elsenham, Stanstead, Bishops Stortford, Broxbourne and Stratford. After which he took an even deeper breath, and added on a desperate, expiring note, 'Change here for Peterborough.'

He then glanced at the clock and flicked a lever with his thumb. The train began to move, gathered speed at a truly phenomenal rate, made a circuit of the room, and vanished predictably through a hole in the wall.

He watched it disappear, and then for the first time seemed to wake to the fact that he wasn't alone. 'My most contrite apologies, madam,' he said. 'When duty demands, one must always heed the call. The travelling public has a right to expect that all Great Eastern traffic will be prompt to the minute. That was the 4.25 up to London, due in Cambridge 5.10. There's a freight train from March arriving here at Norwich at 4.58. So until then, dear lady, I can truthfully say that I am utterly, indeed irredeemably, yours.'

8

'And now, Constable, provided you've no objection,' Mrs Wellbridge said, 'I'd like to go and get dressed.'

She was out of the room before Harris could stop her.

Wellbridge threw out his hands in a gesture of impotence. 'Take no notice,' he said. 'She's got a thing about this boy.'

Harris frowned. 'What sort of a thing? Has he been pestering her in some way?'

'Not that I know of.' Wellbridge shook his head.

'Then what makes her think he's to blame for all this?'

'My wife has a strong imagination, Constable. She gets these ideas, but it's all in her mind.'

'What ideas, Mr Wellbridge?'

'She says he watches her, follows her around.'

'And you don't think he does.'

Wellbridge shrugged. 'He may do, but I haven't any evidence to prove that he does. He's never approached her, at least to my knowledge.'

'But he makes her feel uneasy in some way?'

'She says that when he looks at her she feels that he's stripping away all her clothes.' He paused and glanced at Harris. 'I suppose, if you're a woman, an impression like that can be very disconcerting. You imagine all kinds of possibilities, Constable.'

'You mean she's afraid of him?'

'Yes, I think she is. He's a big lad, he's strong, and as far as she knows he could turn out to be violent. I don't know enough about him to be able to judge. Is he likely to be dangerous?'

'Never has been, sir, as far as I'm aware. He's a simple soul, Danny. Born a bit backward, but he's harmless enough.'

'I'm right then,' said Wellbridge. 'Deirdre's just letting her imagination run away with her.'

'If she thinks he's going to rape her, yes, I'd say she is. That just isn't Danny. But he could well be frightening to someone who doesn't know him. I can understand that.'

'Perhaps you could have a word with him.'

Harris nodded. 'I'll do that, sir, yes, but explaining to Danny's a difficult job, and strictly speaking he's not doing anything illegal. It's not against the law to look at a woman. If it were, then three parts of the male population would end up in gaol. It's just that with Danny he likes pretty things. Women and sea shells and little furry animals, they're all much of a muchness as far as he's concerned. He spends half his time collecting shells on the shore. He's got quite a collection. Keeps them in an old tumbledown hen house up at the farm.'

'Then . . .'

'What, sir?'

Wellbridge seemed to hesitate. 'You say he's got a yen for pretty things. What about a prayer-wheel set with coloured beads? Would that catch his eye?'

'Well, it might, sir, yes,' Harris admitted.

'Then suppose he was nosing round the house while we were out. If he looked through the windows, he'd be able to see it lying there on the desk . . . It's only a thought, Constable, but mightn't it be worth while following it up?'

Harris looked at the windows, then at the desk. He still seemed doubtful. 'It could be, sir,' he said, 'but I can't see Danny Sprot breaking into a house and tearing it apart. It just isn't like him to do such a thing . . . Leave it with me, sir. I'll go up and see him . . .'

'And take a look at his hen house?'

'I'll do that, sir, too, and I'll get someone down to fingerprint the room.'

'So you want me to leave it exactly as it is?'

'For the moment, sir, yes.'

'And you'll let me know how things go?'

'We'll keep you informed, sir.' Harris turned towards the door, then he stopped. 'There's just a couple of things puzzle me, Mr Wellbridge,' he said. 'If someone looked through those windows, caught sight of the prayer-wheel and wanted to steal it, why didn't he break in here instead of in the kitchen? And once inside, why didn't he simply take it and go? Why create all this havoc?'

Wellbridge gave another shrug. 'Constable,' he said, 'between you and me I just haven't a clue.'

9

'Now, you said you wanted to ask me some questions.' Burcham seemed to be mildly amused. 'I can't really think why, but fire away, dear lady. You've all my attention.'

Sue Gradwell decided to waste no time. 'You've heard about the woman who was found on the beach, sir?'

Burcham wrinkled his brow. He was clearly at a loss. 'A woman? I don't think so. What was she doing? Wandering?'

'I'm afraid not.

'You mean . . .?'

'She was dead, Mr Burcham.'

'Dead? Good heavens! No, indeed, I hadn't heard. You see, dear lady, I don't venture out much. The trains have to run. I haven't been out since . . . when was it? Let me think . . . Sunday . . . Dead, eh? The poor creature. Drowned, I presume.'

'We think she may have been murdered, Mr Burcham.'

'Murdered? Well now!' Burcham stroked his chin. 'Here? In dear old Medford? That's a turn-up for the book. It most certainly is. Tell me, dear lady, when did this happen?'

'We don't know for sure, sir. That's why we're here. We're hoping that someone may give us a lead.'

'Ah, yes. A lead.' There was a pause as the 4.25 Up on its way to Cambridge exploded from a tunnel, made a circuit of the room and vanished once again. Burcham traced its path intently before he resumed. 'A lead,' he said. 'Of course. The eternal point of departure. The Paddington of all detective investigation. You want me to say I saw a dark-bearded man, dressed in a cloak, lurking in the shadows. But I didn't, dear lady. I see little of the village and it rarely sees me. As general factotum of the Great Eastern Railway, my time is at a premium. Public safety has to be the prime consideration. That and public service. Wouldn't you agree? Signal boxes must be manned, rolling stock inspected, and of course the timetable has to be rigorously adhered to. It leaves me no time to plod the village streets or to gaze out of windows. In other words, dear lady . . .'

'You've seen nothing unusual going on in the village.'

'No, I'm afraid not. It grieves me to disappoint such a charming guest, but the village of recent days has been to me, you might say, nothing more than a shuttered casement. Its comings and goings have passed me by.'

Sue Gradwell sighed. 'Then I'm doing no good here, am I, Mr Burcham?'

'No, perhaps not' – Burcham watched the train as it made yet another rumbling circuit – 'but it seems a shame for you to leave empty-handed, don't you think? You see, dear lady, we don't get many visitors. How about a cup of Great Eastern tea? We have a refreshment room below stairs.'

'I don't think so, Mr Burcham, thank you very much.'

'We serve a wide selection of differing brands. The travelling public requires us to offer a choice.'

'I'm sure it does, sir, but I really haven't the time.'

Burcham sighed in his turn. 'Ah, well, that's a pity. It is indeed.' He pondered a moment, then looked at her hopefully. 'Perhaps you could ask me a few more questions.'

'I don't think so, sir. It wouldn't be much use.'

'I suppose not, no.' He took another deep breath. 'These inquiries of yours. They're confined to the village, I presume. Am I right?'

'In the main, sir, yes.'

'You wouldn't, perhaps, be interested in the marsh?'

'Only after dark.'

Burcham's face brightened. 'After dark, eh? When in particular?'

'Monday, Mr Burcham. But . . .'

'Wait, dear lady.' He raised a mottled hand. 'Please say no more till I've checked on the schedules. Now let me see.' He ran a finger down one of the lists on the wall. 'Today we're operating on the 1872 timetable. Yesterday was 1870. That means Monday must have been 1868.' He peered at the list more closely. 'Yes, it was undoubtedly Monday. I thought perhaps it was.'

Sue Gradwell was puzzled. 'What was?'

'The light.'

'What light, sir?'

'The light on the marsh.'

'You saw a light on the marsh? On Monday night?'

'Correct, dear lady. That was the day of the Foresters' excursion to the Crystal Palace. We ran a special train from Cambridge to London and

59

offered cheap fares. Eight shillings the first class return, four shillings covered cars. 6.15 from Cambridge. London nine o'clock. Returning 8 p.m. Cambridge 10.45.'

'You run the trains at night?'

'Needs must, dear lady, when the public demands. Dark or not, the schedules have to be maintained. We can't have travellers stranded in the small hours. That would be a dereliction of duty.'

'Then you were here in this room on Monday night, Mr Burcham?'

'Had to be, yes. Till the train reached Cambridge. The darkness makes for difficult running, of course, but verisimilitude has to be preserved.'

Sue Gradwell glanced at the curtainless window.

'You don't switch on a light?'

'Goodness me, no!' Mr Burcham seemed surprised that such a question should be asked. 'That would be destructive of authenticity. The stations are lit and the carriages too. And the signals show red and green. That's enough.'

'Then you can see quite clearly out across the marsh?'

'Of course. Not that there's normally anything to see.'

'But on Monday you saw a light?'

'Oh, yes, dear lady. No doubt about that.'

'What sort of a light was it?'

'No more than a pin-point. Bobbing about.'

'You're sure it wasn't marsh gas?'

'A will-o'-the-wisp? No. Not erratic enough.'

'What about a boat?'

Burcham shook his head.

'Moved about far too fast for a boat.'

'Then what would you say it was?'

'Looked to me like a torch. Though why anyone would want to be out on the marsh at that time of night, heaven only knows.'

Sue took out her notebook.

'What time was it, Mr Burcham?'

'Let me see.' He turned back to the lists on the wall. 'I remember it quite clearly. The train had just left Stanstead. Now when was it due? Ah, yes. 9.50. It would be round about 9.52, dear lady. Eight minutes to ten.'

'You're sure about that, sir?'

'Oh, yes.' Mr Burcham was quite decisive. 'I'd just switched the down signal at Stanstead station back again to red. The train was running to time. Due at Newport 10.05. Chesterford 10.20 Shelford 10.37 Cambridge 10.45 ... Now how about that cup of tea? And a muffin perhaps? I can assure you, dear lady, the Great Eastern serves its customers the most delicate muffins in the whole of East Anglia.' He looked at her expectantly.

Sue Gradwell slipped the notebook back in her pocket. She ventured a smile.

'Well, maybe just one, Mr Burcham,' she said.

10

At much the same time as Sue Gradwell took her first sip of Great Eastern tea, Lubbock unlocked the door of the cottage at Kettle Hill and stepped inside. Tench followed him in.

'You say there's nothing of hers here at all?'

'As far as I can see, not a solitary thing.' Lubbock waved a hand around. 'There's no sign that she was ever a part of the place. Whoever the chap was, he's cleared out the lot.'

'What did she bring with her?'

'Just a case, that was all.'

'And you've no idea what was in it?'

'Not the faintest, laddie. The usual things, I expect. Clothes, toilet articles. Whatever she'd be needing for a fairly short stay.'

'You say she came in a taxi?'

'That's right. From Holt.'

'How d'you know she came from Holt?'

'Saw the name on the cab. Gresham Cars. They've got a garage out on the Cromer road. Might be a good idea to try and trace the driver. Find out where he picked her up. If it was the station, then there's always the chance she'd just got off a train.'

'Probably from Norwich. That won't get us very far.' Tench was less than optimistic. 'Still, it's worth a try. What was he like?'

'Short, stocky chap. Fortyish, I'd say. Dark hair, heavy stubble. Spoke with a Scots accent. Glaswegian, at a guess.'

'Right. I'll get someone out there. Shouldn't be difficult to track him down.'

'He might have talked to her, too. You know what taxi drivers are. Not that she'd be likely to tell him anything useful, but odd things slip out. You might pick up a clue. Follow every trail that presents itself, laddie. That was always my rule. In a case like this, you never know your luck. Something that seems to be completely irrelevant may prove to be vital.'

'You haven't got a phone here?'

'No, not yet. It's the next thing on the list, but the restoration work had to take priority, so there's no chance of tracing any calls she may have made. Pity, but there it is.'

Tench looked round the room.

'You say the last time you saw her was Thursday?'

'That's right.'

'But I thought you'd arranged for the mill to work at weekends. Weren't you here then?'

'Should have been, yes, if everything had gone according to plan, but it didn't. Had to run down to Diss to look at some burr stones, and fixed up with Joe Rogers to take over from me. He worked the mill at Billingford before the war, and lives out at Glandford. Trouble was he cried off, so I had to cancel the whole thing.'

'Then we're starting with a blank sheet, aren't we?' said Tench. 'We don't know who the woman was, we don't know what she did or why she rented the cottage, and there's nothing to tell us exactly where she died.'

Lubbock was undeterred.

'True laddie, true, but there are worse ways of starting a murder inquiry. At least we're not lumbered with a lot of preconceptions. If we've nothing to go on, we can hardly begin by jumping to wrong conclusions. That's easy to do and it wastes a lot of time. Far better to start with an open mind.'

'I'd sooner start with a few solid clues.'

'Well, you haven't got them,' said Lubbock, 'so just be patient. Let the case simmer. It'll come to the boil in its own good time.'

'It won't even simmer till Lester arrives. God knows where he's got to. I told him to meet us here.'

Lubbock was irritatingly bland.

'Perhaps there's been another murder.'

'God forbid,' said Tench. 'We've got enough on our hands already.'

11

Perversely enough, at that precise moment, Bill McKenzie, parked in a police car at the end of Deep Lane, tossed his cigarette stub through an open window, put the car in reverse and swung it round in an arc till it faced the village.

If anyone had told McKenzie that his attitude to life was persistently cynical, he'd have raised his bushy eyebrows and flatly denied it. To him it was nothing but sheer common sense. Long experience of investigating violent criminals had taught him to be wary, not to say pessimistic. Life in the force was a dicey business. There could well be someone waiting round the next corner to clobber him with a crowbar or something that was equally hard and unyielding, and he'd long ago come to the firm conclusion that to hope for the best was to court disaster. He therefore made a point of expecting the worst, and consoled himself with the ever-present thought that if the worst didn't happen, that would be a bonus and the best that existence was likely to offer.

Faced with an afternoon's house-to-house in Medford, he'd decided at the outset that knocking on doors in such a dead-alive hole was more than likely to prove unproductive, and since the day was warm, tramping from end to end of the village would offer little beyond a mounting frustration and much in the way of sweat; so, reading through the list of residents providentially provided by Constable Bates, he'd elected to knock on those doors that bounded the village extremities, and had commandeered Gregg's police car for comfort.

His wanderings had taken him from Greystoke Farm on the Blakeney road, back through the middle of Medford to Choosley House on the Warham side of the Sibthorpe fork, and then through the village once again and down Deep Lane to the edge of the marsh. Once there, he parked the car, lit a cigarette, leaned back in his seat and stared at the flat desolation ahead.

It mirrored his mood and reflected his afternoon. A waste, nothing more. A mass of dull brown weed stretching out as far as the eye could see. Featureless, boring, barren and drab.

Patience had never been a virtue that Bill McKenzie had taken much trouble to cultivate. It was typical of him that, presented with a pint, it took him no more than a couple of gulps to empty the glass. It irked him to see the level of the beer remain static, and staring at the Medford marshes evoked a similar kind of progressive irritation. Their unchanging sameness was a pain in the neck. The sooner he got back to Norwich the better.

He was already rolling forward to gather speed down the long, straight stretch that led to Liggerbeck Hill and thence to more civilized parts of Norfolk, when there were three urgent thumps on the roof behind his head.

Braking hard, he looked round to see a thin, pallid, bespectacled youth, shouldering a rucksack and breathing heavily.

'You a policeman?' he panted, bending down to the window.

McKenzie was in no mood to answer such a question. He glared. 'What d'you think this is, lad?' he said curtly. 'A corporation dust cart?'

The youth fell back a pace. 'Well, no. But . . .'

'What?'

'I think I've found a body.'

For the first time since he'd driven into Medford, McKenzie's eyes gleamed. He pushed open the door and stepped out of the car. 'You think? Aren't you sure?'

'No, I can't be.'

63

'Why not?'

'Well, it's out on the marsh. In what looks like a sack.'

McKenzie's eyes positively sparkled. 'Show me,' he said.

III
THE SACK

Let every man carry his own sack to the mill

French proverb

1

It lay half-submerged in a tangle of marsh grass some three hundred yards along the coastal path that led walkers to Wells. Perhaps twenty feet out, it was way beyond reach.

McKenzie peered at it. 'It looks like a sack,' he said. 'Someone must have stood here and slung it out. Dumped it.'

The youth dropped his rucksack down on the path and pointed. 'There's something sticking out.'

McKenzie narrowed his eyes. 'You could be right, lad,' he said. 'What d'you reckon it is?'

'A hand?'

'Looks to me to be more like a foot. Difficult to tell. You can't see for the weeds. We'll have to get it hauled in.'

'You'll need ropes and hooks.'

McKenzie eyed the brown mass of weed, the water channels running through it and the mud oozing up.

'I can see that, lad,' he said. 'You stay here. I'll be back.'

An hour later he stood watching with Tench and Bates as two men with grappling hooks dragged the sack clear of the marsh and set it down on the path. Projecting from the open neck was what was clearly a man's hand.

'Empty him out,' said Tench.

The two men pulled the sacking clear of the body, and then stood back.

Tench turned to Bates. 'D'you know him?'

'Aye, sir, that I do fer sure.' The constable needed no more than a glance. 'Knowed him fer nigh on twenty-five year, an' he be drunk as a polecat most o' the time.'

'What's his name?'

'Craske, sir. Eli Craske. Lives on Liggerbeck Hill, but he ent one fer spendin' much time in the parlour, not to my way a' thinkin'. More like he'll be proppin' up the bar in the Old Dun Cow. Landlord turns him out o' there every blessed night, an' he ent much fer findin' his way back home. I've bin tellin' him more'n once as he'd end up flat on his belly i' the marsh.'

Tench looked down at the grizzled, mud-spattered face. 'Well, he ended up there. You were right about that, but one thing's for sure: he didn't crawl into that sack and do a hop, skip and jump. Ledward's on his way and we'll have to wait till he gives his opinion, but unless I'm much mistaken the man's neck's been broken.' He turned back to McKenzie. 'Mac,' he said. 'I want this path closed and taped off. No one's to touch him till Ledward arrives. He's on his way now, and Lester and his team are ready to move in as soon as he's finished ... Where's this lad that found the body?'

McKenzie waved a hand towards the end of Deep Lane.

'Told him to wait in the police car. Said you'd want to have a word.'

'Who is he?'

'Told me his name was Alexander King. He's a schoolboy. Sixth former at Mountfield School at Holt.'

'Then what's he doing down here?'

'Said he was just walking. Some school expedition.'

'Did he now?' said Tench. 'Well, I'd better have a talk to him. You hold the fort. Bates can do the taping.'

He opened the car door and eased himself into the driving seat.

'Alexander King?'

'Alex. That's right.'

'Detective Chief Inspector Tench ... You're at Mountfield?'

'Yes, sir.'

'Then what's all this about a school expedition?'

The boy blinked at him. 'Expedition?'

'You told Sergeant McKenzie you were on a school expedition.'

'Exercise, sir.'

'That's different?'

'Yes, in a way.'

'Then tell me about it.'

'Well, it's no big deal, sir, not really. There's just half a dozen of us, all sixth formers. We're walking the coast from Holme to Cromer, and I'm doing the leg from Holkham to Medford. We're studying the way that the shoreline's changed. It's a geographical exercise.' He unbuckled the ruck-sack resting on his knee. 'I can show you my notebook.'

Tench flicked through the pages. He recognized the school's coat of arms on the cover. 'You've finished your stint then?'

'Yes, sir. Ends in the village.'

'Didn't expect it to end quite like this though, did you?'

'Not exactly, sir, no.'

'You're feeling all right? Not sick or anything?'

'No.'

'Where d'you live, Alex?'

'Saxlingham, sir. Field Dalling Road.'

68

'Then someone must be picking you up here in Medford. Am I right about that?'

'Yes, sir. Mr Dalton. Six o'clock at the church.'

Tench glanced at his watch.

'Then it looks as if I'd better run you there,' he said 'We don't want Mr Dalton to be hanging around, do we?'

'No, sir.' The boy made it only too clear that that was the last thing he wanted to happen.

'Bit of a tartar, is he, this Mr Dalton?'

'Doesn't like us to be late, sir. Says punctuality's the politeness of kings.'

There was a nod from Tench.

'Louis the Eighteenth.'

'What, sir?' The boy was puzzled.

'Louis the Eighteenth. It was his favourite saying.'

'Wasn't he the one who was guillotined, sir?'

'No,' said Tench. 'That was his brother, but we'd better not risk it, had we? Wouldn't want to see your head rolling round among the tombstones. Come on. Let's go.'

2

Steve Harris parked his motorbike at the gate of Astley Farm, picked his way through the farmyard muck, and tramped across a field till he came to the hen house. Its rickety door, the hinges hanging loose, was propped open against the wall by an old wooden box. He stepped inside. There was no sign of Danny Sprot.

Sunlight filtered down through the broken roof, and laid out on the floor was a line of much-corroded biscuit tins spaced out with a precision that was almost worthy of Constable Bates. Behind them was an equally meticulous line of miscellaneous objects that, at one time or other, had caught Danny's eye and proved to him to be irresistibly attractive. There was a glass case containing a stuffed red squirrel, a brightly coloured German beer mug embossed with a picture of Alpine huts against a background of mountains, a picture of Ginger Rogers cut from a film magazine and stuck on a piece of cardboard, a red rear reflector from a bicycle, and a snow scene containing a top-hatted snowman which, when shaken, produced a cascade of flakes.

Harris shook it and watched the flakes feathering down. He waited till the last had settled, then carefully replaced it and looked around. Apart from the tins and Danny's few treasures the shed was bare. There was no sign of a Buddhist prayer-wheel, and no obvious place where it could have been hidden.

Except, perhaps, for the tins.

He squatted down beside them, removed the lids one by one and riffled through the contents. Not that he didn't know what to expect. He'd seen inside all of them. Danny was only too eager to show them to anyone expressing even the mildest interest. In the first were his cockleshells – the famous Medfords; in the second his whelks; in the third a selection of scallops and trough shells. The fourth held Venus shells, carpet shells and razors, while the fifth was a jumble of sea urchins, brittlestars, seamats and starfish. There was also, somewhere among them, a lone, rigid seahorse retrieved by Steve himself from a Cornish beach and, much to Danny's delight, presented to him to swell the collection.

Not that he always remembered their names, although Steve had looked them up in a seashore book and identified them for him. Danny's memory, like much else about him apart from his physique, was, to say the least, underdeveloped. Sixteen years old, broad and sturdy, he was mentally still little more than a child, and a simple one at that; but not one, in Steve's experience, who was likely to smash people's windows, let alone attack a defenceless woman.

He hadn't expected to find Wellbridge's prayer-wheel hidden among the shells, collectable even though it might be, and it took him no more than a matter of seconds to prove he was right. He was just about to return the lids to their rightful tins when the pattern of light in the shed seemed suddenly to change, and turning round he saw Danny standing in the doorway blocking out the sun.

'Hello there,' he said.

Danny smiled at him happily. 'You lookin', Mist' 'Arris?'

Steve nodded. 'Just looking. You've got some beautiful shells.'

The boy came closer. 'Pretty,' he said. 'See.' Rooting in his pocket, he pulled out an old fur mitten and held it up between his finger and thumb. 'Pretty,' he repeated. He stroked it, then rubbed it against his face. 'Soft,' he said.

As Steve well knew, there was only one way to deal with Danny Sprot, and that was to praise his treasures, however outlandish they happened to be. 'Yes, Danny, that's really pretty,' he said.

Danny beamed at him 'More, Mist' 'Arris.' He felt in his other pocket and this time produced a silver propelling pencil. 'Shiny,' he said, and turned it so that it flashed in the light.

'Oh, that's even prettier.' Steve made all the right noises and held out his hand. 'Can I see it?'

'Look? You look, Mist' 'Arris?'

'Yes, Danny, look.'

The boy handed it over. Steve examined it. Engraved on the shaft were two letters; 'D.W.' He frowned. 'Tell me, Danny,' he said. 'Where did you find it?'

'Find?' Danny screwed up his eyes as if trying to remember what the word meant.

Steve laid the pencil down on the ground. Then he peered at it and picked it up. 'Find, Danny. Where?'

Light dawned.

'Danny show,' the boy said. 'You come, Mist' 'Arris.'

3

He led Harris across the field, through the farmyard and down the road.

The constable trailed him, though not without misgivings. There was no way of telling where Danny might be taking him. His notions of time and distance were somewhat erratic, and his daily wanderings in search of shells led him to far-flung places along the coast. He was well known to all the drivers of lorries, vans and tractors within fifteen miles, and all he had to do was to stand and wait at the side of the road till one of them picked him up. Any effort to trace him during daylight hours would have involved a process of progressive elimination. He might be trawling any shore from Cromer in the east to Burnham Sands in the west, and there'd even been days when he'd tracked the cockle women out to Blacknock.

It was therefore only natural for Steve Harris, as he followed him down the road towards Blakeney, to wonder what, in a rash moment, he'd let himself in for. He had a momentary vision of two weary travellers marooned on a beach with night coming down, and made up his mind that, if Danny seemed determined to lead him much further, he'd go back and fetch his bike.

But at that moment, opposite the end of the drive that wound between trees to Sparrow Hill House, the boy stopped and turned back towards him.

'Here,' he said, 'Mist' 'Arris. Find pretty here.'

Steve handed him the pencil and pointed to half a dozen different places. 'You show me where.'

Danny hesitated for no more than a fraction of a second. He walked to the grass verge at the side of the road, set the pencil down and smoothed the grass over it. Then he straightened up and smiled. 'Find,' he said. 'Here.'

'Good, Danny. Well done.' Steve picked up the pencil and held it out between two hands for Danny to see. 'Look,' he said. 'Letters.'

The boy looked and nodded. 'Lett-ers, Mist' 'Arris.'

'Not Danny's letters.' Steve shook his head. 'Bad thing, Danny keep.'

A look of disappointment crossed the boy's face. 'Bad, Mist' 'Arris?'

'Yes, Danny. Bad. Very bad . . . This' – he held up the pencil and pointed to the drive – 'this belong lady. Live in house. There.'

The boy looked at the pencil and then at the drive. 'Lady, Mist' 'Arris?'

Steve took a deep breath. 'You know lady? Live there in house?' He pulled out his notebook and, using the pencil, drew the outline of a girl with a figure like an egg-timer. 'Lady. Live there.'

Danny's eyes brightened. He nodded three times and smiled. He was happy again. 'Pretty,' he said.

Half an hour later Steve Harris was back at Sparrow Hill House. He rang the bell, and this time it was Deirdre Wellbridge who opened the door. She was wearing a white, pleated skirt and a lemon-coloured blouse, and her ash-blonde hair was swept back in a pony-tail. She folded her arms – a gesture that doubled the thrust of her breasts – and eyed him with a mixture of amusement and irritation.

'Back again, Constable?' she said. 'What now? Don't tell me you've already arrested that cretin.'

'Not yet, Mrs Wellbridge, I'm afraid.' Steve forced himself to sound apologetic. He held out the pencil. 'I'd like you to take a look at this and tell me if it's yours. It's engraved with your initials.'

She only needed a glance. 'Yes,' she said, 'it's mine.'

'Did you know it was missing?'

'Of course I knew it was missing, Constable,' she said impatiently. 'I lost it the day before I went off to Lynn.' She looked up at him sharply. 'That boy, Daft Danny. He took it, didn't he?'

'I wouldn't think so, ma'am.'

'You wouldn't? Well, I would. It's just the sort of thing he'd be likely to do.'

'Have you any idea, ma'am, exactly where you lost it?'

'No, Constable, I haven't. It just disappeared.'

'Where from? A handbag?'

'No, I keep it in the glove compartment of the car.'

'Then your husband might have borrowed it. He could have lost it.'

'He has his own car. He doesn't use mine.'

'Do they stand outside at night?'

'Yes, they have to. We haven't got around yet to building a garage.'

'But you do keep them locked?'

'Normally, yes.'

'There are times when you don't?'

'Odd times, I suppose, but only during the day. In a quiet place like this . . .'

'It's always best to lock a car, Mrs Wellbridge.'

'You mean with folk like Daft Danny hanging around? All right, Constable. I'll remember in future. I suppose he said he found it lying around. Did he tell you where?'

Steve looked her straight in the eyes. 'It was at the end of the drive,' he said. 'On the grass verge. I was searching for clues. I just happened to see it, ma'am, and picked it up.'

4

Ledward was squatting beside the body. He glanced up at Tench.

'I suppose,' he said, 'you want to know when he died.'

'We need to know, Doctor. We can't begin to piece things together till we do.'

'It's impossible to be accurate at this stage, Chief Inspector. You realize that?'

'Of course, sir.'

'I can only give you an estimate, but I'd say death occurred between thirty-six and forty-eight hours ago.'

Tench did some swift reckoning. 'That means somewhere between six thirty Monday night and the same time Tuesday morning ... You can't narrow it down any more?'

'At the moment, no. I may be able to once I get him on the slab. Till then you'll just have to bide your time in patience.'

'What's your verdict? Broken neck?'

'Appearances suggest it.' Ledward was back to his old cautious self.

'Anything else that's significant?'

'Not at first sight. Don't press me for more, Chief Inspector. Not yet.'

'I wouldn't dream of it, sir,' said Tench.

The doctor packed up his bag. 'I'll be off then. Get him back to Norwich as soon as you can.'

'How long before you can give me more details?'

Ledward looked at his watch. 'Ring me tomorrow lunchtime. Not before that. And don't expect miracles.'

'I never do, sir,' said Tench. 'I was born in a rectory.'

He waited till the doctor had stumped away down the path, then he turned to Sergeant Lester. 'Get the rest of the photographs,' he said. 'And once the medics have taken him away, I want the whole path searched from the end of Deep Lane as far as the next tracks that lead back to the main road.' He swivelled to face Bates. 'Where would they be, Constable?'

'This side, sir. By the old army camp.'

'How far from here?'

'About a quarter of a mile, sir.'

'And the other way? Towards Blakeney?'

'Meals Lane, sir. Maybe six hundred yards.'

'Close the path between both of them. All the way.'

'Right, sir.'

'Do a lot of people use it?'

'Some of the village folk, walkin' their dogs, sir. Hikers too, but they be mainly at weekends.'

Tench narrowed his eyes. 'Suppose that sack had been tossed out from here late on Monday night. Could it have gone unnoticed till a couple of hours ago?'

'Doubtful, sir, but maybe Eli's hand weren't a-stickin' out then. There's no tellin' just when it worked itself free, an' there's not many folk as'd worrit themselves about a dirty old sack out there on the marsh. Not if they couldn't get close enough to look.'

'I suppose not, no . . . This Eli Craske. Something of a dipsomaniac, was he?'

'Aye, fond of his ale, sir. Many's the time I've been leadin' him back to Liggerbeck Hill an' puttin' him to bed.'

'Trouble, was he?'

'More of a noosance, sir. Reglar like. That'd be my description.'

'Enough of a nuisance for someone in Medford to want to see him dead?'

Bayes looked down at the body.

'Wouldn't say so, sir, no. Made a lot o' noise often, late of a night, when the landlord turned him out o' the pub. There be folk as didn't take too kindly to that. But it were like to be irritation, no more.'

'What kind of a noise?'

'Singin', sir, mainly. Once he'd had a skinful, Eli were fond o' lettin' rip wi' a song. He were more'n a bit partial to "John Brown's Body". Many's the night he'd be moulderin' in the grave all the way through the village, right from Liggerbeck Hill to St Mary's church. But he weren't ever violent, sir, not to my know.'

Tench frowned. For a moment he seemed to be deep in thought, then he picked up the sack and handed it to Lester.

'Sergeant,' he said, 'make sure that that sack goes straight to the lab. I'll give the boffins a ring . . . Mac!'

'Sir.' McKenzie stiffened.

'Round up Gregg and Sue Gradwell. Get them back to Norwich. I want everyone in my office first thing tomorrow morning. See that they know.'

'Right, sir.'

Tench turned back towards Bates.

'Now, Constable. Once Sergeant Lester's finished here on the path, you'll be in charge. I'll get someone down to help. And we're going to need a separate incident room. D'you know of any place we could use?'

'There's an empty cottage on Drove Street, sir. Belongs to the church. I'll have a word with the rector.'

'Good. If it's available, give the Duty Sergeant at Norwich a tinkle.'

'I'll do that, sir, for sure.'

McKenzie pointed towards the end of Deep Lane.

'Looks like the snatchers are here, sir,' he said.

Two men were making their way along the path, carrying a stretcher.

'Then we'd better get clear,' said Tench, 'and leave them to Lester. There's little enough we can do here tonight.' He stared down at the body. 'Two murders, Mac. Are we looking for two different killers or one?'

McKenzie shrugged. 'Could be either. I've a two-headed penny. D'you want me to toss?'

'No, not for the moment.' Tench knelt down by the body and peered at it closely. 'I've a strange idea,' he said, 'that our friend Mr Craske can give us the right answer. Before you start spinning coins I think we'd better ask him.'

5

By that time Lubbock was back at his cottage below the church at Cley. Indeed, at that precise moment he was leaning with his arms on the front garden gate, smoking his pipe.

On the road signs the village was Cley-next-the-Sea, but the sea had for centuries been in retreat, and the shingle bank on its fringe was now a full three-quarters of a mile from the windmill on the quay, and from Lubbock's cottage all of a mile and a half.

He'd bought the cottage, Umzinto, some years before the war when his wife was still alive, and it had long been his practice, on warm summer evenings, to lean on the gate, light up his pipe and dream of those days when the Green below the church had been the hub of a far-flung maritime trade.

Even the cottage itself, as he'd once taken pains to explain to young Tench, drew its name from the time when Cley had still been a port. 'Believe it or not,' he'd said, pointing with the stem of his pipe towards the Green, 'for hundreds of years, Mike, this broad stretch of grass that runs down to the river was a bustling quay. Then some profiteering local bigwig, with an eye to the money he could make from grazing, built an embankment and drained the marshes. Well, of course, the river silted up, the quays here were abandoned, and the port moved to where the windmill stands now, much closer to the sea. Ships were still trading there sixty years ago, though the bigger ones, the steamships, anchored three miles out, in the channel that's still known as Blakeney Pit. There the freight was transferred to lighters that were poled all the way out and back again to Cley. Fourteen hours it took them, there and back; they did it for years; but when at last the railway builders reached Holt, that was the end. The port simply died, and now all that's left is a quiet little village on the edge of the marshland, a mile from the sea.

'But that's not quite all. Some of the very last ships to trade here were owned by a firm called the Rennie Line. They operated a regular service to Natal, and gave their vessels strange African names. One of their captains, when he retired, settled down in the village and bought properties here. And so, incredibly and yet delightfully, laddie, the streets of Cley still sprout houses with names like Umtata, Umgeni and Umvolusi, even Umzinto – all Zulu names, the names of territories, townships and rivers in South Africa – and puzzled students of all that's absurd in the world come inquiring why names as outlandish as these turn up on the edge of Norfolk.'

Umzinto had been Lubbock's retreat from the turmoil of Norwich, and now, in his retirement, it was still a retreat: a place where he could put his feet up, smoke his pipe and doze without constant fear of interruption; where, of a summer evening, he could loll on the gate and muse. Which was why, that warm May evening, he was still lolling there, still smoking, still lost in fancies of tall-masted vessels tied up within yards of his garden gate, when a police car drew up in front of the cottage and Tench stepped out.

He slammed the car door. 'Coffee,' he said. 'And make it strong and black.'

Lubbock straightened up and knocked out the dottle from his pipe.

'How about a cup of tea?'

Tench shook his head. 'Coffee.'

'Poisonous muck. I've told you that before, laddie. Stultifies the mind, dries up the tongue and rots the extremities. You'd be far better off with a pot of Darjeeling.'

'Coffee,' said Tench. 'And don't pretend you've run out. There's a tin in the larder. You know damn well there is. And I'm the only one who drinks it.'

Lubbock opened the gate. 'Right,' he said cheerfully. 'If you're still determined to die in the full bloom of youth, then coffee it is. But when your socks shrivel up and your toes drop off, don't say I didn't warn you.'

6

Tench drained his coffee.

Lubbock poured himself a third cup of tea. 'If you want my opinion,' he said, 'it's odds on that the same man did both.'

'Let's hope so,' said Tench. 'If we're looking for two different killers, we're going to need reinforcements. We could have done without this additional complication.'

'There is another side to the business, laddie. If it is the same chap, a second murder could help. Killers aren't infallible. They may think they've successfully covered their tracks, but they leave clues behind. You'll have double the chance of running him to earth.'

'If he did both.'

Lubbock waved his pipe. 'Look at the evidence, Mike. How long did Reg Ledward say our Mallalieu woman had been in the water?'

'Between eight and twelve hours.'

'And when was she found?'

'Roughly around half-past nine Tuesday morning.'

'That means he dumped her round about midnight.'

Tench shook his head. 'No, it must have been earlier than that. Low water that night was just before eleven. By midnight the tide would have covered Blacknock.'

Lubbock shrugged. 'Well, let's say eleven. And this Craske chap was murdered at much the same time. Late Monday night. Near the end of Deep Lane. No, laddie, it's too much of a coincidence. There must be a link.'

'The trouble is we're not sure just when Eli Craske died. Ledward's estimate leaves us with a twelve-hour span. He could have been killed at any time after half-past six on the Monday night. Someone could have done him in long before the woman's body was dumped.'

'It's possible, yes, but let's face the facts. It's not exactly probable. If I were you, I'd be looking for a solitary killer, at least until something turns up to prove me wrong.'

'I'd sooner be sure.'

'Well, you can't be. Not yet. Patience, Mike, patience. I've told you before, patience is the key to solving all murders. You can't rush a case. All you can do is nudge it along. Let it simmer for a while. Leave it to the lab technicians for the moment. You'll get their reports. Till then, ask questions and listen for clues. Work on a theory, but don't assume anything. If you're proved to be wrong, just start again from scratch. It's patience that counts, patience and persistence. Sooner or later, in ninety-nine cases out of a hundred, they'll uncover the truth.'

'You've been telling me that,' said Tench, 'ever since the first time we met.'

'Because it bears repetition. You were always impatient. Wanted to be two jumps ahead of the field. The sad truth is, laddie, that sprinters don't often win long-distance races. It's staying power that counts. Take it from me.'

'All right.' Tench nodded. 'You said work on a theory.'

'I also said don't assume that it's right.'

'Fair enough. Let's work on one that may very well be wrong. Let's work on the theory that whoever killed your lodger carried her body out to Blacknock at low water on Monday night. Let's suppose that he carried her out from Deep Lane. That provides the shortest route across the marsh, so once he'd dumped the body he'd come back the same way . . . Are you with me so far?'

'Every step, laddie.'

'Right. Let's suppose a bit further. Let's suppose that he carried her out in a sack, tipped her out at Blacknock, returned across the marsh and reached the end of Deep Lane still carrying the sack. By that time he'd have been pretty sure that he was safe, and that no one had seen him. Then suddenly in front of him, blocking his way, was a drunken old villager doing his best to rouse the whole of Medford. What would he do?'

'Deal with him,' said Lubbock.

'Deal with him swiftly, stuff the body in the sack, sling it across his shoulder, walk a few hundred yards up the coastal path and toss it out on the marsh.'

'That's your theory?'

Tench made a non-committal gesture. 'It's the first that comes to mind. Could be right, could be wrong.'

Lubbock reached for his pipe. 'If it's right, then so am I. Killers always leave clues, and he's made a free gift of one. Use it, laddie. Send the sack to the lab and tell the boffins what to look for. If there's one single hair from the woman, they'll match it.'

'I've done that already. They'll be working on it now.'

'Then at least you'll have the answer to one vital question: whether you're looking for one man or two. That's a start.'

Tench nodded. 'It's a start, but we need to know more. That's the reason I'm here.'

Lubbock filled his pipe methodically, rolling the tobacco between his palms. 'Go on,' he said.

'You remember the fire at Kettle Hill?'

'I could hardly forget it.'

'You told me then that the boffins at Norwich were experts on sacks.'

'So they are. Our forensic department knows more about sacks than any in the country. They've lived for God knows how long surrounded by scores of windmills and thousands of farms. They've examined more sacks than you'll ever see.'

'Then they could tell me a good deal more about this one.'

'They'll give you a potted biography if you want one.'

'Somehow,' said Tench, 'I think I'm going to need one. Even if they can prove that that sack was used to carry the woman's body out to Blacknock, we're still working in the dark. We don't know who she was, and we don't know who killed her and dumped her on the sands, so we can't even start to guess at a motive or make any links. At the moment there's only one feasible way of tracking him down, and that's through the sack. I want to know where it came from. Have they got the resources at the lab to tell me that?'

7

Lubbock was in no hurry to reply. He spent half a minute lighting his pipe, and then wafted away a cloud of blue smoke. 'Sacks are made of jute,' he said, 'and most of it comes from India – Bengal or Assam. The boffins in Norwich have built up quite a formidable dossier about it. It's grown in the main on a stretch of the Ganges north-east of Calcutta, and processed in one of the mills on the Hooghly. Send a sack to the lab and they know more than enough about the fibres of jute to tell you exactly where it was grown. They can narrow it down to a matter of miles on the same stretch of river, and if you find that you need the ultimate refinement they'll pin-point the particular mill near Calcutta that processed the stuff. It could be any one of a couple of dozen, or it might even be one by the Tay in Dundee. Wherever it is, they can tell you. They're experts on jute. Norfolk's a farming county. We've had to call on them time and time again to analyse sacks.'

'Fine,' said Tench, 'but I don't want to know where it came from in India. What I need to know is where it came from in Norfolk.'

'They can help you with that. They know which importers deal with which mills and which types of sack. They can give you their names and the names of the wholesalers they trade with.'

'I don't want to know who sold it. I want to know who bought it.'

'Then it's a case of elimination, Mike. The wholesalers can tell you which retailers they deal with.'

'It's a hell of a long process.'

'It's one that needs patience. That proves my point. But unless you're

79

lucky and some other piece of evidence turns up to help, it's the only possible way. I can tell you one thing though. If that sack contained a body, it wouldn't be the sack that most millers use now – the ten-stone type. It'd be the old standard twenty-stone sack. It'd have to be, for size. That could help you to trace it.'

Tench pushed aside his cup. 'Then tell me this. Who still uses the old type?'

'Farmers and some of the long-established millers. Those who have the knack of handling them. And there aren't too many of the old millers left. It's not easy to shift a standard sack. When it's filled with grain or flour it weighs half a hundredweight. Not the sort of thing to be shouldering around.'

'Then yours at Kettle Hill are all the smaller type?'

'Every single one, so if you've got some wild idea that our murderer picked up a standard sack when he cleaned out the cottage, forget it. All the sacks at Kettle Hill are the ten-stone type. They're locked in the granary. And before you ask, laddie, no, there aren't any missing. I've already checked.'

Tench took a deep breath. 'Then it looks as if we're up against a bit of a problem. We've a nameless victim, a faceless killer, no weapon except for a couple of hands, and the only clue that's so far presented itself is a sack that may prove impossible to trace.'

'There's always the cottage,' said Lubbock. 'When are Lester's men coming to dust it?'

'First thing tomorrow, but at this stage fingerprints aren't much use. Not unless we've already got them on file. Before we can match them we're going to need a suspect, and at the moment there isn't one within sight.'

'There probably won't be a print in sight either. From the look of the place it's as clean as a whistle. But remember what I said. Killers aren't infallible. Even the cleverest. They miss little things. It's our job not to make a similar mistake. All you have to do is be a mite more thorough than the man you're tracking down. That shouldn't be too hard. You've a good deal more time than he ever had. And anyway' – he blew out another cloud of smoke – 'what detective worth his salt wants an easy case to solve?'

'I do,' said Tench. 'It'd make a pleasant change for once in a way.'

Leaving Umzinto, he didn't take the road to Holt and from there back to Norwich. He drove down to Cley village, turned left on the coastal road and, passing Blakeney and Kettle Hill, made his way into Medford; then, winding through the village, he swung right at Deep Lane and parked his car on the edge of the marsh.

Lester and his team were still searching the path.

'Found anything?' he asked.

The sergeant shook his head.

'Nothing of any significance, sir.'

Tench looked towards the sun, low down in the sky.

'Will you be finished here tonight?'

'Not a chance, sir, no.'

'The print men. Where are they?'

'One of them's here, sir. The other's at Sibthorpe. There's been a break-in there at Sparrow Hill House.'

'I need both of them over at Kettle Hill first thing tomorrow. They're to dust the mill cottage from end to end. Murder comes before a break-in. Get word to the chap at Sibthorpe ... And join them as soon as you've finished the job here. I want that cottage combed: fingerprints, footprints, tyre marks, the lot. If there's a single scrap of evidence we need it unearthed.'

'Right, sir.'

'Mr Lubbock'll be there to meet you. He knows what to look for.'

'Still detecting, sir, is he?'

'Sergeant,' said Tench, 'Mr Lubbock was detecting before you were born. He's up every morning at five o'clock, takes his cherrywood stick and covers five miles before he cooks breakfast. And if ever he loses the use of his legs, he'll be detecting from a wheelchair for every waking moment of the rest of his life ... Clear?'

'Very clear, sir.'

'Right. Carry on.'

He walked back along the path to the end of Deep Lane, and stood for a moment looking out across the marsh. The landscape was one of flat desolation stretching away beyond the range of his vision: just a tangle of dull brown saltmarsh grass intersected by twisting, watery channels that merged with the grass and then lost themselves out in the featureless waste. It wasn't land, it wasn't sea, but an indeterminate mixture of both, lonely and sullen as the light began to fade.

In front of him a track curved out across the marsh, broad and firm for perhaps a couple of hundred yards, then gradually narrowing till it seemed to peter out. He glanced towards the west. The sun, red as fire, was already touching the line that divided land from sea. In another half-hour it would have vanished from sight.

There was little time left, but the need to do something positive drove him to take the risk. He took two hesitant steps, then began to stride out, following the track as it wound across the marsh. Once it began to contract and the wilderness seemed to be closing in around him, he slowed down, searching ahead with more care. Five minutes went by, then ten. He pressed on. A quarter of an hour . . . and then suddenly all that remained beneath his feet was a tenuous muddy path no more than a yard wide, twisting away towards a pair of rotting planks flung in haphazard fashion across the face of a creek.

Under the darkening sky the grim flatness of the marsh still seemed to stretch away without end, but somewhere beyond in the gloom was the sea, the receding tide, and hidden beneath the sea was the sand and Blacknock.

He turned and looked back. All he could glimpse of Medford were pinpoints of light winking out here and there and then disappearing, as the villagers closed their curtains and shut out the savage emptiness beyond.

He thought of Mary Bunn, sobbing in wild despair as the waters rose around her, and suddenly felt all the chill loneliness of his own isolation.

He remembered what Bates had said. 'If ye're out on Blacknock in a blanket o' fog, ye may as well sit down an' sob till ye die. There's not much else ye can do.'

He shivered and began to walk back, picking his way step by step, testing the ground, the light failing around him and the path lost in shadow, till at last it broadened out and he could see the black line of the coast up ahead.

It was dark when he reached the end of Deep Lane, and Lester and his men had long since shouldered their equipment and gone. He started up the car, turned it towards the village and drove off at speed. Then, as the dancing headlights picked out Liggerbeck Hill, he wrenched the wheel left towards Holt and Norwich.

He hadn't even set eyes on Blacknock, but for one day at least he'd seen more than enough of Medford and its God-forsaken marsh.

As he followed the winding road past St Mary the Virgin, Leo Wickstead, in his bedroom above the baker's shop, shrugged on his nightshirt and, with much heavy breathing, dragged off his socks.

His wife loosened her stays, and scratched her barely discernible waist.

'Reckon as ye'll need ter be tellin' him,' she said.

'Tellin' who?'

'On'y one ter be tellin', boy. Ol' Jack Bates.'

'Tellin' him wha' like?'

'Yew know. 'Bout they sacks.'

Wickstead rolled into bed. He grunted. 'Aye, well, mebbe . . . sometime,' he said.

IV
MANY MANSIONS

Wyd was his parisshe, and houses fer asonder

Geoffrey Chaucer: *The Canterbury Tales*

1

To say that Billy Stormer was an ideal pupil would be straining the truth. His teachers at Chalk Hill Senior, if asked for their opinions, would have classed him as one of those boys who could do better. Some might have described him as lazy, others as indolent, while the more charitable among them would possibly have conceded that he was bright but disinclined to make sufficient effort.

There was, however, one daily task that he enjoyed and at which he'd proved to be tolerably efficient. Every morning, before school, he collected the daily papers from Medford Post Office and General Store, and rode through the village delivering them. The only trouble was that, once his round was completed, there were days, particularly warm days in summer, when he felt it would be folly to spend time in a classroom. On such occasions he selected some deserted tract of country, propped his bike against a hedge, stretched himself out on the grass in the sun and promptly went to sleep.

Since he was always in the rudest possible health and unlikely to have suffered a stroke overnight, it was rightly concluded at Chalk Hill Senior that if young Billy Stormer failed to answer his name when the register was called, he was up to his old tricks; and that being so, it was only proper that the local constable should be briefed to keep a sharp lookout and apprehend the absentee should he find him snoring somewhere in the sunshine when he should have been in the shade, imbibing a refreshing cocktail of English grammar and mathematical equations.

It therefore came as no surprise to Constable Bates at half-past nine the following morning, as he rode up Liggerbeck Hill and out on the Wells road towards Elderberry Farm, to find Billy Stormer stretched out on the verge with his hands behind his head, snoring like an underpowered donkey engine.

Nonetheless, he was more than a little surprised at what was lying on the verge beside Billy and his somewhat dilapidated bike.

Extending a size-eleven boot, he alerted the boy to the presence of the law. Then he nodded towards the grass. 'What's this, lad?' he said.

Billy sat up and blinked. 'Found'n, Mr Bates.'

The constable was unimpressed. 'Stole it more like.'

'It weren' nobody's, Mr Bates. It were lay there, jus' waitin' fer someone ter pick it up.'

'And you picked it up.'

'It weren' doin' nothin', Mr Bates, an' tha's truth. Saw it there Monday mornin'. It were still there terday.'

'Oh, aye?' The constable eyed him with evident mistrust. 'An' where would that be?'

'Up i' Swallernest Wood.'

Bates took him by the ear and hauled him up on his feet. 'Reckon ye'd best be showin' me, lad,' he said, 'an' if ye're a-tellin' me a load of ol' squit, ye'll be gettin' such a clip roun' the lug as ye'll hear swallers singin' inside it fer weeks.'

The boy looked up at him.

'Ye wouldn', Mr Bates.'

The constable bent down. He peered straight into Billy Stormer's face. 'Well, mebbe not, lad,' he said, 'but ye're still enough of a doddy little mite to be turned arse-uppards an' tanned as a babby. So ye'd best lead the way an' look sharp about it, else reckon ye'll be choosin' to walk that bike all the way back to school.'

2

When Mike Tench addressed his squad in Norwich that morning, he knew nothing of Constable Bates's encounter with the somnolent Billy Stormer, and he was completely unaware that Emmy Wickstead had developed a disturbing preoccupation with sacks. He was more concerned with the few facts he did know, and the plans he had in mind to unearth a few more.

He pointed to a set of photographs on the pinboard behind him.

'First victim,' he said. 'A woman, early thirties, five feet two inches tall, roughly eight stone, green eyes, auburn hair, name unknown. Found on the sands at Medford at approximately 9.30 Tuesday morning. Identified by ex-Detective Chief Inspector Lubbock as the woman who, a week yesterday, paid him a fortnight's rent on the Phoenix Mill cottage at Kettle Hill. Gave her name as Veronica Mallalieu and an address in Southampton, both of which were later found to be false. Last seen by him on the following day, and we have at the moment no further sightings.

'Dr Ledward's report states that she didn't drown, nor did she die from vagal inhibition or the shock of immersion. His conclusion is that she died from anoxia, deficiency of oxygen, produced by someone placing a hand over her nose and mouth and keeping it there. In other words she was suffocated, and already dead when she was dumped on the sands. Death was certified at 11.58 on Tuesday morning, but Ledward's estimate is that she died between twenty-four and forty-eight hours before that, and she'd been in the water at least eight hours but no more than twelve.'

He turned back to the pinboard. 'Victim number two,' he said. 'Eli Craske, a notorious drunkard and resident of Liggerbeck Hill in Medford.

His body was found in a sack on Medford Marsh at 4.45 yesterday afternoon. The autopsy report isn't available yet, but indications are that someone snapped his neck and then dumped him. The estimated time of death is between thirty-six and forty-eight hours before discovery.

'Now, if Ledward's correct in his diagnoses, it would appear that the woman was left on the sands sometime between sunset and midnight on Monday, and this is corroborated by the evidence of a Mr Burcham who says he saw someone with a torch moving about on the sands just before ten o'clock. It also coincides roughly with the time when Eli Craske must have been murdered. We're therefore assuming, at least for the present, that the crimes could be linked, and that means we're looking for the same individual in connection with both . . . Are we all clear so far?'

There was a murmur of agreement.

'Right,' he said. 'Now, a word about the sack that held Eli Craske's body. We've sent it to the lab for analysis. It's possible that it may have been used by the killer to carry the dead woman out to the sands. If it was and the boffins report to that effect, then the link between the crimes can be proved, but we have to wait until they've completed their work; and even if they do come up with confirmation, we still know very little. We don't know who the woman was, where she came from, or what was the purpose behind her visit. We don't know who killed her or what was the motive behind the crime; and if the lab doesn't come up with the confirmation we need, we'll know even less. We'll be looking at two unrelated crimes and two separate killers, and we won't know whether the woman was dumped from Medford or dropped in the water somewhere else along the coast.'

He paused. 'If you've seen the *EDP* this morning, you'll know that Dave Ransome's given us a front-page spread with an artist's impression of the woman and an appeal for help in identifying her. We can only hope that someone recognizes her and comes forward with information. In the meantime the most fruitful line of investigation seems likely to lie in tracing the victims' movements, particularly those of the woman. We know she arrived at Mr Lubbock's cottage a week yesterday in a taxi from Holt, so we need to trace the driver and interview him. The taxi was hired from Gresham Cars on the Cromer road, and the driver was roughly forty years old, short and stocky with dark hair and a heavy stubble. He spoke with a Scots accent.

'We also know that Mr Lubbock arranged for bread and milk to be delivered to the cottage: the bread to be supplied by Leo Wickstead, the Medford baker, and the milk by the Boldings at Morston Bottom Farm. We need to contact them too, and the postman from Blakeney. He's an elderly chap by the name of Fred, but the Boldings must know him because he delivers there too, and has done for years.

'Now we've no idea what this woman's intentions were, but she took good care to hide her identity, so she must have had some secret purpose in mind. The cottage at Kettle Hill is some distance from the road. There's a bus service, yes, but it may well be that she hired a bicycle. We therefore need to contact the cycle dealers in the area, and the nearest one for her would be Bretland's in Blakeney. It's essential we track her movements and find out what she was up to, and you know what these Norfolk villages are like. A strange woman on a bicycle, probably asking questions, would be bound to raise a question or two herself.

'We'll need to scour the area from Blakeney to Wells, and that means a hell of a lot of hard work: far too much for us to cope with on our own. I don't like asking for help, but it's better than having the Met on our backs. I've seen the Chief Super this morning, and he's in full agreement, so we're drafting in a team from the local forces to assist where required. They'll be based here in Norwich.

'Now to what we do ourselves.' He looked round the squad. 'We're setting up an incident room in Medford. It's an empty cottage in Drove Street by the bridge across the river. We've rigged up a phone line, and Lock's already there. He'll be in charge to collate information, so see that you report all findings to him.' He turned to face McKenzie. 'Mac, it's your job to chase up the taxi driver. That should be easy. There can't be many Scotsmen driving taxis in Holt. See what he remembers about the woman . . . OK?'

'Right.' McKenzie nodded.

'Andy!'

'Sir,' said Gregg.

'Get down to Morston Bottom and talk to Walter Bolding. Find out what he's seen when he's delivered the milk. And don't be deceived into thinking he's stupid. He's a simple soul is Walter, but he doesn't miss much, I can vouch for that. He's been useful to me on more than one occasion . . . Take Sue Gradwell with you. Find out what he knows about Fred the postman, then drop Sue off in Blakeney. After that, go back to Medford and see Leo Wickstead. You've met him already, so you're the one to deal with him. He must have delivered his bread to someone at the cottage. See what he's got to say.'

Gregg was clearly none too happy at the thought of tackling Mr Wickstead twice in the space of twenty-four hours.

'He didn't say a lot that was useful yesterday, sir.'

'Maybe not.' Tench grinned. 'He's a cantankerous old sod. Did he give you a lecture on how to bake a loaf?'

'Something like that, sir.'

'And I bet he told you to sample Emmy's butterfly cakes.'

'That too, sir,' said Gregg.

'Then he hasn't changed much even though he's moved shop . . . Did you buy any?'

'Yes, sir.'

'How many?'

'Half a dozen.'

'Did you enjoy them?'

'Didn't get the chance, sir. Sue commandeered them. She said they were delicious.'

'Good. Then you know what to do. Buy another half-dozen and find out what he knows . . . Sue!'

'Yes, sir?'

'When you get to Blakeney, track down the postman. He must live locally. See if he delivered any post to the cottage, and ask him if he noticed anything unusual . . . Now, the rest of you. You, Bob, George and Steve.' He turned to the three detective constables: Ellison, Rayner and Spurgeon. 'Take some of these.' He laid his hand on a clutch of photographs. 'They're copies of the artist's impression, the one in the *EDP*. Split Medford between you and do a house-to-house. We need to know if anyone's seen this woman around the area. And find out where Eli Craske was on Monday night. Folk may not have seen him, but they probably heard him. Once he's had a skinful, he rouses the village, so start at the pub. Right?'

'Sir.' The three constables nodded as one.

'And by the way' – he held up the photographs – 'you're all going to need a few of these, so collect them before you go . . . We're having posters printed and, once we get them, they'll be displayed in all the salient places . . . Now, any questions?'

Sue Gradwell raised a hand. 'What about Bretland's, sir? D'you want me to call there as well?'

Tench shook his head. 'No, we're leaving that to Constable Harris at Blakeney. He's got a motorbike. If he draws a blank there, he'll be doing a round of the cycle shops . . . Anything else?'

'The incident room,' said McKenzie. 'What's the phone number?'

'It's here on the board. Everyone make a note of it . . . I'll be there myself for most of the time. If I'm not, then Lock'll know where to find me . . . Now, any more queries?'

He waited. There was silence.

'Right,' he said. 'Get cracking. We need a lead on this woman. That's the first priority. Until we know who she is, we're just fumbling around in the dark without a torch.'

3

Steve Harris's bike was a Velocette 'Noddy' with a maximum speed of fifty miles an hour. It was new, silver-grey and spotlessly clean, but McKenzie would have viewed it with utter disdain. Its limited power would have left him as deeply depressed as if he'd been condemned to live the rest of his life in Medford.

His own pride and joy was a machine of a different colour and calibre: an ageing 490 cc Norton which he swore had once won a TT race in the Isle of Man. Painted bright red, incredibly noisy and spitting clouds of acrid blue smoke, it could still be coaxed to reach a sweet sixty on a straight stretch of road; and though Gregg had once described it as a death-trap on wheels, and Tench had more than once compared it to Lubbock's burnt-out old briar, it was, to him, a jewel to be treasured.

It was unfortunate, perhaps, that Mr Wilfred Saxby, the owner of Gresham Cars, was in no mood that Thursday morning to sympathise with such an unnatural assessment. Mr Saxby, the night before, had attended the annual dinner of the Norfolk Licensed Victuallers Association, of which his brother, the landlord of the Cock and Bull at Great Yarmouth, was the president elect. It had been a night of considerable celebration. Staggering into bed at three o'clock in the morning, he'd been wakened at six by a sense of acute nausea and a conviction that all the windows in the house had been shattered. The dawning realisation that what he'd heard was nothing more than the clank of milk bottles deposited on the doorstep had done little to make him feel any better, and the sharp shaft of pain that had stabbed him behind the eyes as he'd moved his head had produced the groaning recognition that he was afflicted by a hangover of monumental proportions.

He was consequently in no frame of mind to welcome McKenzie's arrival in Holt, accompanied as it was by an ear-splitting racket that sounded to him like a battery of machine-guns, and when the sergeant hammered on the door of his office, flung it open with a clatter and clumped into view, he raised a pair of haggard eyes and scowled at the intruder. 'What the hell are you driving?' he said. 'A Flying Fortress?'

McKenzie was a man who, for all his addiction to tankards of Norfolk ale, was immune to hangovers. He recognised the symptoms at a glance, but ignored them. 'Mr Saxby?' he said cheerfully.

Wilf Saxby gave a reluctant grunt. 'So what if I am?'

The sergeant produced his card. 'Detective Sergeant McKenzie.'

Saxby closed his eyes. 'Not this morning,' he said. 'Come back this afternoon.'

McKenzie showed no compassion. 'I need to talk to one of your drivers.'

'Can't it wait?'

'No, sir, it can't. Not unless you want to be charged with obstruction. We need to talk to him. Today.'

Saxby sighed wearily. 'Right. What's his name?'

'We're hoping you can tell us.'

'You're asking me to trace a driver and you don't know his name? Well, that's bloody helpful.'

'Short and stocky,' McKenzie said. 'Round about forty. Speaks with a Scottish accent.'

'Sounds like Sandy.'

'Sandy who?'

'Sandy McLeish. Fits his description. Came here from Glasgow. Why d'you want to talk to him?'

'We think he may have evidence that'll help us,' McKenzie said.

'Not in trouble, is he?'

'Not as far as I've heard. Should he be?'

'Can't think why.'

'Then where can I find him?'

Saxby shrugged. It was clear that he wished he hadn't. 'No idea at all,' he said, closing his eyes again.

McKenzie began to bristle. 'What d'you mean, no idea? You run this firm, don't you?'

'Today's his day off.'

'It would be . . . So where does he live?'

Saxby took a deep breath. Even that, it seemed, occasioned him a good deal of pain. He eased a drawer open gently, took out a file and ran a wavering finger down a column of names. 'Old Kelling,' he said. 'Bodham Cottage.'

'Where's that?'

'A mile away. Turn off the Cromer road . . . But it'll just be a waste of time.'

'Why?'

Saxby sighed. 'Because he won't be there.'

'Then where will he be?'

'Search me,' Saxby said. 'His wife kicked him out a fortnight ago. He's still looking for lodgings.'

'And you don't know where?'

'No . . . Your guess is as good as mine.'

'Well, thanks a million,' McKenzie said. 'You've made my day.'

Saxby looked up. It cost him an effort. His eyes were twin pools of alcoholic stupor. 'My pleasure,' he said, wincing. 'Don't slam the door.'

4

Mike Tench's objective that morning was modest: to uncover some scrap of evidence that might help him to put a name to the unidentified woman found on Blacknock; but he was hardly prepared for the fact that by mid-afternoon he felt even more confused than he'd felt six hours earlier.

Not that his day at Medford didn't start with the promise of better things to come, but the promise was vague, its fulfilment a matter of mere speculation, and it left him wondering, even so early, whether the few facts he'd learnt had any relevance at all to the answers he required.

His arrival at the incident room by the bridge coincided with that of Constable Bates and a small, ginger-headed boy of scruffy appearance who was wheeling a bicycle.

Tench looked at him, then at Bates.

'And who've we got here, Constable?' he asked.

'Name o' Billy Stormer, sir. Thought as I'd best bring him along to see you.'

'What's he been doing?'

'Truantin' from school among other things,' said Bates. He took Billy by the ear. 'This is Detective Chief Inspector Tench, lad,' he said. 'Now you tell him what you bin a-doin' of an' sharp.'

Billy looked down at the tarmac of Drove Street. 'Ent bin doin' nothin'. Found'n a did, an' tha's truth, Mr Bates.'

'Found what?' The constable gave his ear a tweak. 'An' speak up, lad. We ent over fond o' bendin' down to catch words.'

'This,' Billy said. He pushed the bike forward.

'One Raleigh bicycle, sir,' Bates explained. 'Seems like as it's new. No crossbar. Lady's model. Frame bears the number' – he took out his notebook – '675243. Boy claims he found it in Swallernest Wood. Saw it there first, he says, Monday morning. Ent shifted since.'

Tench examined it carefully. 'Where's Swallownest Wood?'

'Off th'Wells road, Warham way, sir.'

'How far from here?'

'Couple o' miles, sir, no more.'

Tench turned to the boy. 'Billy,' he said, d'you remember where you found it?'

Billy nodded mutely.

'D'you think you can you show me?'

Another nod.

94

Bates tweaked his ear again. 'Show some respect, lad. Got a tongue, have you?'

'Yes, Mr Bates.'

'Then wake up an' use it.'

Billy rubbed his ear. He looked up at Tench. 'Yes, sir,' he said.

Twenty minutes later they stood by a clearing in Swallownest Wood. Billy pointed to a hollow behind a fallen tree. 'It were there,' he said.

'It were there what?' Bates glared at him. 'It were there . . . sir.' 'Louder.' Billy sighed. 'It were there, sir.'

'Better,' said Bates. 'Reckon you be learnin' a mite this morning. An' nex' time, lad, remember, else ye be wantin' a sharp word wi' me.' He turned towards Tench. 'Said as it were lyin' there, like as if someone had tossed it down an' then gone for a walk.'

'Then it wasn't really hidden?'

'If ye choose to believe the little warmint, then no, sir. Seems it were jus' dumped.'

Tench laid a hand on Billy's shoulder and steered him away from Bates. 'Billy,' he said, 'I need you to help me. So don't be afraid. Just tell me the truth . . . Will you do that?'

The boy looked up at him. He seemed to hesitate, then nodded his head.

'Good,' said Tench. 'Now this is very important. You say you saw the bike here on Monday morning. What time was that?'

'Afore school . . . sir.'

'So why didn't you tell Constable Bates about it then?'

'Thought as it belonged ter someone.'

'You thought they'd gone walking somewhere in the woods?'

Billy nodded again.

'And they'd come back and pick it up?'

The boy nodded a third time.

'Then what did you think when you saw it again this morning?'

A shrug of the shoulders. 'Didn' belong ter nobody.'

'You thought whoever owned it had thrown it away?'

'Yes, sir.'

'Right. Now was it in the same place as when you saw it on Monday?'

'Yes, sir. Jus' lyin' there. Back o' th'tree, sir.'

'It hadn't been moved at all?'

Billy shook his head.

Tench squatted down and turned the boy round to face him. He looked straight at him. 'Did you find anything else here, Billy?' he said.

Billy swallowed hard. He seemed for all the world like a very small animal caught in a pair of headlights.

95

Tench held him there. 'It's very important, Billy. I need you to tell me.'

'Come on, lad,' said Bates. 'Out with it an' sharp. Mr Tench ent one fer askin' ye things more'n once.'

Billy's hand moved slowly. It burrowed deep into the pocket of his short grey trousers, and came out clutching something that glinted in the sunlight. He held it out for Tench to take, then he looked up at Bates. 'Weren' meanin' ter keep it, Mr Bates,' he said, 'honest. Jus' savin' it ter look at a while, tha' were all.'

5

McKenzie was having a more frustrating day.

Old Kelling was nothing more than a cluster of cottages dotted round a church, but the trouble was that none of them appeared to have names, and it wasn't immediately evident which of them belonged to a taxi driver called Sandy McLeish.

After a circular tour that yielded no firm sighting of Bodham Cottage, he swore vehemently beneath his breath, parked the Norton beside the wall of the church and, selecting one of the dwellings at random, pushed open the wooden gate, walked up the garden path and rapped on the door.

It was opened by a grizzled old man, leaning on a stick.

'Good morning, sir,' McKenzie said, summoning his shreds of courtesy. 'I wonder if you can help me. I'm looking for somewhere.'

'Oh, aye?' The man shifted his stick a couple of inches, and listed more to the right.

'I'm trying to find Bodham Cottage.'

There was a moment's pause.

'Which be tha'? Bodham Old or Bodham New?'

'Are there two of them?'

The old man nodded.

'Tha's right, bor. Two on 'em. Allus bin two.'

'I'm looking for a chap called Sandy McLeish. Drives a cab in Holt.'

The man peered at him suspiciously. 'What ye wantin' him fer?'

'He's an old friend,' McKenzie said promptly, wise to the ways of Norfolk.

Another long pause.

'Tha'll be needin' Bodham New then.'

'And where's Bodham New?'

'Fur side o' th' church . . . He'll none be there though.'

'You're sure about that?'

'Aye. Flitted a week agone. Dassn't come back. Reckon as Minnie gan him a ding o' th'lug.'

'Minnie? That's his wife?'

'Aye. Minnie McLeish. Minnie Jelf as was.'

'Will she be there?'

'Like as not, mebbe. Lives there, don' her?'

'D'you think she'll know where he is?'

'Reckon she ent fretted. Telled ol' Geoff Bunn as she'd not be moithered ower much an he druv off Cromer Pier.'

'No love lost between them, eh?'

The old man chuckled. 'Aye, an' that ent fur wrong.'

McKenzie took a deep breath. 'Doesn't anyone know where McLeish has gone?'

'Oh, aye.

'Who then?'

'Mos' folk, a reckon.'

'Do you know?'

Another chuckle. 'A could mek a good guess.'

'Then maybe you'd care to make one.' McKenzie was already beginning to smoulder.

'Dolly Monement.'

'Dolly who?'

'Dolly Monement, bor.'

'And who's Dolly Monement?'

'Her as he's a-keppin' wi'.'

'He's living with her?'

'Reckon so.'

'Where?'

'Her place, o' course.'

'And where the devil's that?' McKenzie was now dangerously close to ignition.

'Webburn way, a reckon.'

'Weybourne?'

'Aye, Webburn. Said so, didn' a?'

'Then what's her address?'

The old man shook his head.

'Ent part o' my know,' he said. 'Not yet it ent. But there ent much ter Webburn. Tha'd best ask about.'

6

Tench looked down at the object in the palm of his hand.

'What is it, sir?' said Bates.

'Looks like a medallion.' Tench examined it more closely. 'Gold, on a chain, but one of the links has come loose. There's an inscription on it too, but it's difficult to read. You've got to get the light at just the right angle.' He tilted it this way and that, peered down at it and frowned. 'Seems to be a verse. God knows what it means though.' He held it up to the sun and, narrowing his eyes, slowly picked out the words. ' "Beneath me doth lie . . . Another that be . . . Much richer than I . . ." Ever heard that before, Constable?'

Bates shook his head. 'Can't say as I have, sir.'

Tench turned to Billy Stormer. 'What about you, Billy? Do you know what it means?'

Another shake of the head. 'No, sir.'

'Where did you find it?'

Billy cast a wary glance up at Bates. 'It were . . .'

'Yes?'

'It were in th'bag, sir.'

Tench frowned again. 'What bag?'

'Bag on th'bike, sir.'

'You mean there was a saddle-bag?'

'Sir.' The boy nodded.

'Then where is it, lad?' Bates glowered at him. 'Ye'd best be sayin'.'

Billy trudged towards a pile of fallen leaves beneath a tree. Brushing the leaves aside, he pulled out a black leather bag and handed it to Tench. 'Weren' hidin' it, sir,' he said. 'Honest a weren'. Jus' keepin' it safe.'

'Aye, mebbe.' Bates was clearly unimpressed. 'Reckon you an' me's due fer a bit of a talk, lad. Quiet like.'

Tench looked inside the bag. It was empty, but there was a pocket at the side that opened with a zip. 'Billy,' he said. 'This medallion. Where was it? Was it in the bag or did you find it in the pocket?'

Billy pulled at the zip. 'It were in there,' he said. 'Felt it wi' mi fingers.'

'Right down at the bottom?'

The boy nodded. 'It were hid.'

'And that was all there was? Nothing else?'

'No, sir.'

Bates was a sceptic where Billy was concerned. His eyes turned to gimlets. 'You sure, lad?' he said.

'Honest, Mr Bates. There weren' nothin'. Tha's truth.'

'It'd better be.' The constable looked down his nose, and then turned back to Tench. 'If ye want my advice, sir, ye'd best be a mite wary o' tekkin' all young Billy Stormer's a-sayin' as gospel. Needs summerin' an' winterin' afore ye do tha'. He ent shanny. Fur frum it. Reckon he be just about as sharp as a pritch, an' pritches is sharp. Rare sharp to my know.'

'Oh, I think we can trust him, Constable,' said Tench. 'You wouldn't lie to me, Billy, would you?'

'No, sir.' The boy shook his head.

'You're going to help me, aren't you?'

Billy looked at him and nodded.

Tench held up the medallion. 'Girls wear these,' he said, 'don't they?'

'S'pose so, sir. Yes.'

'And girls don't wear trousers, do they?'

'No, sir.'

'They've no trouser pockets.'

Another shake of the head.

'Good. Now this is gold. It's worth quite a bit. Suppose you were a girl, and you were riding a bike with this round your neck, and the chain broke. What would you do?'

Billy looked up hopefully. 'Put it some place safe?'

'And you haven't a trouser pocket. So where would you put it?'

'In the bag, sir?'

'Right. But you want to make sure you don't lose it, so where's the safest place?'

Billy pointed to the zip. 'In there, sir.'

Tench nodded. He seemed surprised. 'Yes,' he said thoughtfully, 'I think you may be right. Well done, Billy! You've been a great help . . . Hasn't he, Constable?'

Bates gave a sniff. 'Sharp as a pritch,' he said. 'Allus were.'

7

If Sandy McLeish had seen the scowl on McKenzie's face as he roared across Kelling Heath and down the hill into Weybourne, he might have thought twice about lying in bed and teasing Miss Dolly Monement's left nipple into a pointedly acceptable state of tumescence. As it was, he was lost in a world of passion when the sergeant raised a fist full of menace and hammered on the door.

Dolly, who was abstractedly stroking his back while studying a patch of damp on the ceiling, stopped in mid-stroke. 'There's someone at the door,' she whispered.

'It doesni matter,' he said. 'It'll no be anyone important.'

'It might be mum.'

Sandy growled. 'It'll no be your mum. Bide still. Let 'em be.'

They lay there, not moving. Silence resumed.

'There ye are,' he said. 'I'm no always wrong, ye know. That was her gone.'

As he spoke the last word, the hammering was repeated.

'I'll have to go,' she said. 'There may be something wrong.'

She wriggled out from underneath him, flung on a flimsy dressing-gown and went to the window. 'It's a man,' she said, 'on a motorbike.'

'It's no a body ye know?'

She tossed her head. 'Never seen him before.'

Sandy McLeish swore loudly into the bedclothes. Then he threw them aside, strode to the window, pulled up the sash and leaned out.

'Away with ye,' he shouted. 'She doesni want to see ye.'

As he slammed the sash down, there was a noise as if someone had thrown a rock at the door.

Swearing even more loudly, he wrenched the window up a second time and leaned out even further. 'Bugger off,' he yelled, 'or I'll call the polis.'

A heavily built man with a straggling black moustache stepped back from the door and glared at him. 'Are you Sandy McLeish?' he said.

Sandy glared back. 'What's it to yous?'

The man held up a card. 'I'm Detective Sergeant McKenzie,' he said, 'so get yourself down here and open this door.' He looked at his watch. 'You've got thirty seconds. If you're not down here by then, you'll be spending a night in the cells at Norwich.'

They faced one another in a much-cluttered parlour, Sandy in nothing but a pair of trousers and the dark, curling hair that matted his chest.

McKenzie eyed him with visible distaste and a good deal more in the way of mistrust. 'Now, Mr McLeish,' he said. 'A word of warning. I'm a man of short temper, and it's already in shreds. I've been chasing you round Norfolk since just after dawn, so don't waste my time . . . You drive cabs for Gresham Cars.'

Sandy had once spent a Hogmanay night in the cells at Kirkintilloch, and it wasn't an experience he was keen to repeat. He weighed the pros and cons and came to the conclusion that it might be better for all concerned to proceed with some caution. 'Aye,' he said warily. 'Just for the noo.'

'And a week yesterday you drove a fare down to Cley.'

Sandy pondered the safe reply, and decided to be truthful. 'Aye, it were a lassie,' he said. 'What's the fret?'

'You remember her?'

'That yin? Och aye, I mind her too fine.'

'Then describe her.'

Sandy shrugged. 'A wee bitty lassie. Ginger heid an' a bag. Tellt me she was biding some place down south.'

'You spoke to her then?'

'Ayed an' nawed, that were all. There wasni much chance.'

'Why not?'

Another shrug 'She wasni for listening.'

'You mean she did all the talking?'

'Aye, all the bloody way. Starts when she sits hersel' doon in the cab an' doesni bloody stop till she gets oot at Cley.'

'Did she talk about herself?'

'Aye, every wee stupit bloody detail.' Sandy drew a deep breath. 'Tricklt like a tap, she did. Niver run dry . . . An' it's no good yous askin' me what like she said. I canni remember.'

'You'd better.'

'For why?'

McKenzie pulled out his notebook. 'She's been murdered,' he said. 'That means I need all the wee stupid bloody details. So start talking. Fast.'

8

If the day had ended prematurely as he emerged from Swallownest Wood with Bates and Billy Stormer, Tench might well have considered that Thursday had been a productive day. He'd been handed an abandoned bicycle which, more likely than not, had belonged to the woman found on Blacknock, and he had, in addition, unearthed a medallion with a verse that could provide him with a clue to her identity. It was a good beginning to what promised to be an illuminating day. As he pulled the car to a halt outside the incident room and stepped out into the sunshine of Medford's Drove Street, he felt a sense of optimism that even Sergeant Gregg would have found hard to emulate.

What he wasn't prepared for was the flood of confusing information that was waiting to assail him.

The first instalment was delivered by Detective Constable Lock as he pushed open the door of the incident room.

'Steve Harris has been in, sir.'

'So soon?' said Tench. 'What did he have to say?'

'No luck at Bretland's, sir. They haven't sold or hired a bike to a woman for more than three months . . . He went on to Wells, but the cycle dealers there weren't a great deal of help. He's on his way now to make inquiries in Holt.'

'You showed him the bike we found?'

'Yes, sir. He took a look at it and made a note of the number.'

'Well, if it is hers – and all the signs suggest that it is – she must have picked it up from somewhere fairly close by. All we can do is hope it was some place in Holt. If it wasn't, then we'll have to start thinking again. I suppose she could have got it from Sheringham or Cromer, but they're pretty far out. I wouldn't have thought she'd have gone all that way.'

Lock stared at the bike that was propped against the wall. 'Could be some small repair shop in one of the villages, sir. One we don't know about.'

'Could be,' said Tench, 'but I don't think it is. Small repair shops don't often keep a stock of new bikes, and if Harris doesn't know about it she wouldn't either . . . Anything else to report?'

'Yes, sir. Sue Gradwell rang up from Blakeney. She's tracked down the postman. He's a chap called Fred Bishop.'

'And?'

'Nothing, sir, I'm afraid. She drew a complete blank.'

'No post for the cottage?'

'Not even a postcard. Bishop said he hadn't been up there since the fire.'

Tench sighed. 'We don't seem to be having much luck, Des, do we?'

'Not a lot, sir, no, but it's early days yet.'

'You sound like Mr Lubbock.'

Lock narrowed his eyes. 'It's just that I've a hunch that something's going to break, and pretty soon, sir,' he said.

The time was then ten to twelve. At a quarter past twelve something did break, but not quite in the way that Detective Constable Lock had been hoping. A raucous spitting sound that died in a cough outside the incident room announced McKenzie's return from the outer, more desolate regions of the sticks.

He flung open the door, collapsed on a chair and vowed in a cluster of sanguinary terms that, if ever he survived to reach the age of retirement, he'd never set foot outside Norwich again. Nor did he wish to see, let alone converse with, anyone who lived in the Norfolk swamps.

He dismissed them all with a searing contempt. 'Dumplings,' he said, 'the lot of them.'

Tench assumed the worst. 'Waste of time, was it?'

McKenzie lay back in the chair and stretched out his legs. He managed a weary shrug. 'Well, now. That depends.'

'On what?'

'On what sort of rubbish you're willing to believe. Wasn't there someone once who asked, "What is truth?"'

'Pontius Pilate,' said Tench.

'Thought it might be a double-dealing sod like him.' McKenzie closed his eyes. 'Well, if I were you, Mike, I'd ask the same question.'

'Go on.'

'This cabby of yours . . .'

'What about him?'

'He's a chap called McLeish. I managed to track him down, but only after chasing three times round the swamps and prising directions out of a set of fumble-tongued oafs who seemed to be intent on obstructing the law.'

'The point is, did he talk?'

'Not right away, no. His mind wasn't exactly riveted on me. It was under the sheets, between a couple of distinctly eye-catching nipples and a pair of shapely legs. But once he'd rolled out of bed and pulled on his pants, yes, he talked quite a lot.'

'About her?'

'Oh, yes. Seems she had quite a tongue, this Mallalieu woman.'

'Was that the name she gave?'

'No, they didn't get quite as far as swapping names and addresses, but she yammered all the way from Holt into Cley, mostly about herself. Seemed determined to give him every stupid wee detail. That was what he said.'

'Come on then, Mac.' Tench was getting fretful. 'Let's be knowing what they were.'

'Don't rush me,' McKenzie said. 'I've had a morning that's left me just about in shreds. I've been battling with semi-literate octogenarians . . .'

'Oh, get on with it.'

'Right.' The sergeant shrugged. 'No rest for the zealous.' He pulled out his notebook and flicked through the pages. 'He didn't pick her up from the station. It was a cab-rank in Holt . . . She was a widow, so she said. Hadn't any children. She'd inherited quite a bit of money from her husband. Used to spend her holidays here as a schoolgirl, and it reminded her of happy times. Because of that, she'd decided to come back and settle in the area. Said she wanted to buy a house, an old one, one with a bit of character. She was ready to spend money on it: that was no problem. Asked him whether he knew of anything that might fit the bill; but of course, being Sandy McLeish from Glasgow, he hadn't a notion. Not to worry, she said. She was staying for a fortnight, maybe longer, and that'd give her time to look around for herself. She hadn't any intention of going back home till she'd found what she wanted: it was too far to travel.'

He glanced up at Tench. 'Well, by this time,' he said, 'McLeish was beginning to feel it was time to give his own voice a chance to be heard, so he asked her where she came from ... And guess what, Mike? She actually told him.'

'And it wasn't Southampton?'

'No, it wasn't. It was Truro. So God knows where she'll end up before we've finished ... You know what I think? I reckon everything she said was a load of old rope. The woman was just an accomplished liar. If you want my advice, you'll forget every word.'

Tench turned towards Lock. 'Mac's probably right, but you'd better check with Truro. There's always a chance she was telling the truth.'

'Want to bet?' McKenzie said. 'It's odds on next time she'll be living in John o' Groats. Or what about a cottage on the cliffs at Cape Wrath? That's just about as far from the swamps as you can get ... Of course,' he added, 'she could have packed a bikini and swum across the Channel. I wouldn't put it past her.'

9

It was a call of nature – though not, it must be said, the sound of Medford's gently trickling stream – that, a few minutes later, spurred him into reluctant activity.

Lock waited till he'd gone. 'Sarge seems a bit grumpy this morning, sir,' he said.

'Understandable,' said Tench. 'It's a frustrating case. We're making no headway. And Sergeant McKenzie isn't blessed with your spark of optimistic faith. If Mac sees a light at the end of a tunnel, he keeps the news to himself in case it goes out.'

'Well, he could be wrong after all, sir, couldn't he? She could be a widow and living in Truro.'

'And her name could be Mallalieu. Yes, it's possible.'

'But you don't think it's likely.'

'No,' said Tench.

Lock picked up the phone. 'I'll get on to Truro,' he said. 'Tell them to ring me back.'

Lubbock, long before, had made his own assessment of Sergeant McKenzie, though he'd never divulged it to anyone but Hastings. Loyal, he said, trustworthy, a man to have close at hand if you were in a tight corner, but lacking in patience, undiplomatic, strong on emotion, but weak when it came to logical analysis. Every one of his opinions needed straining through a sieve to get rid of the flaws.

There were some folk, he said, who proved to be almost invariably right, while others were more than frequently wrong. But McKenzie was different. More often than not he was both right and wrong: right in his sweepingly broad diagnoses, but wrong in most of those vital particulars that needed a far more incisive mind.

It was a truth that, inside the next quarter of an hour, was borne out to the full once Constable Bates arrived on the scene.

'Arternoon, sir,' he said.

Tench looked up. 'Back again, Constable?'

'Aye, sir. Back again.'

'More about Billy Stormer?'

'No, sir. Yelda Thober.'

'Isn't she one of the cockle women?'

'Aye, sir, that's right. More forrard than most when it comes to mardling, though that ent saying much.'

'You've spoken to her?'

'Aye, talked to all of 'em, sir. An' shown 'em the picture. Asked 'em if they'd mebbe set eyes on the woman.'

'And Yelda Thober said she had?'

Bates nodded stiffly. 'She did, sir, aye. Friday forenoon it were. She's a cottage out on the Sibthorpe road, an' she were on her way down to Medford to tek her daughter an apple pie – that's the one, sir, as lives on Liggerbeck Hill – an' she sees this furriner – a woman it were, sir, riding a bike – a-coming down from Sibthorpe.'

'She was sure it was her?'

'Said as she were positive like, sir, aye. Then, a couple o' minutes later, up on Main Street, she sees the bike a-propped up by the Post Office wall. So, when she tells me this, I puts two an' two together, sir, an' reckons it be time I be paying a call on ol' Maisie Tackleston.'

'Who's she?'

'Maisie Jelf as was, sir. Runs the Post Office along wi' the general store . . . So I sees her an' asks has a furriner been in, a woman. Aye, she says, more 'n one, so I shows her the likeness.'

'And she recognized her?'

'Aye, sir, that she certainly did. A fair talkative mawther, that were what she said. Holidaying like an' renting a cottage. Wanted a local map. Said as she weren' over familiar wi' the place.'

'Did she say where she was from?'

'Aye, sir. Not as Maisie were like to be asking. Said as she were coming from some place called Pendle. Can't say as I've heard of it, but that were what she said.'

'It's in Lancashire,' said Tench. 'As a matter of fact, it's not very far from where I was born.'

'Aye, well, an' that'd be right, sir,' said Bates. 'Maisie, she reckoned it were somewhere up north, an' she be known as a knowledgeable body, be Maisie. More'n most, that is.'

'Pendle!' said Tench. 'Where the hell next? And what, of all places, made her choose Pendle?'

'Don't know it, sir,' said Lock.

'Pendle Hill, Desmond. Home of the infamous Lancashire witches. Old Chattox and Demdike. Agents of the devil. One died in gaol and the other was hanged.'

'Well, at least it fits,' said Lock. 'In the last few hours she's been in Medford, Southampton, and after that in Truro. And now she's up in Lancashire. Reckon she'd need a broomstick to whizz round that fast.'

10

With McKenzie already despatched into Medford to round up the three detective constables, and Lock on his way to the Wicksteads' shop in search of bread rolls and pasties in lieu of a midday meal, Tench dragged the phone towards him and rang through to Ledward.

The doctor had clearly suffered a restless night.

'Yes,' he said sharply, implying with a single three-letter word that he was grossly overworked and hadn't time to spare to be answering casual callers on the phone.

'Chief Inspector Tench, sir.'

'Well?' The tone of voice revealed a growing impatience.

'The autopsy report on the Blacknock woman.'

'It should be on your desk. I sent it first thing this morning.'

'I'm in Medford, sir. It hadn't arrived when I left. Can you give me a run-down?'

Tench heard a deep sigh.

'D'you think I've nothing better to do, Chief Inspector, than repeat ad nauseam what I've already written?'

'It would be helpful, sir.'

'Not to me,' Ledward said. 'I've two suicides and three sudden deaths in the fridge, and young Mason's off sick.'

Mason, his long-suffering assistant was at least forty-five.

'A brief résumé, sir?'

Another sigh.

'All the findings confirm what I told you yesterday. Death from anoxia.'

'What about the time?'

'What about it, Chief Inspector?'

'Death was certified at Holt at 11.58 on Tuesday, but you said you thought she'd died some twenty-four to forty-eight hours before that. Is it possible to be more accurate?'

'No, Chief Inspector. My original estimate still stands. The stomach contents showed a partially digested meal of bread, cheese and pickle, but it's quite impossible to say precisely when it was consumed.'

'So that means she died sometime between midday on Sunday and the same time on Monday.'

'I'd say so, yes.'

'What about Craske?'

'Nothing about him at the moment, Chief Inspector. Five minutes ago I made the first incision to open the thoracic and abdominal cavities. I was just about to start my examination when I was called to the phone – gratuitously, it seems. So I suggest if you require any further information you put an immediate end to this pointless conversation and let me proceed.'

Tench swore beneath his breath and rang off. He sat for a moment, staring at the phone; then, recalling the operator, he asked to be connected to the lab.

The phone clicked several times and he heard Merrick's voice.

'Ted,' he said. 'It's Mike.'

'Hello, Chief Inspector.'

Ted Merrick was the analyst working on the sack. Younger than Tench himself – Ledward would have classed him as an infant-in-arms – he was, nonetheless, an expert in his field. More than that, he never suffered from morning melancholia, didn't regard his findings as classified material, and was normally cheerful, which made him more forthcoming than the doctor was ever likely to be.

'Anything yet on that sack?'

'Well,' Merrick said, 'it's one of the old type, a standard twenty-stone. We've taken a sample and first indications point to jute from Faridpur. We haven't got around yet to where it was processed.'

'Where's Faridpur?'

'It's on the Ganges, about a hundred and fifty miles north-east of Calcutta.'

'That's as far as you've got? Nothing so far to prove a link with the woman?'

'Not yet, sir, no, but we're working on it.'

It was Tench's turn to sigh. 'OK. Let me know if anything turns up.'

'Don't worry, sir. We will.'

*

Don't worry. Be patient.

He dropped the receiver back on its hook and swore again. How long was it now since Ledward had rung him yesterday morning? He looked at his watch. Nearly twenty-seven hours. Twenty-seven hours of niggling investigation, and what had he got to show for it? Not much at all.

He'd got a woman who might or might not have been murdered, whose name might or might not have been what she claimed, and who might or might not have lived in three different places hundreds of miles apart and even further from Medford.

He had an old dipsomaniac whose killing might or might not be connected. He had an empty sack that might or might not prove the link. He had a bicycle that might or might not have belonged to the woman, and a gold medallion with a puzzling inscription that might or might not have any significance.

In other words, all he'd managed to achieve in twenty-seven hours was a load of speculation based on a multitude of still unanswered questions.

What he needed was one solid, cast-iron clue: a fingerprint, a hair, a single incontrovertible statement, none of which, so far, had emerged from the dark, oozing mud of Blacknock.

He knew very well what Lubbock would have said. 'Work and wait, laddie. Let the case simmer. It'll come to the boil when you're least expecting it.'

Well, maybe it would, but it seemed to be taking a bloody long time to show the first signs.

He took the deepest breath that he'd taken all day, pushed back his chair and threw open the door. Once outside the cottage, he made his way across the road, leaned on the bridge and stared down at the river.

Its unhurried flow as it trickled towards the sea didn't exactly inspire him with patience, but at least it made a change from staring at the phone.

McKenzie's mange-ridden mongrel sniffed at its favourite milestone and lifted its leg.

Medford, oblivious, drowsed in the sun.

11

It was half an hour later, while he and Lock were sampling Emmy Wickstead's potato pasties, that Steve Harris arrived back from Holt on his two-stroke.

'Don't tell me,' said Tench. 'No one in Holt's ever heard of a woman's bike.'

'Not exactly that, sir. There are three cycle dealers. They all sell women's bikes and one of them hires them, but that's about it. None sold in the last few weeks and only one hired, and that to a local councillor's wife in the town. She returned it a week last Monday.' He paused and scratched his head. 'But there is something else.'

'Go on.'

'Well, sir, there was a break-in at Sibthorpe yesterday. Sparrow Hill House. It's owned by a Mr Wellbridge.'

Tench nodded. 'Sergeant Lester mentioned it. Said one of his men was taking prints over there . . . What was taken?'

'That's the strange thing about it, sir. Only a prayer-wheel.'

'A what?'

'A prayer-wheel. It's not very big. It's just a small copper drum on the end of a stick. Holds a set of prayers. Buddhists carry them about.'

'You mean this Wellbridge is a Buddhist?'

Harris grinned. 'Wouldn't think so, sir, no. He'd just picked it up as a bit of a curio.'

'Valuable?'

'No, not according to what he says.'

'Then why steal it?'

'That's the puzzle. He doesn't seem to know. But whoever took it wrecked the place.'

'Criminal damage?'

'Yes, sir. A lot of it. Just in one room.'

'And you think there's some connection?'

'There could be, sir, yes. Mr Wellbridge runs a timber business in Holt, so while I was there I thought I'd pop in and tell him what the print man had found – not that that was much help: just his own and his wife's prints, and one or two others that weren't on the files – but then I showed him the woman's picture, the Blacknock woman, and he took one look at it and said, yes, he'd seen her.'

'Where?' said Tench. 'Inverness . . . Folkestone . . .?'

'No, sir.' The constable shook his head. 'Said he'd seen her on board ship.'

There was a moment's silence.

'Coming from where?'

'Bombay, sir,' Harris said.

V

LIMBO

Such . . . are your sex – part truth, part fiction;
Some thought, much whim, and all a contradiction

Richard Savage: *Verses to a Young Lady*

1

The site of the Wellbridge timber yard in Holt was cramped and inauspicious, but the business appeared to be prospering and the office occupied by Wellbridge himself was relatively spacious.

'Please take a seat, gentlemen,' he said. 'What can I do to help you?'

McKenzie chose an armchair; Tench a round-backed metal one close to the desk.

'You had a visit,' he said, 'this morning, sir, from Constable Harris.'

Wellbridge nodded. 'Yes, that's right.'

'You identified a woman in a picture he showed you.'

'Yes, I did.'

'You couldn't have been mistaken?.'

Wellbridge raised his eyebrows. 'You think I might have been, Inspector?'

'Not really, sir, no. But there's always a chance, and we have to make sure. Appearances can be deceptive, particularly where artists' impressions are involved, and everyone has a double – an approximate double – somewhere in the world.'

Wellbridge smiled and shook his head. 'Not in this case, Inspector. I've no doubt at all that the woman in the picture was the one that I saw.'

'On board ship.'

'On board the *Strathaven*. She's a P&O liner. Sailed from Bombay 25th October. Docked at Liverpool November 10th.'

'You were sailing back from India with your wife?'

'She was on the ship, yes, but she wasn't my wife, Inspector. Not at that time. It was a shipboard romance. We were married a month later.'

'Then she may have seen this woman as well.'

Wellbridge gave a shrug. 'She may have done, yes. On the other hand, she may not. The *Strathaven*'s a large vessel. Twenty-six thousand tons. Troopship in the war. Recently reconverted. She was carrying a lot of passengers.'

McKenzie stirred in his seat. 'This was six months ago, sir?'

'Roughly that, yes.'

'It's a long time to remember the face of a fellow passenger. How can you be so certain?'

'Because, on a couple of occasions, Sergeant, I shared the same table with her at dinner. That was early in the voyage, before I met Deirdre. Deirdre Thompson she was then. Now she's Mrs Wellbridge.'

'So this woman. You got to know her quite well?' said Tench.

'I wouldn't say well. We passed some idle chit-chat. That was about all.'

'Did she tell you her name?'

'Yes. Miriam something. I didn't ask her surname.'

'Did she say where she came from?'

'Regretfully, no. We didn't get as far as swapping addresses, but I had the impression it was somewhere in Kent.'

'Why was that, sir?'

'Just that she talked a lot about it. Mentioned places like Penshurst and Tunbridge Wells.'

'Means nothing,' McKenzie said. 'She could have been there on holiday.'

Wellbridge nodded. 'Yes, she could, but it's the best I can do.'

'Then perhaps you could describe her for us,' said Tench. 'There are things that aren't apparent in an artist's likeness.'

'Such as?' Wellbridge frowned.

'Things like approximate age, weight and height. Colour of hair. Colour of eyes.'

There was a pause.

'It's always difficult, Inspector, to guess a woman's age, but I'd say she was round about thirty, small and slim, auburn hair cut short and neatly waved . . . As for the eyes, that's a bit of a problem. Hazel I'd say, but they had a green fleck. I remember thinking they went well with her hair.'

Tench switched his line of questioning. 'This break-in at your house, sir. It happened yesterday morning?'

'Yes, that's right.'

'While you were here in Holt, and your wife was somewhere on the way back from Lynn?'

'Correct, Inspector.'

'There was considerable damage, so Harris was saying, but the only thing taken was a prayer-wheel that wasn't particularly valuable.'

'It wasn't valuable at all. Worth a pound or two perhaps, but no more than that.'

'And you can't explain why the thief chose to take it?'

'No, Inspector. I told the constable I couldn't.'

'You know, of course, sir' – Tench held up the picture – 'that this woman was found dead on the sands at Medford. On Tuesday morning.'

'Yes, he said so.'

'That means she couldn't possibly have been responsible for the break-in.'

Wellbridge looked surprised. 'I never thought she was.'

'Yet it's very strange, isn't it? If this is indeed the woman you saw on board ship, then she travelled with you from India, and six months later she turns up at the very place where you've chosen to rent a house.'

'And,' McKenzie added, 'she turns up dead.'

Wellbridge stared at him. Then he looked back at Tench. 'You're not suggesting . . .?'

'No, sir, we're not. We're just trying to find some rational explanation.'

'Well, there's only one, isn't there? The whole thing's just an inexplicable coincidence.'

'Or else,' said Tench, 'you've made an honest mistake.' He held out the picture. 'Take another look.'

Wellbridge crossed to the window and held the portrait to the light. He turned it this way and that. 'No,' he said at last, 'I've made no mistake.'

'You still say this woman was on board the *Strathaven* and shared your table at dinner?'

'I'm positive, yes.'

'Then if it isn't too much trouble, sir,' said Tench, 'I'd like you to come and identify the body.'

Wellbridge pushed himself up.

'Willingly,' he said. 'But it won't make any difference, Inspector. Not a jot. I know that I'm right.'

A quarter of an hour later, they stood by a sheeted body as a mortuary attendant uncovered the face.

'Look very carefully, sir,' said Tench.

Wellbridge peered down. Then he stood back and nodded.

'Yes,' he said, 'that's her. That's Miriam. I'd know her anywhere.'

2

'He's wrong,' McKenzie said as they walked to the car.

'He seemed pretty sure.'

'He may have been' – the sergeant shook his head with some vehemence – 'but that doesn't make him right. He's made a mistake, he must have. Southampton I can take, and Truro. Pendle, too, at a pinch. But Bombay's stretching things a bit too far. He's mixing her up with somebody else.'

Tench unlocked the car and leaned on the roof. 'I'm not saying I haven't some doubts myself, Mac, but look at it this way. This is the first sighting – all right, alleged sighting – we've had of the woman outside the Medford area . . .'

'Yes, way outside.'

'And there's another thing, too.'

'Tell me,' McKenzie said.

'If, as he says, she was on her way from India, it seems very strange that the only thing missing is something that came from that part of the world. A Buddhist prayer-wheel.'

McKenzie gave a shrug. He was clearly unconvinced. 'Well, I'll go along with that,' he said, 'but deep down I'm a simple, uncomplicated soul, so just explain to me one thing. Veronica or Miriam, or whoever else she turns out to be in the end, was found stretched out dead on the Medford sands last Tuesday morning; and our personable friend, Dr Reginald Ledward, tells us that she died at least a day before that. So just explain to me, Mike, how she could have nicked a prayer-wheel, whatever that is, sometime on Wednesday.'

'I can't.' Tench opened the door and eased himself into the driving seat.

'Resurrection?'

'No. Not very likely.'

'Reincarnation?'

'Forget it.'

'So what do we do now?'

'I think,' said Tench, 'we indulge ourselves. We do a little detour on our way back to Medford, and make the acquaintance of Mrs Deirdre Wellbridge. Let's see what she has to say.'

She had plenty to say. She made that very clear as soon as Tench flashed his card.

'Mrs Wellbridge?' he said.

She was in a tight-fitting, lemon-coloured blouse and a pair of blue slacks. Both were designed to show off her figure: an effect they achieved to some advantage and McKenzie's all too obvious fascination.

She looked down at them from the top of the steps. 'Yes,' she said. 'What?'

Tench held up the card. 'I'm Detective Chief Inspector Tench ... And this is Detective Sergeant McKenzie.'

'About time,' she said. 'You've arrested him then?'

'Who, ma'am?' Tench looked blank.

'Daft Danny. That half-wit up at Astley Farm.'

'I'm afraid ...'

'Don't tell me you haven't.' She gave them a glance of withering contempt. 'Can't the police round here do anything at all? Isn't it your job to protect the public?'

'Part of it, ma'am, yes.'

'Then why don't you get up there and arrest him?'

Tench strove to be patient. 'I'm afraid, Mrs Wellbridge, that's not why we're here.'

'Then it should be,' she said. 'He's a menace. Lock him up.'

'At the moment, ma'am, we're concerned with something else.'

'Are you indeed? And what would that be?'

Tench seemed to hesitate. 'May we come in?'

'If you have to.' She stepped aside grudgingly, led them down the hall and showed them into a room at the back of the house. It was spacious, with oak-panelled walls, a three-piece suite, a heavy oak table and a knee-hole desk. French windows, wide and high, revealed an unkempt garden.

On the desk was a carved wooden box made of teak. She flipped open the lid, took out a cigarette and lit it with a gold-plated lighter. Then, blowing out a cloud of smoke, she turned to face them. She made no move to offer them a seat.

'If you're not here,' she said, 'to talk about that brainless young zombie, then what have you come for? I hope you're not simply wasting my time.'

'We never work without a purpose, Mrs Wellbridge.'

'No?' She made her doubts very clear. 'Then what is it?'

Tench turned to McKenzie. 'Sergeant, show Mrs Wellbridge the picture.'

McKenzie pulled it out of an inside pocket and handed it to her. 'D'you recognize that woman?' he asked tersely.

Her answer was equally short and direct. She took one glance at it and handed it back. 'No,' she said.

'Please look very carefully, ma'am,' said Tench.

She took a deep breath and looked a second time.

'I've told you,' she said. 'I don't know her. Who is she?'

'She's the woman who was found on the sands at Medford.'

There was a flicker of interest, then she shrugged. 'I still don't know her.'

'Your husband does,' said Tench.

She gave a little laugh. 'Now why doesn't that surprise me?'

'I don't know, Mrs Wellbridge. Suppose you tell me.'

'I don't see why I should. It's no business of yours.' She looked straight at him. 'Let's just say that my husband mixes with a great many women.'

'Women you don't recognize?'

'Rarely, I'm afraid.' She glanced at the picture again. 'Did he say where he met her?'

'On board the *Strathaven*, Mrs Wellbridge, so he told us.'

'Did he now?' She held it up and studied it more closely. 'Then I must have missed her. She's hardly what you'd call remarkable, is she?'

'You never saw her on board ship?'

'No, I didn't.'

'And you haven't seen her round here?'

'How many more times do I have to say this, Inspector? No, I've never seen her. I never saw her on the voyage and I haven't seen her here.'

'Well, thank you, ma'am.'

'Is that all?'

'Yes, I think so. For the moment.'

'And what about this Daft Danny creature?'

'What about him, ma'am?'

'When are you going to lock him up?'

'We can't lock people up without a good reason,' McKenzie said. 'What's he supposed to have done?'

She turned on him. 'Supposed?' she said. 'Supposed? There's no supposed about it, Sergeant. He did it.'

Tench intervened. 'Did what, Mrs Wellbridge?'

'You wouldn't need to ask if you'd seen this room when I got back yesterday. He wrecked the place, didn't he? I told that man of yours . . . What's his name?'

'You mean Constable Harris?'

She nodded. 'That's the one. Harris.'

'We'll have a word with Constable Harris, ma'am,' said Tench. 'I'm sure he's reported it.'

She stubbed her cigarette out on the top of the desk. 'Then you're a good deal more confident than I am,' she said.

'Nonetheless, ma'am . . .'

'I'm to leave it to you?'

'Rest assured, Mrs Wellbridge. We'll make inquiries.'

'I hope so, Inspector. For your sake,' she said. 'Because if you haven't arrested him by this time tomorrow, I'll be making a complaint to someone a good deal higher up than you.'

'That's your privilege, of course, ma'am,' said Tench. 'No.' He raised a hand. 'Please don't trouble yourself to move. We'll see ourselves out.'

3

McKenzie took the wheel of the car. He raced down the twisting drive, clipping tree branches, turned on to the main road and then, without warning, jammed on the brakes.

'Bitch!' he said.

Tench relaxed his grip on the dashboard. 'Why the hell did you do that?'

'She's a bitch,' McKenzie said. 'I thought she was, and I was right.'

Tench stared at him. 'You've met her before?'

'Haven't met her, but I've seen her. Yesterday, down in Medford, while you and Bates were closeted with Surly Sarah. She disturbed my long contemplation of the river. Walked across the bridge, wiggling her hips. I was looking straight at her and she simply ignored me. Can you believe that?'

'Difficult,' Tench said drily, 'but I suppose it's possible. You can't be her type.'

'Well, if Wellbridge is, God help him, that's all I can say. Why would anyone in their right mind marry a malignant harpy like that?'

'Easy. She's got curves in all the right places and probably a ton of money stowed away somewhere.'

McKenzie snorted. 'She'd need to have both, and a hell of a lot more than I reckon she has, for me to take her on.'

'So . . . which of them's mistaken?'

'Not her. She's lying.'

'You think so?'

'I know so, Mike. I've met her kind before. She could lie the pants off a Sumo wrestler, and do it without so much as a flick of an eyelash. If Wellbridge was right, and I'm beginning to think he was, then I'm ready to bet she nicked him from right under Miriam's nose, and wants to forget that she ever existed.'

'Even so,' said Tench, 'we'd better check on this Daft Danny business. Drop me off at Medford and run down to Blakeney. Harris should be back there by now. Get hold of him and find out what's been going on.'

As McKenzie drove away across the bridge and swung the car towards Blakeney, Lock appeared at the door of the incident room. 'Mr Lubbock, sir,' he said.

'What about him?'

'He's here to see you. Been here half an hour. Said he'd better wait. It was something urgent.'

'Did he say what it was?'

'No, sir. Just that you needed to know.'

'Right. We'd better find out what's troubling him,' said Tench.

Once he opened the door, he'd have known, even if Lock hadn't warned him, that his old Chief was waiting and had been for some considerable time. The room reeked of smoke, clouds of it rolled towards him, opaque in the shafts of sunlight, and deep in the haze he glimpsed a flickering match.

He wafted away what he could of the gloom. 'When in hell's name,' he said, 'are you going to get rid of that God-awful pipe?'

Lubbock was unmoved. He blew a thunderhead of smoke towards the ceiling of the cottage and tossed the match in a waste bin. 'Not yet,' he said, 'laddie. Bought it some place in Aylsham before the war. Never found another quite like it since.'

'And you won't. It's just a corroded old stump.'

'It's singed a bit. That's what gives it its flavour.' Lubbock stretched out his legs. 'You worry too much, Mike. Sit down and relax ... Any news about the sack?'

'Nothing conclusive. The boffins are still working.'

'And what about my lodger?'

'I'm glad you asked that,' said Tench. 'According to her she's got homes not just in Hampshire, but in Lancashire and Cornwall, and we've turned up a witness who swears she was on a ship coming back from Bombay.'

'Well, that's something. You're making progress.'

'If we are, we're just wandering round in a maze. The only real clues we've uncovered are that bike' – he pointed to it, propped against the wall – 'which may be hers or may not ... And this.' He pulled open the drawer of a filing cabinet, took out the medallion in its cellophane wrapper and slid it across the table. 'Found in a pocket inside the saddle-bag. There's a verse on it, but no one seems to know what it means.'

Lubbock laid down his pipe, hoisted himself with a grunt from the chair, carried the wrapper across to the window, held it to the light and peered at it closely. Not for long: a few seconds. Then he looked up. 'It's from Swaffham,' he said.

'Swaffham?' Tench blinked. 'How can you tell?'

'The old stand-by, laddie. A spot of local knowledge. This engaging little trinket's a keepsake from Swaffham. Shops there sell them. You can get them either in gold or silver. Or one of the baser metals. I've seen larger versions too, carved out of wood, to hang on the wall.'

'And you only get them in Swaffham?'

'Oh, I expect you can pick them up in Thetford or Dereham. Places close by. But yes, most of them come from there.'

'Why Swaffham in particular?'

Lubbock retrieved his pipe and bit hard on the stem. 'It's the pedlar,' he said. 'A bloke called Chapman. Went around with a packhorse selling his wares ... Don't say you've never been inside Swaffham church.'

'You know damn well I haven't.'

'It amazes me,' said Lubbock, 'just how much you've still to learn about Norfolk. I thought everyone had heard about old John Chapman.'

Tench closed his eyes.

'Go on,' he said. 'Tell me.'

4

Lubbock tossed the wrapper down on the table, eased himself back into his chair and tapped the medallion with his pipe-stem. 'That verse,' he said, 'has a story behind it.'

Tench nodded. 'I thought it might have.'

'D'you want to hear it?'

'Why not? Listen and learn. That was what you said ... Right. I'm listening.'

His old Chief took a clasp knife out of his pocket, scraped the bowl of his pipe, knocked it out in the waste bin and, producing an old leather pouch, rolled a wedge of tobacco between his palms. 'Once upon a time,' he said, '... and that's the only honest way to begin this tale, because part of it's fact and part of it's legend, and no one knows for certain just how much there is of each ... Once upon a time, there was a pedlar, John Chapman, living in Swaffham. He traded round the villages, selling pots and platters. It was a devil of a tiring business tramping from place to place, and after one particularly strenuous day he went to bed early. But he didn't sleep too well. He kept dreaming and waking and dreaming again. He was meeting a stranger who told him that if he made his way to London and stood on London Bridge, he'd hear something there that would make his fortune. The dream was so vivid that it kept coming back to him all the next day, and when he dreamt it twice more in the nights that followed, he decided to chance his luck and go up to London. Well, of course, his wife told him she thought he was mad ...'

'I'm not surprised,' said Tench.

'As a matter of fact' – Lubbock tamped the tobacco down in his pipe – 'neither am I. She was probably a good, solid, sensible Norfolk woman, but that's beside the point.'

'He didn't take her advice?'

'Of course he didn't. He was a good, solid, sensible Norfolk husband. He took his dog with him and tramped up to London, made straight for London Bridge and waited there for fortune to make itself known. Well, he waited three days, strolling up and down and chatting to passers-by, but no one told him anything that was likely to make him rich. Then, late on the third day, so the story goes, one of the local tradesmen couldn't contain his curiosity any longer. "Friend," he said, "I've seen you walking up and down now for three whole days. What on earth are you doing?" It was an honest enough question, so the pedlar gave him an honest enough answer. "I had a dream," he said, "that if I waited on London Bridge, someone would tell me something that would make my fortune."'

'And this remarkably omniscient tradesman just happened to tell him where to find it.'

'Yes, he did,' Lubbock said, 'but not right away.'

'It sounds an unlikely tale,' said Tench, 'but carry on. Don't let me spoil the finale.'

'Well, this chap heard him out without interrupting, which is more than I can say for some folk. Then he gave a little laugh. "Friend," he said, "you'd be far better off to go back home. Dreams mean nothing. If I paid any attention to what I dreamed, I'd never get any work done. Why, a few nights back I dreamed that if I went to the house of a pedlar who lives in Norfolk, and dug under an apple tree in his garden, I'd find a pot of gold. Did you ever hear such nonsense?"'

'Amazing,' said Tench. 'So he dug and he found.'

'Are you telling this tale, or am I?' Lubbock said. 'Yes, he did. He unearthed a brass pot full of gold coins. But there was more to it than that. There was an inscription in Latin engraved round the bowl, but since he wasn't a Latin scholar and couldn't read anyway, it meant nothing to him. He simply thanked his lucky stars for the gold that he'd found and put the empty pot among his wares to be sold. Then, sometime later, a would-be purchaser who happened to know Latin translated it for him. And there it is.' He pushed the medallion back towards Tench. '"Beneath me doth lie/ Another that be/Much richer than I."'

'So he dug a second time?'

'And found a much larger pot crammed to the brim with gold and jewels ... Of course, it's all nonsense, but it makes a good yarn, and the people of Swaffham have been repeating it ever since. It's become a local legend. You can buy medallions like that in jewellers and curio shops all over the town. Some have a picture of the pedlar and his dog embossed on the back. Others just the pedlar without any verse.'

'And there never was a John Chapman?'

'Oh, yes, there was. You'll find him in the parish records at Swaffham. He was a churchwarden there in 1462. Reputedly a wealthy man. Paid for the splendid north aisle of the church: seven bays and a clerestory with thirteen arched windows; and he's carved on one of the pew ends with his dog. But no one seems to know how he made so much money. Maybe at least a part of the story's true, and he turned up some long-buried Roman treasure. On the other hand he could have dabbled in smuggling gold – a lot of it was done – and made up the tale to explain his sudden wealth. But we'll never know the truth, whatever it was.'

Tench waited. 'That's all? That's the end?'

'What else did you expect? A codicil to his will?'

'Not much help though, is it? It doesn't exactly solve all our pressing problems?'

'Well, it does establish a connection with Swaffham.'

'A possible connection. No more than that.'

'Look on the bright side, laddie. You've just acquired another bit of Norfolk folklore. Stow it away in the memory bank.'

'I'd feel better,' said Tench, 'if I could stow away just one indisputable fact about this woman of yours. She's turned up in Southampton and Truro. She's toured the Lancashire witch country. Added to that, she's sailed to Bombay and back, and now she's had the gall to pop up in Swaffham.'

'Well, at least she's come to rest in God's own country.'

'She may have done,' said Tench, 'but all I'm doing is wandering in Limbo . . . And don't tell me to be patient. This kettle of a case has been simmering long enough. It's time it began to whistle . . . So, what was so urgent it spurred you here to see me?'

'Ah, well,' said Lubbock, 'that's a different tale.' He struck a match and lit his pipe, producing in the process half a dozen turbulent billows of smoke that all but obscured him. 'That sack. Did the lab say what type it was?'

'Merrick said it was the old standard type. Twenty-stone.'

Lubbock nodded. 'Thought it must be . . . You remember I asked Joe Rogers to stand in for me at the mill last weekend?'

'Yes, so you said.'

'Well, Joe's one of the old style millers. Prefers to work with the standard sack, and he's still got some left that he brought from Billingford. I dropped in to see him at Glandford this morning after I'd had a word with Lester and his team, and he mentioned that last Friday he took an armful of them over to Kettle Hill. There was nobody about and the granary was locked, so he left them in the stables. They weren't used, of course, because he had to cry off, so he picked them up on Monday evening – there was still no one around – and took them back home. The trouble is they were just an armful. He never bothered to count them, so he can't say for sure whether any were missing.'

'Fine,' said Tench. The word was heavy with irony. 'So whoever killed your lodger and cleaned out the cottage could have picked up a sack while he was there and used it to take her body out to Blacknock.'

'He could have done. Whether he did, laddie, that's another matter.'

'Did you ask Rogers where the sacks came from?'

'He couldn't remember. It's a long time ago. He left Billingford before the war. Said he thought it might be some firm in Suffolk that's closed down since then. But he bought his sacks from a number of different places. Might have been any of them.'

'That's the trouble,' said Tench. 'Everything's a case of might or might not.'

Lubbock blew a smoke ring and watched it twist away. 'You've got clues,' he said. 'What more d'you want out of life? An unsolicited confession?'

5

It was half-past four by the time that Lubbock started up his old three-wheeler and turned right beyond the bridge towards Cley, and if Tench was left in a state of some frustration it was nothing to what he felt at eight o'clock that night. By then he wasn't merely disconcerted. He was thoroughly confused.

It wasn't that the returning members of his team had nothing to report. It was rather that what they had to say was of such a conflicting nature and the pattern of developments so unexpected that he began to wonder just what malevolent spirit had suddenly possessed the sleepy village of Medford.

Gregg and Sue Gradwell were the first to report.

'Mainly negative, sir,' said Gregg. 'Walter Bolding delivered a pint of milk to the cottage every day from Thursday till yesterday morning.'

'What time did he deliver?'

'Usually round about seven o'clock Never saw anyone there and left the milk by the doorstep. It had always disappeared when he turned up next day.'

'And what about Wickstead?'

'Pays a lad called Tommy Grimes to make his bread deliveries. Drives a small van. Said he usually reached there about ten o'clock, but only saw the woman once. That was Thursday morning. Every day after that the place was locked up and he left the bread outside. Said much the same as Bolding. Someone took it in, and apart from the first day there never seemed to be anyone about.'

Tench turned to Sue Gradwell.

'And the postman made no deliveries at all?'

'Not even a card, sir. Never went to the cottage, but he did mention a couple of things that seemed strange.'

'What were they?'

'Well, sir, he has to pass the mill on his way to Morston, and he said that one morning he saw a van turn off the main road and drive up to the cottage.'

'What day was that?'

'He said he thought it was Thursday. Round about half-past ten in the morning.'

'Did he describe it?'

'Yes, sir. Said it looked like a railway delivery van . . . So, if the woman was there at ten o'clock on Thursday as Grimes says she was . . .'

'She may have been waiting for the van to arrive?'

'Seems likely, sir, doesn't it . . .? And there was something else he said. He couldn't remember which day it was, but one morning late last week a woman in a car pulled up beside him on that long stretch of road between Morston and Medford. She asked him if he knew where she could get hold of some sacks. He told her he didn't, but the best thing to do was try one of the farms.'

'What was she like? Did he say?'

'Yes, sir.' Sue Gradwell checked her notebook. 'Smartly dressed, attractive, long dark hair. Looked to be in her thirties.'

'And the car?'

'A red sports car. Open-topped. Couldn't say what make. It drove off towards Medford.'

That was at 4.45.

At five o'clock the three detective constables, Ellison, Rayner and Spurgeon, reported back from their house-to-house in the village. They'd apparently elected Ellison as the spokesman.

'Well?' said Tench.

Ellison scratched his head. 'We collected quite a lot of gen, sir,' he said, 'but I don't know what you'll make of it.'

'Why?'

'Taken all in all, sir, it doesn't add up to much.'

'You mean no one in Medford set eyes on the woman?'

'I wouldn't exactly say that, sir, no.'

'Then what would you say?' The Detective Chief Inspector was growing more frustrated with every second that passed.

'Well, between us, sir, we covered all the houses and spoke to as many people as we could, but when we showed them the picture, most of them said no, they were sure they hadn't seen her. There were something like half a dozen who said yes, they had, then they took a second look and said they couldn't be certain; and in the end there were only two that stuck to their guns and said yes, it was definitely her that they'd seen.'

'Who were they?'

'One was Mrs Thober, sir, the woman who was gathering cockles on Tuesday morning.'

'Yes, we know about her. Who was the other?'

'A Mr Britiffe, sir. Peter Britiffe. He lives on the Sibthorpe road and runs a greengrocer's business in Wells. Collects a lot of his produce from a market gardener up in Sibthorpe. Drives up there in his lorry every morning round about six o'clock. He said that last Friday, on his way up the hill, he saw the woman sitting on fallen tree by the side of the road. There was a bicycle lying on the grass close by.'

'He drove past her?'

'Yes, sir.'

'Then he could only have caught a glimpse of her. How could he be sure?'

'He drove back an hour later and she was still sitting there. She held up a hand and stopped him. Asked him if there were any empty houses further up the road, and he told her there were only two between there and Sibthorpe – Astley Farm and Sparrow Hill House – and both of them were occupied. Were there any, she said, in Sibthorpe itself? Well, all he could say was he didn't really know. She'd be better off making some inquiries in the village.'

'You asked him to describe her?'

'Rayner did, sir. He was the one who spoke to him.'

'And . . .?'

'The description fitted what we know, sir,' Rayner said. 'Late twenties, short and slim, auburn hair . . . But there's just one thing. She said she was a stranger and didn't know the area. Didn't know much about the countryside at all. She'd spent every bit of her life in London.'

6

It was twenty past five when Wickstead appeared.

Wearing a blue-striped shirt with a red bow tie, black trousers and a pair of maroon-tinted braces, he stood for a moment in the doorway, monumentally spherical, blocking out the light. Behind him, barely visible, was Constable Bates.

'Mr Wickstead, sir,' he said. 'Came over to see me, so thought I'd best bring him around here like. Ye'll mebbe care to listen to what he has to say.'

Tench sighed, but with a smile. 'Yes, indeed. Why not? Good afternoon, Mr Wickstead. Please take a seat. It's a long time since we met. You look more prosperous than ever.'

'Fairish, sir. Fairish.' Wickstead eased his prodigious bulk on to a small wooden chair, wiped his pince-nez on a large flowered handkerchief and clipped them on his nose.

'You've something to tell me?'

The baker shifted himself to a more comfortable position. 'Aye, it were Emmy.'

'Your wife? How is she?'

'Fair ter middlin', sir. Complains as she gets a mite breathless at times, but we ent as young as many o' them tha's around.'

'None of us are, Mr Wickstead,' said Tench. 'So what's she been doing?'

'Doin'?'

'You said it was Emmy.'

'Oh, aye. Tha' be right. It were she as says I should go an' tell Bates.'

'What about?'

'Old Eli Craske, sir, an' him bein' found in a sack on the marsh.'

'Go on, Mr Wickstead.'

'Well, sir, it were this way like. We gets a furriner in th'shop, a-quizzin' us whether we got any sacks ter be sellin'.'

'When was this?'

'Reckon as it were mebbe las' Thursday.' Wickstead paused, closed his eyes and appeared to be deep in thought. 'Aye, Thursday,' he said at last. 'That'd be right. Noontime thereabouts.'

'This foreigner, Mr Wickstead. Was it a woman?'

'Not as ye'd be sayin', sir, no, an' tha's a fact. Not lest they be mekkin' 'em wi' bristles a-spruttin' out o' their chins.'

'A man with a beard?'

'Some might be callin' it tha', sir, aye. A tufty little thing an' a bash ter go with it, an' not a whisker where it should be. Bald as a new-laid egg up on top.'

'Tall was he, Mr Wickstead?'

'Aye, ye could safely say tha', sir, a reckon. Six foot if an inch, an' up an' down straight like a yard o' pump water.'

'How old would you think?'

'Mebbe knockin' on fifty, thereabouts like.'

'And how was he dressed? Can you remember?'

'Smartish, sir, for sure. A white shirt an' blue tie an' they loose sort o' things as some folk calls slacks. Not as left ter me I'd be wearin' 'em, mind.'

Tench stifled a smile. It cost more than a little effort. 'There's no accounting for tastes, Mr Wickstead,' he said.

'Right, sir, aye, an' that ent far wrong.'

'This man. Did he tell you why he wanted the sacks?'

'Aye, that he did.' Mr Wickstead nodded sagely, and shook like an oversized jelly on a bread board. 'Not that Emmy an' me was for askin' like . . . Said there was rubbish he needed ter be rid of.'

'So, did you sell him any?'

'Hadn't none ter sell, sir. Flour, it comes in from Wells every Wednesday mornin' reglar as clockwork, an' driver, he teks empties back ter th'mill. An' this furriner, he be wantin' big sacks, not they duzzy little buggers we gets delivered now. So I looks at Emmy an' she looks at me, an' we tell him he'd best be tryin' at one o' th'farms.'

127

'And what did he say to that?'

'Said not a word, sir. Jus' give us both a nod, an' druv off through th'village in his little red car like as if Jack Mellon's ol' bull were bruck loose an' a-poundin' towards him down Liggerbeck Hill.'

'And you haven't seen him since?'

'Not a hide nor a hair, sir, no, an' tha's a fact.'

Tench pushed back his chair. 'Well, thank you, Mr Wickstead. You were right to come and tell me. You've been very helpful.'

'Aye, mebbe so,' Wickstead took a deep breath, heaved himself up, rocked from side to side and grabbed the edge of the table to steady himself. 'It be like this, sir,' he said. 'Old Eli Craske weren' everyone's cup o' tea, not by th'length of a double-size pritch. If his brains was dynamite, they wunta blown his cap off, but as Emmy were sayin' on'y yestereen abed, when dead uns starts turnin' up all ower Medford, then it gits ter lookin' dark atop o' Will's mother's, an' ye needs ter bring out yer considerin' cap.' He paused and treated himself to an even deeper breath. 'Ye'll be agreein' wi' tha', Mr Tench, sir, no doubt?'

'Oh, entirely, Mr Wickstead. Entirely,' said Tench.

7

He watched them go, Wickstead rolling from foot to foot through the doorway with Bates in stolid attendance behind him. Then he picked up the phone, dialled a number and waited.

There was a buzzing on the line and a couple of clicks.

'*EDP*?' he said. 'Put me through to Dave Ransome. Tell him it's Chief Inspector Tench.'

He waited again, tapping the table impatiently, till he heard Ransome's voice. 'Yes, Mike? Developments?'

'Little enough at the moment.'

'No response to the picture?'

'So far, not a whisper, but I need another favour. Is there still time to get a few lines in tomorrow's edition?'

'Just about,' Ransome said, 'but we'll have to move fast. What's it about?'

'Sacks,' said Tench. 'You know the old man's body was found in one. Well, we've had reports of a man and a woman wanting to buy them. Made separate inquiries. Drove a red sports car, make unknown.'

'Can I use that?'

'Yes, use it by all means, but add an appeal. Say the police want to hear from anyone who's been trying to buy sacks in and around Medford. Say we need to eliminate them from our inquiries. And we'd like anyone who's been asked about sacks to ring either Norwich or the incident room in Medford. You've got a note of both numbers.'

'OK,' Ransome said. 'I'll do what I can, but a word to the wise. The big boys are on to the story. There'll be headlines tomorrow in a clutch of the nationals. You know the kind of thing. GRISLY DOUBLE MURDER SHAKES QUIET NORFOLK VILLAGE. Be prepared for a gathering of wolves in the morning.'

Tench sighed, and not for the first time that day. 'Well, it had to come,' he said. I'm surprised they've not cottoned on before now ... Right, leave it with me. I'll see Hastings and arrange a press conference for sometime tomorrow. Not that there'll be much to tell them, but it may at least keep them off our backs for a while. I'll let you know the time.'

'Nothing more I can use?'

'Sorry, Dave, no. Between you and me, and not for publication, we still don't know for certain who the woman was, or whether the crimes were linked. We need all the assistance we can get from the public, so make a point of that. Just say that we've had a number of leads and we're following them up.'

'Is that true or just flannel?'

'Oh, it's true right enough. We've had a good dozen, but they're all of them pointing in different directions. And no, I'm not saying what they are at this stage. But don't worry. If anything really significant turns up, you'll be the first to know.'

It was Ransome's turn to sigh. 'It's a good job I'm patient, trusting and utterly devoid of ambition,' he said. 'But you'd best be prepared. Come tomorrow morning somebody's going to be asking awkward questions.'

'Such as when are we going to call in the Met?'

'Well, are you?'

'Over my dead body.'

'Now that *would* be a scoop, Mike. LOCAL POLICE CHIEF VICTIM OF SILENT KILLER ... Let me know in advance.'

'And God bless you, too, Dave,' said Tench.

He pushed the phone aside.

It rang again immediately, and Lock picked it up. 'Yes, sir,' he said, 'he's here ... Inspector Darricot, sir.' He passed it back to Tench.

Graham Darricot was Tench's second-in-command. More experienced in the city than out in the sticks, he'd been left in charge at Norwich. 'That you, sir?' he said.

'Yes, what's the trouble?'

'There's a woman turned up here from Thetford, sir. Said she'd seen the picture of your Blacknock wench in the *EDP* this morning, and thought it was her lodger. Wanted to see the body.'

'You arranged it?'

'Yes, sir. Wasn't any point in bringing you back if it was just a false alarm, but she says yes, it's her.'

'She's certain?'

'So she says.'

'Is she still with you?'

'Yes, sir. I've taken a statement.'

'Then hang on to her. Take her to the canteen. Give her a cup of tea, but don't for God's sake let her out of your sight. I'll be with you just as soon as I possibly can.'

He rammed the receiver back on its hook.

'Something interesting, sir?' said Lock.

'Could well be,' said Tench. 'It's hard to believe, but we may have got a positive ID . . . At last.'

8

He called in Gregg, Sue Gradwell and the three detective constables. 'There's nothing more you can do here tonight,' he said, 'so get back to Norwich . . . George and Steve, you can travel with me . . . There'll be a briefing in my office 8.30 tomorrow. Everyone there.' He turned back to Lock. 'You'd better hang on here for the moment, Des. When Sergeant McKenzie turns up, tell him to wait. As soon as I know what's happening, I'll give him a ring. Once he's here, you can sign off as well. Use the other car.'

'Right, sir,' said Lock.

The traffic that evening was heavier than usual, and it was well after seven o'clock when he swung through the gates into the compound at Norwich.

Darricot, a tall, slim man with a pencil-line moustache, was waiting to meet him at the head of the stairs.

'Who is she?' Tench asked.

'A Mrs Dracopoli. Felicity Dracopoli.'

'Peculiar name for Norfolk.'

'She's a peculiar woman,' Darricot said.

'In what way?'

130

'You'll find out. But a word to the wise. Don't expect too much. I wouldn't say she was the answer to all your prayers.'

'Where is she?'

'Still in the canteen with a WPC.'

'Best bring her up to my office,' said Tench. 'I'll speak to her there.'

Darricot showed her in.

She was dressed in the height of fashion: a knife-pleated silver lamé sheath with a velvet collar and belt, a small black close-fitting hat and an equally small but strapless handbag. At a guess, Tench thought, she was in her late forties, but her figure was still that of a twenty-year-old.

'Mrs Dracopoli,' he said, and held out his hand.

She ignored it. 'You're Detective Chief Inspector Tench?'

'That's right.'

'Then you're the one who's responsible, are you?'

'Responsible, ma'am?'

'For keeping me waiting in this hell-hole for an hour.'

Tench raised his eyebrows. 'Please sit down, Mrs Dracopoli.'

'I prefer to stand,' she said curtly. 'I've no intention of staying here longer than I have to. So if you've any questions to ask, make them as short as you possibly can.'

'I must apologize for taking so long to get here. I had to drive a long way.'

'In your job,' she said, 'you should learn to delegate authority. I've already told the facts to your colleague here, and I fail to see why I should have to repeat them to you.'

'I happen to be in charge of the investigation, ma'am. I regret that you've had to wait.'

'Then the best thing you can do is to waste no more time. You're not the only one, Chief Inspector, who's had a long journey. I've come all the way from Thetford and I have to drive back. So say what you have to say. Otherwise you'll be driving to Thetford to see me.'

Tench glanced across her shoulder at Darricot. The inspector gave a shrug.

'Inspector Darricot took you to the mortuary, ma'am.'

'He did.'

'And you identified a body.'

'I did, and it wasn't exactly a pleasant experience.'

'I appreciate that, Mrs Dracopoli,' said Tench. 'The woman you identified. Who was she?'

'My lodger.'

'And what was her name?'

'The name she gave me was Westmorland. Mrs Jean Westmorland.'
'And you're sure it was her?'
'Positive,' she said. 'I'd know the woman anywhere, dead or alive.'

9

'Tell me about her.'
'I know very little. I made that clear to your colleague.'
'You run a lodging house?'
'No.'
Tench frowned. 'You said this Mrs Westmorland was a lodger of yours.'
'So she was. In the sense that she lodged in my cottage.'
'She shared a cottage with you?'
Mrs Dracopoli took a deep and exasperated breath. 'No, she did not. Are you being purposely obtuse, Chief Inspector?'
'I'm trying not to be, ma'am, but you'll have to explain.'
'Then I'll put it very simply. I'm a widow, Chief Inspector. I own a large house on the outskirts of Thetford. It has a cottage in the grounds that I let from time to time.'
'Then this woman was your tenant.'
'No, she was my lodger. There was no contractual agreement between us. She had no rent book. She merely paid me to lodge in the cottage for a month. The payment was in cash and she made it in advance.'
'She came to you and asked to rent the cottage for a month?'
'Yes, she did. The vacancy was advertised in the local press. She told me she'd seen it.'
'When was this?'
'A week last Saturday. I showed her the cottage, she paid a month's rent and I gave her the key.'
'Did she say where she'd come from, this woman?'
'No, and I didn't ask her. There was no cause for me to do so.'
'Then you don't know her home address.'
'No, I don't.'
'She didn't give you her ration book?'
'Why should she do that? I don't supply food. She merely rented the cottage and arranged to feed herself.'
Tench thought for a moment.
'You knew she was missing?'
Mrs Dracopoli took another deep breath. 'No, I didn't, Chief Inspector.'
'But she must have left your cottage in the middle of last week.'
'I was well aware of that, but I didn't know she was missing. I visited

her twice in the first few days to see that she was settled, and then on the Tuesday she came to the house and told me she intended to go to the coast to visit a friend. She said she'd probably be away about a week, but it might be longer. She'd let me know when she was back . . . She was a free agent, she'd paid the rent, so I thought no more about it. It wasn't till this morning, when I saw her picture in the paper, that I connected her with the woman found dead on the sands.'

'And you know nothing more about her?'

'No, nothing at all.'

'You haven't been in the cottage?'

'Not since a week last Monday, Chief Inspector . . . Now is there anything else you have to ask, or can I go?'

Tench leaned back in his chair. 'There is just one question, ma'am. You couldn't have seen this woman more than three or four times, yet you said you were positive that she was the woman you were shown in the mortuary. How could you be so sure?'

'Quite simply, Chief Inspector. I recognized her face.'

'Looks can be deceptive, Mrs Dracopoli.'

She frowned and shook her head 'You mean everyone has a double? Not in this case, Chief Inspector. The woman I saw was undoubtedly Mrs Westmorland . . . I was a beautician for twenty years. I'm used to studying faces, and she had one very distinctive blemish: a mole on her forehead right on the hairline. It was quite unmistakable. Hadn't you noticed?'

'To be honest, ma'am, no, but I've still to see the autopsy report.'

Mrs Dracopoli, at that, seemed to thaw just a fraction. 'Then I have at least made some little contribution. I suppose you might say it was worth the journey. And the very considerable inconvenience . . . Am I now free to leave?'

'You've always been free to leave, ma'am,' said Tench, 'but thank you for waiting. We may, of course, need to speak to you again, and we'll have to search the cottage, so please keep it locked. There'll be two of my men down first thing tomorrow to ask for the key. You can stay with them while they search if that's what you wish.'

He held out his hand. She seemed surprised, but she took it.

'Oh, I'm sure they can be trusted with the silver,' she said. 'But don't set a time. If you do, then they're bound to arrive an hour late, and in the meantime I might have contrived to lose the key. And you wouldn't want that to happen, Chief Inspector, now would you?'

She flashed him an unexpected smile.

'No, ma'am,' said Tench.

10

'That,' said Darricot, 'is one very strange lady. I'll bet she's tied up a few men in her time . . . D'you believe what she says?'

'Why not? I've no reason to think that she's lying. The trouble is she hasn't added much at all to the little we know. She's just made things more confused.'

'You've got a firm ID.'

'Yes, but we've had two equally firm ones already. In the first she was a woman called Veronica Mallalieu, in the second she was a Miriam and now she's Jean Westmorland.'

Darricot pursed his lips. 'So what does it all add up to? What have you got so far?'

There was a helpless shrug from Tench. 'What we've got,' he said, 'is one dead woman who's turned up with a fresh identity in half a dozen places all over the country, and one dead man who was apparently so drunk that he couldn't have seen who it was broke his neck.'

'And couldn't tell you if he did . . . What about suspects?'

'At the moment practically everyone in Medford, not to mention one or two that live out on the fringe and strangers that keep popping up out of nowhere.'

Darricot stroked his chin. 'Then I'd say you're in a bit of a pickle, to put it mildly.'

'Put it any way you like, it's one hell of a mess. We've got a quiet little village out in the sticks where nothing ever happens year after year, and all of a sudden it's plunged into mayhem. Why? That's the question.'

'Well, there must be an answer somewhere.'

'There is,' said Tench, 'and I can't help feeling it's staring us in the face. It's under some stone that we've passed umpteen times and never turned over. But where and which one?'

Darricot shrugged. 'D'you want to know what I think?'

'Is it going to help?'

'It might . . . D'you want to know what your trouble is?'

Another shrug from Tench. 'Go on. What is it?'

'You've got a crossword complex.'

'And what the devil's that?'

'It's a form of tunnel vision. It works like this. You're stuck on a clue and you rack your brains for hours trying to find an answer. But it's just a waste of time. Your thoughts are lodged in a particular groove that's never going to lead you to the light at the end . . . So what d'you do? You fling it aside, forget all about it and flop into bed. You sleep like a top, and when you wake up next morning the answer's as clear as the sun that streams in through the bedroom window.'

'You mean the best thing to do is take a night off and sleep on the problem.'

'Why not? At this stage it can't do any harm, and it might provide the answer.'

Tench summoned up a grin. 'You know what?' he said. 'I might just do that. There's not much . . .'

The phone rang, shattering his words. Darricot lifted the receiver, listened and then passed it across the desk. 'It's Lock,' he said. 'From Medford.'

Tench gave a sigh. 'Yes, Des, it's me. What's the panic now?'

'I think, sir, you'd better get back here,' said Lock. 'We've found another body.'

11

As ill luck would have it, two lorries were locked together on the road south of Glandford, and he was forced to turn round and make a detour through Sibthorpe. By that time the sun had already disappeared and the bright Norfolk light was fading into dusk; but speeding down the slope beyond Sparrow Hill House, it was clear that he'd stumbled on yet more mayhem.

Outside an isolated cottage on the hill he saw the scene-of-crime vans. Ledward's car was there with McKenzie's ageing Norton propped on its stand, and the cottage itself was ablaze with lights. A couple of police photographers were standing by the door, nursing their cameras, Lester's men were unloading their equipment from the vans, and out in the road McKenzie was in deep conversation with Bates.

As Tench drew to a halt he bent down beside the car. 'Looks like we've got another one, Mike,' he said.

Tench stepped out and slammed the car door. 'Who is it this time?'

'Chap called Joe Grice. Mid-sixties, thereabouts. Spent most of his life fishing for whelks out of Wells. According to Bates he was a quiet sort of bloke. The inoffensive type.'

'Who found him?'

'Bates did. He'll give you all the details.'

'Is Ledward inside?'

'Been here half an hour. Must have nearly finished the job by now. You'd better come in and take a look for yourself.'

The cottage had no hall. The front door opened straight into the parlour. It was a small room, barely furnished, but there were two other doors. One was closed, but clearly led to the back of the house; while the second, wide open, revealed a twisting flight of stairs, and lying at the bottom the body of a man. He was clothed in a frayed pair of cotton pyjamas and an old woollen dressing-gown, and lay face down with his feet stretched out towards the stairwell, his head at a peculiarly twisted angle and his arms at his sides.

Ledward was kneeling beside him, packing his bag. He looked up as the two detectives came in, and it was clear from his expression that he wasn't in one of his mellower moods.

'Ah, Chief Inspector,' he said, 'you've arrived at last. And about time, too. I didn't intend to wait.'

Tench was hardly in the right frame of mind to be diplomatic. 'I was in Norwich,' he said curtly.

'So was I . . . Resting.' The doctor looked at his watch. 'But I've already been here for three-quarters of an hour.'

'There was a pile-up on the road. I had to take another route.'

Ledward raised his eyebrows. Then he fastened the clasp on his bag and stood up. 'And now,' he said, 'I suppose you want answers.'

'Just tell me what you can.'

'Cause of death, broken neck. Much the same as the case you were kind enough to bring to my attention yesterday. At a guess, someone grabbed him by the head and wrenched it back sharply. Done with sufficient force, the cervical vertebrae would snap like a twig.' He looked down his nose. 'But don't quote me on that.'

'He couldn't have fallen down the stairs?'

'No, he couldn't, Chief Inspector. Take a good look at the position of the body. If he'd fallen, he'd have put out his arms to break the fall, but it's clear that he didn't. He was dead to all intents and purposes when he fell.'

'Could he have had a heart attack or a stroke?'

'All I can say is that none of the visible signs are present.'

'So when did he die?'

'At the moment I can only make the roughest of estimates. Some sixteen hours ago. Possibly eighteen.'

'The early hours of this morning.'

'It would seem so,' said Ledward.

'Nothing more you can tell me?'

'Only that this spate of unexplained deaths is a gross inconvenience.' The doctor was equally curt in his turn. 'You know the form well enough. You'll have to wait for my report . . . Death was certified at 8.02 p.m. . . . You can ring me tomorrow lunchtime. If I've anything else to say, it won't be before then. Just get him back to my place as fast as you can.' He picked up his bag. 'It's time you got your act together, Chief Inspector. This village is becoming a charnel-house . . . Pray allow me to wish you a very good evening.'

Tench waited till he'd gone. 'And a very merry Christmas to you as well,' he said.

12

McKenzie jerked his head towards the door. 'Doesn't improve, does he? Has to be his usual curmudgeonly self.'

Tench shrugged his shoulders. 'We can hardly expect a lot of sweetness and light. It's the third time we've called him out here in three days. Let's hope we don't have to make it a fourth.'

'From what I've seen of this idyllic little corner of the Norfolk sticks,' McKenzie said gloomily, 'that's more than possible.'

'God forbid,' said Tench. 'We can't afford a fourth . . . Come on, Mac. Let's get out of here and make room for the workers.'

As the photographers moved back with their cameras and tripods, he walked across the road to Constable Bates. 'Now, Constable,' he said. 'Tell me what happened.'

Bates removed his helmet and scratched his head. 'Well, sir, it were this way like. Ye'll remember as we were mentionin' guides on the marsh?'

'That's right.' Tench nodded. 'You said you wouldn't fancy crossing it without one. If a man tried to do it, he'd need to know the way.'

'Aye, sir, so he would, an' I be gettin' to ponderin' who there might be in these parts as knows the way across. Apart, ye might say, from the women as gathers the cockles out there. An' I reckons there could be three.'

'Who are they?'

'Well, sir, the first be Danny Sprot as lives up at Astley Farm.'

'The one they call Daft Danny?'

'Aye, sir, the same. Daft Danny Sprot. Keps with his mother up at the farm, but accordin' to my reckonin' she ent much fer watchin' arter the lad. Wanders around a deal all on his own does Danny, an' many's the time he's bin a-followin' the cockle women out to Blacknock. But I looks at it this way, sir. No one's a-goin' to ask Danny how to get there. He'd not be understandin' 'em, an' even if he did he couldn' be a-tellin'.'

'So you'd rule him out, would you?'

'Aye, sir. He's simple like, but he's harmless.'

'Then who are the others?'

'Well, there's Jem Stuart, sir, as lives by the sluice on the Morston road, an' then there's Joe Grice. Him as is lyin' there stretched out inside.'

'He was one of the guides?'

'Off an' on, sir, aye, since the day he sells his boat an' quits fishin' fer whelks. An' Jem Stuart's bin tellin' me as Joe's bin a-talkin' around to folk, an' sayin' as how this furriner's bin askin' him questions, like what was the best way to get to Blacknock. So I says to miself, Jack, tha'd best be seein' Joe. An' come this evenin' I teks a stroll up here an' finds him dead as a doornail, an' I reckon that's like to be viewed as mighty strange, sir. Wouldn' you be sayin' so?'

Tench frowned. 'You mean he may have known too much and was babbling about it? Yes, Constable, I would. Sounds suspicious to say the least . . . This foreigner. I take it Joe had never seen him before?'

'Seems not, sir, no.'

'When did he speak to him?'

'Accordin' as Jem Stuart tells it, sir, it were Sunday arternoon. This chap, he comes a-knockin' at Joe Grice's door.'

'And did Grice tell him how to get to Blacknock?'

'He did, sir, aye, as Jem was a-hearin'. Offers Joe a tidy sum from all accounts jus' to show him the way. An' he weren' one to be turnin' down a fiver, weren' Joe, so he teks him out that very same evenin' 'cross the marsh to the edge o' the sand.'

'This was Sunday?'

'It were, sir, so gossip say.'

'Would the tide and the light give him time to do that?'

'Sunday, sir? Aye. There'd be more'n enough o' both. Tide'd be clear o' the marsh by six o'clock, an' sun weren' a-settin' till near half-past eight.'

'Did Grice tell anyone what this man looked like?'

'Seems like he weren' sayin', sir. An' I were all fer askin' him that very same question till I gets here an' sees him a-spread on the floor.'

Tench glanced towards the cottage that Lester's men were already taping off. 'Well, we can't ask him now, so you'd better get a statement from Stuart right away. Let me have it in the morning, and yours as well . . . You can leave this place to us. There's enough of us here. And thank you, Constable. You did what was right.'

'Too late, sir, I'm afraid.'

'Oh, I don't know,' said Tench. 'He's been lying here for something like eighteen hours. If it hadn't been for you, we mightn't have found him for another two days.'

'Aye, sir, that be true.' Bates stared at the cottage and shook his head sadly. 'There be times,' he said, 'when Medford's a desperate strange kind o' place. One day there'll be curtains a-twitch all the way up Main Street an' word it gets around like the speed o' the wind, an' the next, so it seems, everyone be struck of a sudden as blind, deaf an' dumb as they three wise monkeys ye'll be hearin' about.'

13

As the constable strode away stiffly down the hill, Tench crossed back to where Lester was chatting to McKenzie.

'Find anything on the marsh path, Sergeant?' he asked.

'Nothing of any significance, sir,' Lester said. 'The usual rubbish. Empty cigarette packets, sweet wrappers, all that junk. I've passed a sackful to the lab.'

'What about the mill cottage?'

'No distinctive tyre marks, sir. The weather's been too dry. And whoever it was that cleaned out the place, they did a pretty thorough job. There weren't many good prints, and most of those we found were Mr Lubbock's or the woman's. Copies of the rest have gone to the lab.'

'Not much to show then for all those hours of work.'

'Not a deal, sir, no, but that's the way it goes.' Lester nodded towards Grice's cottage. 'We may find something here.'

'Let's hope so,' said Tench. He turned to McKenzie. 'What did Harris have to say about this lad Daft Danny?'

McKenzie gave a shrug. 'Seems to know him well enough. Swears Lady Wellbridge has got it all wrong. Says he's childlike, yes, but he's never been violent. Not the sort of lad to go wrecking folk's houses. Reckons he's just too trusting. Thinks everyone's just as gentle as he is and full of good intentions. He'd never understand this obsession of hers.'

'Did Harris call it an obsession?'

'Said Wellbridge told him she'd got some kind of fixation about the lad. Stared at her, she said. Undressed her with his eyes. Well, and so what? I've done that myself. I bet Wellbridge has done it. It's hardly a crime.'

'He's a big lad?'

'Big and broad, so Harris was saying.'

'You didn't see him yourself?'

'No. We went up to the farm, but he wasn't there and Harris said it was no use trying to find him. He could have been anywhere on the coast between Burnham and Cromer.'

'Well, if he's big and broad he could frighten a woman, and according to Bates he knows his way across the marsh, so we'd better keep an eye on him just in case . . . What about having a word with his mother?'

'Not much point from what Harris says, and if anyone has to keep an eye on him, he's the one to do it. He seems to know more about the lad than anyone else, and he can at least communicate with him. If you ever want to talk to him you'll need Harris there.'

'Right.' Tench nodded. 'I'll get on to him tomorrow. It looks like being another long day.' He jerked a thumb across his shoulder. 'Is Lock still down at the incident room?'

'Was when I left.'

'Then leave him to me. You get off back to Norwich. Get a night's sleep. We're all going to need one.'

Lester had disappeared back inside the cottage, so he ducked under the tapes and followed him in.

The sergeant was labelling plastic bags. He looked up as Tench came in. 'I wouldn't hang around, sir,' he said. 'We're going to be here for hours, and there's nothing you can do. We'll have to leave the back garden till tomorrow when it's light.'

'Just do what you can, Sergeant,' said Tench. 'Leave the rest till the morning. There'll be a couple of men down from Norwich to relieve you ... Found anything of interest?'

'Only this, sir,' Lester said, 'and I wouldn't know whether it's important or not.'

He threw open the door that up to then had been closed. 'Take a look, sir,' he said.

Picking his way round photographers and fingerprint men, Tench walked across the room and stood in the doorway. Beyond was a scullery with a floor tiled in stone, and lying on the floor was a white paper bag. Its contents had spilled out and scattered across the stones.

'D'you know anyone here who collects shells, sir?' Lester said.

Tench stared at them: cockleshells and whelks, mussels and razors, scallops and sea urchins. 'I haven't a notion, Sergeant,' he said.

VI
ASKING AND GIVING

El dar es honor, y el pedir dolor
Giving is an honour, asking is a pain

Spanish proverb

It was McKenzie who told him. 'Danny Sprot collects shells,' he said.

That was on Friday morning, and Friday was the day when everything changed; when what had started out as the simple case of a woman washed up drowned on a Norfolk beach, assumed of a sudden a totally different aspect and threatened to become part of an international conspiracy.

It was the day when representatives of the national press descended on Medford; and Tench, in Norwich, faced a barrage from avid reporters clamouring to know all the details of the case, demanding to be told what progress, if any, the police had so far made, and asking the pointed questions: how many more murders were there going to be in Medford before he discovered who the first of the victims was, and what steps was he taking to uncover a motive?

It was the day when the county's Chief Constable made an early morning phone call to Detective Chief Superintendent Hastings and expressed his concern in no uncertain terms, and when Hastings, arriving at HQ well in advance of his normal time, immediately called in Tench and relayed that concern, though in somewhat more temperate tones.

'He's worried about press reaction,' he said.

'Aren't we all, sir?' said Tench.

'You've seen the morning papers?'

'Most of them, yes.'

'They don't exactly shower us with compliments, do they?'

'They don't give us a great deal of credit, sir, no, but none of us are happy about the way things are going. We've just got to take the flak, and hope we get a break.'

Hastings leaned back in his chair. 'The trouble is, Mike, we can do that for just so long and no longer. The powers that be are distinctly shorter on patience. They fret when nothing seems to be happening. Three murders in three days is too much for them to take. You know what the next step's going to be, don't you?'

'Oh, I think so, sir, yes. They'll give us instructions to call in the Met.'

'They will, and that's the last thing I want, and you too I'd imagine. We don't need a lot of bright young things from the smoke swarming all over us, so we'd better get cracking . . . What's the state of play?'

Tench gave him a run-down. 'If I had to make a guess, sir, I'd say that all three cases were linked.'

'The same killer each time?'

'It looks like it, sir. He murders the woman, puts her body in a sack, carries it across the marsh and dumps it at Blacknock, and then on the way back he comes across Eli Craske. The man's roaring drunk and making enough noise to rouse the whole of the village, so he strangles him, stuffs his body in the sack and throws it out on the marsh. And we know that the last victim, a chap called Joe Grice, knew enough about the marsh to act as a guide. He'd been spreading the tale around that a stranger had approached him and offered him money to be shown the way across . . .'

'And you think he was killed because he knew too much and was talking about it.'

'It looks that way, sir, yes.'

'But it's all just speculation, Mike, isn't it? You've no hard evidence.'

'None, sir, I'm afraid. We're hoping that the lab can give us a lead, but we're still waiting for them to come up with results.'

'Well, we can't afford to wait for very much longer. We need to know who this woman was and what she was doing here on the coast. She obviously didn't come here just to buy a house. If that was all she had in mind, she wouldn't have taken such pains to lay a confusing trail.'

'No, she wouldn't,' said Tench, 'but there's another point, too. We're not the ones she was hoping to confuse. As far as she was concerned, there was no reason for us to become involved at all. She was laying the trail to confuse someone else, but the question is, who?'

'And we can't hope to find the answer to that till we know who she was.' Hastings pushed back his chair, walked across to the window, stood there for a moment looking out across the city, and then turned to face Tench. 'This woman's the unknown factor, Mike,' he said. 'She's the key to the case. We have to track her down, probe every scrap of evidence she's left on the trail. So what d'you plan to do?'

2

It was a day that began for Mike Tench at half-past six in the morning, when he sat down at his desk and reached for the reports that, in his absence at Medford the day before, he hadn't yet seen.

He read them through, one by one, but they yielded no joy.

There were two autopsy reports from Ledward. The first, on the woman, added little or nothing to what he already knew. The doctor had been characteristically cautious. Beyond saying that she hadn't drowned, but had died of anoxia, he'd ventured no opinion on the manner of her death; and while detailing the stomach contents, he'd refused to speculate on when her last meal had been consumed. Though she wasn't a virgin, there were no signs, he said, of sexual interference or recent sexual activity, but he did confirm the presence of a mole on the right anterior hairline. There was also a second on the lower left abdomen and, in addition, an appendectomy scar.

The second report, that on Eli Craske, offered little else but the fact that he'd died from a fracture of the cervical vertebrae and had, in the hours preceding his death, consumed the equivalent of eight pints of beer.

There was also a note from Detective Constable Lock. The police at Truro had checked the electoral roll and reported that there was no Veronica Mallalieu. Nor did she appear on those for the Pendle area of Lancashire.

He tossed all three aside. Underneath them was the report from the three detective constables, Ellison, Rayner and Spurgeon. It repeated Peter Britiffe's account of his meeting with the woman on Sibthorpe hill, and went on to detail the result of their inquiries about Eli Craske. He'd apparently arrived at the Old Dun Cow at just after six o'clock on the Monday evening, and remained there as usual till 10.45 when the landlord had turned him out. No one in the village remembered seeing him after that, though many had heard him singing in his usual drunken fashion at various points along the Main Street between the pub and the church. The last to hear him had been an elderly widow, Amelia Curl, who lived on Deep Lane. She'd heard him stumble past her house and down towards the marsh, bemoaning the fact in a raucous voice that he was a lonely little petunia in an onion patch. She'd been in bed half an hour, so she hadn't got up. She'd just switched on the lamp and looked at the clock. It had shown twenty past eleven.

He tossed that aside, too. He still wasn't any wiser about who the woman was, where she'd come from, or what she was searching for up on the coast.

He opened a drawer, pulled out a notepad and pencil, and sat there staring at the blank sheet of paper.

Just what did he know about this enigmatic woman?

He picked up the pencil and began to make notes.

Mr Wellbridge had identified her as someone called Miriam who'd sailed from Bombay on October 25th. Mrs Dracopoli had identified her as a Mrs Jean Westmorland who, on Saturday, 28th April, had rented a cottage from her in Thetford. On Tuesday, 1st May, she'd told Mrs Dracopoli that she was going to the coast to visit a friend and might be away for something like a week. His old Chief, John Lubbock had also identified her, but this time as a woman called Veronica Mallalieu who, the following day, had rented the Phoenix Mill cottage at Blakeney. She'd travelled by taxi from Holt and had paid him a fortnight's rent in advance. The only luggage she'd brought with her had been a suitcase, and she'd told the taxi driver that she was a widow without children who was looking to buy a house, an old one with character, because she'd spent her holidays on the coast as a schoolgirl and had always retained happy memories of the place.

On Thursday 3rd Tommy Grimes had seen her at about 10 a.m. when he'd delivered the bread from Wicksteads', and at half-past ten the postman had noticed what appeared to be a railway parcels van turning up to the cottage. Sometime later that day Lubbock had paid her a visit, and the next morning Peter Britiffe had seen her sitting on a fallen tree by the side of Sibthorpe Hill. There was a bicycle lying on the verge beside her, and later that morning Yelda Thober had spotted her riding into Medford. From there she'd apparently ridden to the Post Office where she'd talked to Maisie Tackleston and bought a local map.

And that had been the last firm sighting of her till approximately half-past nine on the morning of Tuesday 8th, when Sarah Clogston had found her lying dead on Blacknock.

He flicked back through the notes. The vital clues, the ones he needed, lay further back in time. What was her real name and where had she come from that Saturday, all but a fortnight ago, when she'd presented herself at Mrs Dracopoli's door in Thetford?

And what had she been looking for in Blakeney . . . or in Medford? A house, so she'd said, but if her purpose had merely been to buy an old house, then why all the subterfuge? Was the tale of the house just a subterfuge, too?

Where was he to start searching?

The obvious place to begin was right at the beginning, but in this particular case that meant Bombay, and with a killer on the loose, who'd already committed three murders, time was of the essence and Bombay was six thousand miles away.

No, it had to be Thetford. If she'd left any clues at all, they were likely to be found in Mrs Dracopoli's cottage.

He drew the notepad towards him and began to work out a plan of campaign for the day.

It was half an hour later that Hastings had rung him from the Chief Super's office. 'I think, Mike,' he'd said in diplomatic tones, 'that you and I had better have a little get-together.'

3

At half-past eight, in the interview room, Tench faced his team, augmented now by the presence of ten constables drafted in from widely scattered parts of Norfolk and two detective sergeants, Keith Varden from Wymondham and Clive Hellyer from Lynn.

Varden was in his thirties, dark-haired, broad of build and seemingly phlegmatic, while Hellyer, some ten years his junior, was tall, fair, lithe and persistently cheerful. Varden, it seemed to Tench, was by far the more thoughtful and likely to prove the more able of the two.

He nodded towards them and then looked around.

'You'll have all heard by now,' he said, 'that there was a third murder in Medford in the early hours of yesterday morning: the victim, one of the marsh guides whose name was Joseph Grice. Now we know that this man was approached, sometime last Sunday afternoon, by a stranger who offered him five pounds to show him the way across the marsh, and that Grice took him out that same evening to the edge of the sand. Apparently he made no secret of what he'd done, and it therefore seems likely that this stranger, probably the man who'd already committed the other two murders, decided to put an end to his gossiping before the story spread any further round Medford.

'Assuming this to be the truth, and we've no reason to assume otherwise unless we turn up conflicting evidence, we can only conclude that this killing and that of the man, Eli Craske, are both of them logical results of the first, the death of the unknown woman found on Blacknock.

'We can't, of course, afford to neglect this last murder. We must follow it up, but until we know who the woman was and what she was doing in the Medford area, we've no hope of uncovering a motive for her murder and that reduces our chance of tracing the killer. Added to which, we're at something of a crisis point. Unless we can produce some tangible results and produce them quickly, we're likely to find ourselves saddled with a team of investigators from the Met, and that's the last thing that any of us wants to happen.

'We have to follow two lines of inquiry, and that, unfortunately, means splitting our forces, but with an expanded team, with the help of Detective Sergeants Varden and Hellyer and our colleagues who've joined us from other parts of the county, we can at least hope to make some progress. So this is what we do.'

He laid out the plans in detail. Gregg was to go to Thetford, collect the keys to the cottage from Mrs Dracopoli and make a thorough search of the

147

premises. Ellison was to trace the railway delivery van, discover what it had delivered to the cottage at Phoenix Mill, where the contents had been despatched from and who was the sender. Spurgeon's inquiries were to take him to Swaffham. He was to seek out all shops that sold medallions of the kind found in Swallownest Wood and ask if they'd been visited by the woman in question, while Rayner was to visit all farms in the Medford area in an effort to track down the man and woman in the red sports car who'd been inquiring about sacks.

Sue Gradwell's job was to interview Jem Stuart, the other marsh guide, see if he could add anything to what he'd already told Bates, and take a statement from him. After that she was to pay Mr Burcham another visit, and question him again about the light on the marsh. 'Try and get him to be more accurate, Sue,' he said. 'He seems to be positive enough about the time, but not the place. I want to know whether that light was on the marsh or out on the sands. See if he can give a more positive location. Get him to point out a line from his window.'

Lock was still to man the incident room in Medford, and McKenzie was to stay in Norwich. 'I need you here for emergencies, Mac,' he said.

He then turned to Varden and Hellyer. 'Your job,' he told them, 'is even more important. There'll be transport laid on to get you out to Medford, and I've arranged for Constable Bates to be there to meet you. Use his expertise. He knows every stick and stone of the place. Split the village between you and do a thorough house-to-house. I want everyone questioned and statements taken. We need to know exactly where they were and what they were doing between midday on Sunday and nine o'clock Tuesday morning, and between six on Wednesday evening and six yesterday morning. We're particularly interested in Deep Lane leading down to the marsh, and Sibthorpe Hill, the scene of the last murder.' He paused. 'And one other thing, a paper bag containing sea shells was found last night on the floor of Grice's cottage, so ask around the village. We want to hear about anyone who goes round collecting them.'

That was when McKenzie raised a hand.

'Danny Sprot collects shells,' he said. Tench stared at him and frowned. 'Daft Danny?'

'Yes. He spends half his time searching for them down on the shore. He's got quite a collection up at the farm.'

Once Tench got a sniff of a worthwhile clue, he wasn't inclined to stand still. 'Then find him. Bring him in.'

'You'll need Harris as well.'

'Then find him too.' The response was immediate, not to say curt. 'I want them both here in double quick time. And tell Steve Harris that I don't give a damn what he thinks about Sprot. Unless he can prove he was nowhere near Grice's cottage on Wednesday night, he's got a hell of a lot of awkward questions to answer.'

4

It was a day when the members of Tench's team, pursuing their widely separated searches, met with varying degrees of success.

McKenzie had no difficulty in tracking down Harris. Blakeney's resident constable, taking advantage of what he thought might prove to be a trouble-free morning, was still loitering over a leisurely breakfast.

'What's the trouble, Sarge?' he asked.

'The trouble,' McKenzie said, 'is your pal Danny Sprot.'

Harris selected a burnt slice of toast and spread it with marmalade. 'What's he supposed to have done now?'

'The Chief thinks he murdered a chap called Joe Grice.'

Harris was unmoved. He bit a slice off the toast. 'And what is it that's given him that crazy idea?'

McKenzie explained.

Harris chewed his toast and listened. 'A paper bag?'

'That's what he said. A paper bag. A white one. Stuffed full of shells.'

'What kind of shells, Sarge?'

McKenzie had overslept and had missed his own breakfast. 'Well,' he said testily, 'they're not likely to be bloody mortar shells, are they? Sea shore shells. What other sort are there?'

'Yes, but what type? Cockles, whelks, scallops?'

'How the hell would I know? I haven't even seen them.'

Harris drained his coffee cup. 'Doesn't sound like Danny.'

'That's beside the point. The Chief wants to see him, and you along with him.'

'He's going to put him through the wringer?'

'That's the general idea.'

'Does he know what he's taking on?'

'He's got a vague notion. That's why he needs you.'

'He's going to need Danny's mother there too. The lad's only sixteen.'

'Then we'll just have to take her along as well, won't we?'

'That may not be easy. You haven't met Mrs Sprot.'

'Bit of a termagant, is she?'

'That's putting it mildly. She'll have your balls for breakfast.'

'If she does,' McKenzie said, 'it'll be a damn sight more that I've had

149

this morning ... Come on. Let's get cracking and get them both back to Norwich. The sooner the better.'

Ellison, whose job was to trace the railway van and ascertain what it had delivered to Mill Cottage, had what he thought was a complicated task.

He didn't know which station had delivered the package or where it had been sent from. Nor did he know the name of the person who'd done the sending. Unravelling the truth was likely, so he felt, to prove a little difficult.

Nevertheless, possessed of a keen intelligence and being something of a scholar in his off-duty hours, he reasoned that the package could well have been despatched from Thetford before the woman left for Blakeney. If that was the case, the delivery station was likely to be Holt.

He rang the parcels department. There was no reply. Nor was there when he tried again, five minutes, ten and twenty minutes later.

Well aware that he was wasting valuable time and cursing British Railways underneath his breath, he commandeered a police car and drove down to Holt. It took him another three-quarters of an hour, but he consoled himself with the thought that inquiries made on the spot might prove to be swifter and more productive than attempts to explain himself over the phone.

The parcels clerk at Holt was a middle-aged man with a heavy moustache and an air of long-acquired boredom. He raised a weary head from behind the glass partition and acknowledged his visitor's rap on the window with a solitary word and a visible lack of interest. 'Yes?' he said.

Ellison held his card up in front of the glass. 'Detective Constable Ellison, Norwich CID.'

The clerk was unimpressed. 'Yes?' he said. 'What?'

'I'm inquiring about a package delivered a week yesterday to Phoenix Mill Cottage at Blakeney.'

'Blakeney?'

'That's right.'

'Name?'

'Whose name?'

'Name of addressee.'

'That's debatable,' said Ellison. 'Could be Mallalieu. Veronica Mallalieu.'

'Spelt?'

Ellison spelt it out. The clerk produced a heavy, leather-bound register and ran his finger down a column. 'No Mallalieu,' he said.

'Well, you must have a record of the consignment somewhere. It was probably booked in sometime on the Wednesday.'

The clerk turned back a page and did another finger-exercise. 'No,' he said. 'No Mallalieu.'

150

Ellison raised his eyebrows. 'Try the address,' he prompted.

The clerk moved his finger three inches to the right and worked it slowly down the page. 'Ah, yes,' he said at last. 'Phoenix Mill Cottage, Blakeney. One bicycle. Booked in at Norwich. Wednesday, 4.15.'

'D'you know who booked it in?'

'Consigner was . . .' A pause. The finger moved again slowly. 'Consigner was Wensum Cycles, St Giles Street, Norwich.'

'And who was it addressed to?'

The clerk took a deep breath as if the effort to speak required it. 'The addressee was a Miss Eleanor Welsby . . . Anything else?'

Ellison made a note. 'No,' he said, 'nothing more. Please tender my thanks to the British Railways board. I think you're all doing a magnificent job.'

5

As far as Sue Gradwell was concerned, interviewing Jem Stuart was a waste of time. He'd already been questioned by Bates, and he wasn't likely to say anything more that was useful. All she'd have to do would be to draft out a statement and get him to sign it. And as for Mr Burcham, he couldn't be expected to point out precisely the position of a light that he'd only glimpsed for a moment across a featureless expanse of marsh. It was just the kind of boring job she'd been expected to do, day in and day out, since she joined the CID.

Rayner, who was doing a round of the farms, dropped her off at the sluice on the Morston road, and from there she walked up the path by the river to Jem Stuart's cottage.

Stuart, a bluff, stocky man in his middle sixties, was hoeing his vegetable patch at the back and didn't seem inclined to abandon the job. What did she want to know? He couldn't tell her anything more than he'd already told Bates. All Grice had said was that some furriner had been quizzing him about routes across the marsh, and had offered him a fiver to show him the way. No, he hadn't said anything else about the man. Just that Sunday afternoon was the first time he'd seen him, and he hadn't set eyes on him since. Seems he'd paid Joe off at the bottom of Deep Lane and told him to forget that he'd ever so much as met him . . . Now if that was all, he'd like to get on with his hoeing.

'We need you to sign a statement, sir.'

'Do ye now?' he said. 'Well, missy, there's a table in the kitchen. You go in and write one, and when ye've got it all writ, bring it out an' I'll mebbe think about signin' it. Right?'

She hesitated a moment. He continued to hoe.

What was the point?

'Right, sir,' she said.

It was all of an hour later when she raised the brass knocker on the door of The Meals, rapped sharply twice, took a couple of steps back and looked up at the attic window.

She'd been right, of course. It was going to be a complete and utter waste of a morning. She took two steps forward and rapped on the door again. To her surprise, it opened to reveal Mr Burcham. He was wearing a frock coat and top hat, a grey waistcoat and tie, and carried under his arm a large leather-bound book, across the front of which, in gold letters, were emblazoned the words BRADSHAW'S MONTHLY GUIDE.

He beamed at her. 'How delightful to see you, dear lady,' he said, his deep voice rolling past her and down to the heart of Medford. 'Do please step inside. You arrive at the most appropriate of times. I was about to take a rest in the refreshment room and regale myself on two of the Company's incomparable muffins. Perhaps you'd care to join me.' He raised his one free hand. 'I beg you, don't refuse. It would give me the greatest pleasure to entertain such a charming guest on behalf of the Railway.'

It had taken her half an hour to climb the hill from the sluice. She was hot and dispirited.

'I wouldn't say no to a cup of tea, Mr Burcham.'

'And a muffin?' He cocked his head on one side and waited.

She summoned up a smile. 'And a muffin,' she said.

'Splendid! Splendid!' He moved aside to let her pass, but once in the house she suddenly stopped and listened. 'No trains?' she said.

Burcham raised a hand and steered her towards the muffins. 'No, dear lady, not at the present time. Perhaps I should explain. This is a quite remarkable day for the Great Eastern Railway. The 1874 timetable. That means we're in the middle of a General Election, and Mr Gladstone has been making a speech here in Norwich. We're transporting him back to London by special train, and I've received instructions direct from Head Office to clear all the lines ... He's due to leave in ... Let me see.' He consulted the gold watch suspended from a chain in his waistcoat pocket. 'Ah, yes. Precisely three-quarters of an hour. Till then every bit of my attention is yours. So step inside and take a chair. The train's ready and waiting, the kettle's on the boil and the muffins are impaled on the end of a fork. We have ample time at our disposal, dear lady. We can therefore, together, consume them at our leisure.'

6

Gregg unlocked the door of the cottage at Thetford, dropped the key in his pocket and stood for a moment looking around.

He'd dropped Spurgeon in Swaffham to search for the shop that might have sold the medallion, driven from there down the long, straight road to Thetford, collected the key from Mrs Dracopoli, and walked the couple of hundred yards to the cottage.

It was small, no more than a lodge at the end of the winding drive that led to the house, and the door opened straight into a comparably small and starkly furnished parlour. There was a deal table with two hard wooden chairs, a Welsh dresser with a sparse collection of crockery, a slim writing desk, a gas fire and, tucked away in a corner, a tall oak stand crowned with a bowl of artificial flowers.

He turned the key in the desk and lifted the flap. There was nothing inside. The pigeon-holes were empty.

He looked round again. There was nothing anywhere in the room to show that anyone had lived there in the past few weeks. Indeed, from all appearances, it could have stood unoccupied since well before the war.

Two doors opened off it. One led into a cramped and claustrophobic kitchen with a gas stove, a sink, a shelf with pots and pans and an ancient clothes-rack suspended from the ceiling. All the pans were clean and scoured. There was no sign that anyone had even boiled an egg, let alone cooked a meal.

The other door led up a narrow flight of stairs to a bedroom. It was dark and drab with a small single bed, a marble-topped washstand complete with a bowl and jug, and a heavy oak clothes-chest, the lid scraped and scarred by generations of use. The only light came through a small casement window that overlooked a minute vegetable garden smothered in weeds.

He raised the lid of the chest and peered inside. It was empty, like the desk.

The bed was draped in a dark blue coverlet. He turned it back and lifted the pillow. There was nothing underneath.

He lifted the mattress, looked under the bed. Once again, nothing.

He sat down and wondered what to do next. If the Chief had sent him down here to find some clue to this mystery woman, then it looked as if the Chief was going to be disappointed. If she'd lodged here at all – a fact he was already beginning to doubt – then it was clear she'd taken everything she owned up to Blakeney. As far as he could see, there was nothing, not even a wisp of hair, to reveal that she'd ever set foot in the place.

Yet surely there must be something. She'd paid Mrs Dracopoli a month's rent in advance, and no one left home for a month with just a small suitcase. There must be another one – a larger one – somewhere around.

He looked up at the bedroom ceiling. There was no trapdoor to a space in the roof.

Was there then a wall space hidden behind the furniture?

It took him another ten minutes to search. He went downstairs to the parlour, stripped the dresser of its crockery and pulled it away from the wall, but his efforts revealed nothing except a dull, dusty stain on the paper behind. Pushing it back and replacing the crockery, he pulled out the writing desk. The result was the same.

There was no possible hiding place in the kitchen. The gas stove, like the fire, was bolted to the wall and impossible to move, and though, back in the bedroom, he dragged out the chest and the bed there was nothing behind them.

He peered through the window. There was no garden shed, no outhouse of any kind. Just a weed-smothered patch of garden.

He sat down again and pondered the problem. The small case that she'd taken with her to Cley couldn't possibly have held all she needed for a month, so what had she done with the rest of her belongings? If he'd been in her position, determined to cover his tracks and leave nothing behind that might yield a clue, what would he have done?

There was, he decided, just one step that he might well have taken. It was at least feasible and worth a quick check.

He locked up the cottage and drove into Thetford.

7

'He's not here,' said Harris, 'so God knows where he is. He could be anywhere on the coast by this time of a morning.'

They stared at the row of biscuit tins, the stuffed red squirrel, the German beer mug and Ginger Rogers.

'What about his mother?' McKenzie said. 'Won't she know where he is?'

Harris snorted down his nose. 'That'll be the day. As far as she's concerned, once he's gone, he's gone. She won't give him a thought till the light begins to fade. She's one simple rule. He's got to be back in the house before dark. She doesn't give a toss what he does before then.'

'Taking a chance, isn't she?'

'Can't afford not to. She's a widow with a farm to keep running.'

'Aren't there any other sons?'

'No. Danny's an only child. After he was born she wouldn't risk a second.'

McKenzie stroked the bristles on his chin. 'Well, at least she'll know about the night before last. Whether he was back before Joe Grice was murdered . . . And we're going to need her, aren't we?'

'I suppose so.'

'You don't sound too keen.'

'Between you and me,' said Harris, 'I'm not. You haven't met her. She's a cross between the Basilisk and Medusa the Gorgon.'

'Never heard of 'em,' McKenzie said, 'so let's go and find her.'

At first sight Mrs Sprot revealed nothing to match Harris's fearsome description. Standing with her back to them, mucking out the cowshed, she seemed to McKenzie to be the last person likely to consume a vital part of his anatomy for breakfast. Not much more than five feet tall in her wellington boots, she was a veritable wisp of a woman, hardly the type designed to produce a son who was six feet tall and broad into the bargain.

When she heard them, she turned, and the look she gave them was more than enough to convince him that Harris could well have been right. Sour-faced and sharp-featured, she leaned on her fork and surveyed them with a mixture of belligerence and contempt. 'Oh, it's you,' she said, addressing herself to Harris. 'And what'll ye be wantin' this time?'

Harris trod carefully. 'Good morning, Mrs Sprot.'

'It were,' she said, 'but no more it ent. Say what ye want. I've work ter be doin'.'

'We're trying to find Danny, Mrs Sprot. We'd like to have a word with him.'

'Ye would now, would ye?' she said. 'Well, ye can't.'

'D'you know where he is?'

'Aye. Mebbe I do.'

'Then perhaps you'll tell us.'

'Wouldn' do any good. He ent speakin' ter no one.'

'Where is he, Mrs Sprot?' McKenzie wasn't prepared to waste any more time.

She ignored him. 'Who's yon gret lummox?' she said to Harris.

'Detective Sergeant McKenzie.'

'Then tell him I ent tellin' him all o' my know. Ent no business of his.'

'Mrs Sprot . . .' McKenzie said.

'Aye?' she said. 'Go on.'

'We're here on official business. We have to speak to Danny.'

155

'Do ye now? Or what?'

'If you know where he is and refuse to tell us, then we'll have to arrest you.'

'Fer what?'

'For obstructing the police. Is that clear enough?'

'Oh, aye,' she said, raising the fork. 'Too clear fer your good, ye botty little bugger . . . So afore I gets ter sticking this pritch through yer foot, I'll tell ye where he is. He's locked in his room an' he's bin there since midnight, which is when he gets home, an' he ent settin' foot outside till I'm good an' ready ter be lettin' him go. Not fer you, nor fer any Chief bloody Constable neither . . . Now get out o' my cowshed. No one comes inside here an' I don' invite 'em . . . Well, go on. Get out.'

She jabbed at McKenzie's foot. He jumped back and she jabbed again. 'Outside!' she said. 'Both o' ye!' Then, raising the fork, she pointed it straight at those vital appendages that Harris had declared she feasted on for breakfast. 'I ent waitin' till Christmas,' she said, 'so get movin' an' make it quick, or ye'll be nursin' a bloody sight more 'n just a couple o' sore feet.'

8

Wensum Cycles was a large Norwich shop devoted entirely to the marketing of bicycles, their spare parts and accessories, and its street door opened on to a spacious showroom, at the far end of which stood a highly polished mahogany table with a telephone, two wire trays for incoming and outgoing correspondence, and a heavy leather-bound ledger that, from its well-worn appearance, had been in use since the firm's establishment sixty years before.

Seated behind it was an elderly, bespectacled man with immaculately styled grey hair and a paunch. As the door bell tinkled and Ellison came in, he looked up, removed his spectacles and rose to his feet with a magisterial dignity. 'Good day to you, sir,' he said. 'My name is Kingsley. Reginald Kingsley. How can I be of service?'

Ellison was a well-mannered young man who'd been brought up to observe the social niceties. Courtesy, he felt, demanded a like response. 'Good morning, sir,' he said. 'My name is Robert Ellison. Detective Constable Ellison.' He produced his card. 'I'm afraid I'm not here, sir, to make a purchase. All I need is some assistance.'

If Mr Reginald Kingsley felt any disappointment, he'd long since trained himself not to show it. 'If you need assistance, sir,' he said, 'then assistance you shall have. Do please take a seat . . . Now what can I do to help?'

Ellison took out his notebook. 'I've reason to believe, sir, that on Wednesday, 2nd May you sold a young woman a lady's bicycle, a Raleigh. The number on the frame was 675243 . . . Would that be correct?'

'Absolutely correct, sir.'

'You remember the woman?'

Kingsley nodded twice. 'I do indeed, Constable. The circumstances were sufficiently unusual to etch themselves on my memory.'

'In what way unusual?'

Kingsley pushed aside the ledger. 'Well,' he said, 'Wednesday is always our half-day closing, and the time had just gone midday. I'd locked the street door and was turning to let myself out at the back, when there was a hammering on the glass and I saw this young woman peering in. I went to the door and pointed to the notice that said the shop was closed, but she pleaded that her business was urgent. She had, she said, to speak to me. Well, it's never been my practice, Constable, to encourage belated customers once I've locked up: the times of opening are clearly specified on the door; but the look on her face was one of such appeal that in this case I relented.'

'You let her in, sir.'

'I did.' He sighed and shook his head. 'It was a decision I had cause to regret more than once. I'd already dismissed the rest of the staff, and it was well after one o'clock before I could get away.'

'But you did make a sale.'

'Yes, indeed, but at considerable cost, let me say.'

'Why was that, sir?'

'Well . . .' Mr Kingsley paused. 'How can I describe her? She was a personable young woman, attractive I'd say to men of her own age, but distinctly obsessive. She seemed determined to tell me all about herself: how she came to be in Norwich, what her intentions were, and why she found it vital to possess herself of a bicycle on that particular day and at that particular time. She never stopped talking. To put it bluntly, Constable, she battered me with words. Once she'd left, I felt constrained to run a glass of water and take a dose of aspirin.'

Ellison gave a faint smile. 'From what we know of her, sir, that doesn't surprise me . . . Can you remember what she said?'

'I'm afraid much of it went in at one ear and out at the other, but yes, there are some things I can still recall. She said she was a private inquiry agent working for a firm that was based in Chelmsford, and her job was to track down a woman who'd abandoned her husband and left him with two small children to care for. This woman had recently been seen around Blakeney, so she'd set out that morning from Chelmsford to drive up by car. Apparently all had gone well till she'd stopped at Swainsthorpe to take a break. She'd parked the car by the side of the road, but while she was away a lorry had backed into it and she'd had to get it towed to a

157

local garage and leave it there for repairs. She had to have transport – that was what she said – and a bicycle was the only feasible alternative . . . She was very particular, examined all the different makes that we had in stock, and asked a lot of questions. I wondered at one stage whether she would, after all, make a purchase; it took her nearly an hour to make up her mind; but at length she decided to take the Raleigh and asked if it was possible to have it delivered. I told her the best station for Blakeney was Holt. They'd deliver it from there by road. To my great relief, Constable, she said that would be fine.'

Ellison frowned. 'Did she give you a name and address?'

'A name, yes.' Kingsley opened the ledger and turned back the pages. 'Miss Eleanor Welsby. But she told me she couldn't at that moment give me an address. She didn't know where she'd be staying. She'd have to give me a phone call as soon as she knew. I pointed out that we were closed for the rest of the day, but she said couldn't I possibly make an exception just for her? It was essential that the bicycle should be despatched that same day. Well, by that time, Constable, I was desperate to close the sale and I knew I had work to complete on the accounts, so I told her that if she phoned between three o'clock and five I'd still be available. She rang me, if I remember, round about four and said I was to send it to Phoenix Mill Cottage at Blakeney, so I had it collected and despatched that evening.'

'And how did she pay?'

'She paid cash,' Mr Kingsley said. 'I offered to take a cheque, but she said no, she never carried a cheque book when she was working. I must admit that I found that rather strange, but she opened her handbag, took out a wad of notes and paid on the spot . . . It was, you might say, a brief encounter but a memorable one. She was, I felt, a somewhat eccentric young woman, graceful and yet completely lacking in grace. One with a mission that excluded all else. Needless to say, I received no subsequent word of thanks. That came as no surprise. She was not, to my mind, the type to give gratitude much of a thought.'

9

None of her colleagues, even the odd misogynist, would have characterized Sue Gradwell as lacking in grace, and Mr Burcham would certainly not have subscribed to such a graceless opinion. It was clear that, to him, she combined all the graces essential to youth and beauty, and that, seated behind his battery of finger-length levers, he conceived it as being no more than his duty to ensure that her every wish was fulfilled.

It was evident, nonetheless, that he was finding the task a difficult one.

'Now let me see, dear lady,' he said. 'I'd just cleared the train to Newport and restored the down signal to its normal position, so I must have been standing' – he moved a pace to the right – 'just about here. I looked up at the window and happened to see the light.'

Sue Gradwell was standing behind him. 'Can you show me exactly where?'

Mr Burcham shifted his head first to one side and then the other. 'When you reach my age, dear lady,' he said, 'memory tends to be a fickle kind of jade. She is, as Goldsmith said, no more than a fond deceiver: she speaks with a double tongue. I can do no more, I fear, than to hazard a guess. You wish me to do so?'

'Please, if you would.'

Burcham narrowed his eyes. 'You see that streak of dust that runs down the window?'

She looked across his shoulder. 'Yes,' she said.

'Well, as far as I remember it was just to the right of that, and about two-thirds of the way up.'

She tried to focus her eyes on the featureless waste. 'It was quite a long way out, then?'

'Oh yes, dear lady, a very long way.'

'Would you say it was on the marsh or beyond that, on the sand?'

Mr Burcham pondered. 'Difficult to tell. At such a distance in the dark one can only conjecture, but hazarding another guess I'd say it was on the sand.'

'And you're sure of the time?'

'Positive, dear lady. The Foresters' excursion pulled into Stanstead dead on the minute. The Great Eastern takes especial pride in its punctuality. Connections are of vital importance to the public.'

'Well, thank you, Mr Burcham. You've been very helpful.'

'Not at all, dear lady. The pleasure was mine.' He seemed to hesitate, then turned towards her. 'I suppose you have a picture of this poor, deluded woman?'

'Deluded?'

'She must have been, surely . . . To drown herself.'

Sue Gradwell frowned. 'She was murdered, Mr Burcham.'

He seemed taken aback. 'She was? Good heavens! I hadn't realized that.'

'I did tell you about it. The first time we met.'

'Did you?' He stared at her. 'How very strange.'

'You said you couldn't have seen her. You were far too busy running trains to gaze out of windows.'

'I did?' He appeared to be genuinely puzzled. 'Well, that was true at least. As general factotum of the Great Eastern Railway . . . You do have a picture?'

'Yes, of course.' She took one out of her document wallet and handed it to him.

He peered at it. Then he carried it to the window, held it out at arm's length and studied it from a number of different angles. This took him a little time, but at last he seemed satisfied. 'This is the woman who drowned?' he said.

Sue wasn't prepared to argue. 'That's right, Mr Burcham.'

'Then yes' – he glowed with pleasure – 'I've most certainly seen her. I thought it was possible, and indeed I was correct.'

'You were?' For the first time she spoke with some misgiving.

'Oh yes, dear lady, no doubt about it. No doubt at all.'

'Where did you see her, and when?'

'Well now, let me see.' He closed his eyes briefly as if trying to remember. 'I wasn't here. . . . Now where was I?' There was a pause. He tapped his forehead. 'Ah yes,' he said, 'now it all comes back. I was replacing a signal lamp down at Saffron Walden. There was a knock on the door, and when I went down she was standing by the turnstile. I asked her what I could do to help, and she said she required a single ticket to Hertford. I issued her with one and told her she'd have to change at Broxbourne. The train was already waiting, so I showed her across the bridge and made sure she was settled in a suitable compartment. She was, I might say, effusively grateful and tendered me a two-shilling piece as gratuity. Naturally, in my capacity as general factotum, I declined in spite of her protests to accept it. She left . . . let me see' – he crossed to the timetables pasted on the wall – 'yes, of course. At precisely 11.35. Though I say it myself, I think she was much impressed by the service we offered.'

She knew the inescapable truth by then. She'd been wasting her time. But she had to ask the question. 'When was this, Mr Burcham?'

The answer came far too promptly for comfort. 'Why, yesterday morning, dear lady, when else? The train was due to pass through Saffron Walden. I had to replace the lamp to ensure its safe passage.' He beamed at her. 'Now . . . how about another of those scrumptious muffins?'

'I don't think so, Mr Burcham,' she said very gently, 'but thank you all the same.'

Once outside, she pounded the stone gatepost hard with her fist. 'Damn!' she said. 'Damn, damn, damn!' And then with a vehemence that Mr Burcham would have found to be disconcerting in one so blessed with the feminine graces: 'Men! Bloody men!'

10

Andrew Gregg rarely swore – as far as he was concerned it revealed a lack of style, not to mention a vocabularian poverty – but standing in the left-luggage office at Thetford station, he was sorely tempted to indulge in a couple of singularly appropriate oaths.

The minor official allegedly in charge – a pimply youth with Brylcreemed hair: anathema to anyone who professed at least a little sophistication – was proving obstructive.

'Can't be done,' he said. 'Ye gotter have a ticket.'

Gregg restrained himself, not without an effort. 'Look again, lad,' he said. 'This is an official folder. Inside there's a card. It states quite clearly that I'm Detective Sergeant Gregg from the CID in Norwich . . . I suppose you can read?'

The pimply youth regarded him with scorn. 'Course I can.'

'You're not deaf?'

'No, I ent.'

'Then I'll repeat myself, and this time listen . . . I'm investigating a murder, and I need to examine any luggage still in your possession that was deposited here a week last Wednesday. Understand?'

The youth gave a nod. 'Ye still need a ticket.'

Gregg took a deep breath. 'How many times do I have to say this? The luggage isn't mine. I didn't leave it. So I haven't got a ticket.'

A shrug. 'Rules is rules. Ye gotter have a ticket.'

'Right,' Gregg said. 'You've a choice. It's up to you. Either you show me the luggage or you'll be spending a night in the cells at Norwich. You're obstructing the police.'

A sigh. 'What is it?'

'What's what?'

'The luggage. What is it?'

'Probably a suitcase.'

'Colour?'

'How should I know the colour? It doesn't belong to me. For all I know it could be red with yellow stripes.'

The youth shook his head. 'There ent one like that. Not as I've seen.'

Gregg leaned forward, the flat of his hands on the counter. 'Look, sonny,' he said. 'Just answer me this. Have you still got any article that was deposited in this office a week last Wednesday?'

'Not usual, that. Them as leaves stuff here comes back the same day. They ent fer waitin' a week.'

Gregg took a second, even deeper breath. 'They can't do anything but wait if they're dead . . . Now just go and check.'

The youth gave another shrug and wandered off through a door at the back. After a couple of minutes he poked his head round the jamb. 'No case,' he said.

'Is there anything else?'

'On'y one thing from Wednesday.'

'What is it?'

'A holdall.'

'Then for God's sake bring it.'

It was dull brown in colour with a zip but no lock. Gregg examined it. No label. He stripped back the zip and began to rummage inside. There seemed to be nothing there but underwear. He pulled the garments out one by one and tossed them on the counter: bras, knickers, underslips, packets of stockings . . .

The youth watched him with a kind of vicarious fascination. 'That ent allowed,' he said.

'Too bad,' Gregg told him.

'Rules is rules,' said the youth, 'an' that's agen the rules.'

'Then report me,' said Gregg.

He continued to rummage. Out came a jar of face cream, a tin of talcum powder and a variety of lipsticks. At the bottom was a writing case. He laid it on the counter and flicked open the clasp. On one side was a sheaf of blue letter paper, on the other the matching envelopes; but underneath the blue paper, tucked out of sight, was a newspaper cutting, and below it was a single folded sheet that didn't match. This one was white.

He unfolded it and smoothed it out on the counter with the cutting beside it, stared at them for a moment and then replaced them both in the writing case. Stuffing the clothes back in the holdall, he laid the case on top and fastened the zip. 'I'm impounding this,' he said. 'It's vital evidence in a murder inquiry.'

The youth opened a drawer and took out a printed form. 'Ye'll have to sign for it,' he declared, 'an' don't think I ent reportin' what you done, cos I am.'

Gregg reached out and patted him on the shoulder. 'You do that,' he said. 'And don't forget. The name's spelt with three Gs.'

Back at the car, he unzipped the holdall, and took out the cutting and the folded sheet of paper.

The cutting had been clipped from the *Eastern Daily Press*. It was Lubbock's advertisement for the cottage at Kettle Hill.

The odd sheet was a middle page taken from a letter. He read it through, whistled softly, then placed both items inside his notebook, started up the car and drove off towards Swaffham.

At least he'd salvaged a little bit of something from an otherwise utterly unproductive morning.

11

Though some members of Tench's team were finding the search for information difficult and, in McKenzie's case, positively dangerous, others had no cause to cajole or persuade. It was offered to them free of any prior solicitation.

While Gregg was engaged in a fruitless examination of the cottage at Thetford, and McKenzie was facing imminent impalement by a Gorgon who was wielding a contaminated pitchfork, a young man dressed in an immaculate lounge suit presented himself to Detective Constable Lock in the incident room at Medford.

'Yes, sir?' said Lock. 'What can we do to help?'

The young man seemed to hesitate. 'It's a bit awkward,' he said. 'You are . . .?'

'DC Lock. Detective Constable Lock. Please take a seat.'

'You're in charge here?'

'Correct, sir.'

The young man pulled out a chair and sat down. 'It's about those murders last Monday night. I think I may know something.'

Lock picked up a pencil. 'Can you give me your name, sir?'

'Chetley. Dominic Chetley.'

'And your address?'

'The Heathers, Ford Lane, Copston.'

'That's near Sibthorpe, isn't it?'

'About a mile to the east, on the Langham road.'

Lock made a note. 'Right, sir. Carry on.'

The young man paused again. 'I wouldn't like any of this to become public property.'

'Of course not, sir, no.'

'The truth is, Constable, I was out with a married woman last Monday night. She wouldn't want to be involved.'

'Just tell me what happened, sir. If it's connected with the murders, we do need to know.'

'Yes, I realize that, but it's all a bit embarrassing.'

Lock said nothing. He waited.

'You see, Constable, we've been going out together now for a couple of months, and we usually drive down here to Medford and park the car by the edge of the marsh.'

'Whereabouts would that be precisely, sir?'

'There's a track that runs off the road to Wells about a quarter of a mile beyond the end of the village. It leads down to the marsh by the old army camp. It's usually quite deserted.'

'But last Monday it wasn't?'

'No, there was a car already parked there.'

'What time was this, sir?'

'It must have been round about quarter to eleven. We'd been down to the Crown at Wells, and we left as soon as the landlord called time. We drove straight from there.'

'Can you describe the car, sir?'

Chetley frowned. 'Not in detail, no. It was moonlight, of course, but still pretty dark, and we didn't get too close. As soon as we saw that someone else was parked there, we backed down the track till we reached the main road ... It was a saloon car, possibly black or dark blue, but apart from that it's difficult to say.'

'You weren't near enough to see the number?'

'I'm afraid not, Constable.'

'And you couldn't see whether there was anyone inside'

'No, it was too dark and we were too far away.'

Lock nodded briefly. 'There's just one thing, sir. Are you sure this was Monday?'

'Oh, yes. Quite sure.'

'You've some reason for saying that? Some way we can double-check without involving your lady friend?'

'I've been worried about that, but yes, I think there is.' Chetley seemed only too eager to oblige. 'I picked her up by the ford at Copston just after nine o'clock. I remember very well because while I was waiting the church clock struck the hour. Copston church has got a carillon. The bells play a different hymn tune every day. On Monday it was "The King of Love my Shepherd Is". You know the one. It's based on Psalm 23. I heard it quite clearly. You can check with the rector.'

'Then I'll do that, sir,' said Lock. 'And thank you for coming in. If we need more information, we will of course be in touch.'

He rang up the rector.

'I believe your church has a carillon, sir.'

'You believe right, Constable.' The voice was mild, indulgent. 'It was a gift from a local benefactor forty years ago.'

'I don't know much about carillons, sir. How does it work?'

'There are twelve bells in the tower cast by Taylor of Loughborough. The clock strikes them mechanically and picks out a hymn tune.'

'That occurs every hour?'

'No, not each hour, Constable. Just six times a day. Every three hours starting at six in the morning. The last tune played is at nine o'clock at night.'

'And the hymn changes every day?'

'Every two days. We have seven different tunes, and the cycle lasts a fortnight. It begins with "The Saints of God" and ends with "Jerusalem on High".'

'Then can you tell me, sir, which tune was played last Monday?'

'Well, now, let me see.' The rector paused and pondered. 'The clock has been out of order. It was only restarted a week last Tuesday.' He counted off the days. 'Tuesday, Wednesday. Thursday, Friday. Saturday, Sunday . . . That means that by Monday we'd have been on the fourth tune, so the bells must have played . . . yes, of course, "The King of Love".'

'Thank you, sir,' said Lock. 'That's all I wanted to know. You've been most helpful.'

'You're sure there's nothing else?'

'Positive, sir.'

'You must come and hear them sometime. The tone is most mellifluous. Just give me a call. I'll be glad to show you round.'

'I most certainly will, sir,' said Lock.

12

Lock wasn't alone in being graced with gratuitous information that morning. Detective Sergeant Clive Hellyer, on attachment from Lynn, was likewise favoured.

It was perhaps fortunate for him that he was, since the irksome process of knocking on cottage doors in Medford had already depressed his normal good humour. It was, of course, true that Joe Grice's house on the Sibthorpe Hill occupied a somewhat lonely position – his nearest neighbour, a sour-faced old hag who'd reluctantly confided that her name was Minnie Marsden lived a couple of hundred yards down the slope – but it was dispiriting, even so, to find that no one, on the night of his murder, had apparently noticed anything unusual.

Medford, so it seemed, was a village whose residents, once the sun went down, wrapped themselves in curtained cocoons, switched on the wireless and closed their eyes and ears to any sight or sound beyond the walls of their parlours.

Other members of Tench's team had already, of course, discovered this for themselves, but to Hellyer, more familiar with the chatter, the traffic and the wholesale bustle that characterized Lynn, the very silence of Medford came first as a phenomenon, then as an irritation, and at length as a dull, depressing mass of cloud that hid his high spirits, even from himself.

His answer was, like McKenzie, to lean on the bridge, stare at the sluggish water and, unlike Gregg, to swear himself back into a tolerable humour.

Not that it seemed to work. He'd run through his whole gamut of expletives one by one, and was about to start again, when an alien sound attracted his attention.

It wasn't, as it had been for McKenzie, the sound of high heels tapping on the road, nor the sight of swelling breasts above a slim waist. It was a slow chugging noise that was clearly mechanical, and what emerged at last from the bend on the hill was no naked Aphrodite, but a dirty farm tractor, scattering mud from its wheels as it made its erratic progress towards him.

Hellyer watched it. When it reached him, it stopped and a corpulent man with unruly grey whiskers, a buttonless shirt and a pair of earth-stained trousers tied up with string clambered down from the seat. 'You!' he said hoarsely. Then he cleared his throat and spat on the road. 'You police?'

Hellyer eyed him warily. 'CID,' he said.

'Same difference, ent it?' The man spat a second time. 'You on these murders?'

Hellyer looked him up and down and didn't like what he saw. 'I could be,' he said.

'Don't ye bloody know?'

'All right. Yes, I am.'

'Then ye'd best come wi' me.'

'Come with you where?'

'Why, up ter th'dome, o' course.'

Hellyer was baffled. 'The dome? What's the dome?'

'It's a bloody dome, ent it? Up at Copston airfield.'

'What's wrong with it?'

'Wrong wi' it? Not a lot. It don't change a deal.'

'Then why d'you want me to see it?'

'It's what's in it like, ent it?'

'And just what would that be?'

'Reckon ye'll see,' the man said. 'Come on then. Climb up. I ent got all bloody day.'

Hellyer sniffed the air. 'No thanks,' he said. 'You lead the way. I'll follow.'

VII
THE SIGNIFICANT THIRD

I always know when Lady Slattern has been before
me. She has a most observing thumb

Richard Brinsley Sheridan: *The Rivals*

1

Mike Tench had heard Lubbock say more than once, when they'd been talking together in the cottage at Cley, that solving a murder was much like the business of cultivating roses. You needed to prune the evidence you'd gathered, discarding most of it as quite immaterial; you scratched yourself from time to time following clues that led absolutely nowhere; and then one day, after weeks or perhaps even months of waiting, the case would open out like a beautiful flower.

He recalled the words that morning as he sat in his office, waiting for McKenzie to produce Danny Sprot. The trouble with this case, he reflected, was simply that he didn't know enough to make a start. How could he prune the evidence and discard the immaterial when he didn't know who the murder victim was? He couldn't even say that he'd followed a useless clue when he'd no tangible guide to what might be useful.

He stared at the files that littered his desk. Who was she, this woman? Where had she come from? Why had she rented that cottage in Blakeney and taken such pains to conceal her true identity? What was she looking for, trundling round the coast on a bicycle, asking questions about houses and investing herself with a different name and background at every encounter? Why was it that her arrival had transformed Medford from a sleepy little village where nothing ever happened into a place of notoriety where three murders had followed one another in swift succession?

And where the hell was McKenzie? He glanced at his watch. Eleven fifteen. What in God's name were he and Harris doing down at Sibthorpe? Milking the cows?

No, said Harris, announcing their arrival twenty minutes later, they hadn't got around to milking the cows.

'Where's Sergeant McKenzie?'

'Down in the charge room, sir.'

'What's he doing there?'

He was, said Harris, charging Mrs Sprot with assault and obstruction.

'Go on. Tell me,' said Tench. 'Why's he doing that?'

Harris explained. 'She turned a bit awkward, sir. Refused point-blank to let us see Danny, and threatened us both with a pitchfork.'

'One of those, is she?'

'Afraid so, sir, yes.'

'So what happened?'

'Well, the sergeant tried to grab it, sir, and slipped flat on his face in a patch of cow muck. While he was down, she emptied a bucket of disinfectant over him.' Harris gave a grin. 'He's in a bit of a mess, sir. Doesn't smell very sweet.'

'I'll bet his temper isn't very sweet either,' said Tench.

'Firing on all cylinders, sir. Spent his time muttering terrible oaths all the way back to Norwich.'

'So where's Danny Sprot?'

'In the interview room with a constable, sir. His mother'll be there as soon as the sergeant's charged her.'

'It's a pity we can't forget all about her.'

'Not advisable, sir. Especially now she's here.'

Tench sighed. 'I suppose not.'

'Knows her rights, does Mrs Sprot, and she's not over fond of members of the force.'

'All right then, Constable. You bring her in. Tell Sergeant McKenzie to go and have a shower and get changed. One bad smell about the place is enough.'

'Before that, sir . . .' said Harris.

'Something you want to say?'

'I'd like to look at the shells, sir. The ones that were found in Grice's cottage.'

Tench nodded. 'OK.' He unlocked a metal filing cabinet and took out two plastic envelopes. The first held the shells, the second the paper bag. He handed them to Harris.

The constable examined them. 'Two things, sir,' he said, 'before we start asking Danny any questions.'

'What are they?'

'This paper bag, sir. Yes, Danny collects shells, but I've never known him use anything else except his pockets.'

'And . . .?'

'The shells themselves, sir. Some of them are mussels. He never picks up mussels. You won't find a mussel among his collection.'

'Why not?'

'He just doesn't like them. He's a simple sort of lad. He collects pretty things, and mussels aren't pretty. Not to him, anyway.'

'So you think we'll be wasting our time.'

'I don't think he was the one who dropped the bag, sir. I've known him long enough, and none of this fits. He just isn't the type to break into houses or to be violent.'

'Not even if he happened to be scared?'

'No, sir.'

'Mrs Wellbridge seems to think he broke into her house. He could have

170

broken into Grice's cottage and been caught in the act. According to what I hear he's a strong enough lad.'

'I wouldn't be inclined, sir, to set too much store on Mrs Wellbridge's opinion. She's got a bit of an obsession about Danny.'

'Unjustified?'

'Yes, sir.'

Tench looked down his nose. 'Well, you may be right. Get the mother in and let's ask him a few questions.'

Harris looked doubtful. 'You won't get much in the way of answers, not from Danny.'

'That's what you're here for, Constable,' said Tench. 'Your job's to interpret. Leave his mother to me.'

2

At that very moment Detective Sergeant Hellyer was standing on the road that ran through Copston airfield staring at an object the like of which he'd never seen before.

'What is it?' he said.

The bewhiskered man climbed down from his tractor. 'It's a bloody dome, ent it?'

'But what was it used for?'

'Search me,' the man said. 'Reckon it were somethin' ter do wi' flyin'. Bin empty since th'war.'

Hellyer walked round the peculiar structure and examined it. It was a concrete dome some twenty feet high and painted black, though the paint was beginning to peel away. It had a heavy steel door with a hasp and a padlock, and low down on one side was a ventilation hole that someone had sealed with a sheet of cast-iron.

'Could have been an ammunition store,' he said.

'Coulda bin,' the man said. 'Bin empty fer years. Point is though: that ent my lock.'

'How d'you mean? Not your lock.'

'Them fliers, they be leavin' it wi' out any lock. Door were standin' oppen. Kids was usin' it ter piddle in, aye an' worse'n tha'. There be fine goin's on, an' reglar like, too, wi' they courtin' couples a-neckin' inside. Farmer Pigott, him as gets ter workin' th'land agen now an' worked it afore th'war, he says ter me, Abe, he says, you see ter the puttin' of a lock on tha' door. An' I does as he says. I finds one an' fits it on sharp as ye please. But that one ent mine. It be same kind, aye, but that one be all bloody shiny an' new. Some bugger's a-gone an' swapped it.'

171

'Why would they do that?'

'Reckon it be cos of what they be shovin' inside.'

'So what have they shoved inside?'

'Ye'll be seein' soon enough.' He fished a key from his pocket and turned it in the lock. 'It's bloody dark,' he said, 'so I'm tellin' ye now. Ye'd best watch yer step or ye'll be trippin' on it like and brekkin' yer neck.'

He pushed the door open, stood in the shaft of sunlight and pointed to the left. 'It be down there,' he said. 'An' no, I ent moved it. Not a bloody inch. Just oppened it up fer ter see what it were.'

The place smelt of damp and dust and urine. Hellyer peered down into the gloom. It took a second or two for his eyes to adjust before they focused on the object dumped on the concrete floor. He dragged it into the sunlight and squatted down beside it. Then he straightened up and turned.

'Leave it where it is,' he said. 'Just lock the door and give me the key. I'll have to go down to Medford and make a report. When I get back I'll need to see you, so where will you be?'

The man scratched his head. 'Tha's a rummun to answer. Carn say fer sure. Depends like, don' it?'

'Depends on what?'

'If I still happens ter be hereabouts like or mebbe gets ter be endin' up some place else.'

Hellyer glared at him. 'What's your name?'

'Abel. Bin Abel now fer forty-five year.'

'Abel what?'

'Lavender.'

'Right, Mr Lavender.' Hellyer wasn't prepared to waste any more time. 'You stay right here. Go and lean on the tractor, and don't stir a yard till I'm back. Understand?'

Mr Lavender cleared his throat and spat on to Copston airfield. He shrugged resignedly. 'Aye, reckon so,' he said. 'But ye'd best not be long. Ol' tractor's gettin' a mite low on gas, an' I ent switchin' her off. Teks half a bloody hour ter get her runnin' this mornin', an' I ent much fer startin' her up twice a day.'

3

The interview room was alternately in sunlight and shade as white summer clouds moved across the sky. Tench and Harris sat on one side of the folding table; Danny and his mother facing them on the other.

McKenzie's wrath and the charges laid against her appeared to have had little or no effect on Mrs Sprot. She glared at Tench.

'Ye can save yer breath,' she said 'I ent sayin' nothin'.'

Tench gave her a soothing smile. 'That's perfectly all right, Mrs Sprot,' he declared. 'It's Danny we need to talk to.'

'What the hell fer? He ent done nothin' wrong.'

'We just need to be sure, ma'am.'

'Sure? What's bloody sure? Sure o' what?'

'We need to know where he was last Wednesday night.'

'Then ye'd best be askin' me, cos it ent a deal o' use ter be askin' much of him. Don' know one bloody day from another, he don'. Never knowed that from the day he were born.'

'We can but try, Mrs Sprot.'

'Then ye'll need ter be a bloody sight cleverer than most.'

She folded her arms and sat back. 'Well, get on wi' it,' she said.

Tench turned to Harris. 'You ask him, Constable.'

Harris produced a calendar, pointed to the date and then to the sky. 'Today, Danny. Now,' he said. 'Fri-day.'

Danny looked puzzled. 'Fri-day, Mist' 'Arris?'

Harris nodded. 'Fri-day.' He moved his finger to a date two days back. 'Wens-day,' he said.

'Wens-day.' Danny repeated the word.

'Wens-day. You,' said Harris, pointing. 'Where? Danny where, Wens-day?'

Danny furrowed his brow. 'Mist' 'Arris?' he said.

The constable repeated the same manoeuvre, but this time in an even more laborious fashion. The result was the same. He glanced at Tench. 'It's no good, sir,' he said. 'He just doesn't understand.'

'Course he bloody doesn't.' Mrs Sprot scowled. 'He ent a bloody genius.'

'Right,' said Tench. He turned on her sharply. 'Since you claim to know all the answers, Mrs Sprot, tell me this. Where was he last Wednesday?'

'Whenabouts Wednesday?'

'From the time it got dark until Thursday morning.'

Mrs Sprot was visibly disgusted. 'Where d'ye think he bloody was? In bed, o' course, snorin'.'

'How can you be certain?'

'Cos if he weren', he'd a bin locked in his room yesterday. He knows bloody well as he's in afore dark, else tha's what he gets fer stoppin' out late.'

'You're willing to swear he was back home before dark on Wednesday night?'

'Aye, that he were. Ets his supper – sausage an' mash it were – then he's off atween th' sheets an' snorin' fit ter wake all the cocks i' bloody Norfolk.'

Tench pursed his lips. 'Show him the shells, Constable,' he said.

Harris emptied the bag of shells on the table. He pointed towards them. 'Shells,' he said. 'Pretty.'

The boy smiled and nodded. 'Pretty, Mist' 'Arris.'

'Danny's shells? Yes? Shells belong Danny?' Harris pointed again, first at Danny himself and then at the table.

Danny looked at the shells, then he shook his head firmly.

'Not Danny's?' Harris said.

Another shake of the head. The constable frowned. He spread the shells out and looked up. 'Why, Danny? Why? You tell Mist' 'Arris. Why not Danny's shells?'

The boy leaned forward and picked one up. He showed it to Harris. 'Muss-el?' he said.

'That's right, Danny. Mussel.'

Danny turned it in his hand. 'Not pretty, Mist' 'Arris,' he said. 'Muss-el not pretty.'

As he spoke the words a cloud drifted clear of the sun, and a sudden shaft of light illumined his face. In that moment he looked to be almost angelic.

Tench took a deep breath. He leaned back in his chair and stared for a moment at both the alleged delinquents. Then, without any warning, he waved a dismissive hand towards Harris. 'Do me a favour, Constable,' he said. 'Get rid of them both. Tell Sergeant McKenzie to bail Mrs Sprot. Just pack them off home. We're wasting our time.'

He watched them out of the room. As the door closed behind them, the phone on the wall rang, shattering the silence.

He lifted the receiver.

'Chief Inspector Tench?'

He didn't recognize the voice. 'Speaking,' he said curtly.

'Sergeant Hellyer, sir. Medford. We've found something here ... Yes, sir. That's right. I think you ought to see it. It's up at Copston airfield out on the Langham road ...'

4

Tench stood and stared. 'What is it?' he said.

'Astrodome,' said Harris. 'Used for teaching the techniques of night flying. Astronavigation. Using the stars. The RAF locked their navigators up in there for hours.'

'Well, sooner them than me. Let's hope none of them suffered from claustrophobia ... Who found it?' he asked Hellyer.

'Farmhand, sir. Name of Abel Lavender. His boss told him to put a lock on the place, but he reckons someone broke in, dumped the stuff inside, and then replaced the broken lock with one of his own. It's the same type, but newer.'

'Where is he, this Lavender?'

'Gone back to work, sir, but I've got his address. Seems to me there's nothing suspicious about him, but I told him we'd probably need to take a statement from him at some time or other.'

'Right. Let's take a look.' They moved forward to the doorway.

'It was a couple of yards to the left, sir,' said Hellyer. 'Had to shift it into the light to see what was in it.'

Tench looked down. On the dusty concrete floor was a blue leather suitcase. The lid was thrown open, and it appeared to be stuffed to the brim with clothes.

'Women's clothes,' said Hellyer. 'Everything down to a suspender belt and a bra.'

'Nothing else?'

'No, sir. No labels on the case, and the makers' tags have been cut off the clothes.'

'OK.' Tench nodded. 'It'll have to be left where it is for the moment. The crime squad's on its way, and the print men'll need to dust it. As soon as they've finished, get it down to the incident room at Medford.'

'Right, sir.'

'And I want this place watched from now on, day and night. Unobtrusively, of course. There's plenty of cover over there.' He pointed to a clump of bushes on the opposite side of the road. 'When you get back to Medford, choose four of your men and tell them to work the job in shifts, two at a time. Whoever broke in could possibly come back. If anyone tries to get inside they arrest them. Understood?'

Hellyer nodded. 'Understood, sir,' he said.

'Constable' – Tench turned back to Harris – 'I'll run you back into Blakeney. Pick up your bike and then take over here till Sergeant Lester and the crime squad have finished. They'll need to comb this place for any signs of evidence. Once they're through, lock it up. By that time Sergeant Hellyer's men'll be here, and you can leave it to them. Just hand the key to him. He'll be down at the incident room in Medford. I'll see you both there ... OK?'

'Clear enough, sir, yes.'

'Right then. Let's go. I'll drop you off at the police house. If either of you want to contact me in the meantime, I'll be over at Cley. Umzinto Cottage. It's right by the church. We need a witness to take a look at that case, and I think I know someone who'll be only too anxious to lend us a hand.'

5

Lubbock was leaning on the gate at Umzinto Cottage, smoking his pipe and gazing out across the unkempt meadows that had once been a thriving seaport. He didn't stir as Tench's car pulled up by the Green, nor as the door swung open and the Detective Chief Inspector stepped out on the tarmac. If he acknowledged his friend's arrival in any way, it was merely by a fractional adjustment of his gaze. His elbows continued to rest on the gate, and the pipe remained firmly clamped between his teeth. 'Coffee?' he said.

'No time.' Tench jerked a thumb. 'I need you down at Medford.'

Lubbock straightened up. 'News on the sack?'

'No, the boffins are still at work. But we've found a suitcase. We think it may be hers.'

'That's interesting. Where?'

'The astrodome at Copston airfield.'

Lubbock nodded. 'That fits.'

'Fits what?'

'Just an idea I've been tossing around . . . Any other developments?'

'We've had reports that a car was seen parked by the marsh late on Monday night.'

'Whereabouts by the marsh?'

'At the end of the track by the old army camp.'

'How far's that from Deep Lane?'

'According to Bates, about a quarter of a mile.'

'And the time's right?'

'Yes, 10.45. Much the same time that we reckon Craske was murdered.'

Lubbock nodded again. 'Then that fits as well.'

'Does it?'

'Yes, it does. You see, laddie, it's like this . . .'

'Save it,' said Tench. 'First things first. I want you to take a look at this case. Come on. Get in the car. You can tell me on the way.'

'It's like this,' said Lubbock as they reached the village and turned sharp left on to the coastal road. 'You've got three murders and no firm suspect. Am I right?'

'Too right.'

'Then perhaps that theory of yours is wrong. Perhaps it's time you scrapped it and started again from scratch.'

176

'You've got an alternative?'

'Let's just say, laddie, that I've been doing some thinking. Thinking back, to be precise.'

'Back to when?'

'It's not so much back to when as back to where. You remember that winter four years ago?'

''47? Yes. It isn't easy to forget.'

'Think back to the end of February. Where were you then?'

'You know where I was. I was wandering round Italy. Doing the job you sent me to do.'

'You weren't exactly wandering, were you now, laddie? You were probing the past in search of a killer. I'd sent you to see that professor in Naples. What was his name? Visco?'

'Giovanni Visco.'

'And if I remember rightly, he drove you out into that wilderness. What was it called?'

'Basilicata.'

'That's it. The land that God forgot. And you learned a great deal about unwritten laws: the two unwritten laws that dominated life down there in the South. One was the law of the vendetta. What did he call it?'

'The Lex Talionis. An eye for an eye and a tooth for a tooth.'

'And a life for a life. Wasn't that what he said?'

'Yes, but . . .' Tench frowned at the road. 'It's no relevance here.'

'I never said it had. I was thinking of the second.'

'Omerta?'

'That's right. What did Visco call it? The conspiratorial silence of the South? When a dead body turns up in the street, no one knows anything, no one's seen anything. People smile and they shrug, but no one says a word. Omerta decrees that that's how it has to be . . . Now think, laddie, think. Think about Medford.'

'Go on. I'm listening.'

'Your theory, right or wrong, was that the killer carried the body of this woman all the way out across the marsh and the sands to Blacknock. How far was that? A mile and a half? It'd need a man of considerable strength . . .'

'Or a woman.'

'Or a woman, as you say. But if it was a woman, then she must have been long accustomed to toting heavy weights, and whoever did it, man or woman, must have had an intimate knowledge of the tracks across the marsh. You accept that?'

'Yes' – Tench nodded – 'but there've been two other murders. On both occasions a man's neck was broken. Could a woman have done that?'

'Why not? If she was strong enough to carry a body that distance, she could well have snapped a neck. And remember. Both the victims were old, and one was almost incapably drunk ... Now, let's go on from there. All the murders have been in or very close to Medford. That points to the probability that the killer's someone local, and if this suitcase of yours turns out to be the one that my lodger brought with her, then the place where you found it – the astrodome at Copston – adds to that probability. The dome isn't something that a stranger to the area would know about. Granted?'

'Yes, fair enough.' Tench gave a shrug.

'And now, laddie, you've added a little bit more – this car that was parked on the edge of the marsh. You're implying that it was used to transport the body, but as far as I know there's no track across the marsh from the old army camp, and it's – what did you say? – a quarter of a mile from the end of Deep Lane? That means our killer had to tote the poor woman not a mile and a half, but a mile and three-quarters ... So what are we left with? A journey of close on two miles with an eight-stone burden across a dangerous stretch of marshland where one false step could mean death in a quagmire. Not very likely, is it?'

'No, but it's possible.'

'All right, it's possible' – Lubbock waved a dismissive hand – 'but have you given any thought to a more feasible solution?'

'Such as?'

'Such as more than one person being involved. If two people had carried the body to Blacknock, the task would have been much easier. And what about three? Or even more than that. Suppose there'd been a whole relay team of carriers ready and waiting, spread out across the marsh. Now correct me if I'm wrong, but it would have been a simple job, wouldn't it, to pass the body from one to another?'

Tench pulled in to the side of the road and stopped the car. 'You're surely not suggesting there was some kind of conspiracy that involved half the population of Medford?'

'Not half the population, laddie, no,' Lubbock said. 'Just a small group. A small group of people who know the tracks that wind across the marsh, use them every day to carry heavy loads, and who are, moreover, the most notoriously tight-lipped clique in the village.'

'So we're back to the cockle women, are we?' said Tench.

'And why not?' Lubbock filled his pipe. 'Ponder it, laddie. From what I've heard of this Surly Sarah and her muscular companions, they're as close a knit group as you're likely to meet anywhere in Norfolk, and they're as tight-lipped as clams. They fit the Neapolitan omerta to a T. So if I were you, I'd scrap that precious theory of yours and start again from scratch. Stir up the mud and scratch for some cockles. They do have to open their shells from time to time, even if it's only to blow their spit-holes.'

*

Once in Medford he turned the case on its side. 'Yes,' he said, 'it's hers.'

'How can you tell?'

'The stitching's worked loose.' He ran a finger along the edge. 'I noticed it when I roped it on the back of the Morgan. Told her one day it was bound to split apart. Yes, it's hers all right.'

'What about the clothes?'

Lubbock picked out a blouse and spread it on the table. 'She was certainly wearing this. I remember the rose embroidered on the front. It's a Damask. I used to grow them in Norwich . . . Take a bit of advice from an old-stager, laddie. When you get all those statements in that you're collecting, set aside those from the Surly Sarahs and go through them all with a magnifying glass. You never know what you might find between the lines. Remember what I said about cultivating roses. This just might be an omen. Who can possibly tell?'

6

At one time Mike Tench would have accepted such advice without any question, but five years of working side by side with Lubbock had taught him to be cautious. He'd realized early on that there were times when his old Chief, quite unaccountably, got a bee in his bonnet and, to mix the metaphors, charged off at random in search of wild geese. This, he was quite convinced, was one such occasion. The thought of Sarah Clogston, Yelda Thober and all the rest of the cockle women spread out across Medford marsh like a relay team seemed to him a far less feasible prospect than one desperate man with a sack on his shoulder treading a moonlit path to Blacknock.

No. Geese, he decided, were not on his menu that Friday afternoon. To mix the metaphors again, he had other fish to fry.

He drove straight back to Norwich and called in the various members of his team.

'So what have we got?' he said.

'Nothing on the medallion, I'm afraid, sir,' said Spurgeon. 'There are five shops that sell them in Swaffham, but only two, the jewellers, stock them in gold, and neither's sold any in the last three weeks.'

Tench turned to Rayner. 'What about the man and woman who were trying to buy sacks? Any better luck with them?'

'Not much, sir,' said Rayner. 'I tracked them so far and then lost the trail. They called at Swans Farm – that's on the Warham side of Medford – and the farmer there told them the best place to go was the flour mill at Wells. The mill manager remembered them. Said he sold them a couple of twenty-stone sacks, but of course he never bothered to ask them their names or where they were from. He did say the man had a beard and moustache and was driving a red sports car, but that was all he could tell me. The mill's on the quay, and he couldn't say which road they took out of Wells.'

'So we're left with a nameless man and an equally nameless woman driving away from Wells with two sacks in a car to nowhere in particular.'

'Looks like it, sir, yes.'

'It doesn't just look like it, George, it's a fact. We're not getting very far ... Right, your turn, Sue. What about those lights on the marsh? You spoke to Burcham?'

'Yes, sir.'

'You don't sound very cheerful,'

'No, sir, I'm not.'

'Don't tell me they've disappeared.'

'Not exactly, sir, no, but I wouldn't like to swear that Mr Burcham ever saw them.'

'You mean he's not a reliable witness? Is that it?'

'I think he only tells people what he knows they want to hear.'

'In other words he's a fantasist.'

'In a charming sort of way, sir, yes, I suppose so.'

'That's a comforting thought. No lights on the marsh. We seem to be making phenomenal progress.' Tench turned a bleak pair of eyes towards Ellison. 'And what about the railway delivery van? Go on. Tell me the postman was fantasizing too, and it never existed.'

'Oh, it existed all right, sir,' said Ellison. 'It delivered the bike we found in Swallownest Wood. Bought from Wensum Cycles here in St Giles Street. Consigned to an Eleanor Welsby at Phoenix Mill Cottage.'

'Eleanor Welsby?'

'Yes, sir. That's the name she gave at the cycle shop. Seems she arrived there at midday on Wednesday, said she needed a bicycle and paid the man in cash.'

'Did she say where she'd come from?'

'Yes, sir. Spun him some yarn about being a private inquiry agent working for a firm in Chelmsford. Said she'd driven up from there, but had had to leave her car at Swainsthorpe for repairs. Told him her job was to track down some woman who'd walked out on her husband and left him with two small children to care for ... Reckon it's just another load of the same old guff, sir. Whoever she is, she's got a strong imagination.'

Gregg was standing beside him. 'I wouldn't be too sure about that, Bob,' he said.

'Why not?' Tench looked up at him sharply. 'Something at Thetford?'

'Something, sir,' said Gregg. 'I'm not sure what it means, but there could be a link.'

'Well, let's hope it's the link we've been missing . . . Go on.'

Gregg pulled out his notebook. 'It was like this, sir,' he said. 'I searched the cottage at Thetford, but as far as I could tell there was nothing of hers there. Whatever she'd brought with her she'd taken away. Seemed to me she'd decided to clear out for good.'

'But she'd paid a month's rent.'

'Yes, sir, that's true, but there wasn't any sign that she'd been there at all.'

'What about the key? Mrs Dracopoli said she gave her a key.'

'Apparently, sir, she handed it back before she left on the Tuesday. Said she'd collect it when she returned . . . But I don't think she ever intended to return, except as a last resort.'

'Meaning what exactly?'

'The cottage was just a staging post, a bolt-hole if you like. It was somewhere to hide out if things went wrong.'

'Fair enough, but what things?'

'She turned up at Cley with a suitcase,' said Gregg, 'but it was only a small one. Not the sort of thing to take if you'd made up your mind to leave home for a month. There had to be another one somewhere, and there was. It was in the left-luggage office at Thetford station. Not a case, but a holdall. I brought it back with me.'

'Where is it?'

'Labelled and locked up, sir, with the rest of the evidence.'

'So? What was in it?'

'A load of women's undies, some face cream, talc and half a dozen lipsticks.'

'Nothing else?'

'A writing case,' Gregg said, 'and these.' He opened his notebook. 'This cutting from the *EDP* about the cottage at Blakeney, and this sheet from a letter. It's a middle sheet, so there isn't an address and there isn't a signature, but a part of it seems to confirm what Bob was saying. It's the bit that's been underlined. I think, sir, you'd better read it.'

Tench frowned at the sheet of white paper. Then he began to read. ' "By the way, I saw Frankie in Blakeney today . . ." '

He paused and looked up. 'There are three exclamation marks after that, and Frankie's spelt the girl's way. ". . . Where? Where d'you think? Walking along the quay right under my window. I tried to wrench it open to call, but it was jammed. So I shot downstairs and out through the lobby, but by that time F had gone. Still, thought you'd like to know. I'll bet that came as a surprise." There's another couple of exclamation marks after that, and then . . .' He ran his eye down the sheet.

'That's the lot, sir,' said Gregg, 'but it's underlined in a different sort of ink, so she must have done it. And she brought it with her, so it must have been important. Looks like she may have been searching for a woman, just as Bob said. Someone called Frankie.'

181

'Frankie. Short for Frances.' Tench looked around. 'Anyone come across a woman called Frances?'

They all looked at one another. Nobody answered.

'Hang on a minute, sir,' said Ellison. 'Before we get too involved, there is something else.'

'Something you haven't told us?'

'Yes, sir.'

'What is it?'

'I rang the police at Chelmsford,' Ellison said. 'They've got three inquiry agents registered in the town. I checked with them all. Only one employs a woman, and she's very much alive. She answered the phone.'

7

It was unusual for McKenzie to say nothing at all. He seemed lost in a world of pitchforks and cow dung, but now, at last, he rediscovered his voice. 'That,' he said, 'doesn't alter what's in the letter. She could still have been searching for this woman called Frankie.'

Tench nodded. 'I'm with Mac. This is the first clue we've had that points to a motive. We've got to follow it up.' He peered at the letter. 'Looks to me like a womanly hand. . . . Andy!'

'Yes, sir,' said Gregg.

'Take this over to the lab right away. Have it photographed and dusted for prints, and get a copy to Dave Ransome. Tell him we need it reproduced in tomorrow's *EDP*. Front page if possible. And couple it with an appeal for the writer to come forward. We've got to find out who sent it and fast.' He looked at his watch. 'It's now 3.45 . . . Bob!'

'Sir,' said Ellison.

'Ring Sergeant Hellyer at the incident room at Medford. Ask him to collect all the statements he's received and bring them back here right away. And tell Lock to bring the rest in as soon as they're available. Once the first batch arrives, I want everyone to check them. If this woman of ours was searching for a Frankie or Frances, then there must be someone of that name in Medford . . . And get hold of Constable Bates as well. He knows everyone in the village. He might be able to save us a lot of hard graft . . . Right?'

'Right, sir.'

Tench looked around. 'Has anyone anything else to suggest?'

'Yes, I have,' McKenzie said. 'I've been thinking about that bag of shells that was found at Grice's cottage. If it didn't belong to Danny Sprot, then

182

who did it belong to? According to Bates, Grice wasn't a collector. So who left it there?'

'Presumably,' said Tench, 'whoever broke in and killed him.'

'You mean the murderer must have panicked for some reason and dropped it?'

'Looks that way, yes. You saw the shells, Mac. They were scattered across the floor ... The bag's already been dusted. We're waiting to see if the lab can come up with some prints.'

'But suppose,' said McKenzie, 'it didn't happen like that. Suppose they weren't dropped by accident. Suppose they were left there on purpose ... to point a finger at Danny Sprot.'

'Go on, Mac,' said Tench.

'Well, he's the obvious candidate for whipping-boy, isn't he? If ever there was a fall guy, Danny fits the bill. He's big and strong, he's simple, he can't speak up and defend himself. Face the lad with a charge of murder and, without some peculiar stroke of luck, he'll find himself swinging at the end of a rope for something he didn't do.'

'Yes, it's possible of course. They could well have been planted ...'

Tench was going to say more, but McKenzie pressed on. 'Then let's assume they were. If we can only get a line on who scattered those shells, that'll give us the link – the one vital link – we've been struggling to find ... Let's use a bit of logic. This is somebody local, who knows Danny Sprot and knows about the shells he collects at the farm. And it's probably someone who'd be glad to see the back of him; someone who thinks he's an irresponsible nuisance, and dangerous with it.'

Tench narrowed his eyes. 'Are you thinking what I am?'

'If you're thinking of Lady Wellbridge' – McKenzie gave a shrug – 'then for God's sake why not? She's a calculating bitch, and it wouldn't exactly be falsifying evidence to say she's got it in for Danny Sprot, would it?'

'No, it wouldn't' – Tench frowned – 'but come on, Mac, face the facts. We're dealing with murder, three separate murders, all of them needing some physical strength. We're dealing with a body carried a mile and a half across the marsh and the sands as far as Blacknock. Don't tell me Deirdre Wellbridge has the strength to do either.'

'I'm not saying she has, but let's face some more facts. If we believe what's in that letter, then this Eleanor Welsby – or whatever her real name happens to be – was searching for a woman. I think it'd be fair to say that Deirdre Wellbridge is a woman.'

'But she was looking for a woman called Frances, not Deirdre.'

'And how do we know Lady Wellbridge isn't Frances? We don't. Her name could be Deirdre Frances Wellbridge. We know nothing much about her. It's possible after all that she may have walked out on a previous husband. She might very well be the woman in the case.'

'But she still couldn't have committed the murders, Mac, could she? Come on now. Admit it.'

'No, maybe not' – McKenzie wasn't to be deflected – 'but you're leaving another fact out of account. The fact that she's not alone. She's got a man in her life. And I'd say that raises a hell of a lot of questions. Like what might have happened if someone was sent to find her.'

'You're suggesting . . .?'

'I'm not suggesting anything,' McKenzie said, 'but I think it's about time we took another look at our lovable Deirdre and this chap called Wellbridge who says he's her husband. It's true they don't seem to be all that close. It's hard to imagine him committing a murder to save her from prying eyes, but I've seen too many suspects fake a relationship to trust what I see. Perhaps the time's come when we should probe a bit deeper. I'd like to know more about Mr and Mrs Wellbridge.'

Tench thought for a moment. 'All right, Mac,' he said. 'I'm not convinced about this. I still think it's a long shot. But let's go and see them. It can't do any harm.'

8

Wellbridge was checking a consignment of timber. He seemed quite unconcerned. 'Gentlemen,' he said. 'Good to see you again. You've some news about the break-in?'

'Not as such,' said Tench. 'We feel we need a little more background information.'

'You think it'll help?'

'We believe it may, sir.'

'Then you'd better come upstairs.' He steered them towards the office. 'Can I offer you a drink?' he asked, once they were seated.

'Not at the moment, sir,' said Tench, 'but thank you all the same.'

'You haven't found the prayer-wheel?'

'I'm afraid not, sir, but we seem to be working very much in the dark. We think you may be able to offer some assistance.'

'Of course. If I can.' Wellbridge appeared to be very much at ease. 'What would you like to know?'

'Well, sir . . .' Tench paused. 'We're still a bit troubled by the presence in Medford of this woman you say you met on the ship from Bombay. You and your wife were on the way home from India. What were you doing out there?'

'Working for the IFS, Chief Inspector. The Indian Forest Service.'

'And what was your job?'

'I was employed by the United Provinces Forest Department. The Forest Research Institute's up at Dehra Dun. My patch was some twenty-five miles to the north in the Himalayan foothills. A place called Shahkot. I was responsible for the cutting and marketing of timber.'

'And how long had you worked there?'

'Roughly five years. Before that I was in Burma.'

'You were happy there? At Shahkot?'

'Reasonably so.'

'Then why did you leave?'

'When I signed up, India was still part of the Raj. Before I left, the United Provinces was Uttar Pradesh. Perhaps I needn't say more.'

'The service was being Indianized?'

'Progressively, yes.'

'So you decided to come home,' McKenzie said, 'and use your expertise to set up a timber business.'

'It seemed the sensible thing to do.'

'Then why did you choose to set up shop in Holt?'

Wellbridge seemed amused. 'Why not?' he said.

'Wouldn't it have been more sensible to choose a part of the county that had plenty of timber? Thetford for instance.'

'As I was feeling at the time, Sergeant, no. I'd lived for years hemmed in by forests and mountains. I needed flatlands and space. And there happened to be a timber yard for sale here at Holt. Does that answer your question?'

'I suppose it's as good a reason as any,' McKenzie said.

'Believe me, Sergeant, it is. You don't suffer from claustrophobia?'

'Not as far as I know, sir.'

'No, you wouldn't here in Norfolk, but there are places, Sergeant, where it grows on you slowly, day by day, till all you want to do is get to work with an axe.'

'Yet you chose to rent a house,' said Tench, 'that's hemmed in by trees.'

Wellbridge shrugged. 'We needed to find a place at short notice, and Sparrow Hill was vacant. It's a temporary base. Once the business is established we don't intend to stay there.'

Tench was cautious. 'Would I be right, sir, in thinking that your wife made the choice?'

'Right, Chief Inspector, and also wrong. She wasn't my wife then, but yes, she found it. At the end of November. We were married a fortnight later.'

'Would you care to tell us where, sir?'

'I can't see why not. Norwich Register Office. It's easy to check.'

McKenzie wasn't one for beating round the bush. 'Was she married before you met her?'

Wellbridge stared at him. 'What on earth gave you that idea?'

185

'Just something we heard, sir,' said Tench.

'Then whoever told you, Chief Inspector, must have been under some strange delusion. No, of course she wasn't. Look up the marriage certificate if you like. You'll find her name and condition. Deirdre Thompson, Spinster. It's there in black and white.'

'Well, that's that,' said Tench, once they were outside. 'He doesn't sound to me like a man with a deadly secret to hide.'

McKenzie lit a cigarette and started up the car. 'Let's go and taunt the wicked witch,' he suggested. 'She's got a short fuse. If only we can strike the right sort of spark, she might blow her top.'

9

She stood framed in the doorway wearing a flower-printed cotton shirt and red tapered trousers. 'Oh, it's you again,' she said. 'You don't need to tell me. You've arrested that moron and now you've let him go.'

Tench looked up at her. 'I'm afraid we had no alternative, Mrs Wellbridge.'

'Typical!' She was scathing. 'Aren't the police wonderful! Why was there no alternative?'

'We've no evidence against him.'

'You've mine. That's enough. What more do you need?'

'We need facts, ma'am.' McKenzie had a different approach in mind. His tone was needle-sharp. 'You accused Danny Sprot, but accusations like that won't stand up in a court of law. Any defence counsel with a shred of ability could make them sound ridiculous. He'd say you were merely prejudiced against his client without due cause.'

Her lips tightened. 'Well, thank you, Sergeant,' she said, 'for those few kind words. I suppose you think a broken window and a vandalized room isn't cause enough. And don't tell me they're not facts because the constable saw them.'

'He did, ma'am, yes, but he didn't see Danny Sprot commit the offence and neither did you. The room and the window have both been checked for fingerprints. We have, of course, found yours and those of your husband, but we haven't found Danny's. We've searched his possessions, what few there are, without any result. There's no evidence at all to link him with the crime. We've no reason to hold him ... Now may we come in?'

She raked him with a glance. 'Why?' she said.

186

'We've another little matter we'd like to discuss.'

'What little matter? Are you going to accuse us of wrecking our own home?'

'Not yet,' McKenzie said.

'I think you'd better leave.' She made a move to close the door. 'If you've anything more to ask, then go and see my husband.'

McKenzie, on occasion, could produce a wolfish smile. 'There is another option,' he said. 'We could charge you with obstruction. The choice is yours, ma'am. You can answer our questions here or in Norwich. Which is it to be?'

She looked towards Tench, but he simply stared back. 'Oh, I suppose you'd better come in,' she said.

She showed them not into the study, but a room at the front. It had a leather settee and two leather armchairs, but she pointedly ignored them. 'What d'you want?' she said. 'I haven't much time.'

McKenzie's response was equally pointed. He looked around, chose the settee and sat down. 'Take a seat, ma'am,' he said. 'Make yourself at home.'

'Now look . . .!'

'Sit down, Mrs Wellbridge.' Tench spoke quietly, but his words carried with them an undeniable authority.

She sat down, with some reluctance.

Tench nodded at McKenzie. 'Ask away, Sergeant.'

McKenzie took his time. 'Where did you first meet your husband, Mrs Wellbridge?'

She sighed. 'I met him on the boat coming home from India.'

'You'd never seen him before?'

'No, of course I hadn't. What's all this about?'

'How long had you been out there?'

'Too long,' she said.

'What d'you mean by that?'

'Simply that I'd had enough of the place. My father was an army colonel. Apart from schooling in England I'd lived there all my life. When the Indians took over, he chose to stay there. I didn't.'

'He was a colonel. What regiment?'

'The Twelfth Royal Gurkhas.'

'Where were they stationed?'

'A God-forsaken place called Abbottabad, and after that at Cawnpore. Another dead-alive hole.'

McKenzie paused. 'How old are you?'

Her lips tightened again. 'That's no business of yours.'

'How old are you, Mrs Wellbridge?' It was Tench who spoke this time.

'If you must know, twenty-two.'

'Where were you married?' McKenzie said. 'Abbottabad or Cawnpore?'

187

She seemed bewildered by the question. 'We were married in Norwich after we got back. We only met on the boat.'

McKenzie was unperturbed. 'I wasn't thinking about your marriage to Mr Wellbridge, ma'am.'

She glowered. 'Then just what the hell were you thinking about?'

'The one before that.'

'There wasn't one before that. What gave you that idea?'

'Simply some information we received, ma'am,' said Tench.

'Then whoever said so was talking about somebody else.' She walked across to the door. 'You should check your facts, Inspector, before you make wild allegations. Your informant was clearly a quite unreliable sort of person . . . Now will you please leave. You're wasting my time and I have to go out.'

'One more question,' McKenzie said. 'Have you another Christian name besides Deirdre?'

'No,' she said, 'I haven't. It's quite obvious you're mixing me up with someone else.'

'Well?' said Tench as they drove away between the trees.

'She's lying.' McKenzie was in no frame of mind to offer a compromise. 'What sort of a car did that courting couple say was parked by the marsh?'

'A dark-coloured saloon.'

'Did you make a note of hers?'

'Yes, it's a saloon, a black Sunbeam-Talbot, but that doesn't mean it was used to dump a body. There must be thousands of black saloon cars in Norfolk. Not to mention blue ones.'

McKenzie was unconvinced. 'She's still lying,' he said.

10

It was half-past six when they got back to Norwich.

Tench's phone was ringing and he grabbed the receiver. The voice was Ted Merrick's. He was speaking from the lab.

'Been trying to get hold of you, sir,' he said.

'You've got some results?'

'Yes, sir. A few. No luck on the paper bag, I'm afraid. We couldn't find any prints. But we did discover some hairs in the sack. They match those of the woman found on Blacknock . . . I hope that helps.'

'Yes, it does.' Tench breathed his relief. 'It's a link in the chain. Thanks a lot, Ted. We seem to be making a bit of progress at last.'

'There's more,' said Merrick. 'The jute was from Faridpur, processed at the Kinnison Mills near Calcutta, and their importers are Simpson, Brand and Ghosh of Dockside Street, Rotherhithe. The wholesalers for East Anglia are Harmon Devenish and Sons of Ipswich. They sell to retailers all over Norfolk, so you'll have to get in touch with them for a list.'

'Fine,' said Tench, but Merrick hadn't finished.

'There's something else, sir,' he said. 'Come down and take a look. I think you'll find it even more interesting.'

There were three screens side by side, each with a blown-up photograph.

'Three identical thumbprints, sir,' Merrick explained. 'The one on the left was taken from the body found on Blacknock ... The middle one's from Blakeney, Phoenix Mill Cottage ...'

'And the third?'

'From the break-in at Sparrow Hill House. That's the clearest of the lot. It was found on a splinter of glass from the window.'

Tench peered at the screens. 'You're sure they're identical?'

'Positive, sir.'

There was silence. McKenzie was the first one to speak. 'That's all we need,' he said. 'D'you want me to bring her in?'

'No, Mac. Hold your horses.' Tench raised a hand. He seemed reluctant to tear his gaze from the screens. When he turned, it was slowly. 'No,' he said, 'not yet. Before we do that, I think I'd like to hear what Mr Wellbridge has to say.'

VIII
THE GAME

Sine periculo friget lusus
Without danger the game grows cold

Latin proverb

1

Deirdre Wellbridge's car had gone from the front of Sparrow Hill House, but her husband's long, white Chrysler convertible was standing on the drive. He opened the door.

'Trouble, gentlemen?' he said, looking at each of them in turn.

'There's something of a problem, sir.' Tench was the one to speak. 'Can we come in and talk?'

'Why not?' Wellbridge seemed totally at ease. He stood aside to let them pass and showed them into the study at the back. 'Deirdre told me you'd called,' he said. 'If the problem's this ridiculous tale about a marriage in India, I'm afraid she's not here. She's spending the night in Wymondham, but I can find you a copy of our own marriage lines.'

Tench shook his head. 'No, sir, it isn't that. We're ready to accept that we may have been misinformed about the marriage, but we do have to check the information we receive.'

'Of course, and you're satisfied?'

'Absolutely, sir. This is something quite different. It seems that we're facing a conflict of evidence.'

'Reliable evidence this time, I hope.'

'Yours, sir,' said Tench, 'and that provided by the lab.'

Wellbridge frowned. 'Then there's clearly some misunderstanding, Chief Inspector. Perhaps you'd better take a seat and explain.'

He pulled out a chair from the table. McKenzie took an armchair and Tench the settee.

'You told Constable Harris that on Wednesday morning you left here at eight o'clock and drove into Holt.'

'That's correct, Chief Inspector.'

'And that when you left, everything here was normal.'

'Perfectly normal.'

'But someone, in the course of the morning, broke into the house through the kitchen window and vandalized this room.'

'They must have done, yes.'

'And at that time the woman you identified as Miriam – the one you say you met on the ship from Bombay – was already dead. She'd been found on the sands at Medford twenty-four hours before.'

'So you told me, Chief Inspector.'

'And we agreed that, in consequence, she couldn't have been responsible for the break-in.'

Wellbridge nodded. 'I also said, if you remember, that I never thought she was.'

'Yes, sir, that's true, but evidence we've now received from the lab seems to tell a different tale.'

'It does?'

'I'm afraid so.'

'And what would this evidence be, Chief Inspector?'

'A thumbprint, Mr Wellbridge. The dead woman's thumbprint. Found on glass from the kitchen window. It proves that she was here.'

'But she couldn't have been here on Wednesday. You said so yourself.'

'No, sir, she couldn't. That's what we find puzzling. But she must have been here at some time or other shortly before she died.'

'Well, if she was, Chief Inspector, it wasn't with my knowledge.' Wellbridge shook his head. 'Of course, it could have been while Deirdre was at Lynn and I was out at work. The house would have been empty for most of the day ... You say this thumbprint was found on the broken glass?'

'A piece of it, yes, sir.'

'But that doesn't prove that she broke the glass, does it? She could have been outside, trying to look in, and put her hand on the window.'

'She could have been, yes, but there's still another question: just why was she trying to look inside? What did she hope to see?'

There was a pause.

'Perhaps ... it was the prayer-wheel,' Wellbridge said.

Tench frowned at him. 'But why? You said it was worth next to nothing.'

'Yes, and that was true. It was, in itself.'

McKenzie leaned forward. 'There's more to it than that, isn't there?' he said. 'Something you haven't told us.'

Wellbridge tapped the table. For the first time he seemed uncertain what to say.

'Is there something else?' Tench repeated the question.

'There may perhaps be a possible explanation.'

'Then why didn't you tell us before?' McKenzie said.

Wellbridge shifted in his chair. 'Simply because it was difficult to believe ... I haven't mentioned it to anyone.'

'Not even Deirdre?'

'Deirdre least of all. I didn't want her to think we might be in any danger ...'

He faltered. The room was quiet.

'Go on, sir,' said Tench.

Wellbridge pushed himself up. He walked across to the French windows and stood there a moment, his hand on the glass, staring out at the unkempt lawn and the conifers. Then he turned to face them.

'Have you ever heard of the Great Game?' he said.

194

2

He didn't wait for an answer. 'No, you haven't,' he said, 'so let me try to explain. Let's go back a hundred years. At that time the Russians were pushing their armies closer and closer to the boundaries of India, and one by one the caravan towns on the old Silk Road fell into their hands: first of all Tashkent, then Samarkand and Bokhara, and finally Khiva. At the beginning of the nineteenth century the Russian and Indian frontiers were two thousand miles apart. By 1900 that distance had shrunk in one region, the Pamir, to less than twenty.

'The Russians always assured us they had no designs on India, but there were many who feared this progressive advance was part of a long-cherished plan to conquer the whole of Central Asia and then seize British India, the richest of all prizes. The Great Game, as it was called, was the British response: an attempt to thwart the Russian plans by sending out secret agents from India, whose job was to find out what their intentions were and to spike the next move.'

He moved away from the windows and sat down again at the table. 'Just after the turn of the new century,' he said, 'it seemed that the Game was over. We signed a treaty with the Russians fixing the boundaries once and for all, but then, ten years later, came the Russian Revolution and with it came Lenin. He set his sights on India, saying quite openly that he intended to liberate it from the British and turn it into a Soviet Marxist state. So the Game began again.

'After Lenin came Stalin, who made no secret of the fact that he cherished the same ambition, and it was only Hitler's invasion of Russia that made him an ally and ended whatever plans he may have had . . . Then just after the war we left India for good.'

'And that was the end of your great little game' – McKenzie had never been just a passive listener – 'so what's all this about?'

Wellbridge measured him with a glance. 'It's about how things change, Sergeant, and how they still remain the same. Someone once said that the Game would only be finished when everyone was dead. Till then it would go on . . . Look at what's happened in the last few years. The Iron Curtain, the Cold War, the Berlin blockade, the conflict in Korea, and now this creeping invasion of Tibet by the Chinese communists. The old rivalries are still there. The Great Game may nowadays take a different form, but believe me, gentlemen, it still goes on, and there are still men in India – expatriates who chose like me to stay on – who recognize the threat and cherish a constantly teasing desire to do something about it . . . Men like Alec Dainton.'

'Dainton?' Tench frowned.

McKenzie was less patient. 'And who the devil was he?'

'Just a friend of mine,' Wellbridge said. 'You wouldn't know him. I used to drink with him in one of the bars at Mussoorie. He was the one who told me about the Great Game. He was an officer in the Gurkhas who'd retired to a bungalow up in the hills. Perhaps I'd better explain a bit further ... The Forest Research Institute at Dehra Dun lies in the Siwalik Hills, some two thousand feet above the Ganges plain. Beyond there the land rises steeply, four thousand feet in less than twenty miles to the hill station of Mussoorie. Shahkot, where I worked, is another thousand feet above that. You approach it by a track, and at the top of the ridge the land drops into a thickly forested valley with a view to the great ice wall, the snow peaks of the Himalayas. I lived there in the Rest House, a wooden bungalow hidden in the trees beyond a sawmill.'

He looked up at them. 'To you, living here on the flatlands of Norfolk, such a place must seem apocryphal, the very stuff of dreams, but to me it was familiar, something seen every day ... Two or three times a week I used to make my way down the track to Mussoorie, and it was there, in the Savoy Hotel bar, that I first met Dainton. Over the years we became friends and drinking companions. He must have been, by then, in his early fifties, and I gathered, from the hints he dropped from time to time, that he'd been mixed up in the Game. He never told me exactly what part he'd played, but one evening there was something about him that was different. An air of suppressed excitement.

'"I'm going on a little expedition, Geoff," he said. I asked him where, but he wouldn't say. "I've had word from the north," he said. "Someone's found Peter's will." Well, of course, I hadn't any idea what he meant, and I told him so. "Peter the Great," he said. "He was the first of the Russians to turn his eyes towards India. Sent his troops to seize Khiva, but never got any further. He died a couple of hundred years ago, but ever since then there've been rumours about his will. No one's ever seen it, but tales about it still persist. It's supposed to contain an order to his heirs and successors to follow Russia's destiny and dominate the world. First Constantinople and after that, India. Think of its propaganda value to the Soviets ... Well, now it's been found. I know where it is."

'I asked him again, "Where?" "Beyond the passes," he said. Beyond the Himalayan passes was Tibet, and beyond that again, Russia ... So who was going with him? "No one," he said. I told him he was utterly, irredeemably crazy, but he wasn't in a mood to listen. "It mustn't fall into Russian hands," he said, "and I'm the only one left who still knows the tracks."

'I did my best to dissuade him, but he'd made his decision.

'The next evening he wasn't in his place at the Savoy.

'I didn't see him again for another six months.'

3

Tench shifted in his chair. He glanced at McKenzie and then back at Wellbridge. 'I hope, sir,' he said, 'that this has some faint connection with the break-in.'

'I hope it has more than that, Chief Inspector.' Wellbridge was deadly serious. 'Otherwise I'm wasting both your time and mine.'

'Then what is the connection?'

'I think it could be the prayer-wheel. As I said, Chief Inspector, I didn't see Dainton again for six months. Then, the night before I left Shahkot for Bombay, something very strange happened. I was ready to start next morning on the long journey home. My trunk was packed, and the coolies had been ordered to take it down the hill before the sun came up. I was reading by the light of a kerosene lamp, making a last-minute check on the accounts, when I heard a low voice call out "Sahib" from the darkness.

'The evening was warm and the doors were still open. Two hillmen were standing on the verandah. They'd set down a litter. On it lay a third man.

'I fetched the lamp and looked down. He was filthy, bearded, and wrapped in a kind of horse-blanket cloak. One hand clutched the wooden beads of a rosary, the other a prayer-wheel.

'The hillmen did their best in gestures to explain. He was a Holy One, maybe from over the snows. They'd found him in the forest, many miles away.

'I got them to carry the litter inside, and then paid them off with a handful of coins. Once they'd gone I knelt down and took a closer look.'

'Your friend Dainton?' McKenzie said.

Wellbridge seemed suddenly restless. He got up from his chair and once again wandered across to the window. He stood for a moment with his hands in his pockets, then he turned and nodded. 'I couldn't be sure at first. The man was dead, that was obvious. He'd probably already been dead when they'd found him. He was thin as a lath, his skin was like parchment, and his dark beard was wild and covered most of his face, but there was something about the cast of his features that disturbed me. With an effort I loosened his fingers from the beads. Then I took them to the table and counted them under the light of the lamp. There were exactly a hundred . . . That was when I knew.'

He pulled out his chair and sat down. 'You see, Chief Inspector, one of the things he'd told me about the Great Game was that the agents despatched from Dehra Dun often travelled disguised as Buddhist pilgrims

197

visiting the holy sites on the old Silk Road. They carried with them, as Buddhist pilgrims always did, a rosary of beads and a prayer-wheel, but the rosary they carried was one with a difference. It had a hundred beads, not the hundred and eight of Buddhist tradition. These men, pundits they were called, were trained to take a pace of a certain length, and at every hundredth pace they slipped a single bead. That meant they could keep a record of the distance they walked ... The man on the litter, strangely familiar but terribly changed, had to be Dainton.'

'So what did you do?' said Tench.

'I unlocked the trunk and stuffed the rosary and the prayer-wheel inside. After that I waited a couple of hours. Then I carried him out into the forest and left him there. Next morning, as arranged, I went down the hill. A week later I boarded the ship in Bombay. It wasn't until a couple of days into the voyage that I examined the prayer-wheel. Inside the copper drum there was normally a roll of paper printed with mantras – Buddhist incantations – but not in this one. Instead there was a folded sheet of parchment covered with what I could only think was Cyrillic script. I put it back in the drum, took the prayer-wheel to the purser and had it locked in the ship's safe. Perhaps it was a good thing I did, because a couple of days later my cabin was burgled.'

Wellbridge gave a shrug. 'At that time I didn't connect it with the prayer-wheel. The only thing that had been stolen was a small amount of money, and other passengers on the same deck had suffered the same treatment. I just dismissed it as a case of petty theft by one of the ship's crew ... I didn't really suspect anything when this woman, Miriam, asked if she could share my table at dinner. I'd no reason to do so. It was only when Constable Harris showed me her picture and I realized she'd been in Medford that I began to have second thoughts.

'What happened after that seemed to confirm all my worst suspicions. First there was the break-in.' He crossed to the desk, the darkest corner of the room, and picked up an object reared against the wall. 'This,' he said, 'is something of a treasured possession. At the time of the break-in, it was hanging on the wall. I removed it before the constable arrived. It didn't seem safe to leave it there with a broken window in the house.' He held it out between his hands. 'It's a hunting rifle, a .275, accurate at up to three hundred yards. Don't worry, Chief Inspector, I've paid for a licence. It belonged to Jim Corbett, the man who killed man-eating tigers in the Kumaon. They called him the Sherlock Holmes of the forests. He helped to train us, and made me a gift of it before I left ... Well, as I said, it was hanging on the wall for anyone to see, but whoever broke in didn't even touch it. Our passports were in a drawer. They weren't taken either, nor was the money in the kitchen or Deirdre's jewellery in her bedroom. The only thing that was missing was that God-damned prayer-wheel ... And now you tell me this woman's thumbprint's been found on the window.'

'You're suggesting, sir,' said Tench, 'that she followed you all the way from India?'

'At the moment, Chief Inspector, I find it hard to conceive of any other explanation.'

'You think she may have been some kind of Russian agent?' Tench's tone of voice made it clear that he found this hard to believe.

'It's possible. All the signs seem to point to the fact that someone was determined to recover the prayer-wheel.'

'Then how d'you explain the fact that she was murdered?' McKenzie asked.

Wellbridge threw out his hands. 'There are dissidents in Russia, Sergeant. People who must have known that the discovery of Peter's will would be a propaganda coup for the Soviet Union.'

Tench leaned back in his chair. 'You suspected this when we talked to you at Holt. Why didn't you mention it then?'

'As I said, Chief Inspector, it was difficult to believe. I was still finding it hard to convince myself. Then you told me about the thumbprint.'

'You realize what you're saying, sir? If all this is true, it means that these murders aren't just a local business. The ramifications are international.'

Wellbridge replaced the rifle. 'I'm very much afraid, Chief Inspector,' he said, 'that that may be true. It appears this woman was dead before the break-in occurred. I can only think she traced me here to Sparrow Hill House, came to take a look and placed her hand on the window. But someone else was watching her, and he was the one who killed her. Then later he broke in here for himself and made off with the prayer-wheel. Whether you'll ever find him I wouldn't like to say. He could well be back in Russia by now.'

'But that doesn't explain the two subsequent murders,' McKenzie said.

'No, but let me finish, Sergeant.' Wellbridge raised a hand. 'I don't know exactly how the woman died – my only source of information in that respect has been newspaper reports – but none of them has mentioned a broken neck, which appears to have been the fate of the two later victims. If it's true that two different methods were used, then perhaps there were two different murderers. That's a matter of logic . . . My own suspicion, for what it may be worth, is that there were two men deputed to track her down. In other words, the one who killed her had an accomplice. The job of the first was to seize the contents of the prayer-wheel and get them out of the country as fast as possible. The other had instructions to cover up the tracks . . . It's only a suggestion, gentlemen, but perhaps it's one you might well consider. Three people have died and the prayer-wheel's disappeared. I'm merely trying to make sense of a series of happenings that otherwise leave me baffled. I've thought about them a lot in the last few days, and I can't explain them in any other way. If you can, I'll be only too happy to hear. It was never my choice to get embroiled in some wild international conspiracy. I've tried to lead a simple, uncomplicated life, and this, to be honest, is something of a nightmare. The sooner the whole business is cleared up, the better . . . And now, if you don't mind' – he pushed aside his chair – 'I must ask you to excuse me. I've an appointment at nine o'clock to meet a buyer in Fakenham.'

Tench made no protest. He seemed, of a sudden, strangely disinclined to take the matter further. 'Well, thank you very much, Mr Wellbridge,' he said. 'No doubt we'll be in touch.'

4

Once outside in the car, McKenzie made his views on Mr Wellbridge very plain. 'That's the biggest load of old rope I've ever stumbled across,' he said. 'Why didn't you bring him in? We could have given him a real grilling.'

'We've no reason to hold him, Mac. We can't charge him with anything.'

'He's lying through his teeth like his dear darling wife.'

'He could be, granted, but as far as the law's concerned he's done nothing wrong. He's just a man who's had his house broken into and vandalized. He's not likely to be making false claims on insurance. He's been robbed of a small memento of no intrinsic value, nothing more than that. He's admitted as much. That's all there is to it.'

'But this yarn about prayer-wheels and wills. It's just a lot of guff.'

'It may be.' Tench pulled out the choke and pressed the starter. The engine stuttered into life. 'The trouble is, Mac, that we don't know enough to say that for sure. And suppose it's true after all. You know what that's going to mean. We can say a swift goodbye to the Blacknock case and everything connected with it. It'll be taken out of our hands, and we'll be overrun by hordes of aliens from the smoke. Special Branch, the Foreign Office, MI5 – they'll all be dipping their fingers in the pie. It'll be worse than being invaded by the Met.'

'And that's the last thing we want to see.'

'It's the last thing the Chief Super wants to see, too.'

'You wouldn't care for a short, sweet spot of advice?'

Tench grinned. 'No I wouldn't, but I've a feeling I'm going to get it.'

'Too right you are . . . Forget the whole thing and get on with the job.'

'We can't, Mac. Suppose there is something in it. Think of the fall-out.'

McKenzie gave a shrug. 'What's a shower of ash? I've survived a lot worse.'

'Nowadays it's likely to be a different kind of ash . . . No, we can't risk it.'

'It's a pity we didn't take a look at those marriage lines.'

'There wouldn't have been any point. If she'd something to hide, she wouldn't have dared to use her full name. We need to see her birth certificate.'

'Well we can't do that till tomorrow, can we? So what's the next move?'

Tench looked at his watch. 'There isn't one. Not tonight. It's quarter-past eight. It'll be nine o'clock when we get back to Norwich, and I've been up and fretting since half-past five. That's enough wear and tear for one day. This child's away home.'

'Then drop me off at the Adam,' McKenzie said. 'This child needs a pint.'

Tench dropped him outside the Adam and Eve, but he didn't go home. He drove straight to headquarters, climbed the stairs to his office and reached for the phone. Five minutes later he was back on the road to Holt.

If, as Mac had said, Wellbridge's tale was just a load of old rope, then the first thing to do was check the strength of that rope, and there was only one way that he might, conceivably, be able to do it.

5

Some three miles out of Norwich he forked off to the right and, reaching the village of Newton St Faith, drew up before a cottage and knocked on the door. It was opened by a tall, gaunt man with a mop of ginger hair. He wore a red shirt, a gaudy yellow tie and a pair of old flannels. 'Come in, Mike,' he said cheerfully. 'Is it coffee, tea or Scotch?'

'Tonight, Lawrence, coffee. I need to stay awake.'

The man looked at him down his nose. 'That sounds ominous,' he said, 'but nil desperandum. Coffee it shall be. Let's go through to the back.'

He led the way into the spacious room that Tench knew all too well from his previous visits: a familiar world of neatness and confusion that was a study, a library, and a place of relaxation all rolled into one. It had a long wall of books, immaculately shelved; two deep armchairs drawn up beside the now-empty grate; a heavy, broad-topped desk by the latticed window, and a typewriter rising like a great black rock from a white sea of paper: the sheets tossed here and there in abandon, bearing no resemblance to the mathematical precision with which Lawrence Bell constructed his plots.

'Make yourself at home,' he said, and disappeared through a door into what Tench knew was an equally spacious kitchen.

Left alone, he ran his finger along the shelves: hundreds of books on Norfolk that seemed to cover every aspect of life in the county: its history, its legends, its buildings, its roads, its trade and its landscape; and the long row of detective stories, first editions, reprints and green-backed Penguins, all with the name of Lawrence Bell, all of them set in some part of Norfolk: *The Mannington Murders, The Gressenhall Affair, The Itteringham Mystery, The Edingthorpe Equation*, and perhaps twenty others to the end of the shelf . . .

It was Lubbock who'd first introduced him to Bell. They'd been lifelong friends from the time when they'd spent their early schooldays together, but while Lubbock had chosen to join the police, Lawrence, the high-flier, the brilliant scholar, had predictably enough won a scholarship to Oxford. With a teaching post at Gresham's, he'd written in whatever spare time he'd had, till the runaway success of his murder mysteries had given him a solid financial independence. It was then that he'd bought the cottage at Newton St Faith, enlarged it by taking in a wilderness of scrub, and shut himself away to concentrate on his own brand of mayhem and murder. After another forty years, he was still tapping out books on his battered old Remington, spelling out the horrors he preferred to imagine, while Lubbock was still probing the messiness of death and seeking him out from time to time to tap his expertise.

'If I need any local information,' he'd once said, 'I always go to Lawrence. He knows more about Norfolk than any man living, and he hasn't often let me down.'

Tench had discovered that for himself. On at least three occasions Lawrence had provided the vital clue that had led him to a killer, but his expertise extended a good deal further than the boundaries of Norfolk. Lubbock had made that clear. 'I don't know whether I ever told you this, Mike,' he'd said, 'but Lawrence was out in India during the First War. While I was wallowing in the mud of the trenches, he was lounging in one of those pillared bungalows soaking up the sun. But he had a job – intelligence – that took him around the country. Wherever British troops were stationed, Lawrence was there at one time or another. He knows a devil of a lot about India, too. That might be worth remembering.'

Which was why, that Friday night, Tench had reached for the phone and asked for a number at Newton St Faith, and why, once they were settled in the deep armchairs, he with his coffee and Lawrence with a Scotch, his first words were, 'Lawrence I need a bit of help.'

Bell raised a couple of quizzical eyebrows. 'Now why was I so sure,' he said, 'that this couldn't be just a friendly social call? It seems the old adage still has a ring of truth. Like father, like son. How is he, by the way, your mentor and torment?'

'Still stumping the shingle with his cherrywood stick and doing his damnedest to solve all my cases.'

'Brimming over with his usual health and omniscience?'

'Too much of both at times.'

'Then confide in me,' Bell said. 'What's this problem that can't be solved even by the wicked old Wizard of Cley?'

Tench sipped at his coffee. 'It's like this, Lawrence. You're the teller of tales, but just for a change I'm going to tell you one. Somewhere in the plot there has to be a flaw. I want you to find it.'

'You're certain there is one?'

'There'd better be. If there isn't . . .'

'You're in something of a pickle . . .?'

'Worse than that. A crisis.'

'As bad as that . . .? Right then, where does the story start?'

'India,' said Tench. 'I'm a man who's working for the Indian Forest Service at a place called Shahkot . . .'

Bell settled back in his chair. 'Shahkot!' he said. 'Well now! You interest me, Mike. Carry on. I'm listening.'

He listened in silence, merely nodding from time to time. At the end he sat motionless, staring at what was left of the Scotch in his glass.

'So,' said Tench, 'where's the flaw?'

Bell stirred himself. He tossed off the rest of his drink. 'First of all,' he said, 'there is a place called Shahkot. I've been there. It's where you say it is, and yes, it has a sawmill. Yes, there's a Savoy Hotel in Mussoorie. It has a dance hall and a bar. Yes, there were men called pundits. They went out into the mountains disguised as pilgrims, and they were equipped with rosaries and prayer-wheels. Yes, their rosaries had a hundred beads, and they used the drums of their prayer-wheels to carry rolls of blank paper to use as log-books . . . Yes, ever since the death of Peter the Great in 1725 there've been rumours about his will. No one's ever seen it, but the contents are believed to be as you describe them. And it's true that the Great Game has ceased to exist. If there's still some intelligence work on the borders, the methods used nowadays are bound to be very different. But it's feasible that a man who, five years ago, was in his mid-fifties could have worked as a pundit and have known all the tracks . . .'

Tench gave a sigh. 'Then there isn't a flaw. The story could be true.'

'It's fantastic, but yes, like the old adage it has a ring of truth.' He paused. 'But there is just one point I'd feel inclined to query.'

'What's that?' Tench was guarded. At this late stage he felt he could hardly hope for a breakthrough.

'This business about Jim Corbett . . . I met Corbett once up in Naini Tal. A simple, modest, friendly sort of chap and a delightful talker. His knowledge of forest lore became the stuff of legend. He was a great hunter too. Renowned for killing man-eaters up in the Kumaon. Nowadays he's a long way away from India. He's taken to growing coffee in Africa, so I'm

203

told.' Bell pushed himself up and poured another tot of Scotch. 'The point is this. He wasn't a Forest Officer. He was employed by the railways. I don't know that he was ever called on to train Forest Officers, but he certainly trained soldiers. Back in '44 he was given a commission. The army made him a lieutenant-colonel, and put him in charge of training men for jungle warfare in Burma. Not that he taught them how to kill. He didn't. Others did that. His job was simply to teach them how to read the signs of the jungle and survive . . . But the men that he trained did learn to kill, and they learnt how to do it silently and swiftly. You say two of your murder victims in Medford died of broken necks. Well, let's put it this way. There was more than one Japanese sentry in Burma who died of a broken neck.'

He smiled.

'It's worth thinking about, isn't it?'

6

It was.

Approaching Newton's sister village, Horsham St Faith, Tench pulled off the road and parked on a track leading up to a farm. There he switched off the engine and sat staring out at the darkness ahead.

When he'd asked Wellbridge how long he'd been working up at Shahkot, he'd said, 'Roughly five years. Before that I was in Burma.' The implication had been that he'd been working there in the Forest Service, and on the spur of the moment he, Tench, had seen no reason to question it, but what Lawrence had told him suggested that the words might have carried an entirely different meaning.

Suppose Wellbridge had, as he'd implied, been working with the Forest Service in Burma. He couldn't have been working there after '42, because that was the year when the Japs had invaded and driven the British out. He'd left Shahkot last October – 1950. If he'd spent five years there, that meant that he'd started there back in '45. So what had he been doing between '42 and '45?

But suppose, on the other hand, as Lawrence implied, he hadn't been doing forestry work in Burma. He'd talked about Corbett. 'He helped to train us,' he'd said. But according to Lawrence, it wasn't likely that he'd trained him for forestry work. It was much more likely that he'd trained him for jungle warfare. That would explain why Wellbridge had been in Burma. If he'd been in the army, he could well have served there between 1942 and 1945.

And he'd married the daughter of a colonel in the Gurkhas. How significant was that . . .?

Tench stared at the darkness. It seemed almost symbolic. The plain fact was that he didn't really know and had no means of telling. Lawrence had opened up a new train of thought, and he couldn't at the moment see where it was leading.

If Wellbridge had been trained to kill, as Lawrence suggested, and to kill silently and swiftly, he'd have found it easy to deal with Eli Craske and Joe Grice. Both had been elderly, Craske had been drunk, and Grice, lured downstairs from his bed, had probably been half asleep. And more than that. He'd have had both the strength and the expertise to kill a small woman of five feet two, in exactly the way that Ledward had described.

But why should he have done so?

McKenzie's theory, based on the letter that Gregg had found in the holdall at Thetford, was that she'd been sent to track down Deirdre Wellbridge, but there was no solid evidence that that was the case, and even Mac had admitted it was difficult to conceive of Wellbridge committing one murder, let alone three, simply to save his wife from a pair of prying eyes. There was nothing indeed to prove that Deirdre Wellbridge had any kind of secret to hide from the world. The little that they'd so far managed to uncover seemed to point in entirely the opposite direction. In other words there was no logic behind the theory, no hard facts to show that Wellbridge had ever met the woman, apart from their brief association on board ship. It was all conjecture, and conjecture that could just as easily be wrong as right.

He lay back, closed his eyes and tried to work out an alternative explanation, but just as he thought he'd reached one it seemed to slip away . . . Perhaps he was tired. Perhaps, as Darricot had said, he needed to forget the whole miserable business and give sleep a chance to provide the answer.

He reached for the starter, switched on the headlights, put the car into gear, and swung it round in a three-point turn to face the main road.

Then he suddenly slapped the wheel. No, Darricot was wrong. It wasn't tiredness that was the trouble. Sleep would merely prove itself as impotent as he was, because sleep, as he did, needed evidence to work on. The plain truth was that he was trying to build an arch without any keystone. He remembered what the Chief Super had said when the case had first broken: 'We're not likely to make much headway till we know who she is.'

Well, he still didn't know who she was. She'd been dead for five days and no one had claimed her. That was the missing keystone, but how was he to find it? How was he to trace the woman's movements backwards from Thetford? . . . Wait and hope? . . . No, he couldn't afford to do that. There must be a connection somewhere that he just wasn't seeing. Some connection between her and someone in Medford . . . But who? . . . Deirdre Wellbridge? And if it was Mrs Wellbridge, where had they met? Had it been in India? Was a part, at least, of Wellbridge's story true? Had this woman, in truth, been on board the *Strathaven*, and had Deirdre Wellbridge chosen to disown her?

He sat there, thinking, the engine ticking over. Then he reached under the dashboard, pulled out a torch and checked the time on his wrist-watch . . . 10.45 . . . Late . . . Was it too late? . . . No, maybe not. He had to take the chance.

He put the car into gear. It began to move forward.

At the edge of Upper Hellesdon, on the outskirts of the city, he drew in by a phone box, lifted the receiver and asked for a London number.

'Jeremy?' he said. 'Yes, that's right, it's Mike Tench. Sorry to trouble you at this time of night, but I need some assistance . . . Yes, it's urgent. I'll send someone down . . . Yes, the same again if that's at all possible. The name's Wellbridge. Geoffrey Wellbridge . . .'

7

At half-past nine the following morning, as Tench and Hastings were preparing to fight their corner against a bevy of critical press reporters demanding to know what progress had been achieved in the face of this 'massacre', as they called it, at Medford, McKenzie was parking his car by the timber yard at Holt, Harris was puttering up the drive to Sparrow Hill House on his Velocette 'Noddy', and Gregg was dozing in a dusty compartment of a train that was taking him to London.

His instructions had been plain. Once arrived, he was to commandeer a taxi and drive to the Archives Section of the War Office where he had an appointment with a Mr Jeremy Clyde, who would, it was hoped, by that time have retrieved from the archives any relevant facts about the putative career in His Majesty's forces of the man who went by the name of Geoffrey Wellbridge.

When, four years previously, Tench, then a sergeant himself, had first visited Clyde on Lubbock's behalf, he'd been somewhat overawed by the corridors of power, but Gregg, as always discreetly optimistic, was a good deal more relaxed in his approach. This was the kind of assignment he enjoyed. All he had to do was ask a few questions, get the right answers, and after that make a leisurely journey back to Norwich.

He was fast asleep before the train reached Cambridge, and didn't wake up till it drew to a halt in Victoria station.

Mr Clyde, a civil servant persistently loyal to the right-wing tradition, continued to advertise his latent hostility to six long years of Labour hegemony. He wore a regulation pin-striped suit with a light blue fleck, a spotless white shirt and a navy-blue tie. Not much older than Gregg himself, he occupied, nonetheless, a room the size of a modern bungalow. It contained a highly polished mahogany desk, half a dozen tall metal filing cabinets, two high-backed leather-seated chairs and nothing else beyond a carpet of thick Axminster pile.

Seated behind the desk, he waved a hand towards the one vacant chair, swivelled round to one of the cabinets, extracted a file and laid it on the desk.

'You,' he said smoothly, 'are Detective Sergeant Gregg?'

Gregg nodded. 'Correct, sir.'

'You have some means of identification?'

The sergeant produced his card. Clyde examined it at length and then handed it back. 'Thank you, Sergeant,' he said. 'It's a routine precaution, no more than that. We haven't met before, so I have to go through the motions, I'm afraid.'

'Of course, sir,' said Gregg.

Clyde opened the file. 'Chief Inspector Tench,' he said, 'was right in his assumptions. There was a Major Geoffrey Wellbridge who saw service both in India and Burma.' He ran his finger down the page. 'Volunteered for the army in 1940. Posted to the Bedfordshire and Hertfordshire Regiment at Kempston Barracks, Bedford. Served with the 8th Battalion, coastal defence in Cornwall, till 1942. Commissioned Second Lieutenant the same year and posted to India. Captain with the Gurkhas 1943. Recruited for Wingate's Chindits 1944. Served with them in Burma. Awarded an immediate MC for conspicuous bravery in extricating his force from an ambush at Indaw. Wounded and flown back to Calcutta for convalescence, then posted to the 12th Royal Gurkhas at Abbottabad. Promoted to Major 1945. Resigned his commission and discharged October 1945.' He paused and looked up. 'I've had a summary typed out for you to give to the Chief Inspector.'

'Thank you, sir,' said Gregg. He frowned. 'Can I possibly ask a question?'

'Is there something that isn't clear?'

'Just one point, sir. I'm sure the Chief would want me to check while I'm here.'

'You want to know why he resigned his commission.'

'Yes, sir.'

Clyde nodded. 'I thought that might bother you.'

'Well, it does seem a bit peculiar, sir, doesn't it? Was he declared unfit?'

Clyde closed the file. He sat back and laced his fingers underneath his chin. 'No, Sergeant, he wasn't. As far as I know, he was perfectly fit.'

'Then what, sir?' Gregg waited.

A flicker of a smile showed itself on Clyde's face. 'It's a case, Sergeant,' he said, 'of *cherchez la femme*. Have you come across a Deirdre Thompson in the course of your inquiries?'

It was perhaps strange that at that very moment Mr Raymond Giles Benedict started up his Jaguar XK roadster, pulled out of the drive of his large detached house at Chandlers Ford, near Southampton, and turned north on the road to Winchester.

8

Deirdre Wellbridge was visibly annoyed. She stood in the doorway and scowled at Harris. 'What now?' she said. 'Can't you leave me alone?'

'Apologies, ma'am.' Harris was diplomatically contrite. 'The Chief Inspector needs a little more confirmation.'

'Confirmation of what? I explained everything yesterday.'

'You told him you were being confused with someone else.'

'I must be. I made that clear.'

'It's just that the Chief Inspector needs to be absolutely sure of his facts, ma'am. You understand?'

'No, I don't,' she said. 'What the hell kind of confirmation does he want?'

'Your birth certificate, ma'am. I presume you have a copy.'

'Yes, somewhere, but offhand I couldn't for the life of me say where. It's probably stuffed away at the bottom of a drawer.'

'Perhaps you'd look for it, ma'am.'

She frowned at him. 'D'you realize, Constable, just how many drawers there are in this house?'

'A considerable number, ma'am, I'd imagine. But I am prepared to wait.'

'Then you'll have to,' she said. 'Finding it may not be as simple as you think . . . You have a car?'

'Just a motorbike, ma'am.'

'Then you'd better go and sit on it,' she said, 'till I'm ready. I'll let you know when I've found it.'

She shut the door and left him standing at the bottom of the steps.

Harris waited, but not for long. He could be patient with those that deserved it, like Danny, but he wasn't prepared to submit to Deirdre Wellbridge without some kind of protest. He waited exactly two and a half minutes by the fingers of his watch and then tugged at the bell. When she opened the door, he gave her a winning smile. 'Have you found it, ma'am?' he asked.

She was tight-lipped. 'No.'

'Then I'm off to Medford,' he said. 'I've a job to do there. I'll be back in half an hour.'

She slammed the door in his face.

McKenzie was far less inclined to show patience. His ration of that virtue was distinctly meagre at the best of times, and the minute amount he was prepared to extend to Geoffrey Wellbridge had exhausted itself in the course of the previous evening.

'The Chief Inspector's compliments, sir,' he said curtly, 'but he wishes to see you.'

Wellbridge stared at him. 'When?'

'Now, sir. It's a matter of some urgency.'

'It's inconvenient to say the least.'

'I'm to tell him that, sir, am I?'

Wellbridge took a deep breath. 'No, Sergeant,' he said. 'If the Chief Inspector wants to see me, then of course I've no choice. Just give me five minutes . . .'

Harris started up the 'Noddy' and rode down to Medford, where he had a few words with Sergeant Hellyer who'd taken over the incident room from Lock. After that he leaned on the bridge and spent a little time surveying the slow-moving waters of the river as they made their sluggish passage underneath the arch. Then, consulting his watch, he drove back up the hill.

She answered as soon as he pulled on the bell, and held out a sheet of paper. 'Is that what you want?' she asked.

Harris read it through carefully. 'That's it, ma'am. Thank you.'

'Oh, don't mention it,' she said. 'It's always a pleasure to confound the police. I assume it's satisfactory.'

'Absolutely, ma'am.'

'Then perhaps you'll convey that belief to the Chief Inspector. It might persuade him to let me have five minutes' peace.'

'I'll do that, ma'am, yes.'

'And you'll return it?'

'Of course.'

'Then kindly start up that peculiar contraption of yours,' she said, 'and get the hell out of here. Go and make yourself a nuisance to my husband. He's the one you should be pestering, not me.'

9

'Where is he?' Tench asked.

'In the interview room.'

'Any trouble?'

'No,' McKenzie said. 'Just made a mild protest, but came like a lamb . . . Any word yet from Gregg?'

'I told him not to ring. He'll be bringing a letter back.' Tench glanced at his watch. 'And if I know Jerry Clyde, he won't be through down there yet . . . Bring Wellbridge up. I'll see him in here.'

McKenzie shrugged. 'If you say so.'

'This isn't a grilling, Mac. It's just a quiet chat. As I said yesterday, we've no reason to hold him. We don't even know if he's lying or not.'

McKenzie sniffed. 'Well, as far as I'm concerned, the whole tale's a pack of lies. He's just romenting, as they say in Norfolk.'

'Romenting or not, I'd prefer to see him up here in my office, so bring him up.'

'Right, sir,' McKenzie said, 'but it's your choice, not mine.'

He showed Wellbridge in, and Tench flicked a hand towards a chair. 'Please sit down, sir,' he said.

Wellbridge sat and crossed his legs. He was almost apologetic. 'I seem to be causing you a great deal of trouble, Chief Inspector. What is it this time? Another conflict of evidence?'

'Partly, sir.' Tench nodded. 'But we have succeeded in resolving one point. According to the lab, the thumbprint on your window was on the outside, so the woman, as you suggested, was very likely looking in.'

'Well, I did say that that was my belief, Chief Inspector.'

'You did, sir, yes, but a couple of other queries have arisen since then . . . You said you were in Burma.'

'That's correct. I was.'

'In the forestry service?'

'Oh, no, Chief Inspector . . . Did I give that impression? I'm sorry if I did. No, I was in the army.'

'Were you, sir?' said Tench. 'Serving with whom?'

'Wingate's mob. The Chindits.'

'And that was why you had specialized training for jungle warfare?'

'Yes, that's right.'

'So where did you train?'

'Chhindwara, Chief Inspector. Down in the Central Provinces.' Wellbridge didn't hesitate. His answer was quite explicit. 'Round the Seeonee Hills and the Wainganga River. It's now Madhya Pradesh.'

'And when was this?'

'Early 1943.'

'And you went into Burma when?'

'March '44.'

Tench pulled a file towards him and opened it. 'You said you were trained by Jim Corbett.'

'He helped in the training, yes.'

'But according to my information, Mr Wellbridge, Corbett wasn't involved until 1944. That was when he was put in charge and commissioned lieutenant-colonel.'

'That's true.'

'Then he couldn't have trained you.'

Wellbridge was unmoved. 'I'm afraid,' he said, 'that your logic's just a trifle at fault, Chief Inspector. I was wounded in the jungle. It was only a flesh wound, but I was flown out to Calcutta. I convalesced there and then returned to Chhindwara. That was when I met Corbett. Unfortunately Wingate was killed in an air crash and his scheme was abandoned, so I never got back to Burma.'

McKenzie leaned forward. 'As a Chindit, you must have been taught how to deal with Japanese sentries.'

'You mean . . .?'

'Kill them, Mr Wellbridge. How were you taught to kill them?'

'Quickly and quietly, Sergeant.'

'By what method?'

'Pressure on the vagal nerve, or simply by snapping the neck. Both methods are swift and silent. We were all taught to use them.' He smiled at McKenzie. 'But we don't make a practice of employing such methods in civilian life, Sergeant, even in self-defence.'

'Were you ever at a place called Abbottabad?' Tench asked.

'Briefly,' Wellbridge said. 'A matter of weeks.'

'With the 12th Royal Gurkhas?'

'Yes.'

'Under Colonel Thompson?'

'That's correct, Chief Inspector.'

'Am I right in assuming that your wife is the colonel's daughter?'

'Yes, absolutely right.'

'Then you must have met her at Abbottabad. Yet you told us that the first time you met was on the ship from Bombay.'

'So it was.'

'Then . . .'

Wellbridge took his time. He seemed to be quite at ease with himself and the questions. 'I'm sorry to say that your logic's at fault again, Chief Inspector,' he said. 'I was posted to Abbottabad during the hot season, so I never met Deirdre. She was up in the hills at Simla with her mother. When she returned, I'd already left.'

There was a pause. Tench glanced across at McKenzie. The sergeant raised his eyebrows.

'Is there anything more, Chief Inspector?' Wellbridge asked.

'No, sir,' said Tench. 'Thank you for coming in. I'll arrange for a car to take you back to Holt.'

Once he'd gone, there was silence. Tench looked at McKenzie and then raised a hand. 'No, Mac,' he said. 'Just don't say a word. We're still in the same position. We've no valid reason to keep him here.'

'Except that he's lying.'

'We can't prove that he is. You think he killed this woman just because she was sent to track down Mrs Wellbridge. But there's no evidence apart from her own wild claims that that's what she was doing. No, Mac. We still don't know who she was or why she came here, and until we do we're just poking about in the dark without a light.'

Ray Benedict could undoubtedly have proffered that light, but Mr Benedict was still a hundred and twenty miles to the south, unlocking the door of an isolated Kentish cottage on the road between Westerham and the airfield at Biggin Hill.

He pushed open the door and stood for a moment, listening. Then he noticed the letter. It lay on a small mahogany table by the hatstand in the hall. He picked it up and read the inscription. Then, with one swift movement, he tore the envelope apart . . .

10

'Birth certificate, sir,' said Harris.

'Does it give us any clue?'

'Doesn't seem to, sir. Just one Christian name, Deirdre. All it does is prove she was telling the truth.'

Tench read it through. A girl, named as Deirdre. Born in Aldershot, 15th

June 1928. Father, James Verey Thompson, Second Lieutenant, Grenadier Guards ... Certified copy of Entry 38 in the Register Book of Births for Sub-district Two of Aldershot in the County of Hampshire, dated 25th June 1928.

'Well,' he said, 'it proves at least one thing more. Her name's certainly not Frances ... So much for theories. That's Sergeant McKenzie's bright bit of conjecture washed down the drain. If the woman was searching for anyone at all, it wasn't Mrs Wellbridge.'

'You know what I think?' said Harris.

'What?'

'She was barmy. Slipped the noose from some private mental home somewhere.'

'Well, it's true that her behaviour wasn't all that rational.'

'If you ask me,' said Harris, 'it was utterly deranged. What sane woman wanders round a strange place deliberately spreading half a dozen different stories about herself? No, sir, she must have been way off her nut. That's the only explanation.'

'But why should someone kill her?'

'She probably reverted to type and lost it completely. Went berserk. Didn't Mr Lubbock say that she might have been killed by accident?'

'He didn't rule it out.'

'So someone tried to restrain her,' said Harris, 'and she died. If we're still working on theories, sir, that's as good as any.'

Tench swept aside half a dozen files and dumped them in a drawer. 'Theories are all we've got to work on, Steve,' he said. 'I wish to God someone somewhere would come up with some facts.'

Lock came up with a few, and Ted Merrick with more, but all were negative.

Lock handed him half a dozen typewritten sheets stapled together. 'We've had those from the shipping line, sir,' he said. 'Passenger list from the *Strathaven*. It's taken them long enough. There were only two Miriams. One was a twelve-year-old girl and the other was the widow of a Bombay merchant. She was in her sixties.'

'No joy then?'

'None, sir, I'm afraid ... We're still checking the statements from Medford, but so far they haven't been much help either. Just a couple of women called Frances. The farmer's wife down at Greystoke Farm – according to Bates she's eighty-two and crippled with arthritis – and Maisie Tackleston at the Post Office. She was christened Margaret Frances.'

'Keep trying,' said Tench. 'It's all we can do.'

Merrick rang him from the lab. 'No fingerprints on the bike, sir. It must have been wiped clean.'

'What about the sheet from the letter?'

'We found the dead woman's,' Merrick told him, 'and one other set. Look to be feminine, but they aren't a match for any we've got in the archives.'

'Keep trying, Ted,' he said.

Everything was negative, frustratingly so. It was all right Lubbock saying that you had to have a negative before you could print a positive, but none of the negatives in this baffling case had so far produced anything but mistily incomprehensible exposures.

He supposed it was possible that Clyde might come up with something. He checked on his watch and reckoned up times. Gregg should have been in London by quarter to ten. How long would he need there? An hour? Could be more. And he had to get from the station to the War Office and then back again. If he was lucky, he might catch the midday train. That meant he'd be in Norwich by when? Three o'clock? ... No, nearer 3.15, and it was now half-past one ... Another couple of hours.

He reached for the phone, rang the canteen and ordered coffee and a sandwich. He needed Lubbock's patience, but, even granted that precious gift, time was going to drag.

He pulled the files from the drawer and dropped them with a thump on top of the desk ...

11

Gregg had indeed caught the midday train, and he should have been back in Norwich, as Tench had expected, by mid-afternoon; but the failure of a points system south of Cambridge left him fretting for an hour in another dusty third-class compartment somewhere on the verge of Essex; and while he was thus marooned, Mr Raymond Benedict, driving at speed, crossed the Norfolk boundary, flashed past the Dutch-gabled inn at Scole and sped on towards Norwich.

Ray Benedict always drove fast. He enjoyed driving fast. That was why, with considerable wealth and a wide range of cars to suit the contents of his wallet, he'd recently invested in a Jaguar roadster. It consumed the twenty miles between Scole and the city in less than twenty minutes, and he ground to a halt in the police station car-park while Gregg's train was still within sight of Cambridge.

Mr Benedict was young. He was fit and athletic. Slamming the car door, he ran swiftly up the steps and presented himself to the Duty Sergeant at the desk. 'My name's Benedict,' he said. 'I need to see the man in charge of this murder case at Medford.'

The Duty Sergeant eyed him warily. 'You do, sir? Why?'

'The woman . . . I think I may know who she is.'

The sergeant reached for the phone. 'Put me through to DCI Tench,' he said.

Tench stood where he'd stood innumerable times before: in the small claustrophobic room in the mortuary.

'Look carefully, sir,' he said.

The attendant drew back the sheet.

'You recognize this woman?'

Benedict looked and gave a nod. 'Yes, I do, Chief Inspector.'

'Then who is she?'

'She's my sister.'

'Her name, sir?'

'Ruth.'

'Ruth Benedict?'

'No.' The young man bent down and placed a chaste kiss on the dead woman's brow. He gazed at her a moment, then he straightened up and turned. 'Her name's Wellbridge,' he said. 'Mrs Ruth Wellbridge. She's married to a Geoffrey Wellbridge . . . Geoffrey Francis Wellbridge.'

12

'Mac!' Tench shouted.

'Sir?'

'Get everyone in here right away. We've a job on our hands.'

'Something turned up?'

'You're too damned right it has . . . That bugger Wellbridge . . . We've had it all wrong, Mac. We should have guessed long ago. He's had us all tied on a piece of bloody string.'

'Well, I told you he was lying,' McKenzie said blandly.

IX
THE STYGIAN FEN

We were as men who through a fen
Of filthy darkness grope

Oscar Wilde: *The Ballad of Reading Gaol*

1

At quarter-past twelve that lunchtime, as Gregg's train was gathering speed out of London and Ray Benedict was accelerating towards Biggin Hill, a police car drew up outside the timber yard at Holt and Geoffrey Wellbridge stepped out.

He watched the car drive away, then he turned and walked towards the centre of the town. Reaching the Midland Bank, he went in and cashed a cheque, and repeated the process at Barclays and Lloyds. He then made for the Post Office, took a picture postcard from his inside pocket, extracted a stamp from a wall machine, licked it, stamped the card and slipped it into the mouth of the posting box.

From there he walked a couple of hundred yards, turned down a side road and, approaching a line of lock-up garages, took a key from his pocket and unlocked the nearest. The doors, as they opened, revealed a dark blue Vauxhall Velox saloon. He checked the contents of the boot and the glove compartment, drove it out on to the forecourt, locked the garage doors behind him and took the road to Norwich.

He drove fast, but was careful to stay within the limit. By half-past one he was in Norwich; by three o'clock Ipswich, and by four he'd reached Chelmsford. On the outskirts of Brentwood he called in at a petrol station and, pleading a shortage of ready money, paid the bill by cheque. At half-past four he was approaching the Dartford Tunnel which led under the Thames to Rochester, Canterbury and the Channel ports of Kent.

At precisely that moment three police cars pulled into the timber yard at Holt. Tench and McKenzie were in the first; Sue Gradwell was driving the second with Lock in the passenger seat; while the third held the other three detective constables: Ellison, Rayner and Spurgeon.

McKenzie pointed to a corner of the yard. 'Well, his car's here,' he said.

Tench saw it: the empty white Chrysler convertible parked at the side of a timber stack. 'Right,' he said 'Let's go and get him.'

They ran up the wooden steps to Wellbridge's office. In the anteroom his secretary, a buxom blonde with red-lacquered fingernails, was unwinding a sheet of copy from the typewriter. She looked up as she saw them. 'Yes, sir?' she said to Tench. 'Can I help you?'

Tench ignored her. He walked straight past and flung the office door open. Then he turned and held up his card. 'Detective Chief Inspector Tench,' he said. 'Where's Mr Wellbridge?'

She glanced from one to the other of them blankly. 'I don't know, sir,' she said. 'I thought he was with you.'

'He was,' McKenzie told her, 'but that was five hours ago. Where is he now?'

'I don't know.' She repeated the words as though she hadn't made it clear the first time. 'I haven't seen him since he left here with you.'

'Constable Walters drove him back. He dropped him outside the yard. He must have been here by quarter-past twelve.'

'Well, I haven't seen him. He hasn't been in.'

'D'you go out to lunch?'

'No, sir,' she said, 'I just have sandwiches. I've been here all the time.'

Tench picked up the phone. 'We'll have to put out a call. God knows where he is. He's got four hours' start . . . Tell Rayner and Spurgeon to hang on here in case he comes back. I'll arrange for the lab to pick up the Chrysler.'

'And the rest of us?'

'Down to Sibthorpe,' said Tench. 'We can at least grab the delectable Deirdre. She may know something . . . I'll get on to Bates and Harris. You start up the car.'

2

He braked to a halt at the bottom of the drive and wound down the window.

Bates was leaning on his bike, and Steve Harris was with him, sitting astride the 'Noddy'.

'She's in, sir,' he said. 'Her car's parked outside.'

'Right.' Tench was tight-lipped. 'You and Bates go round the back. We'll take the front.'

He led the way up the drive, waited for Bates to position himself, and then pulled on the bell.

Deirdre Wellbridge was wearing the same close-fitting, lemon-coloured blouse that, two days before, had proved such a source of fascination to McKenzie; but this time, when she spoke, it was with an indolent resignation and a lift of her eyebrows. 'And what the hell d'you want now?' she inquired.

'I think,' said Tench, 'that we'd better talk inside.'

She sighed, gave a shrug and led them into the study. 'Now,' she said, 'perhaps in your plodding, inarticulate way you'll explain why you persist in disturbing my peace.'

'Shut the door, Mac,' said Tench. 'Sit down, Mrs Wellbridge.'

'I like standing, Inspector.'

'You may well do . . . Sit down.'

She looked at him and perched on the edge of the settee.

'You asked what I wanted, Mrs Wellbridge. I want the truth.'

'I've always told you the truth.'

'Then do me a favour. Tell me the truth again . . . Where's your husband?'

She looked him straight in the eyes. 'I haven't the faintest idea,' she said.

'Oh, I think you have.'

'He doesn't keep me informed about his business appointments.'

'I doubt very much if his present appointment has any connection at all with his business.'

She sighed again wearily. 'You mean he's out with some woman? Well, that's more than possible. It wouldn't be the first time.'

'No, Mrs Wellbridge, not a woman. Not this time. If I had to make a guess, I'd say Mr Wellbridge was very much on his own.'

'Then I'm afraid I can't help you,' she said. 'I think you'd better leave.' She crossed to the door, held it open and waited.

The two men exchanged a glance. Neither of them moved.

'You refuse to say where he is?'

'How many more times do I have to say this, Inspector? I don't know where he is.'

'Then you leave me with no alternative, ma'am,' said Tench. 'I'm arresting you for conspiring to murder Ruth Wellbridge sometime between the 4th and the 8th of May. You are not obliged to say anything unless you wish to do so, but whatever you say will be taken down in writing and may be given in evidence.'

She stared at him open-mouthed. 'What the hell is all this? And who the devil's Ruth Wellbridge?'

Tench didn't even look at her. 'Take her away, Mac,' he said.

Once outside he called the team together and spoke to Ellison and Lock. 'I want the place searched. And take charge of that rifle that's hanging on the wall . . . I don't think he'll be back, but there's just a slim chance, so get the car out of sight . . . Steve, you keep watch. I'll get a couple of Varden's men to relieve you.'

He turned to Bates. 'What's the state of the tide, Constable?'

'Coming in fast, sir. High water's due at twenty past seven.'

'When was the last low water?'

Bates pulled out his tables. '1.07, sir.'

'Then it's possible he might have made for Blacknock.'

'Might have done, sir. But if he did, he must have known he'd be caught by the tide. Once it starts coming in, it fills the creeks fast.'

'It'll be dark at next low water?'

'It will that, sir, for sure. Half-past one tomorrow morning.'

'And the next after that?'

'Ten to two in the afternoon.'

'Right. I want the marsh and the sands searched as far as Blacknock. Get the cockle women out and Jem Stuart as well. If there's a body to be found, I need them to find it.'

Bates nodded his head. 'Leave it to me, sir. I'll round 'em all up. Reckon they'll be only too willing to help.'

'Sue!'

'Sir,' said Sue Gradwell.

'In the back of the car with Mrs Wellbridge ... Mac, you drive, and sound the bell all the way. Let's get her back to Norwich as fast as we can. I want to see Clyde's report before we put her through the mill.'

3

Gregg was waiting in the office. He handed over a buff envelope.

Tench seemed strangely reluctant to open it. 'We've arrested Deirdre Wellbridge, Andy,' he said. 'But it's a gesture, nothing more. We still need evidence. Is there anything in here that's likely to help us?'

Gregg was non-committal. 'I think you'd better read it, sir.'

Tench slit the flap, removed the two typewritten sheets and glanced at the top one. 'That's interesting,' he said. 'Won a Military Cross, did he? ... "Conspicuous gallantry" ... Well, he didn't show much gallantry towards his own wife.'

He turned to the second sheet and frowned. 'Why did he resign his commission? Did you ask?'

'Yes, sir,' said Gregg. 'Mr Clyde wouldn't put the facts in his report ...'

'But he told you?'

'Yes, he did.'

'Go on.'

Gregg pulled out his notebook. 'Well, according to what he said, it was like this, sir ... As you'll see from the report, when he was wounded in Burma, Captain Wellbridge was flown out to convalesce in Calcutta; and after that he was promoted to Major and posted to the 12th Royal Gurkhas in Abbottabad. His commanding officer there was a Lieutenant-Colonel Thompson, and the Colonel had a daughter named Deirdre. Deirdre Thompson.'

'Deirdre Wellbridge.'

'That's right, sir ... Well, it seems that Major Wellbridge seduced her. Got her pregnant.'

'Did he, by God? He swore to me that he never met her while he was there. Said he never had the chance. She was up in the hills at Simla.'

'Well, she couldn't have been, sir, could she? Not all the time. He could hardly have got her pregnant by pigeon post.'

'No, he couldn't ... Tell me more.'

'Well, from what I gathered from Mr Clyde, Colonel Thompson wasn't too chuffed at the prospect of suddenly becoming a grandad. The girl was, after all, only just seventeen. She had to have an abortion. He insisted it was nothing but rape and said Wellbridge would have to pay. The trouble was his record. He was a distinguished officer, decorated for bravery, so they gave him the option of either facing a court martial or resigning his commission. You know the set-up, sir. Conduct to the prejudice of good order and military discipline, bringing the regiment into disrepute, and all the rest of that malarkey ...'

'So he chose to resign.'

'Apparently, sir.'

'Did Clyde know what happened to him after that?'

'Said he'd heard that some friend wangled him a job in forestry. Apart from that, sir, no. As far as the army was concerned, he just disappeared from sight.'

'And surfaced again at Shahkot.'

'Looks like it, sir, yes.'

Tench folded the report and slid it back in the envelope. 'Well,' he said, 'at least we've got something to throw at Mrs Wellbridge. She's always backed him up. Swore they never met till they were on the way home.' He paused. 'I wonder, Andy ... Why *did* they come home?'

'It's anyone's guess, sir.' Gregg gave a shrug. 'Perhaps, as he said, India for the Indians just wasn't his cup of tea.'

'Maybe,' said Tench. 'Then again, maybe not. I'm reaching the point where I wouldn't trust a word that either of them told me ... Perhaps we ought to try and trace Colonel Thompson.'

'We can't, sir,' said Gregg. 'I was coming to that. He and his wife were killed back in 1947 driving down a steep hairpin road from the hills.'

4

The Chief Super rested his elbows on the desk and clasped his hands beneath his chin. 'So where do we stand?' he said. 'We've got a woman in the cells and a man on the run ... Have we any clues to where he might be making for?'

'No, sir,' said Tench, 'and the trouble is he's got a good four hours' start, but we've put out a general call. All local and national forces have been briefed, and the ports and airports are all being watched.'

'You've got the house and the timber yard covered?'

'Yes, sir. Rayner and Spurgeon are watching the yard, and Constable Harris the house. Ellison and Lock are searching the place. I'm withdrawing all Varden's men from Medford. They'll take over and also keep an eye on the marsh. That'll be scoured tomorrow as soon as the tide permits. I've arranged for the incident room at Medford to be manned night and day – Hellyer's men'll do that – and they'll have a direct line to me here in Norwich ... I don't honestly see what else we can do, sir. We'll just have to wait.'

'You're going to question Mrs Wellbridge, of course?'

'Yes, sir, we'll be doing that later on tonight, but we haven't enough evidence to charge her at the moment, and she's not the type to offer us gratuitous clues.'

'Denying everything, is she?'

'Playing the innocent, sir. Says she knew nothing of what was going on. Claims she knows nothing about a Ruth Wellbridge.'

'Have you told her she's been tricked into a bigamous marriage?'

'No, sir, not in so many words. I need to get more details from Mr Benedict first. He's booked in for the night at the Maid's Head Hotel. I'm going down there to see him ... Before we question her again, we need all the ammunition we can possibly muster.'

'But you think she knows already.'

'She must do, unless she's as innocent as she says.'

'And you don't think she is.'

'No, sir, I don't. I think she's as guilty as hell. The problem is how to prove it.'

Hastings leaned back in his chair. 'Well, if all we have is suspicion, we can't hold her for long ... What have you got in mind?'

Tench took a deep breath. 'I want to let her go, sir.'

Hastings looked down his nose. 'You're sure of that?'

'Yes, sir. We'll question her again tonight after I've seen Mr Benedict. If we don't make any headway – and I doubt if we will, because she's not exactly the sort to cave in – we'll lock her up for the night and try again in the morning. And if she still persists with this tale that she's pure as the driven snow, then it seems to me, sir, that we've only one chance of digging out the truth. I'm certain she knows where Wellbridge has gone, and she's planning to join him. So we let her walk out, keep her under surveillance, and when she makes her move, we tail her. It's the best chance we have of tracking him down.'

The Chief Super pushed himself up from the desk. He crossed to the window and stood for a moment gazing out over Norwich. Then he turned. 'It's risky,' he said. 'We don't know where he's gone. We might have to trail her for hundreds of miles. We could easily lose her.'

'We've alerted all the forces in the country, sir. By tomorrow they may well have picked up his trail.'

'He's had four hours' start. He could be out of the country now and heading for Spain. We haven't got an extradition treaty with Spain.'

'If he's made for an east coast port like Harwich, sir, yes, it's possible he could have slipped out on a ferry. If he's heading for the Channel ports he could be too late, but I've a feeling he doesn't intend to do either.'

'Intuition, Mike?'

'No, not entirely, sir. Wellbridge is shrewd. He's the kind of man who'll calculate the odds in advance and he must know that the first thing we'll do is put a watch on the ports. He may head that way, yes, just to throw us off the scent, but he isn't the type to walk into a trap. Somewhere or other he's going to double back. If he's planning some kind of Continental excursion, it won't be just yet. He'll lie low for a time till the hubbub's died down.'

'And wait for her to join him.'

'That's right, and if she does she'll not only lead us to him, she'll convict herself. If she knows where he's gone, then she's not the innocent she's claiming to be.'

Hastings was doubtful. 'It'll need a lot of organizing. Co-operation with other forces. We're going to need their assistance.'

'Once Varden's men are in place we'll have the numbers to cope.'

The Chief Super took his time. 'All right,' he said at last. 'Go ahead, Mike . . . But on two conditions.'

'Sir?'

'If she shows any sign of boarding a boat or taking a plane, I want her rearrested. If she gets across the Channel, we'll have lost her for good. In spite of Inspector Maigret my faith in the French police isn't all that strong.'

'Agreed, sir.'

'Good. And there's one thing more. I reserve the right to call off the scheme at any time I choose . . . Keep me informed of developments. I'm always available, even if it's three o'clock in the morning. And if you have any problems, get in touch right away.'

'I'll do that, sir. Thank you.'

'Don't thank me,' Hastings said. 'Save your thanks for the next time you meet John Lubbock. And let's hope your intuition's as sound as his used to be.'

They chose a quiet corner table in the Maid's Head lounge. Tench and Benedict took coffee, McKenzie a tankard of Norfolk ale. 'If I'm going to be up half the night,' he said, 'I need it.'

Tench sat back and looked at Benedict. 'Now, sir,' he said, 'tell us about your sister and Geoffrey Wellbridge.'

Benedict lit a cigarette. 'Let me make it clear first of all, Chief Inspector. I never blamed him for walking out on her. Married life with Ruth must have been absolute hell. A double hell, in fact, both for her and for him.'

Tench frowned. 'You mean they were incompatible?'

'Not in the sense you intend, Chief Inspector. When he married her, they were both of them very much in love, and we had no doubts that the union would prove a successful one. But it wasn't to be. Fate decreed otherwise.'

'Fate in what sense, sir?'

'Fate, Chief Inspector, in the sense that my sister developed an illness, one that was incurable and tore the marriage apart. She was a victim of what's known as manic depression. It's a genetic disorder that distorts rational thought, produces violent swings of mood from high exhilaration to savage depression, and in many cases utterly destroys the will to live. The trouble is that the initial signs of its onset are difficult to read. Looking back, we might have read them. She was a pretty girl was Ruth, but even at school she was emotional, highly volatile and subject to moods. We assumed such things were normal in an adolescent girl, and in time she'd grow out of them. You see, Chief Inspector, we lacked the medical expertise to diagnose the truth. As far as we were concerned – her immediate family – she was just highly strung. When she married we had no inkling of what was to come. Nor had Frankie – she always called him Frankie, not Geoff. He was as much in the dark as we were.'

'Then the subsequent developments were entirely unexpected.'

'Entirely so, yes, both to us and to him.'

McKenzie set down his tankard. 'How did they come to meet?'

'By sheer coincidence, really, considering we lived hundreds of miles apart. We had a large house at Eastleigh close to Southampton where my father ran an import and export business, and the Wellbridges owned one of the more expensive hotels on the shores of Lake Windermere. In 1936 we booked in there for a holiday, and Ruth and Frankie met at a dance. She was eighteen, he was eight years older, but before we left they were both hopelessly in love. They were married at Romsey Abbey later that year.'

'And she went up to the Lakes?'

'For a few months, yes, but his father had long been planning to set up Frankie on his own. He bought a small country hotel in Kent and sent him down to run the place. They took a cottage close by, just north of Westerham, and settled down there.'

'And then things began to happen?'

'Almost immediately, yes. You see, Sergeant, manic depression is a progressive disease. Unless treated, it gets worse and the attacks become more frequent. In Ruth's case, it must have been simmering for years. There were periods of psychotic mania when she talked very fast and developed quite irrational enthusiasms for things that her mind, quite wrongly, told her were important. She went on shopping sprees, compelled it seemed by a wild sense of urgency, spending money she could ill afford on things that she didn't need. These manias lasted for weeks, sometimes for months, but they were inevitably followed by long, lacerating periods of black depression when she felt an overwhelming sense of inadequacy, couldn't cope with even the simplest tasks and woke in a morning filled with dread at the prospect of facing another day.'

He paused for a moment, took a sip of his coffee and then resumed. 'I hardly need to tell you, Chief Inspector,' he said, 'that such recurring cycles are hell to the sufferer and hell to a husband who has to watch and care and try to understand. Like most of us, Frankie had had no preparation for dealing with madness. Oh, he did his best. She was in and out of hospitals, staying for perhaps a fortnight at a time, and when she came out she was better for a while, but then the whole sorry cycle reasserted itself. She gradually got worse, began to suffer delusions, saw blood on the curtains and carpets, imagined situations that never existed, and fell into fits of rage that made her physically violent. Twice, in phases of black depression, she tried to kill herself by cutting her wrists.'

He looked at each of them in turn. 'It's a sad truth,' he went on, 'that no amount of love, however strong it may be, has the power to cure madness, whereas madness in the end has the power to kill love. Frankie stuck it for four years. Then one day – it was early on in the war – he turned up at my office, quite out of the blue. Ruth, he said, was in hospital again. She'd accused him of sleeping with a girl he'd never met, broken up the house and attacked him with a bread knife. "I'm leaving her, Ray," he told me. "I can't stand it any more. I've got to get away." I tried to dissuade him, but he was adamant about it. "I'm going for her sake as well as for mine," he said. "If I don't, then there's going to come a time when I'll reach the end of my tether, and once that snaps I won't be able to help myself. I'll kill her, Ray, I'm sure I will. So just let me go. It'll be better in the long run for both of us if I do."

227

'There was nothing I could do. I watched him start up his car and drive away from the office.

'That was more than ten years ago. The little boats, I remember, were bringing back the troops from the Dunkirk beaches.

'I haven't seen him since.'

6

'And after that?' said Tench.

'For a while she was quite beyond understanding. Then she plunged into deep despair. She was paralyzed with shame and fear, and broke into fits of uncontrollable sobbing. She had to be watched in the hospital night and day. They kept her in for six weeks, and when at last they discharged her she came to stay with us at Chandler's Ford. I was married by then, and though my wife was always staunch in her support, it was a difficult time. Ruth was slow to respond. The pills she'd been given didn't cure her. There was and there still is no recognized cure for manic depression. All they could do was moderate the intensity of her moods. We tried to make sure she took them, but sometimes she deceived us into thinking she had, with disastrous results. She had Frankie in her thoughts all the time. She said he had to come back. He must surely come back, and she had to be at the cottage at Westerham when he did. It became an obsession. She said she couldn't stay with us. She had to be where he'd find her when he returned. Eventually we just couldn't take any more. We had to let her go, though it wasn't without deep misgivings.'

'And since then?'

Benedict shrugged. 'Things followed the pattern I expected them to take. While she stuck to the pills, she learned to cope with her swings of mood. When she didn't, the whole savage cycle took charge of her again. I can't remember how many times she rang me up in a black suicidal depression, and I had to down tools and race off to Westerham. All we could do was keep our fingers crossed. For months at a time she was almost normal, and then crash! The whole nightmare was back.'

McKenzie emptied half a pint of ale down his throat. 'So what brought you here today?'

Benedict stirred his coffee. 'Since my father died I've run the business on my own. That means I have to keep in contact with overseas firms, and for the last three weeks I've been in New York. I got back in the early hours of this morning, and the first thing my wife said was that she was worried about Ruth. She'd seen a picture in one of the national dailies: a woman who'd been found drowned on the Norfolk coast. The resemblance to

228

Ruth, she said, was quite uncanny. She'd rung the cottage, but there'd been no reply. She'd been trying all day. She showed me the picture. What she'd told me was right. It did look like Ruth. I snatched a couple of hours' sleep and then rang one of her friends at Westerham. She said the last time she'd heard from her was a fortnight ago, when Ruth had rung her up. She'd talked very fast and seemed very excited. Said she'd heard from an old friend who'd invited her to stay, so she was taking a little holiday. She might be gone for a week or two, but she hadn't said where.'

He picked up his cup and cradled it between his hands. 'I read the signs,' he said, 'and they were all too familiar, so I drove straight to Westerham. I've always had a key to the cottage, and I let myself in. There was an envelope addressed to me on a table in the hall, and a note inside it: "I've had a letter from Valerie. She's seen Frankie! Yes, it's true! At a place called Blakeney. It's somewhere in Norfolk. I'm off there to find him. Don't worry. I'm fine."'

'Who's this Valerie?' Tench asked.

'I haven't the foggiest idea, Chief Inspector. She must be one of Ruth's friends, but if she is, I've never met her. I wouldn't know where to start searching for her . . . You say you've found the relevant part of the letter?'

'Yes, we found it in the holdall she left at Thetford station. We've put out an appeal for the writer to come forward, but so far we haven't had any response.'

'And Frankie? He's still missing?'

'I'm afraid so, yes, but don't worry, we'll track him down. Every force in the country's on the alert.'

McKenzie leaned forward. 'After he walked out, did you ever try to find him?'

'Not at first,' Benedict said. 'I wasn't sure what it might lead to . . . But I did try once later on in the war. Ruth insisted that I did. He was an only child, and I knew he must have kept in touch with his family; but they'd cut themselves off, blamed her for what had happened. I went up to the Lakes to see them, but it proved a waste of time. His father was courteous, but he showed me the door. Said he didn't know where Frankie was, and wouldn't be prepared to tell me even if he did . . . I was in the army myself by that time, and it seemed a pretty fair bet that, if Frankie was still alive, he must be in one of the services. I did all I could. Wrote a whole string of letters to the powers-that-be, but it was wartime and information was difficult to come by. In the end I gave up. It was like pleading with a wall.'

'D'you think it's possible he's up there now? In the Lakes?'

Benedict shook his head. 'His mother died suddenly just after the end of the war, and the old man sold off both the hotels. Went to live somewhere in Yorkshire, I believe. I don't exactly know where.'

'And wherever the old man is, you don't think Frankie's with him.'

'No, he can't be, Sergeant.' Benedict tossed back the rest of his coffee and set the cup down. 'The old chap died of a heart attack nine months ago. I heard it on the grapevine. I think that's why Frankie came back from India. To deal with all the business of his father's will. He must have been left a tidy sum of money, so wherever he is he won't be short of cash.'

'So where the devil is he?' McKenzie said as they drove back through the city.

'Could be anywhere, Mac, between here and Timbuktu. We'll just have to hope someone picks up his trail.'

'Or screw something out of darling Deirdre.'

'Or that,' said Tench, 'but don't hold your breath. I reckon she's out to prove that the cockle women aren't the only ones with tight lips in Medford.'

7

Whether she proposed to be tight-lipped or not, she seemed composed, almost nonchalant, as she faced Tench and McKenzie across the scarred wooden table in the interview room. Seated on a chair some distance away, right leg crossed over left, right toe pointed down, and her skirt drawn up to the level of her knee, was a young woman constable, armed with a pencil and a memorandum pad.

Deirdre Wellbridge ignored her. She glanced scornfully at McKenzie and then looked straight at Tench. 'Now, Inspector,' she said, 'perhaps you'll be good enough to tell me why I'm here.'

Tench opened a file that lay on the table. 'You are Deirdre Thompson?'

'No,' she said, 'I'm not. That was my maiden name. I'm now Deirdre Wellbridge.'

'You live at Sparrow Hill House, Sibthorpe?'

'You should know,' she said. 'You've been there.'

'Please answer the question.'

'There's not much point, is there?'

'For the record, Miss Thompson.'

'Correction,' she said. 'Not Miss Thompson, Mrs Wellbridge. And yes, for the record, I live at Sparrow Hill House.'

'Where were you last Sunday?'

'I've told you that already . . . I was over at Lynn.'

'What were you doing there?'

'Eating, sleeping, shopping, drinking and smoking. Not to mention a few other harmless activities.'

'Why did you go there?'

'I went there, Inspector, to eat, sleep and shop . . .'

'You know what I mean.'

'I went to visit a friend.'

'Male or female?'

'Female, of course. I don't go chasing round Norfolk after men.'

'This friend. What's her name?'

'You won't believe me if I tell you.'

'Try me,' said Tench.

'All right. Mary Smith.'

'You're sure about that?'

She took a deep breath. 'I'm positive about it. We shared a room at school . . . If you must know, Benenden . . . She was then Mary Jones. Now she's married, she's Mary Smith.'

'Her address?'

'The Larches, Castle Rising Road, North Wootton . . . Check with her if you like.'

'We intend to, Miss Thompson.'

'Mrs Wellbridge, if you please.' She turned to the WPC with the memorandum pad. 'Make a note of that,' she said. 'I expect the amendment to be duly recorded.'

'It will be.' Tench nodded. 'When did you go to Lynn?'

'A week ago today. Saturday.'

'And you returned to Sibthorpe when?'

'Early Wednesday afternoon.'

'Not before then?'

'No. Why should I?'

'Mrs Smith will confirm that?'

'I can't see any reason why she should lie.'

'Where were you last Wednesday night?'

She sighed. 'How can I possibly answer a question like that? You really should try to be more precise, Inspector. What time on Wednesday night?'

'Let's say from dusk until dawn on Thursday morning.'

'I went to the cinema in Norwich.'

'On your own?'

'On my own.'

'At what time?'

'I went to the second house. It started at 8.30.'

'What film did you see?'

'*All About Eve*. Bette Davis.'

'And when did you get back home?'

'Just before midnight.'

'And Mr Wellbridge? Where was he?'

'In bed. Fast asleep . . . So I went to bed, too.'

231

'You do sleep with him then, Miss Thompson?'

She gave him a look of utter disdain. 'If you're trying to provoke me, Inspector, you won't succeed. Of course I sleep with him. We happen to be married.'

'So you slept beside Mr Wellbridge until dawn the next morning.'

'Yes, I did. I've been led to believe that cohabitation is a natural thing between husband and wife.'

'Did he leave you at any time during the night?'

'Not to my knowledge.'

Tench glanced at the file. His tone, when he spoke, was deliberately casual. 'You realize, of course, that this man, Geoffrey Wellbridge, isn't your husband?'

Her eyes, for a moment, showed a flicker of anger. 'That's ridiculous,' she said. 'We were married in Norwich just before Christmas.'

'I'm afraid not, Miss Thompson. It's true that you went through a form of marriage, but Mr Wellbridge was already possessed of a wife. He married a lady by the name of Ruth Benedict at Romsey Abbey in Hampshire in 1936.'

She gave a little shrug. 'So?' she said.

'You were aware of that fact?'

'Naturally. He told me. They were divorced before we met.'

'I don't think so, Miss Thompson.'

'Then, Inspector,' she said, 'it's a pity you can only think, because I know for certain. I've seen his army records. There was no such woman mentioned. His next-of-kin was his father, a Mr John Wellbridge. He lived up at Windermere in the Lakes.'

8

Tench sat back in his chair, and slid the file across the table towards McKenzie.

The sergeant took his time. He opened the folder and slowly turned the pages, scanning each with some care. Then at last he looked up . . . 'You told us you first met Geoffrey Wellbridge on the boat coming home.'

'That's right. The *Strathaven*.'

'But you weren't exactly telling the truth, Deirdre, were you?'

She regarded him much as she would some noxious species of insect. 'Mrs Wellbridge to you,' she said. 'I reserve my Christian name for intimate friends.'

McKenzie was unperturbed. He accepted the snub with apparent good grace, and rephrased the question. 'You were lying, Mrs Wellbridge, weren't you?'

She raised her eyebrows. 'I'm not exactly sure what you mean by that. You suffer from the same radical fault as your inspector. You'll need to be more specific.'

'Then perhaps I can explain.' McKenzie was smooth, almost placid. 'When you met Mr Wellbridge on board the *Strathaven*, that wasn't your first encounter with him, was it?'

'Wasn't it?' she said. 'You do surprise me, Sergeant. Now where could I possibly have met him before?'

'At Abbottabad, ma'am?'

'Abbottabad?' She frowned. 'It seems most unlikely. According to my recollection, when he was there I was up in the hills at Simla. That's – let me see – more than three hundred miles away.'

'Quite a distance, Mrs Wellbridge.'

'Indeed, Sergeant, yes.'

'Then enlighten me, ma'am. How did Major Wellbridge manage to make you pregnant? Did he project his sperm along a telephone line?'

She turned towards Tench. 'Is it your practice, Inspector,' she said sweetly, 'to encourage your underlings in gratuitous crudity?'

Tench was impassive. 'Answer the question, Miss Thompson.'

'Very well . . . No, he didn't.'

'Then perhaps you'll be kind enough,' McKenzie said, 'to explain how he did it . . . You see, ma'am, I find the situation perplexing. If Major Wellbridge was three hundred miles away, how could he possibly have raped you?'

'He didn't,' she said.

'Your father apparently had that impression.'

'He was mistaken.'

'Was he? Then tell me. How did you manage to be pregnant? By immaculate conception?'

She gave him a lazy smile. 'Ingenious, Sergeant, but not strictly feasible . . . Have another guess.'

'You've been lying to us, haven't you?'

'Oh, I'd hardly call it a lie, Sergeant, no.'

'Then what would you call it?'

She thought for a moment. 'A diplomatic untruth?'

'As far as I'm concerned, that's the same as a lie. Major Wellbridge was with you at Abbottabad, wasn't he?'

'You certainly seem to be convinced that he was.'

'You had an affair with him, didn't you?'

Another lift of the eyebrows. 'You show a lamentable lack of perception, Sergeant. If I did, you could hardly expect me to admit it.'

'Couldn't I? . . . Why?'

She looked him straight in the eyes. 'Suppose what you say did happen to be true. Think about it, Sergeant. Imagine the situation. A girl of seventeen, the daughter of an army colonel, brought up in a society with a rigid moral and social code, finding herself pregnant by an officer under her father's command! D'you think she'd be happy? Proud of what she'd done? Isn't it far more likely that, looking back now, she'd want to forget it? Consign it to oblivion? Pretend it never happened? . . . I would, if I'd found myself in such a position.'

'But you did, Mrs Wellbridge, didn't you?' McKenzie said.

Her lips tightened. 'If that's what you believe, Sergeant, then by all means believe it. You'll get no confirmation from me.'

McKenzie turned back a page in the file. 'When we arrested you at Sparrow Hill House, you pretended not to know who Ruth Wellbridge was.'

'Did I?'

'Yes, you did. You said, "Who the devil's Ruth Wellbridge?" That was another lie, wasn't it? You knew who she was. You knew very well she was your husband's first wife. He'd divorced her, hadn't he? You told us so.'

She sighed. 'For a detective, Sergeant, your lack of perception's truly alarming. What if I did know? Surely you don't expect me to admit to a crime that I've never committed.'

'I expect you to tell the truth, Mrs Wellbridge, not to lie at every turn.'

'And what is the truth?' she said. 'You profess to know it, so tell me.'

'Willingly, ma'am.' McKenzie leaned forward. He didn't raise his voice, but it cut through the room like the blade of a razor. 'This is the truth, so listen. It seems to be something you find hard to recognize, so I'll take you through it slowly, step by step . . . While you were at Lynn you received a telephone call. It came from Mr Wellbridge at Sparrow Hill House. He told you to make some excuse to your friend, Mrs Smith, and come home right away. He had to see you. It was urgent. He wouldn't keep you long. Perhaps half an hour, an hour at the most. After that you could go back to Lynn . . . So you conjured up some pretext that left you free for the rest of the day, and drove back to Sibthorpe. When you reached there, your husband told you that Ruth, his poor demented first wife, had turned up out of the blue and made a terrible scene. She'd attacked him, and when he'd tried to restrain her, she'd suddenly collapsed. It was a terrible mistake. He hadn't meant her to die, but he needed your help to cover things up . . . So you hatched a plot between you to do exactly that. An elaborate plot. And that's the reason why, on every occasion since then, you've been telling a string of lies. You knew Geoffrey Wellbridge was never divorced. You're a bigamist, Deirdre, and not only that. You're an accessory to murder. That's the truth of the matter, isn't it?'

234

She gazed at him for a full five seconds and then shook her head. 'No, it isn't,' she said. 'You couldn't be further from the truth if you'd dreamed it all up in an alcoholic haze. It sounds more like a chapter from *Alice in Wonderland*.'

Tench intervened. 'Then what is the truth, Miss Thompson?'

'I've told you already. If this unfortunate woman was in fact murdered, I know nothing about it.'

'Then I'm asking you again . . . Where's Mr Wellbridge?'

'And I'm telling you again. I haven't the faintest idea.'

'And that's your last word?'

'It has to be, Inspector. There's nothing more I can tell you.'

Tench pushed back his chair, stood up and closed the file. 'Then I'm detaining you here, Miss Thompson,' he said. 'I'm not satisfied with your statement. You'll be questioned again tomorrow . . . Take her away, Sergeant. Lock her up for the night.'

'My pleasure,' McKenzie said.

She gave him one brief, contemptuous glance and then turned back to Tench. She seemed almost amused, but when she spoke, the words dropped like sharp spikes of ice. 'How deliciously revealing, Inspector!' she said. 'Your sergeant's a sadist as well as a masochist. D'you think he'll lock the door of my cell and try to rape me?'

9

'Stuck-up little bitch!' McKenzie said savagely. 'She was never raped. She lay back and begged for it . . . So where's this murderous sugar-daddy of hers?'

Tench threw out his hands. 'Your guess is likely to be just as good as mine. Land's End? John o'Groats? The Costa del Sol? Give them a shuffle and pick one . . . Could be anywhere, Mac.'

'Then what's your bet?'

'I've got a peculiar feeling he's still around somewhere.'

'Here? In Norfolk?'

'Why not? He's shrewd. He's not the sort who'll make a dash for a sun-drenched beach. Not yet, at least. Not till things have settled down.'

'Then wherever he is, he's going to have a long wait.'

'Maybe. Maybe not. We can't keep a watch on the ports for ever. He's banking on that.'

'So where's he hiding out?'

'As your darling Deirdre says, Mac, I just haven't the faintest. Norfolk's teeming with places where he might have gone to earth. Ruined country houses, abandoned windmills, churches that are crumbling away into dust. They're too numerous to count, and searching them all could take the best part of months ... At the moment I feel as helpless as old Mary Bunn. Out in the dark, groping around on that filthy marsh with the mist coming down, and losing all sense of which way to turn ... We need a speck of light. Something to point the way. Let's hope someone somewhere can provide one, and fast.'

McKenzie gave a sour grin. 'Well, I've never been one for poking round churches. I tend to steer clear of them except for weddings and funerals. But amen to that. And God help him if I get my hands on the bastard. He's cost me too many hours of good drinking time. Whenever I think of him, he's standing between me and all those pints of ale lined up on a bar. I'll strangle the bugger if he gets in my way again.'

'So where is he,' said Lubbock, 'this Francis Frankie Wellbridge?'

Tench wafted away the smoke. 'This cottage of yours gets more like a kippering shed every bloody day.'

'Don't change the subject, laddie. I asked you a question. Where d'you think he's got to, this chap you've suddenly decided to charge?'

'I was hoping you might have some original idea. Don't say you've lost your intuitive spark, though that wouldn't surprise me. Not in this fug.'

'To get a spark you need a flint. Intuition needs a clue to spark it into life ... Tell me something about him.'

'Ex-army major. Served in India, and then with the Chindits in Burma ...'

Lubbock waved his pipe. 'No, laddie, I don't want things like that. I want local connections. I've told you before. They're the things that count.'

'All right ... He lives at Sibthorpe. Runs his own timber yard over at Holt ...'

'Whereabouts in Sibthorpe?'

'Sparrow Hill House. It's on the road above Medford.'

'Tudor? Sixteenth century? Stepped gables and those peculiar twisted chimneys?'

'That's right. Polygonal ... You know the place then?'

'Of course I know it, laddie. Took a stroll up there last summer. Rambling old place. It's been empty for years. Must be riddled with dry rot and woodworm. What on earth made him pick on a place like that?'

'He'd just got back from India and needed somewhere to live. His girlfriend spotted it. At least that's what he said.'

'He bought it?'

'Rented it.'

'Short of cash, was he?'

'I wouldn't have thought so. He'd just inherited a ton from his father.'

'Strange,' said Lubbock.

'Why?'

'Well, let's put it this way, laddie. If you were gifted of a sudden with the money to buy anything you wanted in Norfolk, would you think of dossing down in Sparrow Hill House?'

'I might,' said Tench, 'till I found somewhere better.'

'Is that what he's doing?'

'So he said ... And what the hell's the point of nattering on about it, anyway? We need to know where he is now, not where he was.'

'So where is he?'

'God knows.'

'No clues?'

'At the moment, not a whisper. We're all of us stumbling around in the dark.'

Lubbock laid down his pipe and pushed himself up. 'Then take my advice, laddie. Push off home to bed. At this time of night there's no point in pattering on about anything. You're lost in the dark and I'm half-asleep. Go on. Push off home. Leave me to go to my little truckle-bed. I'll see you tomorrow.'

Tench sighed. 'I suppose you're right.'

'Aren't I always?' Lubbock said.

He watched the car drive away. Then he picked up the phone, dialled the operator and asked for a number.

There was a pause, then a mumbling sound.

'Hello,' he said. 'It's John ... Yes. What other Johns are there? ... Are you still awake in that cosy little nook on the edge of nowhere? ... What d'you mean? Barely ... Then go and make yourself a strong black coffee. I'm coming down for a chat.'

X

LIGHT OUT OF DARKNESS

Nothing comes fairer to light than what has been
lang hidden

> Scottish proverb

1

At ten past nine the following morning, Sunday, Mr Anthony Balham, an estate agent in Holt, walked into Holt police station and volunteered the information that, six days before, he had rented a lock-up garage on Beeches Close to Mr Geoffrey Wellbridge.

Yes, he knew Mr Wellbridge. They'd done business on several previous occasions.

Had Mr Wellbridge said why he needed the garage?

Yes, said he'd just bought a second-hand car and wanted somewhere to store it.

Had he said where he'd bought the car?

Mr Balham shook his head. No, he hadn't, but he did know Mr Wellbridge had bought his Chrysler from Dickinsons, the motor dealers out on the Cromer road.

Since it was the Sabbath, Dickinsons was closed, and Mr Dickinson lived at Bodham, three miles out of town. It was consequently close to eleven o'clock by the time the Holt police confirmed that on the previous Monday morning Mr Geoffrey Wellbridge had purchased a blue Vauxhall Velox saloon with the registration number CL 7238; and it wasn't till half-past four that a constable from the Kent force, on foot patrol, reported that he'd found it parked on Marine Drive at Dover.

By that time Deirdre Wellbridge, still protesting her ignorance of any misdemeanour committed at Medford, had been released from the cell in Norwich police station where she'd passed a somewhat uncomfortable night. Detective Constable Spurgeon, relieved from watch at the timber yard by one of Varden's men, had driven her back to Sparrow Hill House, and once the door had closed behind her, the members of Varden's surveillance team had moved stealthily in to take up their positions: two men in the trees, one at the front and another at the rear of the house; two more in an unmarked car stationed on Sibthorpe Hill within sight of the drive; and another four in two cars by the road intersections at Medford to the north and Copston fork to the south.

Once in place, they waited and watched for the move that Tench was hoping she'd be tempted to make.

2

Tench waited too, but at least with more confidence than he'd felt the night before. It was just possible, he thought, that he might have a clue to which direction she'd take.

That same morning, at much the same time as Mr Anthony Balham had pushed open the door of the police station at Holt, Sergeant Varden, on watch with a colleague at Sparrow Hill House, had intercepted a postman on the point of dropping a card through the letter-box.

He'd examined it, made a note of its contents, and waited for the postman to drop it through the slot.

Half an hour later, Tench had taken a call from Sergeant Hellyer at the incident room in Medford.

'An ordinary picture postcard, sir,' the sergeant had said. 'The sea front at Cromer. Addressed to Mrs D. Wellbridge at Sparrow Hill House. No written message, just a six-figure number. 816827. Could be a map reference. If it is, then it's probably somewhere in Norfolk.'

Lock had produced a set of ordnance maps from one of the metal cabinets in the CID room, and he and Tench had spread them out on a table.

'Must be somewhere Thetford way.' Lock had peered down at the numbered squares. He'd traced the lines with his fingers until they'd converged. 'Yes, sir. It's here, in the middle of Thetford Warren. Right at the junction of these two tracks. And there's an old warrener's lodge. It's marked as a ruin . . . D'you think it might be a rendezvous point?'

'It could be.' Tench had nodded. 'Whether it is or not, we'll have to work on that assumption.'

He'd called in Ellison and Rayner and handed them the map. 'Get down there,' he'd said. 'I want the place covered. If they show, then pick them up.'

They waited and watched: Varden's men stationed in the grounds of the house and covering the roads that led to Medford and Sibthorpe; Hellyer's team down in Medford itself; the two lonely figures crouching in a copse by the astrodome at Copston; and Ellison and Rayner, forty miles to the south, hidden among the trees that enfolded the warrener's lodge at Thetford.

The hours dragged on, the clouds built up, there were rumbles of thunder away to the west. A breeze, perhaps the first sign of an approaching storm, began to rustle the leaves around Sparrow Hill House, but apart from that everything was still.

In the control room at Norwich, Tench and McKenzie glanced from time to time at the large-scale map of Norfolk taped to the wall, and tried to fathom which route the black Sunbeam-Talbot was likely to take.

'If she's making for Thetford,' McKenzie said, 'she'll take the Fakenham road, then by Swaffham and Mundford. That's the shortest way.'

'She could take any of half a dozen different routes,' said Tench. 'She knows the road to Lynn. She might make for there just to throw us off the scent.'

They waited. It was all they could do. Then, at five o'clock, as a premature twilight descended on Norwich, as lightning flashed and the rain began to fall, Desmond Lock, who was manning the phone in the control room, took a call from the Kent police to say that they'd found the Vauxhall abandoned in Dover.

'He's got away, damn it,' McKenzie said. 'We're stuck here in the rain and he's sunning himself on the shores of the Med . . . So where's she going to run to now? Tell me that. Sunny Spain or wet Thetford?'

'God only knows.' Tench was tight-lipped. 'We'll just have to be patient and wait till she moves.'

'And when the devil d'you think that's going to be?'

'When it's dark,' said Tench. 'She's waiting for the dark.'

The rain pelted down on the city for an hour, then the sun came out again, silvering the roof tops, glinting off the slates. Camp-beds were commandeered and set up in the annexe; Lock relinquished the phone; Sue Gradwell took his place. Then, just before half-past seven, the Duty Sergeant rang through from the desk.

Sue Gradwell covered the mouthpiece and turned towards Tench. 'Mr Lubbock's here, sir. Says he needs to see you. It's urgent.'

Tench took a deeper breath than he'd taken all day. 'I'd better see him,' he said. 'Tell the sergeant to send him up to my office.'

'Now what?' McKenzie lounged back in his chair.

Tench stretched and yawned. He seemed reluctant to move. 'I think perhaps he's had a sudden flash of intuition, and it's told him where Wellbridge is hiding out.'

'You think so?'

243

'Yes.' Tench pushed himself up. 'He's built a cosy little treehouse for two down in Thetford Forest ... Come on, Mac. Let's drag ourselves upstairs and find out. At least it'll pass the time.'

4

Lubbock wasn't alone. With him was a tall, gaunt man with a mop of ginger hair.

Lubbock waved his pipe vaguely 'You know Lawrence,' he said. 'No need to introduce you ... We'd have been here before, but we've had a long day.'

'Hello, Lawrence,' said Tench. 'Find yourself a seat.' And then to Lubbock, 'A long day where?'

'First at Stow St Mary and then down at Mattisham.'

'What on earth for?'

'Trying to solve the problem that was driving you close to distraction last night. If a murderer somehow disappears without trace, where in heaven's name can he possibly be?'

'And you've found the answer?'

'We don't know yet. We still need to check.'

'I thought that was what you'd been doing all day.'

'Then you were wrong, laddie, weren't you?' Lubbock examined his pipe and then, with a clatter, knocked it out in the waste bin. 'Since nine o'clock this morning we've been tracking down an indispensable piece of evidence. Once we found it, it led us to draw certain conclusions. We now have to test them ... That's why Lawrence is here. He's the one to explain.'

Tench looked across at Bell. 'I think you'd better,' he said. 'If you don't, we'll be here all night.'

Lawrence produced a folded sheet of notes from his pocket. 'It's like this, Mike,' he said. 'About ten years ago I did some work for a friend who was writing a book about Tudor houses in Norfolk. We did a tour of the county, making a list of the most interesting ones, and one of the places we looked at was Sparrow Hill House. I undertook to do some research to help him out, and last night, when John happened to mention the name, I remembered one particular aspect of it. The trouble was this. The information was there, in partial form, in my head, but I couldn't recall exactly where it was that I'd read it. You see, Sparrow Hill House was built in 1584 by a Francis Clifford, the younger son of a well-known Catholic family. Their family seat was Mattisham Hall, near Diss, but at the time of my research the archives were held by one of Francis Clifford's direct descendants, Sir Roger Clifford, who lived at Stow St Mary. That's close to Downham Market on the edge of the Fens.'

He gave a rueful smile. 'I knew the relevant passage was somewhere in the archives, so first thing this morning we drove over to Stow, but the papers I'd studied were no longer there. They'd all been transferred to Mattisham Hall. That meant that we had to trail all the way back to Diss, and then it was a case of tracing the one vital sheet among thousands of documents. It's taken us all day. It was a hell of a job.'

'But you found it?' said Tench.

'Eventually, yes.'

'So why was it so important?'

'It may not be,' said Bell. 'We're guessing, that's all. But we think we may know where this Wellbridge character's hidden himself away. It's possible, no more than that, that he's still at Sparrow Hill House.'

'He can't be.' McKenzie dismissed the idea. 'The place has been searched.'

'Nonetheless, he could still be there.'

'There's a priest's hole,' said Lubbock, 'and we know where it is.'

McKenzie was baffled. 'And what the devil's a priest's hole?'

'It's a small room,' Lawrence told him, 'hidden behind a sliding panel in the wall. They're common enough in large Catholic houses built in Tudor times.'

5

'You see,' he went on, 'during Elizabeth's reign there were numerous Catholic plots to overthrow the Queen, not least those that were devised by fanatical supporters of Mary Queen of Scots. Because of that the practice of the Catholic faith was forbidden in Britain, and those who refused to take the Oath of Supremacy and attend Church of England services were adjudged to be guilty of treason. But the Catholic faith remained strong among many old aristocratic families, and priests came from abroad, landing illegally on lonely stretches of coast like the ones in North Norfolk, and secretly celebrating mass in isolated country houses.

'Government agents, known as pursuivants, armed with the powers of search and arrest, were deputed to track them down, and so Catholic families building houses at that time took the precaution of adding priest's holes where the priest, together with his vestments and other accessories, could be hidden at a moment's notice if word was received that pursuivants were on the way.'

McKenzie frowned. 'And you know for sure that there's one at Sparrow Hill House?'

'Oh yes,' said Lawrence. 'There's a note in the archives that Nicholas Owen was there in 1585.'

McKenzie looked at Tench. 'Have you ever heard of these priest's holes?'

'I've heard of them,' said Tench. 'I've even seen one at Boscobel House in Shropshire. Charles the Second hid there after the Battle of Worcester. As Lawrence says, they're common enough. I believe there's a place near Kidderminster that has eight of them, scattered around the house. But I've never heard of this Nicholas Owen. Who was he?'

'He was a genius,' Lawrence said, 'a Jesuit brother who was also a highly skilled carpenter and stonemason. He spent most of his life constructing priest's holes all over Britain, and he was such an expert at the job that many of them still remain undiscovered. The pursuivants were trained to be thorough. They demolished some walls, measured and tapped others, raised parts of the floors and often lifted the roof tiles, but in some cases all their efforts came to nothing. His methods were so ingenious that the holes he'd constructed were never detected.'

'But they did find the one at Sparrow Hill House?'

'No, it wasn't uncovered till the middle of the last century when some renovation work was done on the place, but since then it's been listed in the documents of sale, and when the ownership of the house changed some fifty years ago its precise location was recorded. And . . .' He paused. '. . . the means of gaining access to it.'

'Then whereabouts is it?'

'There's an old recessed fireplace in the large ground-floor room at the rear of the house, and one of the oak panels at the side has a spring. It can only be activated by applying a particular type of pressure. That opens up the panelling. Behind it there's an iron pivot runs down through the masonry. If you push hard on one of the stones, the inner wall swings aside. Behind it is the priest's hole.'

'And Wellbridge would know about it?'

'That's more than possible, if he rented the place.'

'The bugger!' McKenzie said. 'I'll bet he's nowhere near Dover. He's back at the house. They'll be hoping to slip away together, the two of them.'

'He couldn't have got back,' said Tench. 'There's been a watch on the place since early yesterday evening.'

Lawrence pursed his lips. 'He could have done, Mike. According to the archives, there's another way in and out of that hole. It was one of Owen's more macabre designs. There's a trapdoor in the floor that covers a shaft with a scaling-ladder. It leads down to a tunnel that comes out somewhere on the edge of the grounds. The trap's weighted, so that it closes automatically, but step on one side of it and it opens. Anyone searching for the hole without knowing it was there could fall twenty feet down the shaft to his death.'

'Do the archives say exactly where the tunnel comes out?'

'No, they don't. I don't think it's even been explored in recent times. It may well have fallen in. On the other hand, it could still provide an escape route.'

'Or a way to get into the house.'

'Yes.'

'That's good enough,' McKenzie said. 'If there's a chance he's still there, hiding out in that hole, let's go and pick him up, and Deirdre as well.'

'No.' Tench shook his head. 'We're just guessing. As Lawrence says, the tunnel could well be blocked. He may not be there at all, and if he isn't we still need her to be free to make a move. She's the only one who can lead us to him.'

'But they could both get away.'

'I don't see how they can. The place is under surveillance. No one's going to leave the house without being seen.'

'Suppose they've slipped out already.'

'Then we can't do much about it. We'll know soon enough. If there's someone still there, then once it gets dark the lights'll go on. If they don't, we'll break in. The next move's up to her. We just have to sit tight and wait till she makes it. It's a risk we have to take ... We'll strengthen the watch. Get on to Hellyer. Tell him to call in his men from the astrodome and all those in Medford. I want them up at the house. They're to ring the whole perimeter. The roads are covered already. Varden's men are doing that. Tell Hellyer that we're on our way down to Medford. We'll use the incident room down there as a base. Once she moves – and she will – we'll search the house and, hopefully, Lawrence can work his magic. If Well-bridge is still there, skulking in that hole, thinking we'll get tired and call off the watch, then he'll find he's got it wrong.' He turned towards Bell. 'You're sure you know how to open it up?'

Lawrence gave a shrug. 'Theoretically, yes. The instructions are clear enough in the archives.'

'But in practice?'

'Well, I can't guarantee there'll be instant success ... It might take a little time.'

Lubbock picked up his pipe. 'What he means is it could be a sleepless night.'

Tench sniffed the air. 'Then do us all a favour. Stuff that corroded old relic away. We don't want to smoke him out except as a last resort.'

Lubbock sighed. 'Why do I sometimes feel that my life's been a glorious failure?' he said.

6

The sun set at 8.35 that evening, but it was hidden behind cloud, the light was already beginning to fade, and by nine o'clock the thick band of trees around Sparrow Hill House had plunged the place into darkness.

At five past nine the closest of Varden's watchers, crouched in the undergrowth at the edge of the gravel some sixty yards from the front of the house, saw the curtains stealthily drawn one by one, but it was too dark inside and he was too far away to know for sure whether the figure he'd glimpsed at a window was a man or a woman.

He waited, scanning the dim wall of stone that blacked out the sky, willing the bleak, blank façade to show some sign of life.

Then it came.

All of a sudden, in an upstairs room, someone switched on a light. It showed as two narrow shafts, one at each side of the mullioned window.

Sergeant Varden himself, watching from the trees on the fringe of the drive, saw the fingers of light through a network of leaves, and crept forward to give himself a clear field of vision.

He, too, waited, his gaze fixed on the window.

Ten minutes passed by, then the light was switched off, but in a matter of seconds another sprang up in a downstairs room in the opposite wing. It survived only briefly, and once it went out, the house was cast again into rustling shadow.

The black Sunbeam-Talbot, parked on the gravel, was an even darker hump against the gloomy stone face of the old Clifford house. Nothing stirred except the breeze blowing in from the sea, and the thousands of leaves that whispered in its wake.

The minutes ticked by. Varden peered at the luminous fingers of his watch . . . 9.35 . . .

How much longer before she moved?

They waited, all of them, flexing their legs impatiently, shifting in their seats: the watchers among the trees and their colleagues in cars on the silent roads that encircled Sparrow Hill.

9.50 . . . Ten o'clock . . .

Then suddenly Varden saw her.

The front door opened and she was there on the steps: a slim figure in her long, dark skirt, carrying a small shoulder-bag and a suitcase. She set the case down, locked the door behind her, stopped for a moment, as he thought, to drop the key in her shoulder-bag, then picked up the case again, turned down the steps and walked to the car. He heard her shoes crunch the gravel.

She put the case in the boot, opened the car door and slid behind the wheel.

The door closed, the engine coughed and then spat into life. As it revved, the car moved forward, slowly at first, then gathering speed as it turned on to the drive, the headlights cutting a swathe through the night. He dropped flat on the ground only seconds before the beam, scything through the dark, swept across his head and was gone.

The car whipped past him, its slipstream stirring the grass against his face.

He saw the tail-lights dwindle, then vanish among the trees, and as they flashed into darkness he scrambled to his feet and began to run down the drive.

When the car reached the gates and turned towards Sibthorpe, an unmarked Triumph Roadster pulled out of a farm track and followed it up the hill as far as the Copston fork, where it veered to the right and took the lane that led to Walsingham.

Ten minutes later, two plain-clothes constables in a Humber Snipe saloon trailed it as it wound through the village, and they were still close behind when it sped past the old manor house at East Barsham and headed out on the road to Fakenham.

7

'We were right,' McKenzie said. 'She's making for that warrener's ruin at Thetford.'

'She could be,' said Tench, 'or it may be just a trick to lead us astray.'

They were gathered, he and McKenzie, with Lubbock and Lawrence Bell, round the old recessed fireplace in Wellbridge's study at Sparrow Hill House.

'Why the hell should it be?' McKenzie was beginning to show signs of impatience. 'We said she'd go that way. Fakenham, Swaffham and then Thetford Warren. It seems plain enough to me.'

'Maybe it is.' Tench conceded the point. 'But we've been led up the garden path so many times in this Blacknock case, I find it hard to believe in simple solutions. Wellbridge is clever. I can't think he's going to make things as easy as that.'

He took a step towards Bell, who was running his fingers across the oak panelling to the right of the fireplace. 'What's the prognosis, Lawrence?' he asked.

'Well, this is the side we have to tackle,' Bell said. 'We can only follow the instructions in the archives and hope that they work.' He took the sheet of notes from his pocket and handed them to Tench. 'You tell me what to do . . . It's the third panel up from the floor. Am I right?'

'Right,' said Tench.

'Read what it says.'

'You have to press on five different points, but in the correct order. Top left, bottom right, bottom left, top right, and then in the centre.'

'OK,' said Lawrence. 'Stand by for the magic.'

He pressed the four corners and stepped back a pace.

'Now the middle,' McKenzie prompted.

'Yes, I know.' Lawrence took out a tape and measured the panel. 'It's just a case of finding the right spot to press . . . You hold the tape.'

McKenzie held it. 'Have a go,' he said. 'We've nothing to lose.'

Lawrence chose a point and pressed.

They waited. Nothing happened.

'Try again,' said Tench.

Lawrence pressed a spot half an inch to the left. Still nothing happened.

McKenzie stepped forward, chose his own spot, and thumped it hard once with the side of his fist.

There was a click and a section of the panelling moved. It creaked upwards slowly, revealing the stone wall behind. When it reached the level of McKenzie's head, it stopped. 'Just needed a bit of coaxing, that's all,' he said.

'It's a good job we brought the magician's assistant,' Lubbock remarked drily. 'They come in useful sometimes, these merchants of beef.'

Lawrence waved a dismissive hand. 'Never mind,' he said. 'Even the best of us can be fallible . . . So far, so good . . . Now, which stone do I push?'

Tench consulted the notes. 'Second from the bottom right.'

'Let the beef merchant do it,' McKenzie said.

He rested his hands on their shoulders, lifted his foot and rammed it hard against the stone. There was a grinding sound, and the wall swung on its pivot. Behind it they could dimly see another stone wall.

Tench handed the notes back to Lawrence. 'Wellbridge!' he shouted 'The game's up. It's over. If you're in there, come out.'

There was silence.

He flicked on his torch and ducked under the panelling.

'Watch out for the trapdoor,' Lawrence called urgently. 'Best look for it first.'

Tench flashed the torch around, stepping gingerly, testing the floor with his foot. 'It's all right,' he said. 'I've found it.'

They saw the beam swing in an arc, probing the darkness, searching the corners. Then Tench squatted down and picked something up. They heard him swear softly.

'What is it?' McKenzie said.

'This.' Tench held it out through the gap.

McKenzie took it and turned it about in his hands. 'I'm still none the wiser . . . What the devil is it?'

Lawrence gave it a glance, nothing more. 'It's a prayer-wheel,' he said. 'Buddhists carry them around and turn them when they pray.'

'And some folk who aren't Buddhists,' said Tench, 'hide them away and then pretend they've been stolen.'

8

They crouched by the open trap in the priest's hole.

Tench played the beam around. 'It's hopeless,' he said. 'I can't see a thing except for the walls.'

McKenzie peered down the shaft. 'Well, one fact's for sure. If he hasn't already done a hop, skip and jump, he must be down there . . . somewhere.'

'Then we've got him.' Tench sounded almost persuasive. 'Even if the tunnel's still open, we've got him. If he tries to slip out, Varden's men'll pick him up.'

'We'll have to drive him out first.' McKenzie was grim. 'If we don't, then he'll just sit tight and stay put . . . And,' he went on, 'it'll be closing-time soon, and if I don't knock a pint back tonight you're going to find me shrivelled into dust tomorrow morning . . . Come on. Give me the torch. I'll flush the bugger out.'

He swung himself on to the scaling-ladder and began to climb down.

They watched him vanish into darkness. Then, deep down, the finger of light flashed again.

The beam wandered around, then settled on one particular spot.

It stayed there, barely moving, for what seemed an age. Then it suddenly flicked off, and they heard McKenzie's feet on the scaling-ladder.

He climbed slowly. Then, when he reached the top, he rested his arms on the rim of the shaft, and looked at each of them in turn.

'Well?' said Tench. 'What?'

In the little stone room, it was too dark to see the expression on his face, but the words, when he spoke them, were menacing enough. 'You're not going to believe this, any of you . . . not in a million years.'

'You've found something?'

McKenzie heaved himself up. 'Yes, you could say that.'

There was a pause. They waited.

'It's not Wellbridge,' he said. 'It's our dear darling Deirdre. And there won't be any need to flush her out. She's dead.'

Tench stared at him for a moment.

'Then . . .?'

'Yes,' McKenzie said.

It was all he needed to say.

EPILOGUE
THE FETCH

There is no people, rude or learned, among whom apparitions of the dead are not related and believed

Samuel Johnson: *Rasselas*

1

Tench put out another call, but too late.

The Sunbeam-Talbot was already in Fakenham where it sped through changing traffic-lights, trapping the two plain-clothes constables in the Humber Snipe behind a set of red lights and a stream of late-night motorists crossing the intersection. By the time the road was clear, the car ahead had disappeared.

It was half an hour later that the Fakenham police discovered it parked by a line of lock-up garages close to the Wells road, and another twelve hours before a message came through from Lynn that a long black skirt, a shoulder bag and a wig had been found in a public lavatory in the centre of the town.

It took another five days before the nationwide manhunt produced a result.

As inquests on all the four victims were opened in Norwich and formally adjourned, the search continued day and night, but without any trace of Geoffrey Wellbridge. He'd slipped through the net that Tench had thrown around him, and vanished, so it seemed, from the face of the earth.

Then at half-past five on the following Saturday, Mr Nathaniel Jenkins, an elderly farmer from the Derbyshire Peak, decided to ease his festering suspicions of the heavily tanned, wiry, middle-aged man who'd recently rented the old limestone cottage that he regularly let to visitors during the summer months. He reported his doubts to the Bakewell police.

The cottage was two miles away from the town, beyond the village of Over Haddon, standing on its own surrounded by fields above the gorge of the Lathkill, and the officers sent to investigate its tenant kept it under surveillance for an hour and a half before they moved in.

Wellbridge offered no resistance. He was briefly questioned, then arrested, taken back to Bakewell and lodged in a cell, while the Duty Inspector rang through to Tench.

Gregg and Ellison were immediately despatched to collect him. They drove through the night, and it was half-past two on the Sunday morning when McKenzie led him, handcuffed between two constables, into the interview room at Norwich, rammed him unceremoniously down on a chair and sent word to Tench that the long search was over.

2

It was a very different man from the one who'd blandly brushed them aside a week before, who faced Tench and McKenzie as dawn broke on the interview room that Sunday morning.

He was no longer the straight-backed, confident figure who'd repeatedly deflected every question they'd asked. In the intervening days he seemed to have shrunk, withered into someone very much older: an unkempt, dishevelled and weary version of the man that they'd known.

He raised a pair of haggard eyes to the two detectives as they pulled out their chairs and sat down on the opposite side of the desk.

'Before you begin,' he said, 'I want to make a statement.'

Tench opened a file. 'You'll have the chance to do that in due course, Mr Wellbridge. For the moment you're here to answer my questions.'

Wellbridge drew a deep breath. 'There's no need to ask any questions,' he said. 'I killed them. All of them.'

'You're ready to admit that you murdered your wife?'

There was one brief familiar flash from the man. The faintest of smiles seemed to play across his lips. 'Which one?' he said.

'You have only one, Mr Wellbridge.' Tench was cold.

'If you mean Ruth, then yes, I killed her, but it was all a terrible, tragic mistake.'

'And the two men, Craske and Grice?'

'I've said so, haven't I?'

'And Deirdre Thompson?'

'Yes . . . If it was her.'

Tench leaned back in his chair. 'You said your wife's death was a tragic mistake. What did you mean by that?'

'We both of us made mistakes, and both of them were tragic. She made the first. She should never have turned up at Sparrow Hill House . . . I made the second. I never intended her to die.'

'But she did, Mr Wellbridge, didn't she?'

'Yes.' The word itself sounded dead.

'Then you'd better explain, hadn't you?'

Wellbridge took another deep breath. 'How can I possibly do that? You'd never understand.'

'Why not?'

'Are you married, Chief Inspector?'

Tench raised his eyebrows. 'Yes,' he said. 'Does it matter?'

'Happily married?'

'I believe so.'

'You're in love with your wife?'

'Yes.'

'And she loves you?'

'She seems to.'

'You live a tranquil life together?'

'I'd say we do, yes.'

'Then you couldn't understand.'

'That may be so' – Tench spoke quietly – 'but I still need to hear your version of what happened.'

'Why bother?' McKenzie said. 'He's already put a noose round his neck. Let the bugger swing.'

Tench ignored him. 'I'm waiting, Mr Wellbridge.'

The man gave a shrug. 'The sergeant's right,' he said. 'I've told you I killed them. Isn't that enough?'

'Not for me,' Tench said, 'no. There are still a great many things that I don't understand. I need to reconcile two very different people: you and a man who gratuitously murders innocent women.'

Wellbridge studied him for a moment. He sighed. 'All right, Chief Inspector, if that's what you want. But at least let me warn you. If your wife hasn't come within a quarter of an inch of stabbing you to death with a kitchen knife, then you're likely to find such reconciliation an almost impossible goal to achieve.'

3

He closed his eyes, bowed his head, and seemed for a while to be deep in thought. Then he suddenly looked up. 'I first saw Ruth at a dance,' he said. 'She was wearing one of those long, swirling dresses that swung from the hips and revealed her trim silken legs to the knee when she spun. She was lithe and slim, and she danced with a kind of serpentine grace that was almost erotic. Those of a cynical turn of mind decry love at first sight, but I loved her then, at a glance. She was electric, candescent, she lit up the floor.

'I couldn't believe that she'd feel about me in the same intense way – I was reserved, undemonstrative, I'd never been handsome and I'd always been shy in the presence of women – but, remarkably, she did. We were happy together. It was a magical time.

'We were married three months later and went to live down in Kent. I thought I must be the luckiest person in the world.'

He paused. The haggard eyes looked through and beyond Tench. 'I wasn't and nor was she. We were both doomed, even then. I because I'd linked myself to a woman who carried the seeds of a progressive, incurable type of madness; she because she'd married a man who could never provide the support that she needed.

'Oh, I knew she could be moody, depressed at times, but I knew what it was. I'd read the books, hadn't I? It was what they called pre-menstrual tension. Most women had it. In my youthful ignorance that was what I thought. It was just something husbands had to tolerate. It would pass.

'I was wrong. It didn't. She got steadily worse. There were two Ruths, the one that I loved and a completely different person that I couldn't understand, and in time came to hate. When I woke in the morning, I could never be sure which of the two would be waking beside me: the happy, laughing, loving girl that I cherished or a sullen, listless, foul-tempered woman who, to me, was a stranger.

'She could change in an instant. I never knew where I stood. One moment she'd be deliriously happy, excited at the prospect of doing something new; the next she'd grow quiet, morose, resentful and petulant. It was just as if a cloud had passed over her sun.

'As the months went by, she got steadily worse. The clouds of depression got blacker, lasted longer. She began to see things that weren't actually there, imagine things had happened that were beyond comprehension. She had fits of ungovernable rage when she tore down curtains, smashed pieces of furniture and, when I tried to restrain her, beat me with her fists.'

He looked across the table at Tench, and gave a sad, hopeless shrug of his shoulders. 'I tried to do, Chief Inspector, what you're trying to do. I did my best to reconcile the two different women who shared my life, but I couldn't. They were too far apart, too contrasting, too discordant: the one that I loved, and the other that I came both to fear and to hate. I kissed one and felt that I could strangle the other, and I knew that one day, when at last I reached the end of my tether, that was what I would do, and that made me afraid.

'One bright summer morning, early on in the war, she woke in a black depression. I had to coax her to get dressed. All she wanted to do was to lie there in bed. Over breakfast she was moody, brooding over something. Then she suddenly came out with it. She mentioned a woman's name, some woman I'd never heard of, spat it in my face, and accused me of sleeping with her night after night. I denied it. What else could I do? She wouldn't believe me, kept on saying I'd betrayed her. The more I protested, the more frenzied she became. She took hold of the cloth, swept all the breakfast things on to the floor and dashed off to the kitchen. I went after her – I had to – but she was waiting behind the door with a knife in her hand. She lunged at me, and I felt the point of the blade against my chest. I gripped her wrists and shook the knife free. There was hate in her eyes, and I haven't any doubt there was hate in mine too. She wasn't Ruth. She

258

was someone I didn't know at all: a stranger, an ugly, wild-eyed, demented woman trying to stab me to death. I could have killed her at that moment. I think I was within a hair's breadth of gripping her by the neck.

'I went upstairs, packed a bag and walked out of the house. I never saw her again till she turned up that Sunday at Sparrow Hill House.'

He shook his head sadly. 'She should never have tried to find me. She never would have found me if some woman hadn't happened to see me in Blakeney. It was the cruellest chance. I'd calculated the odds. Fifty million to one.

'It was midday on Sunday. Deirdre was in Lynn. I was alone in the house when the door bell rang. When I opened the door she was standing there: Ruth. It was so much of a shock to see her that I simply let her in. She seemed normal enough. I thought we could talk. But once inside the study I could tell it wasn't Ruth. It was the stranger with the knife, the woman I thought I'd banished for ever from my life. She saw the picture of Deirdre that I kept on the desk, flung it down on the floor and stamped on the glass. Then she threw herself at me, hammering me with her fists and screaming that I was nothing but a common adulterer. She'd find this woman if she had to search for the rest of her life, and when she found her she'd kill her and kill me too.

'I had to stop her from screaming. I held her tight with one hand and clamped the other across her face. She struggled for a while and then she suddenly went limp. When I released her she simply dropped to the ground.'

He closed his eyes again. His head tossed from side to side. 'I never meant to kill her. I swear I didn't. I'd been trained to kill in the army. I could have done it in a second, silently and swiftly. Just a snap of the neck ... All I wanted to do was to stop her screaming ... And then it was too late ...'

He brushed a hand across his eyes. 'You can't hope to understand,' he said. 'If I were you, I wouldn't even try.'

4

'And I suppose,' McKenzie said, 'that you didn't intend to kill darling Deirdre either.'

Wellbridge stared at the table top. 'It wasn't Deirdre that I killed.'

Mckenzie was harsh. 'But she's dead, Mr Wellbridge, isn't she? We found her at the bottom of the shaft in the priest's hole. Her neck had been snapped. Just like Eli Craske's. Just like you'd dealt with old Joseph Grice. Killed in the way you'd been taught to kill before you went into Burma.'

Wellbridge looked up at him wearily. 'I've told you, Sergeant. It wasn't Deirdre.'

'But you've already confessed to killing her, Mr Wellbridge. Are you telling us now that you didn't? That you killed someone else? That there's another body hidden somewhere in Sparrow Hill House?'

The words came out slowly. 'No, there's no one else.'

'Then just what the hell are you trying to say?'

Wellbridge sighed 'I'm trying to tell you the truth, Sergeant. Let me put it simply. Yes, I wrenched her head back. Yes, I broke her neck. But it wasn't Deirdre's neck. I never intended to kill Deirdre. It was Ruth.'

McKenzie flung himself back in his chair. 'You've lost me,' he said. 'You'd already killed Ruth. How could you possibly kill her twice over?'

'I don't know, but I did.'

McKenzie turned to Tench. 'The man's mad. He must be.'

'No, I don't think he is.' Tench was quiet, composed. He leaned forward and rested his elbows on the table. 'Tell me exactly what happened, Mr Wellbridge.'

For a moment there was silence in the room. Wellbridge stared at his hands. Then he suddenly began to speak, at first in a slow expressionless monotone, then faster, louder, the words at last spilling out of him, charged with a strange emphatic emotion.

'You never knew Deirdre, though perhaps you thought you did. She knew nothing. She loved me and trusted me, God knows why. And she was loyal. Too loyal perhaps. I never told her what had happened that Sunday. As far as she was concerned, it was a plain case of vandalism. Someone had broken into the house and wrecked the study. That was all there was to it . . . She was an innocent. I never for the life of me thought you'd arrest her. But you did.

'Heaven knows what you told her, but it changed her. She wasn't Deirdre. She was bewildered, unbelieving. Then bewilderment turned to hate. I saw it in her eyes. She stood in front of me, accusing me. She said I'd betrayed her. She wasn't shouting, she wasn't screaming, but I saw her mouth moving. It was twisted, like Ruth's. Then she came at me, pounding me with her fists . . . She wasn't Deirdre. She was Ruth.

'I can't tell you what happened. I don't know myself. I can only tell you what I saw, what in that split second I believed to be true, and believed it with such conviction that it banished every other thought from my mind.

'I saw Ruth. Not the Ruth that I'd loved, but Ruth's other self. I knew it couldn't be her, and yet it was her: the mad, malign part of her come back to haunt me. It was her fetch, her earthbound spirit, still clinging to what she believed was her own.

'I knew if I didn't rid myself once and for all of that last surviving shred of her, I'd never be free. She'd return from the grave to torment me time and time again. To claim me, wherever I happened to be.

'It was only when she fell and I knelt down beside her that I knew I'd killed Deirdre.'

McKenzie was in no mood to show compassion. 'So you threw her down the shaft,' he said, 'and turned tail and ran. You wanted to save your own miserable skin.'

Wellbridge gave him one brief contemptuous glance. 'I've made my confession. That's all I have to say. If you want to know the rest, work it out for yourself. You'll get nothing more from me.'

5

It was a week later, just before sunset, that an old Morgan three-wheeler put-putted past the church of St Mary the Virgin, threaded the narrow, twisting road through Medford, turned to the right off Liggerbeck Hill, and made its way down Deep Lane to the edge of the marsh.

Once there, it creaked to a halt and two men climbed out.

They leaned on the fence. One of them lit a pipe, and they both stared at the seemingly endless expanse of scurvy grass and purslane, pools and winding creeks.

'And did you?' Lubbock asked.

'Did we what?'

'Work it out.'

'Most of it,' said Tench, 'but whether we got it right, that's another matter. We grilled him for three whole days, but even so we were left with a lot of unanswered questions.'

'We always are.' Lubbock blew out a cloud of smoke that drifted back in the gentle breeze towards Medford. 'It's rare for a murder investigation to end with everything tied up neatly. The killer's dead or he lies or, like Wellbridge, he simply refuses to talk. We have to guess at the answers, and try to make them credible. I suppose you did that?'

'As best we could, yes.'

'And he dropped a few hints?'

'Odd ones from time to time, and we managed to unearth some further clues ourselves.'

'Then start at the beginning, laddie. Tell me all about it. You believe what he said about never intending to kill his wife?'

'It's a credible explanation. If he had meant to kill her, he'd have done it the way the army taught him to kill. With a jerk of the neck ... That was the method he used on the others.'

'So what did he do when he found she was dead?'

'According to him, he panicked.'

261

'But you don't believe he did?'

'I think he did, but not for long. His first move stemmed from panic. He knew she'd come on a bicycle, so he dashed outside and brought it in . . . Then he sat down to think. He had to get rid of the evidence: her body, her bike, the clothes she was wearing, anything that might show that she'd visited the house . . . He knew that Deirdre wasn't due back until Wednesday. That gave him three days . . . And he knew about the priest's hole. When he'd rented the place, the agent had shown him inside, and he'd explored it more than once.'

'So,' Lubbock said, 'he took the obvious step. He opened it up, stowed the body inside, along with the bike, and then closed up the wall.'

'Correct,' said Tench.

'And after that?'

'Well, he knew he couldn't keep the body there for too long. He had to get it out of the house. The problem was where to dump it. He had to hide it where it couldn't be easily found and, more important, where it wouldn't be linked with Medford. That was why he chose to take it out to Blacknock. He thought the tide would carry it further down the coast.'

'But that night it didn't.'

'No, he thought he'd worked it all out. Dump it in the dark when the tide was on the turn, and if it was washed up it'd be somewhere miles away to the east. He must have known it'd be a dangerous and difficult job, but he was strong and he'd been shifting heavy timber for years. He'd heard about the guides, Jem Stuart and Grice, and he reckoned that once he'd been shown the way across the marsh he could find it again with the help of a torch. Moonlight would be a bonus, but he couldn't rely on it. He had to take a chance. As Bates said, if a man was desperate enough to be rid of a woman he'd like as not murdered, he might well try to do it. And Wellbridge was such a man.

'He said that he'd had it in mind for some time to do a trek across the marsh, and he'd already found out where Stuart and Grice lived. He'd never met either of them, but he chose Grice because his cottage was close to Sparrow Hill House; and that same afternoon, once he'd checked on the tides – they're posted up, as you know, on the quay at Blakeney – he took a stroll down the hill and offered him a fiver to take him out that evening to the edge of the sand. Of course, Grice agreed. He wasn't likely to turn down an offer like that. All he had to do was make a trip he'd made countless times before and say nothing about it.'

'But he spoke out of turn.'

'And paid for it,' said Tench, 'but that was much later. I don't think Wellbridge was worried about him just then. He had other things on his mind. In the few lucid moments before she'd spotted Deirdre's picture, Ruth had told him she was staying at Phoenix Mill Cottage. He knew he'd have to clear it of all her things and find somewhere to hide the bike, and have the lot done before daylight next morning.

'He took the key to the cottage from the pocket of her dress, put the bike in the Chrysler, drove to Swallownest Wood and dumped it among the trees. He must have checked the saddle-bag, but somehow, in the dark, he missed the side pocket that held the medallion. Not that that proved to be a vital mistake.'

'Well, at least you learnt about the pedlar of Swaffham. And you never know,' said Lubbock, 'it might come in handy if someone tries to smuggle gold out of Norfolk.'

Tench took a deep breath. 'D'you want to know what happened or don't you?' he asked.

'Yes. Carry on, laddie. I'm just slipping in the pertinent comment, that's all . . . You were talking about the cottage.'

'He drove to the cottage from Swallownest Wood. It was then just after midnight. He donned a pair of gloves, let himself in with the key, closed all the curtains and switched on the lights. No one was likely to see them – Morston Bottom Farm was a mile away – and if anyone did, they'd simply think Ruth hadn't yet gone to bed . . . He scoured the place, packed all her clothes in the case she'd brought with her, and then checked the outbuildings. All of them were locked except for the stables, but he found the sacks Joe Rogers had left and took one away with him. It was just what he needed.

'He had the money available to fund whatever he decided to do, and we know for sure what he chose to do the following morning, Monday. He rented a lock-up garage from Anthony Balham, a friend with an estate agent's business in Holt, and bought a second-hand car, a dark blue Vauxhall Velox, from Dickinson Motors. We believe that, after that, he left his Chrysler at the timber yard and drove the Vauxhall down to Sparrow Hill House.'

'And used it that night to take the body to the marsh.'

'Yes, we think he did. We're only guessing, but we don't think he went through Medford. He probably took the back lanes to Warham, then from there to the Wells road and down the track to the old army camp. The courting couple from Copston saw it parked there round about quarter to eleven.'

Lubbock straightened up and knocked out his pipe on the fence. 'Are you still trying to tell me he carried the body a quarter of a mile along the coastal path as far as Deep Lane, and then did another mile and a half to Blacknock? That's hard to believe, laddie. It's just that little bit too far to be credible.'

Tench nodded. 'You may be right, but we have an idea that that isn't what he did. The Vauxhall had a roof-rack. We didn't know that till it was found down in Dover, but according to Dickinson the roof-rack was what persuaded him to buy it, and when Lester's men were let loose on Sparrow Hill House they found a wheelbarrow stored in a garden shed. They tested it and discovered some fibres from the sack.'

Lubbock pulled out his pouch and began to refill his pipe. 'Ah well,' he said, 'that's different. You think he used it to wheel the body to the end of Deep Lane.'

'We think he may have done, yes. Before he started out from Sparrow Hill House, he probably stripped her of the rest of her clothes, packed them in the case and left it in the priest's hole.

'Then he stuffed the naked body in the sack. Rigor mortis would be beginning to wear off by that time, but, even so, he may have had to break a few bones ... He put the sack in the boot, strapped the barrow to the roof-rack, and drove by a roundabout way to the marsh. Then he wheeled the barrow along the path, hid it among the trees at the end of Deep Lane, shouldered the sack and set out across the marsh.'

'And when he got back, there of a sudden was old Eli Craske, drunk as a fiddler and hollering fit to rouse the whole of Medford.'

'Unfortunately for Eli Craske, yes,' said Tench.

'Right, laddie. No need to elaborate. We know what happened after that. Just carry on from there.'

'Well, he'd got rid of two bodies, and there was nothing to connect them to Sparrow Hill House, but he still had to deal with the rest of her clothes. We don't know precisely when it was that he hid them in the astrodome, but it must have been at night. He'd driven past it often enough. He knew it was always locked, and, as far as he could tell, no one ever went in. It was the ideal place, but he didn't reckon on Abel Lavender having a pair of such very sharp eyes. He spotted the change of lock and reported it to Sergeant Hellyer.'

'Fair enough.' Lubbock turned his back on the breeze, struck a match, lit his pipe at the third attempt, and blew another cloud of smoke towards Medford. 'But what about all this business of the prayer-wheel and the will? Did he tell you about that?'

'As a matter of fact, he did. It was the only thing he seemed to be keen to explain. Said he wanted to protect Deirdre.'

'Ah yes, Deirdre.' Lubbock stared at the long, straight stretch of Deep Lane. 'He called her an innocent, didn't he? Said she knew nothing ... Just how much did she know?'

6

Tench gave a shrug. 'To quote your pal Ledward, that's where we enter the realm of the imponderables. We know next to nothing about their relationship. Oh, I suppose we could track down some of the people who knew them in India, but what's the point? She's dead and he's likely to go to the gallows. It's not worth the trouble.'

'Then what's your opinion? Don't tell me you haven't one.'

'I'm only guessing.'

'Then guess.'

'I think on his side it was purely a physical attraction and one that cooled quickly when it was out of the tropics, but on hers it was something more. I think he was telling the truth when he said that she loved him. Maybe she was blind, but she accepted his story about the divorce. I know they never appeared to be close, but perhaps in her case it was a front she assumed. He said she was loyal, and maybe she was. He said she knew nothing, and maybe she did. We checked with her friend in Lynn, and we know she never came back to Sparrow Hill House before Wednesday: the day when she found the study wrecked and the window smashed. She'd no reason to believe that what had happened was anything more than a break-in, and her irrational feelings about Danny Sprot merely strengthened that belief . . . as he intended they should.'

'On the other hand,' said Lubbock, 'they could have been in cahoots from the very beginning. She might have been playing his game all along.'

'She might have been, yes. We'll never know, will we? But I don't think Deirdre Thompson was the kind of woman who'd have agreed to a bigamous marriage. Ruth Wellbridge, to her, was just a shadowy figure from the past. She'd never met her. She didn't know what she looked like. When we showed her the picture, she was probably telling no more than the truth when she said she'd never seen her and didn't know who she was.'

'And when she did, that was when she began to suspect.'

'Not immediately, no. The story of the break-in had already taken root in her mind, and I think it was only when we offered her proof that he'd never been divorced that at last she began to put two and two together.'

'Then what about the prayer-wheel?'

'When we found it in the priest's hole, it was clear that he'd concocted the tale about the break-in. It had a dual purpose: to hide the truth from Deirdre, and to throw us off the scent. He knew that, with all the hoo-ha in Medford, it wouldn't be long before we'd come knocking at Sparrow

Hill House, as we were knocking at every other house in the village. What better way to deceive us than by calling us in before that occurred, reporting a case of theft, adding vandalism of the kind that young Danny Sprot might well have committed, and covering himself with a watertight tale that we couldn't really question?' Tench paused. 'It was clever. You've got to admit it was clever.'

'Too clever by half,' Lubbock said. 'We were bound to catch up with him in the end.'

'We did, but by that time Deirdre was dead.'

'As he intended she should be.'

'Yes, he'd grown tired of her. By that time she'd guessed too much. He had to break her neck to save his own from being broken.'

Lubbock pondered. 'This tale about the will. Was it all imagination?'

'No, strangely enough. He said that most of it was true. He did have a friend called Dainton who'd been a part of the Great Game, and it was Dainton who told him the story one evening when they were drinking down at the Savoy Hotel bar. He just adapted it to suit his purpose. And it was virtually flawless. If he hadn't added that bit about Jim Corbett's rifle, even Lawrence couldn't have questioned its truth.'

'Then he wrecked the room himself?'

'Yes, he told us he got up early on the Wednesday morning, smashed the window in the kitchen, wiped the fingerprints off everything he knew Ruth had touched, and then donned a pair of gloves and set about the study. He drove into Holt at the usual time, and simply waited for Deirdre to discover the mess . . . It could well have worked. His one mistake was to miss the print on the window glass, but he couldn't possibly have known about that.'

'And then Grice began spreading the gospel.'

'And went the same way that Eli Craske had gone. Wellbridge had to stop him. We can only guess at what happened, but we know Deirdre called in at the Post Office on her way back from Lynn. That was when McKenzie saw her, crossing the bridge. The coast road's too narrow to park a car, and she'd probably parked it on Sibthorpe Hill. We think Grice may have been in the Post Office too, gossiping to Maisie Tackleston, and Deirdre spilled the beans. After that it was easy. She went to see a film in Norwich that evening, and didn't get back till midnight. Wellbridge was in bed, snoring so she told us. When you're wide awake, waiting, it's easy to fake a snore. They had twin beds, she'd be tired, and the first two hours' sleep are always the soundest. She probably never knew he'd been out of the house. He just walked down the hill to Grice's cottage, and didn't even need to break a window to get in. There aren't many folk in Medford who bother to lock up at night. He told us he just opened the door, stationed himself at the bottom of the stairs, made a bit of noise and waited there in the dark for Grice to come down . . . And it was a good chance to throw more suspicion on Danny Sprot. All he needed was a bag of shells that he'd gathered from one of the local beaches.'

'But things didn't quite work out as he'd planned.'

'No, they didn't. It was all down to Harris. He made two telling interventions. He pointed out that the bag contained mussels, and they were the one type of shell that Danny never collected; and that same afternoon, Thursday, he called in at the timber yard and showed Wellbridge the picture of Ruth. That was when he knew we were sniffing at his door. He had to throw us off the scent. It was time to cover his tracks by using Dainton's tale about the prayer-wheel and the will. So he told Harris yes, he recognized the woman. He'd met her on the voyage home from Bombay. And when we questioned him about it, he added weight to the tale by identifying the body when we took him to the mortuary.'

'And,' Lubbock said, 'it was a good enough tale, at least for a time, to provide him with answers to all the questions thrown at him.'

'Yes, it was, but he must have known we were getting closer to the truth, and it was only a matter of time before his brother-in-law, down in Southampton, put two and two together. Then, on Friday afternoon, when we turned up at the timber yard and began to ask about the marriage, he knew he had to disappear. He'd planned it all down to the finest detail, but to do it successfully, he needed to do two other things first: he had to lay a false trail and he had to get rid of Deirdre.

'The following morning, once Constable Walters had dropped him off at the timber yard, he went to three separate banks and drew enough money to last him for weeks. The Vauxhall was back in the lock-up at Holt. He drove it down to Dover, leaving clues on the way that he hoped we'd pick up – paying by cheque, for instance, at a garage in Brentwood – and abandoned it on the sea front in a line of parked cars.

'We don't exactly know how he got back to Sibthorpe, but we think it must have been by train as far as Holt, and then by a taxi that dropped him off somewhere close by, but we know he cut across the fields and approached the house from the back.'

'But how did he get in? The tunnel was blocked and there were men watching the place.'

'Yes, he'd explored the tunnel and knew the roof had fallen in. And yes, two of Varden's men were on guard. But this was the early hours of Sunday morning, and we hadn't yet brought in the rest of the team to ring the perimeter. There was just one man at the front and another at the back. He said getting in was easy. It was just a matter of waiting. The man at the back went round to have a chat with the one at the front. He was only away perhaps a couple of minutes, but that gave Wellbridge time to slip in through the back door; and once inside, he crouched low enough not to be seen and made his way upstairs to the bathroom. The window there was frosted glass and he was safe from detection.

'He didn't know, of course, that we'd picked up Deirdre. He thought she was asleep in the bedroom, and when he found that she wasn't, he was in a bit of a pickle. He couldn't close the curtains, because that would tell the watchers someone was in the house. That meant he couldn't open up the priest's hole and hide himself in there, so he had no option but to stay where he was. He banked on the fact that, wherever Deirdre happened to be, sooner or later she'd be coming back home, and when she did she'd come up to the bathroom . . .'

'So that was where he killed her.'

'According to the statement he made to us, yes. Then he waited till dark, closed the curtains, taking care not to be seen, opened up the priest's hole and dropped her body down the shaft. After that, he sat down to think. The men outside were waiting, but what were they waiting for? There seemed to him to be only two possibilities. Either they were hoping he'd return to the house, or they thought that Deirdre knew where he'd gone and intended to join him. If that was the case, and it seemed far the more likely, then they wouldn't rearrest her once she left. They'd simply follow her at a distance. He said it was a gamble, but he had his escape planned. His firm owned a lock-up garage in Fakenham. They used it from time to time to store odd supplies of timber, and earlier on in the week – which day he didn't tell us – he'd driven over to Fakenham – it's only a dozen miles – bought a small second-hand Ford pick-up van and stowed it away there. All he had to do was get out of the house, take Deirdre's car, lose his pursuers somewhere *en route*, pick up the van, drive to Mr Jenkins' farm in the Peak, and pick up the key to the cottage he'd already rented by phone.'

'And after that,' Lubbock said, 'it was all too simple. He chose a few of Deirdre's clothes and one of her wigs, and did a midnight flit under your very noses.'

Tench pursed his lips. 'Yes, I'm afraid he did.'

Lubbock stared at the marsh. 'Well, laddie,' he said, 'it all sounds credible enough, but it leaves a few loose ends. What about that postcard with the map reference on it?'

'We didn't bother to ask him. He'd confessed to the murders, and that was that. I suppose he thought it possible we'd intercept any post. I think it was meant for us. Just another trick to lay a false trail. I can't think it would have much meaning for Deirdre.'

'And what about that couple who were trying to buy sacks? The man and woman in the sports car?'

'We never traced them,' said Tench.

'And Valerie? The one who wrote the vital letter that sparked everything off?'

'Oh, she turned up. A couple of days ago. Far too late . . . She'd been touring Scotland with her husband.'

268

Lubbock sniffed. 'If she talks like she writes, it's a wonder he survived
... One more thing. The prayer-wheel. You opened it up?'

'Yes.'

'And what was inside it?'

'Just the usual roll of paper. Buddhist mantras,' said Tench.

7

The sun, as it set, was flooding the clouds above the sea with ragged bands
of colour: streamers of orange, grey and lemon, impenetrable black and
crystalline blue that turned the tidal creeks on the marsh into ribbons of
gold.

Tench rested his arms on the fence, and gazed at the bright desolation
that stretched to the sky. 'You know, somehow,' he said, 'I can't help but
feel a shred of sympathy for Wellbridge.'

'Well, don't,' said Lubbock. 'He killed them, all four of them, that's clear
enough. The rest of what he told you could be just a pack of lies.'

'Yes, it could.'

Lubbock mused. 'Murders. They're all the same. We can only uncover
two-thirds of the truth. However deep we probe, we're always left with
that unresolved third that we can never be sure of.'

'And never will be,' said Tench. 'In practically every case, there's one
vital moment that lacks corroborative evidence, and that's the moment
when the murder's committed ... There are only two witnesses. One of
them's dead and the other's the killer. And we can never be sure that a
killer's confessed to the whole of the truth. It's as simple as that.'

'It's my experience,' Lubbock said, 'that in this life you can never be sure
of very much at all. Look at that sky. It's magnificent, isn't it? There's
nothing anywhere else to compare with the sunsets seen across the coastal
marshes of Norfolk. You'd think tomorrow was bound to be a glorious
day. But I'll wager that by the morning the mist'll be so thick you'll see
nothing from here but a few dull patches of tangled brown grass.'

Tench shivered and rubbed his shoulders. 'Mist on the marsh and not a
single speck of light to serve as a guide ... It makes me think of that cockle
woman, old Mary Bunn, trapped on the mud with the tide seething round
her, and the men on the whelk boats, unable to help, hearing the sound of
her sobs from Blacknock.'

Lubbock tapped out his pipe. 'There's a moral in that,' he said: 'one that
all good detectives should keep stowed away in their memory banks ...
Never believe every little thing that you're told ... I know a chap who
used to fish for whelks out of Wells, and last week we got to talking about

the cockle beds at Medford. He told me that one misty night when the moon was at full he put ashore at Blacknock. The air was still. It was quiet out there, and he swore to me that he heard the cockles blowing their spit-holes in the mud. They were all around him, he said, thousands of them, and they sighed and sobbed for all the world like a woman lost in despair.'

He turned his back on the marsh. 'Best be a sceptic, laddie. It always pays ... Let's go back to the cottage. I need a cup of tea ... I suppose you'll want coffee.'

'Why not?' said Tench.